Books by Jenny Kalahar

The Turning Pages series:
Shelve Under C: A Tale of Used Books and Cats
The Find of a Lifetime
Bindings

One Mile North of Normal and Other Poems
This Peculiar Magic
All the Dear Beasties
I Imagined a Dragon
The Soggy Doggy

Lumi's Curiosities series:
Lumi's Curiosities
The Great Restoration

Lumi's Curiosities

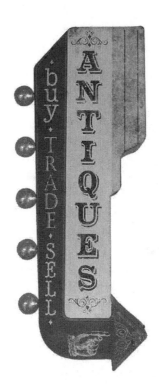

Jenny Kalahar

Book 1 of Lumi's Curiosities

Thank you to my dear, tireless husband Patrick, who makes my writing possible. Thank you to the friends who inspire and support me. Special thanks to Alisa Orr, David Allen, Kathy Jo Carter, Judy Young, Joyce Zephyrin, Michael Strosahl, Theresa Timmons, Sharon Scott, Wanda Smith, Leif Anderson, Dana Anderson, Ben Cornwell, Josie and Carter Herndon, Michael Joyce, my parents, beloved Last Stanza Poetry Association members, the Poetry Society of Indiana, and to everyone who helps and encourages any author along their creative way.

Chapter One

"Horrible! I've never seen anything *like* these." Maddy Rasmusson, her gray, braided bun hanging dangerously loose above the collar of her purple blouse, sank onto a floral cushioned wing chair. She nodded toward a chunky rolltop desk hulking against the center of her wall. "I've always kept my stereocards in my desk. I haven't bought or been given any in many, many years. I've always had exactly ninety-eight travel images and costume scenes, but now I have these five *terrible* cards, too." She pointed at the rectangular, double-image card attached to the viewer and then at the four on the lace-covered tea table separate from those stored in an oak box.

Curious, Lumi Leski picked up the ornate French stereoscopic viewer, peered through its lenses, and then nearly dropped the fragile antique. "Well, these are freakishly nothing like the rest of your cards." She took another look, her scowl deepening. "What in the *heck,* Maddy? How did *these* end up in your collection?" Lumi lowered the stereoscope back onto the table. She glanced at Maddy's life-size folk-art statue of Harry Houdini and noticed he also looked astonished. "And how did you discover them?"

"The new paper delivery man was here, and I offered to let him look around while I counted up some cash to pay my bill."

"Are you still paying for your paper in person?"

Maddy reinserted an escaping hairpin into her bun, then nodded. "You know I don't have any of those computer or internet gadgets, Lu. I like giving my money to living, breathing people, not to screens." The pin fell out almost immediately. "Anyway, the paper man asked about my viewer, so I got out my cards to show him how to use it. Tim from next door was here, too, to return some empty recycling bins. We were all happily talking and looking at my cards like the world wasn't going to spin upside down at any moment, and that's when I saw those ... *terrors*. We were viewing the first couple of cards from the front of the box—my scenes from Holland—then I pulled a handful from the rear. As soon as I really absorbed what the photos showed, I immediately flipped them over and shooed the men out. 'Lumi will know just what to do,' I thought." She paused, her eyes pleading. "What should we do?"

Lumi crossed the room to stare through one of the room's tall windows at her own newly purchased Victorian home. The freshness of the cream-and-blue running trim and spandrels on its narrow front porch contrasted with the cracked sidewalk and the many scraggly, white-headed dandelions in her yard that looked like the snow of summer. Feeling overheated, she gathered her long, golden hair in one hand and secured it with a band into a ponytail behind her back. Turning to her friend, she asked, "Was anything stolen? Has anything been moved or added?"

The older woman pulled a tissue from her sleeve and glanced around at her neatly arrayed antique furnishings, paintings, and display cases. "I haven't noticed anything."

Lumi bit the corner of her lip. "Does anyone have a key to your house?"

Maddy removed her tortoiseshell glasses and used the tissue to wipe her eyes. She thought for a moment before answering. "Well, there's Ralph the Schwann deliveryman, the mail lady in case I get a package that should go inside if it's storming, and Steve from the pet food store who carries in my big bags of cat food. My daughter Jem, of course. And … oh, Tim from next door. And his wife. And their son."

"Maddy!"

Ignoring Lumi, she went on, "And Rachel, two doors down. If she runs out of things while cooking or baking, I let her borrow ingredients whether I'm here or not." Maddy stuffed her tissue away, adding, "I think an electrician I hired once a few years ago forgot to return a key. He needed to be in here while I was gone to visit my friend in New York. Oh, and Magnus Sanders—I don't know *how* I almost forgot about Magnus. I gave him a whole set of keys when I left my car at his repair shop early this morning. That's my spare set of keys—I have another set in my purse."

Lumi shook her head, sighing. *"Far* too many keys have left your hands."

Maddy stood, putting on her glasses again. She joined Lumi at the sunny window to look out at the houses around hers. Her lips trembling and her eyes moist, she asked, "Who would *take* my things? Haven't I been generous? Haven't I given enough away to charities and fundraisers these past fifty years I've been collecting antiques? Why come into my home to … threaten me? If I am being threatened. I don't know how to classify this weird turn of events."

"Well, someone *has* been in here—with a key or without one. I'm not happy at what they've left behind, but I think you should feel lucky that nothing was taken—at least not that you know of. But you need to be more *careful.* Our town is growing larger by the year, and not everyone knows and loves you the way folks in this neighborhood do."

Mrs. Rasmusson smiled at Lumi's last words. "I guess you're right, Lu. Still, I don't want to feel afraid in my own home. I don't want to lock the doors every time I go out to my garage for a piece of sandpaper." She took a step toward the tea table and the offending cards but seemed unwilling to get very close. "Can you guess why anyone would do this? I am heavily, mystifyingly puzzled."

Lumi went to reexamine the five stereocards. "Well, *this* is strange. Now that I look closer, I can see they're *pretending* to be old, but they're not. They're copies of vintage photos that were glued down to thick yellow paper. This was not a professional job."

"No?"

"No. Here—look. The images on the fake cards are duplicates of each other. True stereocards are not just two of the exact, same photo placed side-by-side. They're made of two shots taken at the same time with a stereo camera that has a pair of lenses two or three inches apart. That way, when you see the cards through the viewer, the two photos appear to be one, three-dimensional scene."

Maddy took one of the cards from Lumi and held it under the brighter light of a mica-shade floor lamp. "I did notice something was off, but I was too upset by the … content of the photos to think much about technicalities. I often show off my viewer and cards—they're almost my favorite things—but I *know* I've never seen these new cards before." She looked up, a crease between her brows, her hands shaking as she lowered the stereocard to the table again. "Should I call the police, do you think?"

Lumi shrugged. "I can't say what's been done is a crime. It's more of a prank. You weren't hurt. I don't see any broken glass or damage anywhere." She pulled her ponytail over her shoulder. "But it might be a good idea to report this—have it on record in case some other oddball thing happens to you or in your house."

Mrs. Rasmusson stepped around the room with suspicion. "Everything else seems the same. The orange draperies with those little flowers I embroidered on them are the same; there are my same antiques on their shelves and showcases; and, as usual, my not-so-old Persian rug is right underfoot." She tapped a pink-sandaled foot on a sunny patch of the darkly colorful rug. "What am I not seeing? What else has been moved or touched in here?" She hugged herself, frowning. "I feel rather helpless now, I'll admit."

Noting the way her friend's hands were trembling, Lumi offered, "Let me take photos of the cards with my cell. I'll do some research to find out what the images represent." She got out her phone but then hesitated. "I honestly feel like this was a prank. A *rotten* prank, but maybe that's

3

all it was." She reached out to hold one of the woman's chilly hands. "Even though you *do* show off your viewer pretty often, maybe you simply missed seeing those five cards until today. They could have been surreptitiously put into your collection a long time ago."

Maddy tugged on the hem of her blouse. "Hmm. I don't think so. The edges of the fakes are a different color. That bright yellow stands out, even stashed in the box." She suddenly inhaled, her eyes widening. "I just remembered something. A few years ago, I snatched up a rare Sparton radio at an auction in Noblesville. The Bluebird model. It's right over there in my curved-glass showcase. See? The art deco one with the round, blue mirrored front. It was a *steal."*

Lumi walked toward the case, then bent for a closer look. "So fabulous! I've never seen high-end Sparton radios except in photos."

Maddy rested a hand on Harry Houdini's shoulder, continuing, "A reporter for *Antique Spectrum* newspaper gave me his card. He asked if I had other Spartons, and we talked about the things here in my house. I specifically remember describing my viewer to him, how it has a black-lacquered wooden body with decorations of incised flowers, and that it looks rather like a folding camera."

Lumi glanced at the viewer at the other side of the room. "Very cool. I've always loved your stereoscope."

Maddy continued, "I told him about my animal-shaped bakelite jewelry, my lion-face Russian nesting dolls, my shelf full of mechanical banks, and the space toys my husband collected."

Lumi turned to look inside another case at an antique typewriter decorated with pink and red rose decals. "I'd love to see your bakelite again."

"I mentioned my steamer trunk full of nineteen-fifties wedding dresses, and those plaster gorilla hands from the set of the original *King Kong* movie."

Lumi stood straighter. "Your dresses are *gorgeous,* as I recall. And where are those gorilla hands? I haven't seen them since I was a little girl."

"Wrapped up in the guest room closet."

"Those things are *awesome.* But Maddy, you really *should* have a security system on your house."

Getting back to her story, Mrs. Rasmusson said, "The reporter couldn't ask fast enough to let him do an article on me and my antiques. He was here two days later with a photographer who took so many photos that it would have taken a *book* to publish them all. They both particularly loved my stereoscope viewer, so shots of it and a few of my cards were included with the article."

Lumi grimaced. "Uh-oh."

"After the interview came out, folks from around the world—it was published online, too—phoned or wrote to me wanting to buy things they'd seen in the photos. I've never sold anything from my home, so I ignored the letters and said 'no' to everyone who called."

Lumi slapped her forehead in dismay. "Maddy! Why would you practically *advertise* that you have this collection? I'm sure you don't have insurance on everything. How did you *dare?"*

The older woman shrugged. "I guess I was flattered to have their compliments. They were impressed."

Lumi crossed her slender arms. "You should have been more careful."

"Well, the reporter said he and the photographer featured a different outstanding collection every week. I felt important. I suppose I *was* rather foolish, but what's done is done. Now, though, there are these ugly, scary cards. Even though that *was* quite a while ago, do you think someone's using my collection to terrorize me?"

Lumi bit her lip. "It's possible. Because, you realize, anyone who saw the article and photos knows you have a collection of stereocards, among other cool things. If that interview was published online, it's probably online for anyone to see—even today."

"Oh, *dear.* But I haven't had a call or letter in *ages."*

After Lumi took a few photos, Maddy gathered the offensive duo-image cards and settled them into the rear of her card box, then shut them away inside her desk.

Lumi asked, "What gives me a chill is wondering about a possible motivation for scaring you." She met Mrs. Rasmusson's eyes steadily. "Maddy, how could someone do this without you knowing?"

The older woman looked sheepish. "I rarely lock up anymore. I mean, when I go out, it's usually only for an hour or two at a time. I lock my house and garage at night, of course."

"With all of these valuables in here? You should be locking up every time you leave the *yard."*

Knock-knock-knock

Lumi walked past the foot of the wide, ornate staircase. A pleasant-looking, muscular, brown-eyed man wearing gray slacks and a white dress shirt stood on the porch. Lumi cautiously opened the wooden door, suspecting the stranger was a salesman.

Mrs. Rasmusson joined Lumi. Seeing who was visiting, her cautious demeanor melted away. "Nolan! Come right on in, dear."

The young man pulled open the complaining screen door and stepped into the foyer. He barely acknowledged Lumi. "Mrs. R? I have your car at the curb. Magnus finished his work on it and asked me to run over here for you. Mag took care of that noise you were hearing, so you'll be rattle-free on the drive back home."

This suggestion seemed to agitate the older woman again. "Oh, dear. Oh, *no*. I couldn't *possibly* drive myself home from way out *there."*

Lumi offered, "How about this? I'll go along to drive you home again. No trouble at all." She waited for her friend to nod, and then said, "Give me a second to run to over for my purse."

"Thank you, babycakes. Such a relief!"

Lumi grinned. "I've been told I know just what to do."

Maddy smiled. She touched Nolan's sleeve. "Nolan, do you know Lumi Leski?"

He shook his head. "Sorry, no." He faintly nodded but didn't extend his hand. Lumi didn't, either.

Maddy seemed to be keeping her nerves in check by letting her fingers remained on Nolan's arm. She said to Lumi, "Dear, you run and get your things and we'll meet you at my car. I'll tell the young Mr. Sanders a little bit about how you came to be my neighbor again."

Lumi hesitated, feeling uneasy. Was the woman about to play matchmaker? "Well, okay. Just don't tell him about that time about twenty years ago when I yanked up your nasturtiums helping you weed your front garden."

Nolan stepped onto the porch to hold the door for the ladies.

Lumi thought she saw a twinkle in Nolan's eye as she passed him.

Maddy winked, seeming to notice that twinkle, too.

Lumi felt anything but comforted by Maddy's wink.

During the drive, Mrs. Rasmusson sat beside Nolan on the front seat of the gray sedan, and Lumi sat behind Nolan, silently observing the back of his head. In the rear-view mirror, she glanced at what she could of his face, wishing she could stare openly at it whole instead of in narrow strips. She met his eyes after she had raised herself an inch trying to see more of his nose and lips, then quickly looked away, embarrassed that she'd been caught admiring him.

As they turned onto Main Street, the older woman glanced at Nolan appreciatively. "You look so nice in your court dress-ups. Thank you for retrieving me. Didn't your brother have any of his workers on hand to come for me this evening?"

Nolan smoothly avoided a pothole. "They're swamped. It's getting close to the Fourth of July, which means everyone planning a road trip is finally taking care of the various automotive issues they've been ignoring. I was at his place getting gas, and he asked if I would fetch you."

"How are things at your own workplace? I read the paper, of course, but I would imagine a lot goes on that never ends up in print." She lowered her window and turned off the air conditioning.

"Things have been hectic since last month. We had a cold winter and cold spring. That made my job easy for a long time, but now that the hot summer is here it seems like we're getting calls constantly. With all the new homes and apartment buildings going up all over, I wish we'd add a few officers to the force. Break-ins are happening more and more around the state; now Barnwood has to deal with an increase in that sort of thing, too."

Realization dawned on Lumi: Nolan must be a policeman. If so, why wasn't Maddy mentioning the fright she'd just had? The young woman leaned forward, tapped her friend on the shoulder, and silently indicated that she should bring up the subject. Lumi got a hard look and then was pointedly ignored.

"I think you *should* add to the force. That is an excellent idea. Does the city have the funding, do you think?" Mrs. Rasmusson asked, not looking again toward the back seat as she continued visiting with Nolan.

Lumi tuned them out. She thought about the cards and what they might mean and wondered why the older woman wouldn't mention their existence to this man who was a friend and who could offer advice from the law enforcement point of view.

When they arrived at the service station, Mrs. Rasmusson stepped from the car to walk into the office. Lumi tossed her purse onto the front seat and got out of the back just as Nolan slid from the front. They each closed their door on the same side of the car, but Nolan didn't walk away.

Lumi considered following Maddy, feeling too shy to stand around waiting with a man she didn't know.

"New in town?" he asked as if trying to get her to stay. He leaned a hip against the car and gave Lumi his full attention, making her blush. Lumi was surprised to see his face had slightly reddened, too.

"Yes and no." She liked his casual naturalness. Nolan's features were playful, yet she could imagine him giving a criminal the impression that he meant business. His short, brown hair tried to curl at its very ends. His

7

large and expressive eyes were his best feature. They made her wish she were bolder so she could keep looking into those brown eyes for a long, long time.

Nolan crossed his muscular arms, waiting for her to go on.

Lumi wished she wasn't wearing shorts. Nolan made her feel more exposed than usual. She swept her long, blonde ponytail around to her front, taking some comfort from the way it covered her upper body. Fighting against her usual awkwardness, she said, "I … grew up here. I went to college, then to work in Indianapolis for Cumphrey Auctions. Now I'm back."

"Well, good," he said, his eyes on hers when they weren't watching the way her lips moved when she spoke.

Lumi wondered if he wanted her to continue or to quit talking. Since he wasn't making a move to leave, she said, "It really is. Living in the city, I was feeling lonely in general. I hope to make friends and figure out how to be happy again. There has to be more to life than working and sitting home alone." Her face felt hot. She knew she'd said far too much to a total stranger.

"I'm sure you will. Be happy, I mean."

"I've got a business downtown—an antique shop."

His eyes widened as if she'd hit an invisible target with her last words. "I'm sure you'll be happy with it." He turned toward the office door, his hands on top of the car.

Lumi looked at his profile quizzically. Nolan seemed to have moved closer even though she hadn't seen him do so. His eyes softened when they met hers again. She said, "I … bought the house across from Mrs. R."

"Nice neighborhood. Lots of Victorians. You should be happy there."

"I grew up farther down the street. My childhood house wasn't available, but I was able to get one in the same neighborhood. Feels like home already." Hadn't Maddy told him any of this? She must be repeating some of what he already knew.

Nolan moved slightly closer. He suppressed a smile, looking boyish and adorable. "I'm sure you'll be happy there."

Lumi's heart was pounding. "There's that 'happy' thing again. Don't you ever say anything else?"

He slid his hands into his back pockets as if reaching for something. "Sure. 'You're under arrest.'"

Lumi's mouth dropped open. *What?*

He continued, "And 'don't speed.' 'Your taillight is out.' 'Didn't your mother ever teach you better?' That sort of thing."

Lumi felt her face relax in relief. He'd been making a joke. "Great. Well, I'm glad we had this little non-conversation." She saw Mrs. Rasmusson wave to one of the workers near the repair bays as she left the office. "Thanks for the ride. I'll take Maddy home now." She reached for the door handle, but Nolan was there first, swinging it open, breathing somewhat harder. Lumi stood in the open doorway, very close to him. She met his eyes, acting more confident than she felt. "Are you *usually* this happy about everything?"

He glanced away and then back at her, seeming less playful. "No, Lumi. Just today."

Lumi got in and let Nolan close the door, then followed him with her eyes as he went around to open the passenger door for Mrs. Rasmusson. A little part of her was disappointed she would have to drive away so soon.

"Are you ladies all set?" Nolan asked, bending to better see Lumi after closing the door.

Lumi held her breath, debating for a few seconds if she should say aloud the response forming in her mind. Trying to keep from smiling, she said, "Yes, officer. And we'll be careful not to speed or have a taillight out or do anything else our mothers taught us we'd certainly better *not.*"

Nolan stepped back, laughing. He rapped his knuckles on the roof of the car for emphasis as Lumi started the engine.

Maddy clicked on her seatbelt. As she pulled the few remaining pins from her messy bun, she asked, "What was *that* all about?"

Lumi reached for her seatbelt, listening for any motor trouble. She put the car into gear and rolled forward. "I just had the oddest talk with that friend of yours." In the mirror, she could see Nolan standing where they'd left him, watching as they slowly left the gravelly lot. To Lumi, he looked like Mr. Darcy from *Pride and Prejudice,* gazing at Lizzy as she bumped along the dirt road from Pemberley in a carriage with her aunt and uncle. Lumi's stomach flipped. It felt flattering that he was watching her drive away.

Once clear of the parking lot, she let her nerves react to the unusualness of what had just happened—to the shock of letting a man have an effect on her, and the shock of liking that he'd had an effect on her.

Or *did* she?

Maybe she hated it.

Maybe she should forget the intimate exchange altogether.

Maddy dropped her hairpins into her purse, snapped its top shut, finger-combed her loosened, shoulder-length gray hair, and freed the bottom of her blouse from under the lap band of her seatbelt. "Nolan's adorable. One of the *nicest* young men. Thank you for coming along. Thank you, also, for not pressing me into talking to him about my scare."

"Why, though? You had a cop right beside you the whole ride here, and yet you never said a thing about the cards or a possible break-in."

Maddy shifted to get more comfortable. She put her hand on top of Lumi's arm for a moment. In a tone that was more emotional than Lumi was expecting, her friend said while looking straight ahead, "I simply *couldn't.* As soon as I stepped from the porch to get into the car, I had a flash before my eyes—a memory that had to do with one of the cards. It … it gave me pause, Lu. I was instantly more afraid of telling Nolan than of facing the fact that my home was violated."

"Which of the cards? What did you see in that flash of memory?"

Maddy's cornflower-blue eyes seemed worried as she looked at the buildings they were passing. "I can't say yet. I feel as though this is an assignment, in a way. Like I have to solve this mystery on my own." She turned toward Lumi. "Or with your help. Will you help me?"

Lumi drove in silence for a couple of blocks without replying, twisting her hands on the steering wheel, still feeling the confusing residual effects of talking to Nolan. Did she have time to help Maddy? Did she want to get involved in what might be a sinister or even dangerous situation? She was used to being on her own, never giving much of her attention or time to anything that wasn't a part of her daily schedule or work. Being independent had always given her strength.

The horrible images from the stereoscope cards appeared before her eyes as clearly as the traffic. Would Maddy be treading into frightening waters alone if Lumi didn't offer to help? "I will," she finally answered. "But you have to promise you won't keep any secrets from me. I'll help because I'm very curious and worried for you, but you'll have to give me every piece of the puzzle as you get them. Memories or other clues. Okay?"

"Yes. Yes. Oh, and Lumi, hon—please make a quick stop at the grocery on Main. I need pickles and olives and cream cheese. And ginger ale. Got to get crackers, of course. Fancy crackers. A lime and lemon, too." She dug around in her purse. "I'll make a list."

It felt like an abrupt change in subject, but Lumi didn't mention the cards again.

Once they were back from the repair shop and grocery store, Lumi carried in the bag of food and helped to put the various items into

Maddy's vintage pull-handle refrigerator and glass-fronted cupboards. She then checked the two main floors of the house for anything suspicious.

"All clear, Maddy." She put her hands into the pockets of her shorts. "I hate to leave you alone. Are you sure you'll be okay? You're not worried about another break-in?"

"Heavens, *no*. I've been without my Ras for years, and although I had a shock seeing those cards, I am perfectly fine on my own. You go on and have your dinner, Lu. Thank you."

Lumi hesitated, still looking around from where she stood. "You're very welcome." She stepped close to the front door. "Be sure to lock up already."

"Oh, pish-tosh. I'm *fine*. Do you want to take home a piece of my cake for dessert?"

After saying goodnight, coconut cake in hand, Lumi walked across the street to her own house on Willow Street in Barnwood. She warmed up leftover stroganoff and lima beans in her cozy kitchen, then ate sitting on her overstuffed dark green sofa in front of the TV, her bare toes sinking into the thick tan carpeting. The sofa, large TV, and black-painted modern coffee table were the only items in the living room. She hadn't even hung her favorite modern art prints on the walls since painting them a creamy white several weeks before. She was waiting to find just the right pieces of vintage furniture and was in no hurry to furnish or decorate since she was the only one who ever entered her house.

During commercial breaks in a Meg Ryan movie, she flipped through the photos of the stereocards she'd taken on her phone, enlarging the too-grainy details and wishing she'd held her hands steadier while snapping the pictures. The images shocked her anew, causing her to worry about Maddy again. What a terrible thing to do, and what a strange way to … what? Hurt the woman? Threaten her?

Before heading to bed hours later, Lumi stood at her front windows and looked across at Mrs. Rasmusson's house, front yard, garage, porch, and garden. To her surprise, a lamp in one upstairs bedroom lit at almost the same moment that a light went on in a bedroom on the opposite side of the otherwise dark house. Did she have a guest staying there for the night? Maybe. The items on her grocery list *had* seemed like food meant for a party, but Mrs. Rasmusson hadn't said a word about entertaining.

The longer she stood staring at Maddy's house, the more she felt certain something was wrong. The agreement between the two women was that there be no secrets.

However, having a visitor likely had nothing to do with the mystery of the cards. And, if it had nothing to do with the cards, Mrs. Rasmusson had a perfect right not to mention a party or having an overnight guest. But why hadn't Maddy even casually remarked that she was going to be hosting a get-together that evening? She'd allowed Lumi to search her house for intruders or toppled furniture, hadn't she? So why not at least say that she was expecting company? When Lumi had left her, she'd told the woman to be sure to lock her doors. Why hadn't she said anything then?

After locking her own back and front doors and turning off the downstairs lights, she went up to the bathroom. Lumi usually took a shower on summer nights, but she felt too vulnerable and uneasy. She undressed, put on a nightgown, and slid between her sheets. Not able to relax, she read a few pages of *Through the Looking Glass* and tried again to sleep. But as soon as she had closed her eyes, she thought of nothing but Maddy and the mysterious lights. Someone was *definitely* in her house. Who? Was it any of her business to find out? Probably not. But … what if the woman was being tied up or strangled? Those visions of horror overpowered her concerns about being nosy.

Lumi pounded and knocked and called. "Mrs. R? Are you home?" She felt around for the doorbell and rang it. Finally, light shone through the windows, and a sleepy Mrs. Rasmusson opened the door.

"What *is* it?" she hissed, looking irritated. "Oh, Lumi! It's the middle of the night! What's wrong? Are you hurt? Come in, come *in*. For goodness sake—you aren't even dressed. You shouldn't be running around outside in your robe and slippers."

Lumi pulled open the screen door and stepped inside the house that was lit by a vintage wrought-iron chandelier over the broad walnut staircase. Wide-eyed, she put her hands on her friend's shoulders and whispered, "Maddy—nod if you're safe. Shake your head if you need help."

Mrs. Rasmusson leaned back in surprise, then wrapped her thin blue cotton robe tighter. "Lumi Leski!" she whispered, pushing a lock of her gray hair behind her ear. "What gave you the idea that I'm in trouble? I'm *fine.*"

"Then why are you whispering?"

Maddy led Lumi into the living room. "I have a friend staying the night. He obviously heard you pounding and ringing the doorbell, but I know him well enough to know that he crashed back to sleep as soon as that ruckus was over. I don't want to wake him up again, though."

He? Lumi's mouth hung open in surprise. "Oh."

12

The woman smiled, then shrugged before explaining, her eyes guilty but defensive, "He and I have ... well, he's a widower who gets lonesome—like I do. One night per week, I go to Chess' house, and one other night per week he comes over here. We have snacks after dinner, play rummy, watch TV, and then we go up to separate bedrooms. It's nice to have that feeling again ... that someone caring is in the same house, even if it is only twice per week. We've known each other forever. We were even in high school together." She grinned but wagged a finger in warning. "This arrangement is our own little secret, by the way."

Lumi sighed in relief, smiling. She swept her hair behind her neck, realizing she had gotten hot from the excitement and worry. "How modern of you, Maddy. I hope I can find a companion in my old age. If I don't have a husband." She grinned. "Okay. I'll go back home now. I'll still be smiling when I drift off, you know."

Maddy put her hands on her hips. "We're just friends. I know he wants us to live together full time, and probably even get married, but this arrangement suits me fine. I feel independent, and yet ... needed." She dropped her arms at her sides. "He has me. I have him. We're in our seventies, so it's not like there's any big rush to run to the altar." She wiped a hint of dampness from her eyes with her fingers. As she aimed Lumi toward the door, she added, "I'm sure you'll have someone in your life as soon as you decide it's what you really want. You're young. You have your business—that's where your focus is. But believe me, as soon as you feel ready, there will be a hundred men lined up to stand beside you through life. You're pretty. You're sweet and funny and smart. As soon as you're ready, your man will be here. *Poof*—conjured up like a rabbit from Houdini's hat."

"I don't think Harry Houdini did that trick."

"I suppose not, but I'm too tired to think of a better metaphor, sorry." Mrs. Rasmusson locked the door behind her, and a moment later, the hall light went out.

Walking across the street to stand on her front porch, Lumi mentally replayed what the older woman had said and denied it all. There would be no man for her. She was never going to be ready for a romance. She was sure of it.

She thought again about the fact that no one ever flirted with her the way Nolan had that afternoon. Not even her college boyfriend, who was a boyfriend in name only. He'd never joked with her, never acted interested in her. She knew she purposely discouraged men from getting romantic ideas. It had worked to repel men her whole life. She sighed. Why hadn't *Nolan* been put off?

13

Going inside, she went into the bathroom to study her face in an unrestored farmhouse mirror. Not bad, she thought. A little makeup would help, but not bad.

Why was she suddenly critiquing her appearance? Why did it matter? She only cared about getting her business going, paying her bills, and furnishing her house. She wasn't interested in anything else—especially not a friendly, handsome cop whose muscles filled out a shirt but weren't too bulky, whose eyes gave away his feelings, and whose face was already becoming etched on her heart.

Lumi went to her orange-walled, comfortable bedroom. She reclined on her bed and switched off the table lamp made from a stack of vintage books and thought about the boys she'd known in school. Which one would she choose to have a companionable relationship with in old age? Other than Cal, a boy she'd had a crush on during her senior year, she felt the others in her class were all like brothers or cousins to her. No one had asked her out, but all of them were kind and friendly. Any one of them would be equally fine as a companion to play cards with in the evening in their dotage, but none of them would feel like a romantic suitor—not even Cal anymore. It didn't seem hard to understand, then, the friendly arrangement Maddy had made with Chess.

Chapter Two

Lumi woke after six-thirty to the sounds of birds that had likely been busy at their work of welcoming impending daylight for some time. She stepped to the window and parted curtains made of thin vintage cotton material that looked as floral and summery as the sunny day that was dawning.

After cutting her lawn with a 1950s reel mower, taking a shower, leisurely eating eggs and toast, checking her email, and watching a few minutes of cable news, Lumi drove downtown in her silver SUV that held at least a dozen boxes of items she'd bought at an antique auction the weekend before. She parked at the rear entrance to Lumi's Curiosities and unloaded everything into her small storage room.

At a few minutes before ten in the morning, she opened for business, noting that the temperature felt like eighty degrees already. Sitting at her wooden worktable, she picked up a soft cloth to start cleaning built-up grime from a ruby red Fenton glass hobnail basket but was interrupted by the jingle of the brass bell over her door. It was Nolan.

"I saw your sign and figured there could only be one Lumi in town." Walking along the aisle that led to her worktable, he asked, "Is that a French name?"

Lumi put down the basket and noticed Nolan was wearing black slacks, a white dress shirt, and a gray necktie. She wondered if he would again be heading into court for the day. "French? Uh, no. Finnish. It means 'snow.' Which is weird, since I was born in the summer."

"It's snow wonder I like it."

"No. Bad," she said, trying to seem disapproving.

"I suppose you've heard every pun about your name by now."

She thought for a moment, then shook her head. "Snow joking—I haven't."

"Well … that's just sad." He shyly met her eyes. "You need to hang around with more punsters, Lumi."

She couldn't think of a response. It had sounded like an invitation.

He browsed the antique dishes, furniture, paintings, figurines, tools, books, and miscellaneous vintage household items on display, paying particular attention to a rustic narrow pantry cabinet. Nolan tested the shelves for sturdiness and glanced at the price tag hanging from a string on the top shelf before moving on to another aisle. Pulling a hardbound from a tall, metal bookcase on the far wall, he said, "Michener. That guy can *write*. My dad started me on his stuff a few years ago." He replaced the book and walked on. Holding a blue enamel World War II British canteen, he looked around approvingly and said, "Great store. Above-average offerings with a lot of variety. Been here long?"

"About three months," she answered as she wrote a price and inventory number on a paper label for the basket. "There are so many antiques for sale online that it's hard to compete, but I think every town should have at least one antique shop. Gives the tourists an excuse to stop and stretch their legs. The auction house I worked for is in Indianapolis, but I grew up here and wanted to come back. Like I said yesterday, I was able to buy a house near the one I lived in as a kid."

He put down the canteen and studied Lumi's face as if really looking at her for the first time. "We must have been in different grades. I don't remember you at all. You seem young to have your own house and business."

She felt like he was trying to find out her graduation year—and age. She smiled to herself, pleased that he was interested enough to fish for personal details. "I am, I guess. I was settled-in and content to go on rising through the ranks at the auction house, and I probably would have stayed there, but my great-aunt passed away, leaving a large estate. My mom and dad inherited half, and my two brothers and I each got a third of the other half. I paid off my debts, quit my job, and the rest is Barnwood history. Most of those funds are gone, so I'm living by my wits again, monetarily speaking."

"Still, you spent it wisely. Set yourself up in an interesting career where you're your own boss. It's admirable."

The teasing tone was gone from his rich baritone voice, giving Lumi a clearer idea of the man's personality.

Nolan returned to the pantry cabinet and placed a hand on its top corner. "I've been looking for something like this. Did you get it locally, or did you bring it here from Indy?"

"I didn't bring anything from Indianapolis except my own furniture and clothes and personal stuff. Everything you see here is new to me. In the past few months, I've bought it, hauled it, cleaned it—all without help. I just unloaded the last group from an estate auction this morning." She looked at the cabinet under his hand. "We have the same taste. I *love* that piece. I found it at an estate sale about a month ago. I was going to repaint it, but once I had it cleaned, I knew it needed to stay the way it was. I almost kept it. It sat on my front porch for a few days, but then I decided its true owner was waiting to find it in the shop."

16

Some emotion flickered in his eyes. "Here I am, Lumi, wanting to buy it. I call that fate." He touched the end of his tie as if remembering he had to be somewhere. "What time do you close?"

"At six. I'll have the silverware and dishes cleared off so it'll be ready when you come back. Want to pay now or later?"

"Now." Nolan took the price tag from the top shelf and brought it to her. He turned away again before adding, "I think when you see something you're interested in, you should take action right away."

Lumi blushed, flattering herself that he may have been talking about her as well as the cabinet.

He didn't look at her when he turned to step closer to the cash register. Lumi saw that his face was also slightly red.

She made a mistake on the register the first time she punched in the price, then stammered and apologized before starting over. "I'll have it ready before closing time. Thank you." She placed dollar bills and coins in his hand, noticing for the first time in a long time that she should file her nails and maybe paint them.

He took his receipt, nodded, and met her eyes for an instant, appearing to be as nervous as she felt. He walked out of the shop as a family of four was coming in.

Lumi exhaled, scowling at herself. She had been skittish and thinking flirty thoughts around Nolan Sanders, and that wasn't her personality at all. She was fierce and independent, and she didn't need a man to make her happy.

But if that was so, why was her heart hammering? Why was she picturing Nolan, his muscles bulging, slowly ripping a price tag from her top … shelf? Why was he having this effect on her? Men of all descriptions had been everywhere on the college campus. Everywhere at the auction house. Everywhere, period. She'd avoided them all skillfully. She never allowed them past her defenses. Why, then, was Nolan getting under her skin?

She didn't like this. She didn't want it. He made her uncomfortable. She wasn't feeling like her old self at all. He was coming back later. She wished he wouldn't. He had no right to look at her the way he did with those eyes of his—those expressive, gorgeous brown eyes.

Sighing, she glanced at the time on her phone.

Why did six o'clock have to be so many hours away?

While eating lunch that afternoon, Lumi thought again about the stereoscope cards. She took out her phone and studied the first of the

17

blurry photos she'd taken. The frightening, horrific image felt like it *was* meant to be a threat to Mrs. Rasmusson. The slow-acting method of such a threat was what made it insidious and strange.

Blackmail wasn't likely. There had been no note with the cards. If someone *was* trying to scare her into admitting a past crime, why weren't they there to witness her reaction? Why not give Maddy the images by hand to confront her and make her directly accountable?

After eating, Lumi forced her thoughts back into the present and went to her storage room for another box of the antiques from the auction. She hadn't been to that auction house since she was a teenager with her mother and was happily surprised at how little money things had sold for when most of the bidders had left late in the evening. She'd purchased all that would fit into her SUV without even looking carefully through the box lots.

She now saw they contained silver-plate flatware, vintage linens, jigsaw puzzles, toy cars and trucks, a dented trumpet, 1970s sheet music, religious books, and a few interesting glass pharmaceutical bottles with their fragile, browned labels intact—including two amber bottles made in nearby Fairmount in the 1890s. No great treasures, but several things would look appealing in the cases that lined the walls or on the top of the many cloth-covered kitchen tables used for displays throughout the shop.

She placed the first box onto the floor at her feet and sat on the cushioned stool behind the checkout counter. The first item she removed was a psychedelic-era Liberace record album. Next was a handful of mid-century kids' Valentines. There were metal cookie cutters and a rolling pin; an unopened package of hairnets; a celluloid hand mirror; two angular art deco compacts; a round, mid-century red, yellow, and green metal serving tray decorated with a dancing, chef-hatted alligator holding barbeque forks and saying, "It's hot dog time!"; and a Flintstones lunch box filled with handwritten letters, postmarked from the mid-1980s through the early 1990s. At the bottom of the cardboard box were several loose bracelets and other assorted jewelry that didn't appear to be valuable or attractive. Lumi put almost everything aside to price later.

She allowed herself time to enjoy the Valentine messages written by very young hands, and their comical and colorful illustrations. She wondered how many kids from the era ended up dating in high school, and how many had gotten married and raised families together.

After an elderly couple shopping for a wedding present left with an expensive ten-volume set of beautiful hand-tooled leather-bound books on American wildlife, Lumi decided to read one of the letters from the

18

lunch box. She checked the recipient's address on several of the pale-green envelopes. Each one had been mailed to the same home on the north side of Indianapolis. The envelope with the earliest postmark was on the bottom, so Lumi flipped the stack before opening the first tri-folded letter.

Dear Jackie,

Home is lonesome without our girl. Even the radishes miss you. They've been growing and growing like mad, taking over the garden. I don't know why we planted so many. I know you love them roasted or pickled, but now that you aren't here to enjoy them I suppose I'll have to drive down to you with a basketful of the red things. Is Marty liking work better now? Your dad says hello. He just walked through the front room and asked who I was writing to. When I said you, he did his half of your secret handshake. He misses you, too. Now that you're a big, grown-up lady and married and gone, we feel like such old folks here alone in this house.

Your grandma and Pearline said they are sacking up clothes and such they want to give away, and I should gather up things, too. I won't touch yours—don't worry. I'm leaving everything in your room exactly as you left it. I even left your record collection all messy like you had it! Your dad thinks I'm sentimental.

I got a call today that the photos your dad and I took at your wedding are ready at the drug store. We should have sprung for a real photographer. I'm worried that we won't have taken any good shots of you and Marty over at the church. I wish we'd bought a couple more rolls of film! Even so, we have our memories of the day. I'll bring the photos down with me the next time I visit. Nadine called the day after your wedding, wanting the pineapple-orange cake recipe. I told her you made it yourself, which she thought was very sweet. I'll let you decide if you want to give out your baking secrets or not.

Dad is walking through the room again. This time he has on his ratty swim trunks, which I guess means he is taking Waller down to the lake for a swim. That hairy beast sure loves that your dad is retired now! Me, too. I'm happy he took early retirement to be with me more. Makes it a lot less lonesome here, but I do miss you, my girl! Waller Bee misses you. He wanders around looking for you, going into your bedroom, sniffing around the TV where you always sat on that giant pillow on the floor making your crafts or reading.

19

Call me on Sunday, Teensa. I want to talk to you about something, but I don't want it in a letter. If you're like me, you'll be keeping all the letters you get now that you're living in your own little house, and I don't want you to have it written down what I want to say. The phone or in person is better. Now, don't get scared. It isn't like we're up here dying or anything. Don't worry. But do call.

Love, Mama
P.S. Dad says goodbye. The dog does, too!

Enclosed in the envelope was a wallet-sized color snapshot of a long-furred gray mutt with a happy, open-mouth smile. He looked soaked to the skin. On the rear was written, "Waller Bee. World's wettest dog."

Waller Bee. Lumi wondered how he'd gotten that name. Wallaby? Had Jackie or Mama or Dad originally named him Wallaby?

The return address was from a house in Frankton, Indiana. No name at all—not even initials—was included with the address. Probably Jackie had eventually moved from Indianapolis to Cicero and had taken the letters with her, and there they had gotten put into a box lot and sold by mistake at the auction.

Lumi looked at the next several letters, comparing the postmark dates to be sure she would be reading them in chronological order.

Dear Teensa,

You didn't phone up on Sunday. I don't know that you got my letter asking you to call us in time. The mail is awful slow nowadays! Like "mole asses" your grandma used to say. Still, it's a good, cheap way to keep in touch. I miss you, baby. We had tons of fun when you were a little thing running around here in braids and skipping rope like a kangaroo. The new neighbor girl, Betsy, comes to visit us now, most every day. I think her mama told her to, that I was lonesome for a little girl around the house. She's funny and bubbly. I think she likes your dad. She took a magic marker out to the garden when he was on his hands and knees and drew a smiley face right on the top of his head in the bald spot! Your dad let her. I think he likes her, too.

You'll have to let us know if you and Marty need extra money for going out at night. I never hear that you're going to a movie or anything now that you're married. Let me tell you something, Teensa—don't stop dating. Ever! A man doesn't like to feel like the romance is over once you've said I Do. Hold his hand. Walk up and kiss him when he doesn't think you're even aware that he's in the house. Things like that matter. You'll find he'll do sweet things for you, too. Men are softer than we give them credit for. Your young married life should be full of blooms and missing shirt buttons. Once a baby comes along, you'll have a lot more work and worry. Enjoy taking off your shoes as often as you can, if you know what I mean.

I packed three brown bags of junk for the thrift shop. Your grandma and Pearline had about ten bags full waiting for me when I got to their house. I went through them once I got them out to my car. I didn't want her giving away anything that meant something to me or that you maybe can use now in your own house. I saved nice bath towels for you, and dish cloths. I had to agree with the clothes they were giving away. I can't believe we ladies used to wear those dresses and things! Ha!

Call me when you can. It doesn't have to be on Sunday. I'm home most of the time when I'm not out for groceries or so on. I can hear the phone if I'm in the back yard, too. I suppose I could call you, baby, but I never know your schedule anymore. I have a dull life compared to yours, don't I?

Say hi to Marty!
Love, Mama

Lumi was disappointed that a photo wasn't included with this letter, and she was getting very curious as to what it was that Mama had wanted to talk to Jackie about all those years ago.

A red-haired woman dressed in navy-blue shorts and a yellow t-shirt stepped into the shop. She nodded in greeting to Lumi and browsed in silence for a few minutes. Twice she went to look at the display windows. "May I please buy that plump stuffed bear?" she asked, walking closer to Lumi while pointing behind her. "He's identical to one I had as a kid. I made the mistake of giving him to my little brother when he had the chickenpox. When he gave the bear back to me, there were red ink spots all over it that never washed out. I *hate* that I got rid of him. The bear, I mean. Not my brother. I regretted it almost immediately. After all— what're a few spots between old friends?"

Lumi walked to the display, lifted the sizable light-brown plush bear from the rocking chair, removed the price tag, and handed it to the woman. "Here. He's yours. No charge. I'm a sucker for a happy ending."

With a look of shocked pleasure, the woman took the toy into her arms and almost cried. She hugged the bear tightly and fought to control her emotions as she stood clutching a facsimile of her long-lost friend.

"Don't let your brother have this one," Lumi advised. "Boys get the dumbest ideas."

"I was silly to let my old stuffed pal go. Girls get the dumbest ideas, too. Are you sure you don't want me to pay for him?"

Lumi shook her head. "I couldn't," she said earnestly. "Now—go home and have a tea party. That bear has been sitting alone in his rocking chair for too long. He looks thirsty."

After getting a drink of water herself, Lumi scanned her wares for another item to put in the front windows on the rocker. She decided on the alligator serving tray. The days leading up to the Fourth of July seemed to be the perfect time to sell anything having to do with cooking out.

The tray was sold in less than thirty minutes when a woman and her adult daughter snapped it up for their kitschy kitchen collection.

"This will look great with the chef's hat-wearing lobster ketchup bottle we got last month from a garage sale," the woman said, admiring the tray in her hands. "I don't suppose you have any unusual mustard bottles or jars in the shop?"

"No, but I'll watch for one." She went to her counter for a pen and notepad. "Here. Give me your number or email, and I'll contact you if I find anything you might like."

The price Lumi had gotten for the tray paid for four full boxes of items she'd bought at the auction. That group was off to a good start, she thought.

She sorted a box of silverware, cleared off Nolan's cabinet, and then opened the next letter from the lunch box.

Dear Jackie,

I was glad we finally talked! See? It wasn't anything bad, after all. A will is important to have, and now that you have a new name and husband, your dad and I wanted to change things legally. I don't like to talk about money in that way, or about what will happen when we pass on, but it's nice to have such a thing all settled. If I go first, I want your dad to live with you, or right next door, if possible. He doesn't do well on his own. Your dad wouldn't let me put it in the will, but I'm telling you, baby—make sure I'm buried with nice, warm socks on my feet. Nothing too tight, nothing too loose. Warm and soft. I hate when my feet get cold! I don't want to run around in heaven always complaining to the angels about being cold-feeted!

22

Your grandma and Pearline came over yesterday in the afternoon. We went to the new shopping mall and you should see the weird clothes they have in the stores now! We had to go in the old lady stores and departments in order to get anything that wasn't neon green or with Pac Man on the front. I have no idea what a Pac Man is, but it looks nothing like a man to me! Anyway, I bought a few spring things and got your dad some new swim trunks and a couple of polo shirts.

We miss you, of course. It didn't feel right having a day out with the ladies without you there, too. We ate at Arby's afterward, but your grandma was suspicious of what they put in the horsey sauce, so she ate her sandwich plain with only the meat and bun. I assured her it didn't have anything to do with horses, but that did no good. Imagine how it was to grow up in a house with your grandma in it!

Okay. Now that the socks have been covered, and now that the will is done, I'll stop being mysterious. I'm tucking a little money in this letter. Go out to eat or to a show. Or go find out what a Pac Man is, you two! You're both young. Live a little!

I want to bring the radishes and wedding photos to you soon. You should see the funny one of you throwing the bouquet to your girl friends! It looks like the camera caught you all in the middle of a disco routine! Let me know by mail or phone when I'll be welcome.

Little Betsy is looking at me through the sliding door, so I'll close now. She has a sad face. I suppose I'll need to find out what's troubling her.

Love, Mama

Lumi put the letter back inside its envelope and stepped into the restroom. When she emerged, it must have been later than she realized. Nolan was in the shop. The knot of his tie was loose, and his sleeves were rolled up. She stood beside the cash register, her heart rate quickening as she watched him walk up the aisle.

It annoyed her that he was attractive. That his eyes were … perfect. He smiled, and it frightened her that he was having a peculiar effect on her stomach. His face was excitingly familiar yet fresh and new. She wished the clock would stop to give her time to compose herself before she would be expected to speak, but the seconds kept on ticking. "Is it six already?" she forced herself to ask, trying to snap out of the spell he was effortlessly casting.

Nolan pulled his phone from the pocket of his black slacks and glanced at it, standing near his purchase. "Five forty-five. I see my cabinet is cleared and ready. Thanks."

Lumi's voice wavered and then recovered. "I'll miss it, but ... I'm glad it's going to a good home."

Nolan seemed to hesitate as if he could sense Lumi was thinking about something other than the kitchen cabinet. "I'm glad you feel that way, Lumi. Believe me—I'll take very good care of it."

Lumi met his eyes, careful to keep from smiling as she closed the lid on the lunch box and slid it under her counter. She then mentally groaned to herself, worried her moves must have looked suspicious. "I don't know why I did that," she said with a sigh. She took it out again. "I think I feel nosy for reading these old letters a mother wrote to her daughter. I got them in a box of miscellaneous stuff at an auction. I wonder what I should do with them."

Nolan looked at the box, stepping close. "How old are they?"

"They're from the 'eighties and 'nineties," she said, pushing the box toward him across her counter. She felt the warmth of his arm next to hers. She noticed the soft hair on his forearm and the careful cut of his fingernails. His fingers were long and looked strong—perfect for holding hands, Lumi thought, then snapped out of her startling fantasy. She looked from his hands to his face, struggling to put her walls up again, afraid of the attraction she felt. She knew her expression must be hardening, but she let it, needing to be able to function again with some sense of control.

Nolan suddenly frowned. His eyes altered from hope to hopelessness in a second, as if giving up a fight he knew he couldn't win before it had started. He opened the lunch box lid. "I think you should consider these lost, not sold. No one puts personal letters in a sale on purpose. If they don't want them, they throw them out. If they ended up in an auction, I'd say it was by accident." He lifted out the top envelope. "Have you thought of trying to find the woman these are addressed to?"

"I hadn't thought that far along, I guess."

"Check online for any Jackie Martinsons in Indiana. Probably there won't be many women with that name."

She nodded, embarrassed that she had read a few of the letters instead of immediately trying to find their owner.

"I'll grab the cabinet and leave you to your investigations. I hope you find her. I'm sure she'll be glad to have them back. Goodnight." His usual good humor had left his voice, and he seemed disinterested in hanging around any longer than necessary once he'd given her his advice.

She watched him easily carry away the heavy piece of furniture she'd had such a struggle getting into the shop a month before. Lumi felt like she'd ruined their friendship before it had even started. Maybe he hadn't approved of her reading someone else's mail. Or, he could have been distracted by thoughts that had nothing to do with her.

Could she have only imagined his interest in her to begin with?

Did she frighten him away when she slammed her walls around her again in self-defense?

On warm and sunny evenings, Lumi occasionally walked three blocks from her home to eat dinner on the outdoor patio of a family restaurant, a newspaper or a book as her companion. This evening, however, she didn't feel like eating, especially not in public. She felt like she'd spoiled her appetite forever.

But why? It wasn't like Nolan had scolded her, and he hadn't said she'd done anything illegal. Was she overreacting? Why was she even bothered by his attitude? They barely knew each other.

Lumi went straight upstairs to her bedroom and switched on the air conditioner. After sitting on her bed to rest and think, she opened her laptop and typed in Jackie's information from the envelopes. None of the internet search results connected the address to her name.

Lumi did a search for "Jackie Martinson Indiana." There were seven matches. She found zero matches for anyone with the nickname "Teensa." She did a name search on Facebook. Four of the many Jackie Martinsons on the site were in Indiana, but only one could have been a young woman in the 1980s. She read that particular Jackie's limited biographical info. It listed her current location as Strawtown. *This has to be her!* Lumi thought. Strawtown and Cicero—the location of the auction—are only a few miles apart. Jackie hadn't posted on Facebook for years. Maybe she wasn't living. Maybe the auction had been of *Jackie's* possessions, not her mother's.

Lumi went to her own homepage for updates. It was strange that over a hundred people routinely shared their stories and photos with her, but none of them had anything to do with her in person. What made a friend a friend on social media, and why didn't a hundred online friends translate into a full social life in reality?

She enlarged her profile photo, wanting to see what the rest of the world saw when they first connected to her electronically. She remembered posing while holding a gavel at the auctioneer's podium, playing around for the camera. It wasn't like her. She had been deliberately, habitually professional at the auction house, but a coworker who was taking photos for the company website had handed her a gavel and told her to smile. Lumi copied the flattering photograph to use as her profile photo simply because nearly no other photo had been taken of her since college.

She studied the woman who was Lumi just a year ago. Her very long, golden hair wasn't the same light, creamy color it had been for most of her life, but it was passably nice and had a bit of natural curl. Was it dumb to keep it long, especially in the summer? Should she get a short cut now that she didn't have to dress up for the occasional fine art auction? Maybe. The auction house owners had often complimented her hair, and she felt that was why she was often asked to work the floor at high-end sales. There was no reason to have a hairstyle or hair length that appealed to anyone other than herself anymore.

Lumi examined her face in the photo. She saw her big blue eyes like her mother's, and long eyelashes that didn't stand out unless she wore mascara, but she didn't like mascara. Her lips were full and pretty enough, but they didn't really pop unless she wore lipstick, but she hated lipstick. Average nose, right in the center. A few freckles. Straight teeth, so those two teenage years of braces had been worth the trouble. She didn't scare anyone out of her antique shop with her looks, and she liked to tell herself that that was all that counted.

Lumi glanced away from the computer and down at her slim body that had gotten stronger since she'd opened her business and had been doing the physical work herself. There was a scar on her knee from a fall while roller skating on the Monon Trail last summer. A scab on her other knee where she banged it hard while moving her brass bed from one upstairs room to another after painting her walls a week ago. She was sure there was nothing remarkable about her appearance, and that had always felt like a good thing. A comforting thing.

Sighing, she looked through public records online and found a telephone listing for the one possible correct Jackie, took out her cell phone, and dialed. "Hello? Is this Jackie Martinson? Did you recently place items into an auction in Cicero? You did? I wonder if you realize a lunch box full of letters sold along with some household goods. I bought them. Would you like them back?"

There was a long pause as if Jackie couldn't decide how to answer. When she did, Lumi was surprised that the woman's voice was angry. "I don't want them. Throw them away. I didn't mean to pack them for the auction, but I don't want to keep them anymore. Mom died. I'd sent her that box of letters a long time ago so she could see what she wrote to me about back in the day, and out they went when we cleared away her stuff. Oh, well. Whatever. I don't care what you do with them now. No one means anything to anyone once they've died. I won't be missed, either. We all wither away until there's no one left who cares if we die or not. Just so much wasted space on the planet."

Jackie ended the call without saying goodbye.

Lumi thought about Mama from the letters, how she was kind and loving, and that she wanted to be buried with warm socks on her feet. She hoped Jackie had asked the funeral home to do that. However, she couldn't picture the Jackie from the phone call taking any extra care to look through her mother's sock drawer to select exactly the right pair for Mama to wear through eternity. She wondered what had happened in the intervening years.

Lumi finally went downstairs to put a square of leftover lasagna into the microwave. She stepped onto her narrow porch to retrieve the mail and newspaper, and, when the microwave beeped, she put her dinner, three bills, two pieces of junk mail, and the paper on her large, oval oak dining table. The TV in the living room was tuned to Jeopardy, and she mentally played along as she ate. Nothing separated the kitchen, dining area, and living room except the half of a wall that housed an oven, cabinets, and the refrigerator.

After eating, she walked to her front window to look across the street at Maddy's house. She thought about visiting, but it was later than the summer evening light made it seem. Was Maddy alone or was Chess there with her? Thinking about the older couple reminded Lumi of her college boyfriend, Brad, and how he had hardly been a boyfriend at all. The last time she had heard from Brad, it was in a short email. He wrote that he was a junior-high gym teacher in Bloomington. He also wrote that he was happy he'd taken the job. He didn't mention a girlfriend or wife, but Lumi felt that he might have one but didn't want to say so in case it would hurt her feelings. It wouldn't have, she knew.

"I'm about a month away from turning twenty-eight years old, I live alone, and I've never been in love." Lumi said this to her faint reflection in the window, her arms folded across her chest, holding in more feelings she wasn't ready to admit to the woman looking back at her. Staying unattached had been a goal for her whole adult life. No serious relationships, no physical intimacy other than nearly bland pecks to Brad's lips or cheek, and no going out except for solo dinners after Brad and she had separated after graduation. There had been nothing but work

27

and study in college, and then very little other than work and reading after college. She had loved the huge, busy auction company in Indianapolis and had liked the people there, but those years had been a means to a singular goal: to become one of the auctioneers.

Inheriting her great-aunt's money had been lifechanging. She was surprised that what she had been working toward meant very little when she was given free rein to stay on her planned course or to set out on her own. She hadn't wanted to start an auction company; that would have meant too much hard work and responsibility. Opening an antique shop in a small town seemed like the perfect way to use her education and experience, and yet gave her more free time to explore the state for interesting items and to relax without the stress of having a boss or employees.

She drew the orange and blue paisley curtains closed thinking about her parents who had moved to Florida after they had sold their home, and about her two older brothers in California, both married with children. When she thought about where she would most like to have a shop and to buy a house, her old hometown of Barnwood felt like the perfect place.

But it wasn't.

Other than Maddy, she had no friends in town. Everyone had moved on, and she was too shy to do what it took to turn customers or unfamiliar neighbors into friends. She had her same, old antisocial life all over again. She had fooled herself into believing that she'd lose her shyness if she moved back to her hometown. Lumi found out it doesn't matter where you live—friendships don't just magically happen. Walls don't fall away on their own. Fears remain fears unless you deal with them. Loneliness feeds upon itself. No one will come to your rescue of you push everyone away or keep them at arms' length.

Chapter Three

Lumi stretched and yawned at seven-thirty the next morning, her temples pounding from a headache. Sitting on the edge of her brass bed, she pushed her fingers into her hair and tried to rub away the pain. She'd fallen asleep half-upright while reading instead of in her usual position, and her head was paying the price. The orange walls and art prints in her bedroom seemed overly colorful and more joyful by far than she felt.

She put her book on the nightstand and turned off her lamp. A memory of Nolan washed over her, and she wondered again if she would ever feel ready for a real romance or to try to make new friends.

The friends she'd had in school who remained in town were busy with husbands and jobs and kids and everything that went along with them. They had work friends and couple friends. No one was going to call up someone they barely remembered from high school who'd been away from town for a decade. Bit by bit, Lumi was discovering that they'd moved on. She'd come back to Barnwood not to start over fresh, but to go back to what was familiar. Her old hometown was never going to feel the same as it had when she was a kid, she now realized.

Lumi took a long, scalp-massaging shower and dressed, thinking about the letters, thinking about the stereocards, thinking about Nolan. There was a new thrill running through her veins she couldn't connect to just one of the three alone—each was an exciting challenge or problem. She hadn't felt this kind of heightened sense of adventure even when she was setting up her antique shop. These feelings were new.

She slipped into a tan short-sleeve blouse and a pair of brown denim shorts, mentally replaying her phone call with Jackie Martinson the night before. Time changes everything, she knew, but what had happened to make the woman seem terribly bitter about her mother? Maybe she was only bitter about *losing* her. Maybe she couldn't get over the loss.

Lumi vowed never to read another letter from Jackie's mom; never to look at another photo. It wasn't right. She should throw them out. There was no point in reading them, anyway. She knew Jackie had moved to Strawtown and that her mom had passed away. End of story. What had been written long ago didn't matter. Lumi wasn't a member of the family. She didn't need to intrude on their privacy. End of story. *End of story*.

She carried the lunch box downstairs and put it on the gray-and-red marble kitchen counter, noting that Fred Flintstone seemed happy to be near the refrigerator. Lumi searched her cupboards for something different to eat for breakfast. She eyed the pancake flour, oatmeal, and corn flakes. Those didn't seem appealing, so she ended up making three boiled eggs, raisin toast, and rooibos tea like she did nearly every morning.

After eating, despite the promises made to herself, she opened the box and pulled out the envelope that was dated a week later than the last one she'd read.

Dear Teensa,

How are the radishes? Tired of them yet? I could have brought you even more than that, but your dad said I was bringing you too many already. I've given a lot away to the neighbors, and now that's that for our radishes this year. I'll plant far less next year. If I plant any at all. Without you here, I think they only make me sad to see their leafy green tops and red heads poking up from the garden soil.

I think I told you when I was down to see you that Betsy broke her arm, poor thing! She is hating having to wear a cast. I painted daisies on it with the acrylic paint you left behind with your craft supplies, so at least her arm looks more cheerful. I told her to have her friends decorate it or write on it, too. She fell off her bike at that dangerous curb at the end of our street. I've complained about that for years. Maybe now something will be done. I remember when I was in two leg casts for months and months from the tragedy. Such an ordeal! At least Betsy can run around fine.

Waller Bee got a summer haircut at last. He sure looks weird! Like a different pup altogether! I'll get a roll of film next time I'm at the drug store and send you a photo. Did I tell you that Waller still sleeps on your bed? You're not there, but he keeps hoping, I guess. I would say that you should come and get him to your place, but your dad would be lost without his furry friend. They do everything together! I think your dad wants to learn how to play golf, but he's afraid they won't let WB on the course, so now he's thinking of doing some other thing where he can take the dog. Maybe fishing or jogging. Loads of people are jogging. We didn't know about jogging in my day. We called it running around. Got to have a new word for it when they sell all kinds of equipment and shoes and clothes for it!

I'm going with Brenda, her sis-in-law, Grandma and Pearline to Ft. Wayne a week from Tues. We're going to a museum to see an exhibition of Andrew Wyeth's paintings. Won't that be nice? Do you want to join us? You could drive this far, and then get in Brenda's station wagon and ride along. We'll eat lunch and go see the art. There are really excellent restaurants in Ft. Wayne. You let me know if you want to go and I'll pay for everything.

What did you think of the scarf? I'm glad your grandma taught you to knit and sew and crochet and all that. She used to win prizes at the state fair for her handcrafts, you know, and now you're so good with crafts, and with your camera, too. Your photos are still in their albums in the living room. You'll have to get those and take them to your home the next time you're here. And, yes, I know it isn't scarf season, but your grandma isn't a fast knitter like she used to be. She wanted to send it when it was done instead of waiting for the snow to fly. There must have been a sale on purple yarn. Purple isn't your favorite color, but you can pretend it is when you see your grandma or write to her. Or, maybe don't. You might end up with a purple sweater, too! Ha!

I've got to go. Your dad put on his new swim trunks, has the dog on his leash, and he's grumbling around in the kitchen cupboards looking for something to eat before they leave. I swear, you can't tell him apart from a bear when he's wrecking up the kitchen!

Love from Mama and Dad

Lumi smiled as she put the letter back into its envelope. What a sad thing that people don't write long handwritten notes like they used to.

She made a vow to herself that she wouldn't throw out the letters, but she would keep what she learned in them to herself. She wouldn't take them out of her house, and she would only read one letter per day.

When personal items had been mixed in with groups of things to sell at the auction house, no one had bothered to try to return them. Everything that entered the building went into the auction; if it didn't sell, was donated away. Old family Bibles, photographs, diaries, wedding rings, personally-engraved silver—everything was sold without hesitation. After reading Jackie's letters, Lumi was determined to try to reunite very personal items with their rightful owners.

She finished her tea and washed the two dishes and a pot, wondering if she should make another attempt to get Jackie to take back her letters now or if it would be better to wait. Walking to her SUV, she heard a "Yoo-hoo!" and turned to find the source of the call. It was Maddy, standing outside her front door. Lumi crossed the street and stood on the sidewalk near her picket fence.

"Lumi! How are you?"

"Fine, Maddy. I'm heading to work. I felt like going in early today. How are you?"

Her neighbor opened her screen door and unlocked the wooden door and pushed it open. "Good. I'm just getting home now."

Lumi didn't ask if she meant that she'd been gone all night to her friend Chess' house or if she had been out on errands already that morning. "I'll maybe pop over after dinner tonight, okay?"

Maddy waved again. "Sounds good. See you then, dear."

The antique shop needed a general clean-up and minor reorganization. Lumi scattered the items she knew sold best throughout the cases and displays to keep foot traffic moving from the front to the back so that more of everything could be seen. She placed an original Mrs. Beasley doll on the rocking chair in the windows after wiping the doll's face clean and adjusting her plastic eyeglass frames.

Her next-door neighbor, a lawyer, rapped at her glass door and waved in greeting. Lumi waved in return. She had that same waving acquaintance with several other downtown business owners, and with the neighbors around her home, too. Never any conversation, but there was a feeling of friendliness between them.

After lunch, she priced more of her auction purchases. A large box was full of 1920s and '30s children's picture books. Instead of shelving the ones with decorative covers, she placed them in prominent locations around the store—propped against a teapot here, by a sturdy vase there, and between a bronze figure and stack of pillowcases. One small book had a particularly beautiful cover and interior illustrations of brown mice and blue dragonflies. She put that one on Mrs. Beasley's lap.

The next box contained colorful metal spice cans and cake decorating supplies, and another was full of sealed decks of cards from decades ago and small boxed games like *Pit* and *Bunny Tiddley Winks*.

When she was closing for the night, the shop seemed fuller and had a better selection of eye-catching items for sale than it had before she'd opened. Fewer customers through the day meant she could spend more time on housekeeping and pricing. She was disappointed that Nolan hadn't returned, but not surprised.

She went into her restroom to wash her hands and said aloud to the mirror, "I need to get out where people are. I'll never meet anyone other than five-minutes-at-a-time customers stuck here in my shop all day, and then sitting alone all night."

Instead of going home, she drove to Sally's, a dance-and-dine restaurant near the intersection of two small highways at the edge of town. As she pulled into the crowded lot, she wished she'd brought a book or newspaper to read. It was disheartening to sit alone in a restaurant with nothing to do but stare at the salt and pepper shakers. Determined to make a fresh start despite a lack of reading material to hide behind, she forced herself to go inside.

Music, laughter, and the smells of greasy food and spices greeted her. "How many tonight?" asked a cheerful, suntanned woman wearing a teal blouse and black skirt as she reached toward a wooden menu rack just inside the main entrance.

"One."

The waitress pulled out an oversized menu and weaved through the packed restaurant to a small table in a corner, Lumi following behind.

It may have seemed like banishment to anyone else, but to Lumi, it felt like she was sitting in the perfect spot. She was mostly out of sight there in the darkened corner, yet she could see nearly the whole room. She looped the strap of her purse over her chair and opened the menu as a Cajun song started to play on an unseen jukebox. Lumi glanced around and saw that the large, softly-lit restaurant had three sections: the bar, the dining area, and a dance floor. She went back to studying her menu, reading the descriptions of the offered sandwiches and substantial entrees.

"Come here often?" asked a man's voice above her.

Lumi looked up, startled. It was Nolan, attractive in tan slacks and a dark blue short-sleeved polo shirt. His expression was openly friendly. Standing with him was a beautiful young woman with shoulder-length, feathery brown hair.

"Um, no. I've never been here before. I felt like a change, I guess. Hello."

The woman he was with didn't acknowledge Lumi as she went on toward the nearby ladies' room.

"Here alone?" Nolan asked, stepping a little closer. He had asked it quietly, and Lumi almost hadn't heard him over the music.

She nodded once, then looked at her menu again. She felt like a social outcast, and she was disappointed that Nolan was apparently on a date. Even though she told herself there was never any reason to hope that—

"Want to sit with us? We're right over there. That's my brother, Magnus, and his wife."

33

Lumi looked where he pointed. She recognized Magnus, who was laughing loudly. She hadn't seen him since he was a boy in school, but he looked almost the same. Another man, taller and lean, was at the table, too. Lumi could feel the pulse pounding in her chest. This was why she'd come out tonight—to meet new people. However, now that she was facing the reality of socializing, it scared her. "Um …"

"Come on. Plenty of room. Don't sit by yourself, Lumi. My sister is here tonight, too. She'll be right back. The guy in the denim shirt is her husband, Mike."

Sister? Lumi's spirit soared, and she was sure her change in mood showed on her face. She reached for her purse and menu. Standing shakily, she carried both with her as she followed Nolan to a large, round table near a low partial wall dividing the dining area from the dance floor. Magnus closed his menu and looked up, smiling.

Taking a chair from a nearby empty table and putting it between two others at his table, Nolan sat at Lumi's right and looked around at the others. "This is Lumi. She's one of Mrs. Rasmusson's friends. Lives across the street from her now."

"I know Lumi, sure," said Magnus. His round, full face and longer, softly curling brown hair were a contrast to Nolan's more slender face and short hair. Their features were otherwise similarly handsome. "I remember you from school. I always thought you were named Lumi because of your luminescent eyes."

Lumi wasn't used to flattery, and she was certainly surprised to hear that anyone had thought she'd had appealing eyes—or anything else—when she was in school. She felt her face heating with embarrassment as she sat between an empty chair to her left and Nolan to her right. "Um, I've never heard that about my eyes, but that's nice of you to say. Lumi is a Finnish name. My dad's father immigrated from Finland. I'm named after a great aunt."

"Really?" asked Magnus' wife, a sweet-faced woman with dark eyes and even darker long hair who was obviously very pregnant. She smiled warmly. "My grandfather came to this country from Mexico. My mother's side has been here for oodles of generations, though. My name is Alisa. Nice to meet you." She glanced up as Nolan's sister sat with them. "Cammie, this is Lumi. She's a friend of Nolan's."

A friend of Nolan's? This was news to Lumi. She felt awkward again. "Hi, Lumi. Wow—love that name. Is it because you glow?"

Lumi was startled again at this question and didn't know how to respond. A waitress brought everyone ice water, a straw, and a roll of flatware cocooned by a napkin. Lumi unwrapped her straw, took a sip of water, and repeated what she'd already said about the origin of her name.

After everyone had ordered, Lumi turned to Nolan to say, "I tracked down the woman who put the letters in the auction. She lives in Strawtown now. I called her last night."

Nolan leaned back, surprised. "That was *fast*. I'll bet she was surprised and glad to hear from you."

Lumi sighed and took another drink, noticing again that she needed to file her nails. "She said she doesn't want them. She didn't mean to put her mom's letters into the sale, but she doesn't want them back. I'm supposed to throw them out."

"Hmm," he said.

The others at the table started talking and laughing, but Nolan and Lumi both sat in silence.

He bit his lip after taking a drink of water.

Lumi openly watched Nolan's white teeth press into the edge of his pillowy lip, enjoying the sight, nearly mesmerized. She didn't dare glance up to his eyes to find out if he was aware that she was staring at his mouth. He just kept biting his lip, almost as if he continued to do so only because she was watching.

"That's a shame," Nolan said after Lumi had finally looked away. "Well, I guess not everyone is sentimental about these things."

"I'm not going to destroy them," she said, still avoiding his eyes. Her cheeks felt hot again, as if she had revealed a secret by watching his mouth for too long. "I-I'm going to call her again in a few months to see if she's changed her mind. She seemed upset about her mother's death. It could be that the pain is too fresh for her to think straight. I don't want her to regret a decision made while she's distraught."

"That's a nice thought, and I agree. But, if you call and she doesn't want them even then, I wouldn't press. Most people don't keep old letters for very long." He paused to take another drink. "I am glad you tried. That's more than most folks would bother doing."

Lumi finally met his eyes for a moment. "I have to agree. I worked for auctioneers who never concerned themselves with returning items that were probably given to them by mistake. If an item crossed the threshold, it was put up for sale. If that item didn't get a bid, it got donated to a thrift shop. Their motto was: 'in, auctioned, out, gone, done.'" She mummified her index finger with the wrapper from her straw. "But I guess that's understandable. We worked at such a furiously fast pace that there wasn't any spare time or staff to handle goods any other way. That fast pace is one of the reasons I left and struck out on my own."

Cammie overheard and asked, "You have your own auction company, Lumi? Where?"

Lumi turned in her chair. "No. I have an antique shop downtown in the center of the oldest block of commercial buildings. The exterior is powdery gray-blue now, with white trim and my banner sign. I need to have a more permanent sign made. I love my building, I'll admit. The last tenant stripped the old carpeting away, exposing buttery-soft floorboards. These fantastic iron ball lights hang from the metal tile ceiling from chains that look like they might have been from a centuries-old ship. I bought up every used kitchen table I could find this spring, and they display most of my antiques. Plus, there are a few bookcases and glass-front cases."

"Sounds impressive. What are your hours?" Mike asked.

"I'm open from ten until six, Wednesday through Sunday. Things are slow but steady. I may try to sell rare or unusual items on eBay, too, if walk-in traffic alone doesn't support the business."

Magnus asked, "What's it called?"

"Lumi's Curiosities." She looked around the table, expecting a disapproving reaction. There wasn't one. "I might change it, though."

"I like it," said Cammie, her brown eyes sincere. "Makes me want to go inside to see what you have that's so darn curious." She grinned. "I'll have to go shopping there. I love vintage stuff like lava lamps and blacklight posters. Oh, and black velvet paintings. And orange … anything. And hot pink anything, too."

"And neon anything. Paint-by-number pictures, strange clocks, fuzzy dice …" Mike added. He sighed, crossing his arms. "Oh, how I suffer."

Lumi grinned. "I'll keep my eyes open. I have something in the shop right now that you might like. It's a two-foot-tall mid-century stuffed vinyl bowling pin with these pink, orange, yellow, and green fringes around its edges. If you like it, I'll give it to you for your collection."

Cammie's eyes brightened. "Oh, *thank* you. I know I'll love it."

"I bought it at a thrift shop in Indianapolis about a month ago. It may have been part of a carnival game. I'll put it behind my counter for you. Come by any day."

The women smiled at each other.

Lumi took a moment to be amazed at how well things were going with these strangers. It almost felt like none of them could tell how nervous she was to be sitting at their table.

After more conversation about antiques, the local crime situation, auto repair, the upcoming holiday, Magnus and Alisa's impending parenthood, and food favorites, their dinners arrived. They ate, talked, and laughed for over an hour. She noticed one particular change over the course of the meal: the position of Nolan's left leg. At first, he made sure he was sitting with his legs together or pointed away from Lumi toward Magnus. As the minutes ticked by, he relaxed, and his knee touched hers occasionally. Each time, he would jerk it away. Toward the end of the meal, he let his knee remain against Lumi's for long moments. She relished the feeling of warmth through his slacks against her bare skin. It was a peculiar form of intimacy that no one around them could see or suspect. Lumi never met his eyes when his leg was touching hers. It would have felt far too daring to pair the touch with a silent acknowledgment, Lumi knew.

As soon as everyone had finished dessert, Lumi pushed away from the table and stood. The restaurant's music had turned louder, and couples were heading for the dance floor where it was almost dark except for reflected red and white lights bouncing from a suspended disco ball. The atmosphere in the place had immediately changed, and the music's volume made conversation almost impossible.

Lumi felt split in two. Part of her wanted to stay with the Sanders clan, but another part felt her social skills had reached their limit for one day and night. She grabbed her purse and bill, saying as she glanced around the table, "It was fun to eat with a group. Thanks for the company. Have a good night and a fun Fourth of July."

Magnus spoke louder to be heard across the table as he invited, "You should come over to our place for a cookout on the Fourth. Nolan—tell her to come over."

Lumi tried to hide her sense of panic. Another social gathering? She couldn't possibly fake her way through a long party like a cookout. "No, I can't. But thanks. I'm going to have my shop open until two or three o'clock to try to lure in the tourists."

"Come over after you close," Cammie said, digging through her purse for pen and paper. "I'll write down the address. We'll be there from about noon until after the fireworks are over."

Lumi hesitated, but a sincere double nod from Nolan encouraged her to pick up the scrap of paper. "Well … I might. Thanks."

She paid her bill and walked to the parking lot. The night was warm compared to the artificially cooled air of the restaurant, and the sudden silence felt like a relief. So did being alone again—being sociable was hard work.

Lumi was disappointed that Nolan hadn't walked out of the restaurant, too. She'd had prickles along the side of her body that had been closest to him as if cosmic energy had sparked between them. She'd kept glancing his way, noticing the shape of his hands, the hair on his arms, the muscular outline of his chest and shoulders, the slight stubble on his chin and cheeks. She could still feel the fabric of his slacks on her leg. She was almost sure he would leave the restaurant when she had. It hadn't been a date, but—

"Oh, no!" She suddenly remembered her promise to visit Maddy after work.

Ten minutes later, she arrived at Mrs. Rasmusson's front porch. No one answered the bell. She opened the screen door to knock on the wooden door, and that's when she saw a note taped to one of its windows. "I'm at a friend's. Talk to you tomorrow. Sorry. I called but got no answer. M.R."

Lumi realized she'd left her phone in her SUV during dinner and that she hadn't yet checked for messages or missed calls.

She dialed her voicemail number and heard, "Lumi, dear? Are you there? No? Oh, I wanted to catch you. Chess is on his way over to get me for the night. We've spent each of these last nights together. Since the card incident, I mean. He worries about me. I'm happy to have a protector. Tomorrow we'll stay at my home, so do come to visit if you have time. And Lu—I never showed Chess the cards. I told him I threw them out. I want to protect him, too. Goodnight!"

Lumi checked for other calls or messages and then opened her front door, heading straight for her freezer to get out a gallon of chocolate ice cream. She wasn't in the least bit hungry, but she scooped out a small serving and watched television for a while, flipping from channel to channel, her mind swirling with memories of all that had been said and done during dinner.

After a shower, she sat on her bed and opened her laptop to search for "old family letters" online. Whole large groups were for sale on eBay, and scans of letters and photos were available on genealogy sites. She settled against her pillows and started reading. They were interesting, she had to admit, but she kept thinking of the letters in their box downstairs in the kitchen. Browsing different family writings didn't keep her from wanting to read what Mama had sent to Jackie. Lumi sighed. She wanted to be able to honestly say to herself and Nolan that she wasn't reading them, that she wasn't invading their privacy. But …

Downstairs she went, feeling guilty the whole way. A moment later, she stomped in her bare feet and summer nightgown and damp hair back up to bed. She found an emery board in her nightstand drawer and filed her uneven nails as she read another letter.

Dear Jackie,

This is your dad for a change. Your mom has trouble with her legs bothering her since the trip to the museum. She shouldn't have tried to walk around all day, but you know your mom. Stubborn! I hope you ladies all had a good time while I was here with Waller. Your mom started to write to you, but her pain won't let her concentrate. She can't even read a book or a magazine. Give her a little while. She'll likely pick up pen and paper in a week.

The dog and I went fishing that day you were gone. When we got home, Pearline called and said they took your mom to the hospital. But you know that part since you were there. Your mom is back home and resting upstairs now. She'll be fine, the docs say. She should not pretend she has gams like she did before the tragedy. She usually knows her limit, but I think the paintings were so fascinating that she forgot to sit down.

I got the grass mowed this morning. There's a stray cat I think the Coopers are trying to coax into their house. He sat in a tree and watched me mow for quite a while. Your mom might be feeding him or her (cat butts all look the same to me—I don't know if it's a him or a her), and maybe we're the ones who will end up with a cat, and not the Coopers. I am neither here nor there about it. Seems like a good cat. Kind of looks like a tiny cow with its long fur in black and white patches. I didn't feed him or her. Not sure what opinion Waller Bee has about felines.

Should I sing you the Waller Bee song like I used to when I tucked you into bed? Why not? Are you ready? You can picture holding WB like you used to, waggling his floppy ears along to the song.

Waller who? Waller hey! Who's the dog who came to stay?
Waller is, the Waller did! Now he won't get off my bed!
Waller Bee, we all agree
Is the dog for you and me!
Waller eats and Waller pees
Waller loves to aim at trees.
Waller snores, but just a bit
Tell him to shake and he will sit
Waller who? Waller hey! Waller Bee is here ... to ... stay!

Your mom is calling me from upstairs. Say hello to Marty. Visit when you can. I know your mom would like it, specially now she's stuck in bed.

Dad and Mom

It was fun to hear from the father, thought Lumi. She was grinning, imagining Jackie as a little girl on her bed with the dog, her dad singing their funny song. She read the song over another time, making up a simple tune to go with the lyrics.

But what was this tragedy that had happened to Mama? She had worn casts on both legs long ago, and then she overdid it at the time the letter was written and had to go to the hospital to get them checked. Lumi wished she could call Jackie again to ask her but knew that it would be a terrible idea. She was told to throw out the letters, not to read them.

A photo included in the envelope showed a smiling Dad in short swimming trunks and a t-shirt. He was holding a fishing pole, wearing a slouchy hat that was full of lures. He looked to be about forty-five or fifty years old. Lumi liked his face. It was a great dad face, full of character and love.

Would they end up with the cat that looked like a cow? Would Mama get up out of bed and be fine again? Who was Pearline? Was she Mama's sister? A friend? A cousin? And why did it matter? She should *not* be reading these letters!

She stared at the photo of Dad a moment longer, placed the letter and photo into their envelope, checked her nails for smoothness, and then opened a novel by Fannie Flagg for an hour's read before giving in to sleep.

In her dream, she sat at the edge of a bed holding a woman's hand, telling her stories to help her pass the time while her oddly-bent legs recovered. Lumi couldn't recall the woman's face when she woke up, but many other details of the dream stayed with her for hours that morning, like a sepia-tinged mood she couldn't shake.

Chapter Four

After a productive day at work and a dinner of salad at home, Lumi knocked again at the house across the street from her own Victorian home.

"Hello, Lu. Come in. Do you know Chess Amberton already?" Maddy asked as she walked with Lumi into the living room. "He volunteers at the animal shelter now, but he used to be an accountant at the tomato factory for many, many years. Don't ask him how they make ketchup or salsa or anything. It gets boring fast."

"Me? *Boring?* Bah." Chess, built like a ruggedly handsome, tall tugboat with a gray-haired-but-balding, age-spotted head, folded his arms across his chest, scowling. He couldn't hold that expression for long before a smile defeated it. "I could tell you lots of interesting tomato facts. However," he glared teasingly at Maddy, *"some* people fail to grasp the nuances and pleasures of my storytelling arts." He winked. "How do you do, pretty young lady? Maddy says you live next door?" He held out a hand to her.

Shaking his superhero-sized hand, Lumi said, "Across the street. I grew up in the four-hundred block in that big house with a willow tree in its front yard. My parents moved to Florida while I was still working in Indy. When I was ready to come back to Barnwood, I wanted to buy my old house, but I missed getting it by a couple of weeks. I love the place I *did* get, though, so I'm happy. This one doesn't have the problems my old house had, like bats in the attic and a very damp basement."

"Well, not batty and not wet does sound like an improvement." He cleared his throat. "You know our little secret, Maddy tells me. About us sort of sleeping together. Are you shocked?" He grinned, clearly delighted to be able to talk openly about his sinful ways.

Lumi laughed once through her nose.

Maddy's mouth fell open. She pushed Chess' shoulder feebly. *"Sleeping* together! Chess! You make it sound like we're in the same *bed!"*

Lumi patted her friend's arm, laughing again. "I'm not shocked. I'm glad she has a companion with her at night. But you two should get married. Why don't you?"

Maddy didn't answer as she walked along her hallway past the staircase.

"I want to," Chess said, pointing at his chest with a thumb, "but I can't talk Mad into even thinking about it. Not yet, anyway. She said

taking one waltz down the aisle was enough. I offered to move in here without getting married first, but she doesn't want to look bad at bingo and church. Kind of *hypocritical,* if you ask me." He shouted that last sentence, but he was smiling.

"Lu? Can you help me find my slippers, dear?" Maddy called from outside her hall closet.

Lumi walked around a box fan and down the hall to join her, asking, "Isn't that them?" She pointed at the floor where there were slippers and rubber garden boots and nothing else.

Maddy pulled Lumi into the back porch and leaned against the white washing machine, her eyes troubled. "I don't know if you got my phone message, but I wanted to make sure you'll back me up. I told Chess I threw away the stereocards or burned them or something. I told him they were gross, and I didn't want such things in my home."

Lumi was confused. "But you *did* keep them?"

Maddy nodded. "I did. But they're hidden for now. I might show them to Chess later, but I know that man too well. If he thinks I have them, he'll pester me and pester me to go to the police or to get other people involved in trying to solve the mystery. I just want your help for now. I feel a little bit more in control this way. Chess is a darling, but he's as tough as any prizefighter. I will take his protection and appreciate it, but I can't stand to feel pressured into reporting the cards as a crime or anything. I'm afraid I'm asking you to lie for me. Can you understand why?"

"I guess so. Okay. We'll play it your way. Did he at least see them before you supposedly tossed them out?"

Maddy shook her head. "No. It's better this way."

"Well, maybe we should have contacted the police from the start."

Maddy's face darkened. "I *can't.* I have guilt and sadness when I see the photos. It hits me in the chest. I'm really afraid that I deserve this … threat. Give me time to think and remember. Please? Chess knows there were faked stereocards. He knows I'm upset. Can we leave it at that for now?"

Lumi shrugged, calling, "I *found* them!" She left the back porch and rejoined Chess, trying to seem casual.

"I don't know how they could have been missing," Chess said. "Those ratty old things are always in that closet."

"They were hiding out in the back porch behind the dryer," Lumi lied, bending to look at the Sparton radio again. "They may have been trying to escape into slipper retirement."

The woman finally reappeared, this time with her shoes off and with formerly fluffy pink slippers on her feet. Her shoulder-length, mostly gray hair had been released from its usual bun, and she had taken off her glasses. Maddy looked less severe—almost soft, Lumi thought. Lovely.

Maddy suddenly glowered, supposedly picking up their banter where they had left off. "I told you, Mister. I am not getting … *look* at that man, will you? He stands there like he fully expects I'm eventually going to give in and live happily ever after, married to that pile of rocks. I'm *not.* I will be a hypocrite, yes, and I will sleep in his house, and he will sleep here, and we'll have card games and snacks and talk through *Wheel of Fortune,* but I'm not getting married again in this lifetime. *No.*"

Chess winked. "Well, I'm ready when you are. I'll just wait." He pulled Maddy to the sofa and had her sit beside him.

She looked pleased to be wanted. "Got plans tonight?" Maddy asked, ignoring the arm Chess was snaking around her shoulders.

"None. Last night I went to a restaurant called Sally's for dinner. I actually ended up eating with Nolan."

Maddy's lips parted for a moment before she asked, "Nolan? Sanders? Did you plan that? I didn't think you two knew each other at all."

"We don't. We were coincidentally there at the same time. Nolan invited me to join his family. I am terribly unsociable, so it felt weird to be asked to sit with strangers. They're all very nice, but I guess you know that. I was invited to Magnus' house for the Fourth, so I might go over after I close up shop."

Maddy's eyes sparkled. "Oh, Lumi—I'm glad to hear you're making friends. We had talked about how lonesome you've been. Well, good! The Sanders are a hard-working and good-hearted family. Those kids have always been nice. I've known the family through church for a good many years now." She softened her expression and tone of voice when she added, "Nolan's a widower. I'm sure he's pleased to have a new friend, too."

Lumi's eyebrows rose in surprise. A *widower?* Nolan? She resisted an urge to ask for details. It didn't feel appropriate. Tears wanted to form in her eyes, but she fought them away.

Chess seemed to notice her sadness at the news. "Want to sit in on a game of rummy? Maddy has homemade cream cheese dip and such. We'll put on a game show for background noise. Whattaya say?"

Lumi paused, enjoying the sight of Chess and Maddy's intimate ease with each other. "Three's a crowd."

"Nonsense! I'll get the card table out of the hall closet. Maddy can grab the grub. Lumi, the cards and notepad and pen are in the rolltop desk. You can play chaperone for the evening." He winked and cocked an elbow into the air with the arm that wasn't holding Mrs. Rasmusson. "Wink wink, nudge nudge. Keep us from doing anything we shouldn't."

"I thought that's what the cat is here to do," Lumi said, smiling.

"Tony knows how to keep his opinions to himself." Chess eyed the black shorthair cat lounging on the other end of the sofa, his tail flipping as if fully aware of the fact that he was being talked about. "You know, I like that cat, but he is no great conversationalist."

"I miss having a cat," Lumi said. "I had Tig when I was a girl. He was a prankster. Used to hide behind the furniture and tackle passers-by. Scared the stuffing out of me *so* many times."

They had played two hands of rummy before Chess brought up the stereoscope cards.

"I'll tell you—it's a horrible world when a lady has to endure someone breaking in and leaving things behind that are upsetting. Terrible," said Chess, nearly slamming his discard onto the center of the table for emphasis. "I'm here to protect my gal, though. She can count on me."

Maddy jumped when Chess slammed his card. She said, "I don't want you to get fired up again. They *are* terrible, I'll agree, but now I wish I could remember what they almost remind me of. I'm scared that someone out there remembers something about me that *I*, myself, don't remember. Like, maybe they're threatening me or trying to blackmail me. But I can't be *fully* threatened without knowing what the images are supposed to be all about. It's maddening."

"Your turn," Chess prompted Lumi before putting his hand on Maddy's. "You leave the worrying to me, hon. I'm here now. I wish I'd seen what's hurting you. It's a shame you burned them." He rubbed his chin. "Probably a kid snuck in here. Did they look like a kid could have made them? Like for a craft project?"

"No," Maddy said. "I thought they were real vintage cards at first glance. Lumi saw right away that they weren't, but no—they weren't crude." She sighed. "Chess, my dear, I'm not two years old. You're sweet, and I appreciate that, but don't act like I'm a helpless old lady."

Lumi had to agree with her. Chess seemed more afraid for Maddy than she felt for herself. Maybe that was the way of men. Or of men in love. "I think he's just—"

"I *know* what he's just trying to do," her friend interrupted, picking up her empty snack plate and pushing away from the table. "But it gets to be a bit much. Especially since we don't even know the finer details of what's going on here." She went into the kitchen. When she returned with more chipped beef dip and crackers, she continued, "Those cards could have been put in my box by Ras before he passed, and I never knew it. He could have meant to tell me about them but forgot. Or … since that makes no sense seeing as how they're nasty images and not even old, and they look quite different even from their edges and I would have known they were there even the last time I got them out … it must be that someone came into my house and put them there to scare me. But scare me into what? And why? I've had no phone calls or notes trying to blackmail me or threaten me. Nothing. *Will* there be more? I don't know. Am I escaping actual harm because I now have a bulldog companion beside me every evening and all night?" She shrugged, her eyes looking frightened. "How can I know?"

"Why don't we report it to the police?" Chess asked, looking back and forth between Maddy and Lumi.

"Report what, though?" Maddy asked. "What has happened, really?"

Lumi felt torn between the promises she'd made, not thinking clearly enough to know how to respond.

"I think Mad knows I'm protection enough. She doesn't want the police involved because I'm here now." Chess stole a cracker and some dip from Maddy's plate.

Tony left the sofa to stand near Chess' chair in case there were accidental snack droppings.

Maddy crunched into a cracker, and both she and Chess chewed in unison for a while. Tony put his front paws on the man's leg, his golden eyes hopeful.

"I don't want to bother the police," Maddy finally replied. Looking at Lumi, she added, "I think you'll remember why I want to keep mum for now." To Chess, she explained, "I have to solve my own mystery. That's what Lu and I have been talking about. I need to figure this out myself. I need my friends, but I need mental space to think this through."

Lumi held her breath, trying to find a way to bring up something that had been troubling her. "Maddy? We never got around to discussing our lineup of suspects. The people you said have a key to your door. What do you know about the new newspaper delivery man?"

"I don't remember his name, or if he said it. He did say he had recently moved to Barnwood, that his wife was expecting, and that the paper route was one of three part-time jobs he had until he could maybe get a full-time position at one of the factories. He drives his route, so the only time I've met him was when he was here to collect my payment. He seems like a good person, and definitely not a man with a lot of leisure time to sit around cutting up photos for grotesque art projects."

"Well, what about the next-door neighbor man?"

"Tim? He's lived beside me since he was about five years old, off and on. He and my daughter, Jem, dated in high school. I think they felt too much like brother and sister to get very romantic. They played together as little kids, too. Tim bought the house when his parents divorced about, oh, twenty-five or thirty years ago. He and his wife and son—who just graduated in May—have been nothing but wonderful to me. They're out as suspects."

"Schwann guy?"

"Known him about a year. I can't imagine why he would want to bother me with those cards."

Lumi tried to remember who else Maddy had named when she'd asked who had keys to her house. "Jem and Magnus are out as suspects, too, of course. Electrician, did you say? Some other neighbor? Cat food person? Who else?"

"No one. No one feels in the least bit like they would be out to do me harm. No one on the planet." Her face drooped. "And yet … I have this fear that I'm forgetting something significant. Or some*one*. Some … awful …." She threw up her hands. "This isn't helping, but I don't know what *can* help."

"Whose turn?" Chess asked, wiping his hands with a napkin.

Lumi brought her mind back to the game. "I guess it's mine. Oh, good—a jack," she said, laying down a trio of jacks.

"Run-breaker," complained Chess, watching Lumi discard. He shook his head. "And then what do you do next? You discard a silly little two of hearts."

"Well, *I* think that's a romantic discard," countered Maddy, taking it into her hand and laying down a run before discarding, herself.

"Not if you don't need twos or hearts," grumbled Chess, reaching for the top card from the stockpile. He discarded and glanced at the television. "Good *God.* There's old Pinky Weasel on the TV."

Maddy looked up at the screen and frowned.

Chess shifted on his chair. "I ran into him a couple of weeks ago at the hardware. He's moved back to town to run for the Indiana Senate. Thinks it'll boost his hometown-roots image to live here again. What a phony. He acted like we were old pals, asking about the gang and our girls. I wasn't buying what he was selling, anyway, but when he handed me a slick campaign flyer before he ducked out of the shop, I knew he was still the same Pinky Weasel."

Lumi saw on the screen that the man's name was actually Joplin Rooney. She looked back at Chess. "Pinky Weasel?"

Maddy explained, "Oh, Chess and his friends always called Joplin that." She frowned again. "That's one face I never missed seeing around town all these decades. He was one of the boys who marched against the war and every other injustice we kids marched against, our banners held high. It was obvious, though, that Joplin and his close friends were only interested in causing trouble. Now I see he's trying to do his troublemaking on a statewide level. Never thought he'd turn into a rich, grinning handshaker."

Lumi was confused. "But why that nickname?"

Chess laughed once, harshly. "Whenever he tried to weasel out of getting punished or blamed, he blustered and sputtered and turned red. Pinky Weasel sounded worse than Red Weasel, I suppose."

"So, was he a friend to both of you?" Lumi asked, putting her cards face down on the table and taking a drink of iced tea.

Maddy and Chess exchanged an odd look. It made the little hairs on the back of Lumi's neck stand up.

"Let's just say he was in our class," Chess said. "And let's just say no more about *that* guy."

Lumi suspected Joplin had been after Maddy in school, but she let the topic drop. There were a few kids from her own high school she wouldn't want to see again. One boy from another class brought a dead rat to school and threw it into the girls' shower room. Another boy habitually called her "Screwy," which was irritating for two reasons. One was that she hated near-rhymes. A spiked-hair, muscular girl loved to drag Lumi up and down the hall outside the lunchroom by her arms. The girl had finally gotten in trouble for it, but it always bothered Lumi that she hadn't stuck up for herself against that bully.

Lumi left Mrs. Rasmusson's house at nine o'clock as another episode of *Family Feud* was starting. She thought about Chess and Maddy while she showered. They'd known each other forever, they teased and laughed all evening long, and there was a look of contentment in Maddy's eyes that usually wasn't there. A stand-up-straight, no-nonsense, let's-get-this-done person, Maddy relaxed around Chess and seemed years younger. However, Lumi could see that Chess was too protective, and that probably was why Maddy resisted making their arrangement permanent, and why she wasn't letting him see the stereocards. What had been a twice-weekly night together had turned into every night since the discovery of the cards. This must mean that, on some level, she *was* afraid and wanted to be protected. But was Chess protecting her so much that she wasn't giving herself the mental freedom to remember what the images on the cards represented?

Lumi toweled off, put on a short, white nightgown, and rolled her long dark-blonde hair in spongy curlers. She hadn't bothered to curl or style her hair for a long time, but she wanted to because …

She pushed away a memory of Nolan smiling as he stood inside Maddy's doorway. "No," she said aloud. "Not him. Too handsome. Too muscular." Lumi then realized Nolan sat right at level ten—a perfect man to date. She was at level one, at best, when it came to dating. In her heart, despite being attracted to Nolan, she wasn't ready to think about being a woman in an intimate, romantic way. She wasn't ready to relinquish her control of her own … what? What was she holding onto? The longer she thought about how to answer that question, the more an answer stayed out of reach. Was she keeping her emotions and intimacy in check for a reason she couldn't even name? Was it merely independence solely for the sake of independence? Resisting what might be fantastic simply because she was used to resisting attraction?

There was something else driving it all—something she didn't want to face and might never face. Might never need to if she successfully avoided seeing Nolan again. Avoided thinking about him.

Visions surfaced in her mind: his hands, his warm eyes with their thick, dark-brown eyelashes. His muscular shoulders, endearing smile, his teeth biting his lower lip. She pictured him in the dim light of the restaurant, in her shop, leaning against Maddy's car, reflected in the mirror while he sat next to Maddy, and in the mirror when she was driving away across the service station parking lot.

With a sigh, she reached for the Flintstones lunch box and pulled out the next pale green envelope. She compared the address on this one to the one she'd read last. The same: all the handwriting on the envelopes was the same. That meant that Mama had likely already addressed the envelope before starting to write a letter that she soon abandoned. Dad must have taken her envelope to use for his letter to Jackie. It was disappointing, though, because that meant there was no name with the return address on any of them.

Dear girl,

I'm up and walking again, thankfully! I overdid it. Grandma kept telling me to take sitting-down breaks at the museum, but I thought I knew better. You're never too old to listen to your mother, are you? Bear that in mind! I'm glad your dad wrote you last week. I started to, but my legs were too painful. I got a pain prescription, but I don't like to take stuff like that. Aspirin helped during the day, and I took half a pain pill each night for a while.

Our washing machine finally gave up the ghost two days ago. I'm not saying your dad did anything dumb that caused it to finally break, but I'm not saying he didn't. That's okay, though. It was older than dirt. Now we have to get a new one. And the sunbathing platform your dad and grandpa built over the back porch? Remember how we used to get into our bathing suits, climb out of the upstairs hall window and suntan all afternoon with our books? I loved getting my legs into the sun like that in privacy. Well, it has to come down now. The roof is leaking in too many places. Dad's going to put on a slanty roof. Not sure if he wants to do it alone or hire it done. So, the washer will have to wait for a new roof. No use getting a new washer if it's just going to get leaked on, right?

Teensa, did you get a letter from Pearline? Recently, I mean. She's been spending a lot of money lately, and none of us knows where she got it from. She hasn't had a job since last spring when she worked at that aggravating gift shop place that wouldn't give her enough bathroom breaks. Where is she getting money? Grandma is not giving her any except for a little if she goes to a movie or something. If you got a letter from Pearline, let me know. Call me up. We are worried she is doing things she shouldn't, or seeing a man that is giving her money like that. And what for? We hate to think. Although she is past her prime and in her forties, like I am, she has a nice face when she makes it up, and when she puts on a dress she has a figure men might like. But if she is not going out at night any more often than she used to, a man doesn't seem likely. Is she stealing from your grandma? Grandma says no. This is very odd and not like Pearline. Grandma won't out-and-out ask her straight out where the money is from. I guess it's not my business, as long as I don't have to visit her in jail!

I often think that Pearline is the reason you wanted to get married young. I married when I was young, too, but not as young as you did. Things were different in my day. I think you didn't want to be like Pearline and live with your mother forever, with no real friends or interests. I don't think there was any chance of that, but maybe her situation scared you. I like Marty, don't think I don't. But I do wish you had dated around more. Made sure he was Mr. Right. Don't think I won't be happy to see you two married for fifty years or more! You know your own mind, I'll say that. But it really felt like you settled on the first man who took you out. I know that eighteen and a half is not a baby.

But you'll always be my baby.

Love to you and Marty
Mama and Dad and Waller Bee
PS call me if you hear from Pearline

Oh, Pearline, what are you up to? wondered Lumi. At least there was good news—Mama's legs were better. But Dad had wrecked the old washer somehow. There was no mention of a cat this time. Where was Pearline getting her spending money? And why didn't she have a job? Was she Mama's sister? That made the most sense since she lived with Grandma.

Resisting an urge to read the next letter, Lumi folded the one she'd read and put it back into its envelope and turned off her lamp. The breathy hum from the air conditioner seemed too loud, so she reached for the remote control and turned it off. The room, suddenly silent, felt lonely and empty.

She tossed and turned. Too many thoughts collided in her head to let her get to sleep: Nolan, Maddy, Chess, Mama, Dad, Waller Bee, Pearline, Grandma, the images on the stereoscope cards, the repetitive clicking sounds of *Wheel of Fortune,* Tony the cat sitting high in a tree with the cow-patched cat of the letters. Mama and Jackie on the suntan platform, reading Harlequin romances. Pearline putting on makeup and a dress to meet a mysterious man who paid her to sit on a barstool looking vaguely pretty. Mama's sore legs, purple-blue and swollen, spread tiredly atop wrinkled white sheets.

Everything in her mind scrambled together for long minutes until Lumi gave in to temptation and curiosity. She turned on her stacked-book lamp and opened the next letter.

Dear Jackie,

Since you never called, I guess you don't know anything about Pearline. Or, if you do, she's sworn you to secrecy. Or you're mad about what I said in my last letter about Marty. I like Marty. I think you know that. He's a reliable, upright young man. I do worry that you married too young, that's all. This is not 1920. You can get your own life and job and live on your own. Your only choices were never between marriage or living with your parents for the rest of your life. That's what I was trying to say. Please don't be mad. I am lonesome for your letter that never did come!

The porch roof is off, and the suntan station is gone now. No new washer yet, but we've gone out to the Sears to look at the new models. Expensive! I've hand washed out underpants and shirts for us, and that's good enough for now. Roof first, washer second. The Soap-P-Suds laundry is disgusting, and I don't want to go down there unless I absolutely need to. Remember the last time we went there together? That grubby man tried to hit on you, and I think he was about fifty and you were only fifteen! Mabel goes there, and I could go along with her, but I really don't want to.

Betsy was over this morning before school, showing me how many names and decorations are on her cast. I suppose it won't be too long before it will be off. She sure is itchy! Waller Bee was very rude. Kept insisting on sniffing at her broken arm like it was either irresistible or offensive. That dog!

Pearline—back to her, now—has stopped spending money loosely, according to your grandma. I think they must have had it out. Apparently P is not getting money from her mysterious source any more, or she is hiding it now that Grandma is openly suspicious.

We have a roof man coming late this afternoon to look over the situation and to give us a rough estimate on what he'd charge to do the porch roof. I hate to think! It is kind of a small room, so maybe it won't be too much. Your dad took off the suntan platform and the roof himself, but putting a new one on is another story!

My legs are still sore at night. I don't know that elevating them helps anymore. I have an appointment with the doctor for a few days from now. I worry I'll need an x-ray, and then if I have one, I worry it'll show that my legs have gotten worse. I don't want to think about that, though. Oh, dear! Pray a prayer. Pray a good prayer, Teensa!

Write me when you get this, okay? I miss hearing from you and I don't want to feel like you're mad. If you don't, I'll call you up. You know you can call us anytime, day or night or 3 am!

Love from all
Mama

Although she was very curious about Mama and Jackie and everyone, Lumi finally did feel tired enough to sleep. Her dreams were of nuns praying on their knees. Cats were all around them in church pews, mewing to statues of Jesus and napping in warm, multicolored sunbeams streaming through stained-glass windows.

As Lumi was putting on her sandals to head out the next morning, there was an urgent-sounding knock on her door. It was Maddy. Her hair was messy and she was wearing her pink slippers, not shoes.

"Chess left before the mail came," the older woman said as she stood on the porch, nearly breathless. Her face was fearful, her eyes moist. Holding the corner of a white envelope, she exclaimed, "This was delivered. Another card, Lu! Another card!"

Lumi pointed to her sofa, indicating that the woman should come inside to sit. She took the opened envelope and pulled out a fake stereoscope card on thick yellow paper. It was another horrible image, clearly from the same person who had made the first five. "I don't like this, Maddy. We really, *really* should call the police."

Maddy hid her face in her hands, her elbows on her knees. In a frightened, childlike voice, she said, "Don't."

Lumi sighed with exasperation. "Why? This makes no *sense*. Why do you keep resisting real help? Chess could help. Nolan could."

Maddy lowered her hands but looked only at the blank television screen. "I can't explain it. When I see these cards, the first thing I feel is that I'm in trouble and that I'll be in even *more* trouble if we contact the police. I hesitated about telling you that this card came in the mail, but I *had* to tell someone, I sure don't want to tell Chess—he's already annoyingly clingy and protective."

Lumi sat next to Maddy and took one of her hands in both of hers. She looked to the ceiling and then back at her friend. "All right. But this means war, as far as I'm concerned. I'm at war against whoever is doing this to you. If you honestly feel you have—oh, I don't know—victimized someone in the past who is retaliating, I guess we'd better wait until you naturally remember, or try to dig it out." She sighed again. "I wish you hadn't given that interview with the antiques newspaper. I wish they hadn't taken photos of the items in your home, too."

Maddy's lashes moistened with more tears that didn't fall, making her look vulnerable. She met Lumi's eyes. "I'm afraid on two levels. I'm afraid I've hurt someone without knowing how, and I'm afraid they may pull nastier stunts when they get tired of their card tricks."

Lumi scowled.

The older woman went on, her voice wavering, "You, know, I pretend to be a churchgoing, upright old lady in my neat and tidy house, but I'm far from perfect. I was judgmental too many times. I was scornful. I gossiped. I looked down my nose. I was hoity-toity. I complained about noise. I wrote letters to the editor. I didn't tip enough. I didn't say 'thank you' when I should have. I've done more things that are likely worse, I can guarantee it." She swallowed. "The blood and gore the cards show are oddly familiar. I almost, almost *do* remember. Which is what *really* frightens me! What evil is hovering in the back of my brain that the pictures hint at but don't draw into the forefront of my thoughts and memories?"

They were both silent for a full minute. A dog barking in the distance roused Lumi from her anxious thoughts. "How can I help? What should I do to solve this for you?"

Mrs. Rasmusson swallowed. "Don't tell Chess another card came. Don't tell *anyone* about any of this, Lumi. Especially Nolan. No, please. *Not* Nolan. Not the neighbors or anyone. I had my locks changed two days ago, and now I won't go around handing out my keys like I have. But that won't keep things like this from my mailbox, will it?" She took a breath. "I'll do the work. I'll get out those other five cards and look at them all day, and I'll study this one. I hate to do it, but I can't hide from whatever is in my past if it's determined to come back to bite me."

"Those crimes you listed are hardly anything to feel all that ashamed about, you realize. You didn't say that you'd done a hit-and-run, or that you'd murdered someone in cold blood, or that you poisoned a dog. You must realize that none of what you listed as your sins are things that warrant this kind of treatment."

Maddy looked at the card in Lumi's hand. "Yet ... I feel it in my bones that I've done something ... *something* to deserve such torture."

Lumi stood. She took a photo of the card with her phone and put it back into its envelope before returning to Maddy. "It's Saturday, so it should be a full, interesting day at my shop. How would you like to come with me?"

The older woman stood, too. She looked through the window to her own house, considering. "I think I'll sit at home and look at the cards like I said I will. I feel how helpful you want to be. I guess I'd better help myself, too."

Chapter Five

The next day, Sunday, was unusually busy. Customers from Michigan, Louisiana, Texas, Ohio, and Colorado had stopped on Main Street to discover just what items were considered curiosities in Barnwood, Indiana. After closing at six o'clock, Lumi drove to an ATM and then went home. Maddy hadn't answered Lumi's phone call in the midafternoon, so she assumed the woman must have gone to Chess' house early or had been running errands.

Lumi ate a dinner of stew and slices of Italian bread to the accompaniment of raindrops drumming on the roof as the sky turned to gray-black gloom. She dashed upstairs to grab a shower in case the power went out during the approaching thunderstorm.

In a short robe and with her long hair twisted over her head in a red-and-white-striped towel, Lumi relaxed against a pile of pillows on her bed, staring for a moment at the five newly hung art prints on her bedroom walls. The poster-size framed prints had been in her apartment for over a year, but they seemed fresh and exciting again in their new home. The Erté work called "The Earth's Dream" was a favorite: a woman in a spreading burgundy art deco gown sleeps, covering a large part of the Earth. She dreams of the moon, a yellow orb of swirling light patterns against a midnight blue sky and icy lace. The print stood out boldly against the background of Lumi's autumn orange walls where it hung above her dresser. Three colorful cat reproductions by Louis Wain hung in the space between two windows. The cats were playing ping-pong in the top print, golf in the one below it, and croquet in the bottom illustration. Henri de Toulouse-Lautrec's "The Bed" hung over the headboard of her white brass double bed. Lumi had found a white brass frame for it in exactly the right size. Looking at the rumpled comfortableness of the subjects always made her yearn for a companion to rest with or talk to before sleep.

Lumi remembered that Toulouse-Lautrec had suffered from leg problems for much of his life, which made her think of Jackie's mother. The bass-drumming sounds of thunder felt like a warning not to read another letter, but she couldn't resist finding out what happened next.

Dear baby J,

Pearline is in bed sick with we don't know what. Maybe pneumonia. A fever and a cough. The doctor put her on antibiotics. She

54

should be okay. Don't worry about sending flowers, I did that in both of our names. Sent a bouquet of daisies and carnations. Pink and yellow are her favorite colors. I remember that from when we were little girls. She couldn't wait for spring to come to get out of winter colors and dress in pink and yellow again. You might send her a get well card. You know she would love that!

Pearline and I used to be close. She was always very sweet to me. But after the tragedy, she was never the same. She felt horribly guilty, and probably still does to some degree. She won't laugh when I'm around now. I don't know how to tell her that I don't blame her in the least. I hope she laughs when I'm not around. I'd hate to feel she carries a weight like that even when I'm not where she can see me and be reminded.

The roof is on! Now we need to get to the Sears and get a new machine. I looked at a used one at a garage sale, but Dad says not to go around buying other folks' troubles. Dad says after we get the machine set up he is going to buy lumber and build me a suntan station in the back yard. What he means is that he'll put up a fence around a small area that's big enough for a lawn chair and maybe a little cup-holding table. There I can't be seen with my legs bare, and I can get good sun rays on them. I told him to build it pretty high so that Waller won't hop over the fence to hog my chair. That dog sure loves to hog chairs!

I worry a lot about Pearline. I feel like what happened with my legs ruined her life. People feel guilty when they're caring, and P was always sweet and caring. She thinks I blame her. I don't! I want her to be happy with her life, and to use her two good legs to make a good life. Even though she's not a spring chicken, and is too old to be having babies, she is young enough to find a nice man and settle down in her own house. Now, though, I think Grandma is reliant on her too much. What can be done, Teensa? What can we do?

I will probably visit her in a day or two. When we're together, I want to have it out with her once and for all. I've avoided the topic long enough. She needs to get over thinking she's done this to me!

Dad and Waller are waiting outside on the front steps, so I'll end now. We are walking together to the Dairy Barn for a treat. I'm supposed to be walking a few blocks every day, the doctor said, and then I should be able to do my usual work and everything eventually. Your dad thinks I need a treat to lure me into walking, and I just smile when he suggests things like the Dairy Barn. Last evening we walked to the park to watch the little leaguers playing for a while. Waller got to whining when we wouldn't let him be helpful and fetch the foul balls, so we had to go home again after a few minutes.

> *Love from us*
> *Mama and Dad and Waller Bee*

Lumi stretched out on her side. What happened long ago to Mama, and why had Pearline felt responsible? The storm grew wildly stronger. Lightning flashed, brightening the windows over and over for a second or two at a time. Her bedside lamp flickered. Great booms of thunder shook the house, and she reached behind her head to grab a pillow to hug for comfort. The air conditioning went off when the lamp flickered a second time. She didn't bother to reach for the remote to turn it on again.

Checking her phone for weather warnings, she saw on the radar that the storm passing over Barnwood would end soon.

She wondered about Pearline again. What was wrong with her? Did she have pneumonia, or was it a contagious disease? Should Mama wait longer to go for a visit? What did Pearline do that caused Mama's legs to be damaged?

She hoped Mama did get to have a nice, long talk with Pearline to assure her that she didn't need to feel any guilt. Lumi thought about her relationship with her own mother. They weren't particularly close anymore. She knew the fault of their estrangement was hers, but also knew there wasn't an easy way to restore their former closeness. Too much time had gone by, and too much had gone unsaid. Maddy was her only real friend, and that friendliness had only come since she'd moved across the street from her childhood neighbor.

While the storm died away, Lumi wrote a long email to her mother detailing what she'd been doing since she moved back to town, about the house and how she was slowly but surely furnishing it, and about having a friendly dinner out with Nolan and his family.

She tried to sleep but kept thinking about Maddy and the terrible stereocards. She should have called during the day to find out if she was okay, and if she'd had any revelations or recollections while studying the cards.

Lumi walked across the street before breakfast. There was no answer to the bell or to knocking. She walked two blocks to a convenience store for a couple of magazines, a bag of potato chips, and a large bottle of soda. On her walk home, she realized why she'd bought what she did: to comfort herself with empty calories and celebrity magazines. She only did that when there was something seriously bothering her.

Almost home, she saw Maddy going into her house with her purse and small brown plaid overnight bag. Lumi jogged to her own home, put the paper bag on her porch, and crossed the street.

"Come on in, Lu, girl. I've only been home a minute. I have cookies and a loaf of that good raisin bread from Miss Allison's bakeshop. I can brew coffee or nuke a mug of water for tea."

Lumi said yes to tea and bread as she followed her friend inside and sat at the round table. While Maddy filled a mug and cut slabs of bread with a practiced hand, Lumi glanced around at the charming assemblage of vintage items in the kitchen: primitive baking accessories, colorful teapots, preserved wasp nests, honey jars full of old buttons and beads, dried flowers in faded hues, and a variety of animal salt and pepper shakers situated in pairs or groups atop the tall cabinets. Lace curtains were aged but clean, filtering sunlight into a golden glow that washed over the white porcelain-topped mid-century cast iron double sink.

"Ferocious storm last night, wasn't it? Were you at Chess' again?"

Maddy placed two slices of bread on a dish, then carried it and a mug to the table. "I was, I was. And yes! Such a downpour at one point! I could hardly sleep. Here. The water's hot—watch out. Want butter? I can toast your bread for you."

"Butter, thanks. Untoasted is perfect. May I have a tea bag, too?"

"Oh, I forgot the tea!" Mrs. Rasmusson stood with her arms on her hips, her hair in a tight bun and her glasses high on her nose, giving her the severe look she usually had when she wasn't around Chess. "I wonder about my memory, sometimes—when I remember to wonder about it." She went to one of her white wooden cupboards and took out three different boxes of tea. Setting them on the embroidered blue tablecloth, she said, "Help yourself."

Dunking a bag of aromatic, spicy chai into her mug, Lumi asked, "What about the cards? Did you remember anything?"

Maddy put milk on the table and sat on a wooden chair across from Lumi, her expression unreadable. "I gave up after a few minutes, to be honest. I did try, but the emotions they stirred up were too much to take. Too much." She sighed through her nose. "And yet, I can't say *what* they cause me to feel, exactly. When I look at them, I want to cry. I want to run into my mother's arms. Isn't that odd? Mom has been gone for many years now, and I'll admit that I never was one to run to her for consoling.

I think I'm sort of stern, but my mother took the *prize* in that department." She held her breath for a moment before slowly letting it out, frowning. "But you know what? Even now, when I get afraid, I want my mother. She had a way of standing firmly beside you that made you believe the devil himself wouldn't dare harm a hair on the head of any child of hers!"

Lumi sipped more tea and took a bite of the moist raisin bread. Swallowing, she said, "I have today and tomorrow free. Maybe it'll help to have someone with you when you look over the cards."

Mrs. Rasmusson stared at her hands. "Chess kept asking me what was bothering me last night. I wouldn't say anything, though. It's going to be hard to keep him from getting suspicious, especially if more of those photos come in the mail."

"Let me get the cards now. We'll look at them together. Please?"

"They aren't in the rolltop anymore. I'll fetch them." Not moving, Maddy asked, her blue eyes meeting Lumi's, "What do you think? Should I tell him? Should I admit that I kept the cards and that I've gotten another?"

Lumi shrugged. "Sure. If that's what you'd like. Or don't. Or play it by ear."

Maddy reluctantly left the table, climbed the broad staircase to the second floor, and returned with the six cards. She sat again and dealt them out on the pink-flowered tablecloth, then took off her glasses. "I almost forget the images when I'm not looking right at them. I don't know why that is. It makes the shock new every time, though."

Seeing the photos again made Lumi cringe. She put the rest of her slice of bread back on its small dish, deciding she'd had enough. "When do you think the original photos were taken?"

"Long ago. Look at the hats, the formal way the bodies are dressed, the …"

"Ignore the gross stuff. Look at the other details. Try to remember, Maddy."

She seemed to be resisting. Not fully cooperating. Not willing to attempt the task at hand. Lumi could see her friend's eyes aiming to the side of each card, only pretending to look at the images. Giving up, Lumi sighed and said, "Give them to me. I'll describe the background details for you."

Maddy slid them along the table before using a napkin to dab at her eyes.

"Have you ever seen a horror movie?" Lumi asked.

"Yes. Well, nothing very scary like a chainsaw madman movie or anything with demons or occult stuff. I saw 'Psycho' and 'The Birds' and a few modern mysteries that got sort of scary. They're not something I would choose to watch at this point in my life, but I have seen spooky films."

"Well, when you watched 'The Birds,' did the bloody scenes make you upset enough to cry?"

Maddy thought, closing her eyes. She opened them again. "I can't say that they did, no."

Lumi swallowed more of her tea. "I can see it isn't merely the horror of these images that's upsetting you to tears. I think you're right. I think they're triggering a memory that's personal to you, and there's guilt, fear, or trauma associated with them."

The older woman nodded. "I even get a little nauseous. Ghostly fingers slide up my spine. I feel ice cold or white hot. I'm as nervous as an Alka-Seltzer hovering over a water glass. It's all very … strange. I don't usually act this way. I—I feel like a lost child inside now." She took in a slow breath, her eyes on Lumi's radiating frailty. "I need help."

"I'm trying," Lumi said, patting her friend's hand. She cleared her throat and drank the last of her cooling tea. She gathered her long hair into a ponytail with one of the ties she always carried with her and spent several minutes describing the scenes on the cards without including their offensive content.

Maddy listened, her eyes closed, her hands on her lap clenched together. "No. Stop now," she said after a couple of minutes. "It *does* help to hear the other details instead of looking at them, and I'm not upset when you're describing the scenes, but I can't say it brings any clarity."

Lumi stacked the cards face down on the tablecloth. "We'll try again soon. Think about what I've said. Maybe something will occur to you when you least expect it."

Maddy stood to clear away Lumi's mug and plate. "I may have to admit my memory problems mean nothing will ever come to me about the pictures. Nowadays, I sometimes forget what I did ten minutes ago. Maybe I've simply totally forgotten whatever happened when those photos were taken."

"Hmm," Lumi said, standing. "Relax for now. This has been enough for today." She hugged Maddy goodbye, wondering how to help beyond what she had already done.

Pouring herself another glass of soda after lunch, Lumi flopped onto her large, dark-green sofa and changed the TV channel. A classic movie's black and white scenes reminded her of the stereoscope cards. The men wore hats, and the women were in dresses, just like the people in the cards. However, Lumi thought, adult styles didn't change drastically from year to year in the middle of the twentieth century. Men wore fedoras for decades, and women wore both pants and dresses for decades, too. At formal events and occasions, dresses and hats were even more common for a very long time.

Turning off the movie, she decided to read in her back yard. Just as she was heading upstairs to grab a novel, a neighbor started a lawnmower, so that idea no longer seemed appealing. Instead, she carried her glass of soda to her bedroom and tossed the Flintstones lunch box onto her bed. Getting out the next letter, she settled comfortably against her pillows with her golden hair high up off her neck.

Dear girl,

I heard about the card and gift you sent Pearline! You are divinely sweet! She is better, like I said on the phone, but stays in bed most of the time with her science fiction novels and that little TV from the sewing room. Dodge brought her a bag full of used books the other day, and she is really having a blast!

I laid out in my new suntan station this late morning. What fun! I had on one of my old one-piece swimming suits (still fits!) under my slacks and then I took my slacks off once I was behind the new box fence. We put the blue and white lawn lounger out there, and that old step stool you used to use to see in the mirror to brush your teeth is now a cup holder table. I hope Waller Bee doesn't do some sort of Olympic feats of jumping to get over the fence and onto my chaise! He knows I'm there, but so far he hasn't begged or insisted on joining me. Maybe he understands that a lady needs her privacy.

Our walk last eve was to Padgie's place. I know, I know—I hate bars. However, your dad likes Padgie's and we kept walking places for treats for me *and I thought he should go where he likes to for a change. It was sort of okay. Sort of fun, really. I had a half of a mug of beer and your dad had a mug of his own and then he finished off mine. I could tell he was happy that I wasn't playing school marm the whole time. I even picked out a song on the jukebox. I chose "I'm Not Lisa." Do you know that one? It's my favorite of the modern songs. Oh, I know. It's not that new, but it's about the only recent song I really enjoy. That and "I Believe in You" by Don Williams. Remember when you bought me his album? I guess I'm an old stick in the mud about tunes and can't get excited about the things they play on the radio anymore. Give me The Beatles and I'm in heaven! I'm having a vision of you and your dad dancing in the kitchen to Rocky Raccoon when you were a little girl.*

Now, I didn't want to talk on the phone about this since your dad was sitting nearby reading the paper, but I did talk to Pearline when I visited her and Grandma. This is hard to write about, Teensa. We cried together. I think it was the first time ever, or at least in many, many years we sisters have gotten tenderly emotional with each other like that. I sat on the side of her bed and I held her hand. I told her (like I have before, you know) that my pain is not her fault. She usually walks off or does something else or changes the subject when I've tried to get personal with her, but I had her trapped there in bed. She wriggled, but seemed relieved by the time we were done. She hugged me hard! I think she's got a long way to go to get over whatever sickness she's got. She's lost weight. Looks like at least ten pounds! You can really tell in her face. Thinner and pale and ethereal now, almost.

I told her that carrying around guilt and hurt does no one any good at all and that I have a wonderful life with a man I love. Your dad knew me when I had good legs, you know, but he fell in love with me and me with him after the tragedy. He doesn't love me any less now that I have flare-up pains and have to be off my feet for spells. I told Pearline that we can't know what God has planned. It was meant to be that I went there instead of her. If she would have gone as she'd planned, maybe she would have ended up numbered with the dead! I get shivers just now remembering the look on Pearline's face when I said that. She seemed almost hopeful that that would have happened! She told me she wished she would have kept her ticket, and that it would have spared me a load of pain. But if she can't get past the guilt, I don't know how I can help her. That's what I said.

I called in Grandma when she passed the room in the hallway. I told her how Pearline was feeling, and we held hands together, if you can imagine that! Grandma tisk-tisked her but didn't really put her down. Grandma lives full time with Pearline, so I can guess that she knows how P feels day in and day out. I asked Pearline to move down to live with me and Dad for a while, while she gets well. I thought it would be a nice thing for her, and we could talk it all out every day and get close again. P says she might, when she feels like packing a bag. I hope she does come live with us. I don't know how your dad feels, but when I told him

61

he just grunted. You know he grunts at most things. I can't tell if he hates the idea or thinks it's fine and dandy. If I want her here, he probably wants me to have her.

The new washer is less sturdily-made than my old machine, but I like it well enough. It's quiet, though, compared to the old chugger that rumbled through half the neighborhood when it hit the spin cycle. Remember that fat-jiggler machine Dolores Mathers had when you were a girl? With the belt that went around your middle? I always said I had one of those for free if you stood up against our washer when it really got going. This new washer is so well-behaved that I guess I'll never jiggle again on the porch unless I purposely jump up and down. (Which with my legs is not going to happen!)

I feel tired of talking about, thinking about, writing about my darn old legs! This last round of pain feels like it's almost over now. May I never have to go through it again and bore everyone with my tales of woe!

Well, that's all the news for now. I didn't ever get around to asking Pearline about the money situation. Maybe if she moves here to us I'll find out. Such a mystery, isn't it? You'll have to come home when or if she comes. Maybe if she gets well enough while she's here she can get a job in town and stay around. I think ten steps ahead all the time, don't I? I already have her married off in my imagination!

Love from us all,
Mama (who should get out of this swimming suit! It's pinching!)

Lumi slid the letter back into its envelope. Mama made it hard not to smile while reading her writing, even if things weren't always light and happy. Like the "tragedy." *What* tragedy? Why was *Pearline* supposed to go to wherever it was long ago, and why didn't she? Could she really have died? How did Mama end up going in her place? Would Pearline recover from her illness? Was she moving from Grandma's to live with Mama and Dad?

Lumi opened her laptop. No reply had come from her own mother, but that wasn't surprising. Her parents weren't on their computer very often, and, even though her mom had a cell phone, she only carried it when she went out of town.

She thought about her childhood years with her parents and with her two older brothers, Curtis and Charlie. Her brothers had always been closer to each other than to Lumi, but she and her mother spent almost every weekend together going to auctions, flea markets, antique shops, and old bookshops. Her mother read aloud to her at night from antique-collecting newspapers as if they were bedtime stories. All the local auctioneers and their workers knew Lumi's name, and they took her bids even though children were usually ignored. The flea markets that were then in business had been as familiar to her as any playground. When her mother rented a booth in an antique mall to sell the things she thought would bring in extra money, Lumi had loved to look up prices online, clean and sort items, and to do the inventory on the household computer.

In college, she'd studied art history and world history, cultures, and communications. She went to auctioneering school. Once she'd graduated from both, she found that she couldn't immediately jump into a job holding a gavel at a major company. She'd have to work as an underling for a long time and work her way up. That had been her plan until she'd received her inheritance and decided an antique shop was the better, less-stressful way to earn a living while surrounded by the old things she loved.

She took out her phone but hesitated. She hadn't had a personal conversation of any depth with her parents for a decade. Were Jackie's mother's letters changing her heart? Why did she have a sudden urge to reconnect in a meaningful way after so long? Deciding not to analyze her motives, she dialed. "Hi, Mom. Did you see my email? That's okay. I was only filling you in on what I've been doing lately. I attached photos of my house and the shop so you can see my progress this past month. It feels weird to be living on this street again but not in our same house. I get disoriented driving home after dark. Feels like I should be going further down the street, heading for our willow. When I get another bed moved in, you and Dad will have to visit me. No, the weather was worse south of here. We had a storm, but Indianapolis had more rain and wind than we did. I'm closed today. Yep. And tomorrow. My news? Well, sales have been pretty good this summer, so I went to a few auctions for new stock. In one box lot were about fifty handwritten letters in a metal lunch box. I tried to get the woman who put them in the sale to take them back, but she won't. I tracked her down on the internet. You guys should really get with the times! Actually carry your cell phone, and actually open up your computer once in a while. Oh, you're not that old! Stop saying that! Anyway, Mom, I wanted you to know that I'm doing okay. I get a twinge of lonesome for the auctioneer and my coworkers, but I'm glad I'm on my own, now. Mom! I will when I'm *ready.* I'm not ready. Besides, I'm having fun living in this house all by myself. I can eat when and what I want, I don't do the dishes every day if I feel lazy, and I have only my own laundry to wash. A man can wait until I'm … well, he can wait. You *have* grandkids, Mom. You might get one from me, too, but not … I'm perfectly happy on my own. Ladies? No, no lady friends, either. Yes, yes—I know what you mean. I appreciate that you're a modern woman. Okay, Mom."

Even though she tried to sound convincing on the phone, Lumi wasn't that convinced, herself. The whole time she was protesting that the single life was for her, she kept getting mental flashes of Nolan smiling, of Nolan not smiling, of Nolan asking her to sit at his table, of Nolan lugging off furniture like it weighed three pounds instead of thirty.

She suddenly realized she wasn't listening to her mother, who had kept talking while Lumi was daydreaming. "Well, I think I'll go look around at the north side of Indy for the afternoon. Hit up a few thrift shops. I wish you were here to go with me, Mom. Uh-huh. Me, too. Say hi to Dad for me. I will. Me, too. I will. Bye."

As soon as the call had ended, Lumi burst into tears. The ease and lightness of that conversation with her mother were vastly different from any they had shared in too many years. She wondered if her mother was crying in Florida now, too, also realizing the change and saddened that they had grown distant since Lumi was a girl.

She blew her nose and decided to put on a pair of brown shorts and an orange-patterned linen short-sleeved shirt. Dressed, she strapped on comfortable sandals and went into the bathroom to put on a light amount of makeup. As she was heading to her SUV with a few empty boxes, she had a sudden idea and crossed the street.

"Lu! How nice to see you again. You look like you're pushing autumn itself to come early in that outfit." She stepped back to let Lumi in.

"Maddy, I'm going to Indy for the afternoon to thrift shop and to get groceries. Want to join me for a day out?"

The woman paused but surprised Lumi by saying, "Let me call Chess and tell him. What time do you think we'll be back?"

"Oh, maybe by dark. Is that too late? We can have a nice restaurant supper together, too. My treat."

"That sounds fun. I'll feed Tony, let Chess know we're heading out, put on my other shoes, and grab my purse and a sweater. Come in and sit down. I'll try to be quick."

On the ride south, they discussed the changes in Barnwood in recent years, the factories that had closed since Lumi last lived in town, and which neighbors had left or were still on their street. She glanced at the fields of tall, richly-green corn they were passing on the flat landscape.

As they slowed at a sweeping curve along the White River, Maddy said, "I have a class reunion coming up next weekend. Wait! It's *this* weekend! I keep forgetting the Fourth of July is this week already. We

64

meet every year now, trying to keep our band together as best we can. Only six other people showed up at the Lions' clubhouse last year. We had expected several more, but between sickness or travels, there were only seven of us."

"I've never been to a reunion—not even a family reunion. How many kids were in your class?" Lumi asked, passing a mail truck that was pulled up to a box at the side of the road.

"I think we had about seventy. Four died from one thing or another before the rest of us graduated. Some died in Vietnam. Now we're all old enough to be dying off from old age. Me excepted, of course. I'm a younger spirit than most of those old farts." Maddy airily chuckled at her own use of a mild expletive.

Lumi smiled. The sun was getting hotter, so she turned the air conditioner higher. "I had eighty kids in my high school class and over two thousand in college. I doubt I'll ever go to a college reunion."

"We had turmoil after turmoil when I was in school," Maddy said, sighing. She lowered her gaze to her hands loosely folded on her lap. "Everything was going on at once, that's for sure."

Lumi nodded. "My school years were tame. I was always waiting for the weekends, waiting for three o'clock, waiting for summer, waiting for it all to be over."

"Do you enjoy yourself now, dear?" Maddy asked.

"Oh, I don't know … I think so. Yes. I can do whatever I like, whenever I like as long as my bills get paid and I stay on the straight and narrow. No kids to feed. No husband hogging up my bed."

"We'll have to fix that," Maddy said, suppressing a smile as her eyes sparkled.

"Not you, too!"

"What?"

"I was on the phone with my mom earlier."

Maddy laughed. "Oh."

"So, tell me about your classmates. Who will you see this weekend? Do you know who's coming?"

The older woman rummaged in her purse for her tin of mints. She offered one to Lumi before answering, "I'm not organizing the reunion, so I don't know for certain. Likely it'll be the same folks who were there last time. Jim Scott Byrum is a strange fellow. He smoked grass in school, then went to Harvard after the war. He moved to Indianapolis to work in a law firm, quit the law, and opened a funeral home. He always frightened me. He's tall, and he liked to loom over me when we were kids, waggling his hairy eyebrows. I don't remember if he picked on me

65

in particular or if he was like that with a lot of kids. And, let's see … Mary Johns worked in a car factory. She's rather ho-hum. I can't think of a single school activity that involved her in any way. She was always in the background, never making herself known, and yet she married and had about eight kids. I guess she must have come out of the shadows at some point."

Lumi smiled, stopping at a red light. "Who else?" she prompted.

"Oh, Ralph Morrison usually shows up. He has a limp from polio. He stayed home from the war because of it, of course. He never married, but he did ask me out a couple of times, and he would stare at me if I passed him in the hallway. He gave up after a while and turned rather cold. Now when I see him, he never says a thing to me. I wonder if he was more serious about me than I suspected. Maybe I hurt his feelings."

"That's too bad, but I think boys get over little rejections pretty fast. Don't they?"

Maddy shrugged as they started up again. "Depends on the boy or man." Her tone changed. "Oh, and there's Sandy Davis. He was *good-*looking! I swooned over him for a long time. He married another of our classmates, Mary Sue … I don't remember her last name. It's been Davis for decades. She was the most beautiful girl! Her nose has just about taken over the rest of her face now, but she was the girl all the boys wanted to date in school. Except Chess. Chess never acted like he noticed her."

"Chess—as in the Chess you have your arrangement with at bedtime?" Lumi asked, surprised.

"Bedtime! Lumi! Of all the ways to describe our innocent companionship!" Maddy pointedly and loudly sucked her mint, pretending to be shocked. "Oh, yes. Chess was in my class. Very smart, very nice. A good kid who worked hard all through school to help his family pay the bills. He married another lady, of course, and I married another man. I never saw Chess as a romantic possibility for me, even though I suspected he liked me that way. We were close for a while. Good friends. He was always this barrel of a guy that looked like he could tackle the whole football team by himself. I should say that the way he looked wasn't why I didn't return his feelings—if indeed he *did* have feelings for me other than friendship. He resented the fact that he couldn't do a lot of what the other kids were doing. Every penny he earned went to his folks. There was no lightness in his spirit. He was very serious. Almost … morose. Like a dark cloud was always over his head. So, being a young woman with problems of my own, I didn't feel like adding another gloomy presence to my life."

"I can understand that. But he's so jolly now—you'd never know he used to be gloomy." Lumi turned into the parking lot of a Salvation Army thrift shop and turned off the engine. She unbuckled and turned toward Maddy. "It's funny how people change. Were you the same in high school as you are now?"

The older woman unbuckled, too, thinking. "No. I don't think so. I had been protected by my parents too much. I was immature. I tried to ignore everything that was going on in the news, and I didn't protest or get political. Until I reached my senior year, that is. The music and clothes were getting wilder, and politics seemed to be a part of every conversation. I changed right along with the times. Protested injustices right along with many of my friends. Oh, I did a few things I wish I hadn't." Maddy closed her eyes, then opened them again, seeming to push something from her mind. "Like any young person, I struggled to find myself."

They got out of the SUV and walked into the shop.

Lumi grabbed a cart and glided it down the center aisle. Every generation has its troubles and fears, she thought. "Is Chess going to the reunion?"

"He usually does. He always went alone. His wife never accompanied him. June liked to visit friends in Michigan over the summer months. He and I went together last year."

After half an hour, Lumi went to the shelves of dishes and glassware where Maddy was still browsing. "I'm ready when you are."

Maddy placed several items into the cart. "I'm done."

They walked to the front of the shop and got in line behind a man with a load of work pants on hangers draped over an arm. "Is it senior discount day here?" Maddy asked Lumi.

"That's on Wednesday. But I'm treating, so—"

"Oh, no, you're not, young lady! I agreed to dinner out at your expense. Nothing else! Why, I won't get a thing if I can't get it with my own cash money!"

Mrs. Rasmusson's suddenly fierce expression seemed to envelop her whole body. It appeared to Lumi that even the woman's loose hair had tightened on its own into a severe bun.

"Okay, okay, okay! I was simply trying to be generous. I didn't mean to insult you."

Maddy exhaled, her eyes softening. She put a hand on Lumi's arm. "I don't like people to think I can't pay my way. That's another failing of Chess'. He's always whipping out his wallet. I am an independent woman. My husband let me earn my own spending money to buy my antiques. He knew I didn't like to have him support my bad habits." She paused, looking over the things in the cart she'd selected to buy. "I have a real fondness for old Chess, but I'm going to have to train him better if we're going to …"

"Going to what?"

She lowered her voice to a whisper so the young woman cashier couldn't hear. "Keep on shacking up."

Lumi caught the cashier's eye. She *had* heard. The two of them grinned at each other before Lumi put her pile of clothes, old dishes, books, and an antique framed print of President Roosevelt's dog, Fala, onto the counter.

Sitting down to dinner at a buffet restaurant in the early evening, Lumi smiled to herself.

"What's that mysterious look all about? Thinking of anyone I know?" Maddy asked, teasing.

"Yes. You and Chess. I remembered what you said about shacking up. It tickled me again."

"I don't know what imp took possession of my mouth when I said that!" She lifted her fork and settled a napkin on her lap. "I can be a little wicked."

"When I was a little girl, you seemed like the prison guard of the whole neighborhood. No one dared say 'boo' around you. I wish that we had been closer back then—that I had known how funny and sweet you are."

Maddy waggled her fork. "I *had* to be tough! It was my only defense against the boys who were around town back in the days when you lived down the street. Having a witch in the neighborhood made them think twice about doing something naughty and probably prevented at least some of their mischief. The kids on our street aren't rough ones now. I don't have to be stern. I've let my guard down these last several years." She looked hurt. "But now you see what's happened? Those stereoscope cards invaded my home."

Lumi sipped her tea. "Let's not talk about them tonight. This is our fun day out, after all, and it has at least another hour to go. Here," she said, lifting her amber glass. "Let's toast our great thrift-shop finds and a delish meal. And our beautiful summer. And friendship. And all the nice things in our lives."

Maddy clinked her cup against Lumi's glass, her lips quivering. "Yes."

"What was the best thing you found today? I love that orange stained-glass frame you bought. My sister-in-law used to make frames almost like it. I think she's on to other hobbies now, but they were nice. That old tennis racket you found has an interesting handle design. Going to take up a new sport?"

Maddy's expression lightened. "Chess has a glass-fronted showcase in his living room full of vintage sports equipment, photos, athletic cards, signed balls, and that sort of thing. The racket should fit in perfectly. He could prop it up behind shorter items." She chewed and swallowed a piece of broccoli. "I think my favorite thing from today would be ... that box of Christmas ornaments. They remind me of the ones my parents would have me bring down from the attic when I was a girl. The clip-on birds, especially." She paused to load her fork with spicy chicken. "I won't wait until Christmas to put my birds out. I'm going to clip them onto the top of my bathroom curtains. What do you think of that idea?"

"Nice! I would never have thought of that. You have a great eye for decorating. Your home is *full* of fun touches. What I want to know is, how did you train Tony not to knock everything off the shelves?"

"Ha! He came to me as an older cat. I got Tony the Non-tiger from the shelter last year. I went when Chess was volunteering for the day, and we picked him out together. I get to keep him at my house, but he's really ours together. Tony must be at least fourteen years old now, but he plays around just like a kitten from time to time. He likes the rings from milk cartons best of all. Loves wads of paper."

"I should go to the shelter. I'd like to get a cat or a dog. I've never had a dog."

"Get both."

Lumi considered as she cut a crispy shrimp egg roll into pieces. "I think I'd better get more settled. Maybe in a few months when I know my income is going to hold steadily enough to support me, let alone a pet or two."

"Wait to see what Nolan wants, right?" Maddy grinned.

Lumi gave the woman a wilting look. *"Stop it!"*

"Well, I think you two could be a darling couple. Why not? He's single. You're single. He has a good job. You'd have beautiful children together, Lumi. You're both very nice-looking." She ate for a minute, then added, "I see your SUV in your drive every evening. I don't think you've been out past dark since you moved back to town. Haven't you dated anyone in town?"

"No. I don't do that sort of thing, Maddy. I never have."

Mrs. Rasmusson nearly dropped her fork.

Lumi sighed. "I like being single and independent."

"You mean you don't date at *all?* Not even when you lived in Indianapolis? Not even in high school?"

Lumi shrugged. "I don't have a bit of interest. I want to be my own person—have my own business."

Maddy reached for Lumi's hand on the table, her eyes sincere. "How very sad, Lu. That is a very sad way to live. Don't put yourself on a shelf like that. It breaks my heart to know you've lived without romance."

Changing the subject, Lumi said, her face feeling hot, "Well, my favorite thing from today is that black-and-pink nineteen-fifties phone-shaped plastic purse from the Treasure Tomb. I've never noticed that shop before, but it looks like it's been sitting on Allisonville Road *forever.*"

"I've never been there, either. Their prices were kind of high for such a run-down place."

"Some things were cheap. The purse was a bargain at five dollars. I'll probably put about fifty on it."

Maddy seemed surprised. "You're selling it?"

"Sure. Of *course.* I have a business to run, don't I?"

The older woman poured tea into her cup from a decorated red pot. "I'm so used to buying things to keep for myself or to give as presents that I never shop intending to making money from antiques. But that's right—you need to make a living." She lifted the teapot lid to see how much was left inside. "Does this mean everything you bought today will be for sale?"

Lumi reviewed her purchases while eating the last bite of her egg roll. After wiping her fingers and mouth, she said, "Yes. Except for the clothes. I bought those for myself. Oh, and the books. The large coffee table books are for the shop, but the novels are for me."

"I used to read at night, but Chess, my ever-present companion, keeps me occupied playing cards. That's okay. Now I set aside an hour or two in the afternoon for my books. I think I'll break out some jigsaw puzzles for our evening entertainment. Mix things up a little. We could invite another couple in for board games or poker."

"Won't anyone you invite over suspect something's going on between you and Chess?"

Maddy smiled as a tiny girl walked past the table, holding her father's hand. "That doesn't have to be a secret. I simply don't want anyone knowing we're spending the whole *night* in the same house." Her smile broadened. "Ha! I can hear Chess now, calling me a hypocrite."

It was after nine o'clock and nearly dark when they returned to Barnwood. Chess was sitting on Maddy's front porch bench when they pulled up to the sidewalk. He helped carry her bags inside after kissing her on the cheek. Parked in her own drive at the right side of her house, Lumi unloaded the clothes and novels she had purchased but left the rest of the boxes in the SUV.

She stood leaning against her door after locking it, keenly aware of the semi-darkness and emptiness of her home and that no one had welcomed her with a kiss. "Hello, house. I'm back. I don't suppose you missed me."

Taking a warm shower, she shampooed and scrubbed and allowed her thoughts to luxuriate in visions of Nolan.

"Nolan's a widower," Maddy had said. How long has he been alone? Lumi wondered. Was he looking for a relationship? Was *she?*

Lumi decided she was acting like a schoolgirl with the start of a crush. She'd had no real encouragement from Nolan. He had been nice to her. He had felt sorry to see her sitting alone at the restaurant. He was just being …

"Arg!" Lumi shouted at the fog-shrouded mirror as she dried off. "Stop this!"

In her bedroom, she put on a robe and opened her laptop computer. She wanted to see Nolan again and hoped he was on Facebook. He wasn't. She found his name in the town newspaper archives. He was on the baseball team in school. He'd found a missing diamond ring in the park and the woman who had lost it was overjoyed, but the boy wouldn't take a reward. He got married. His wife died after "a brief illness," and Nolan was listed warmly in her obituary. There were a few mentions of him in crime articles after he joined the police force, about arrests he had made, and court appearances. But never any photos with the news items. Maybe that was typical of police officers and detectives—it kept them from being targeted, perhaps. Or maybe there were no online photos because Nolan was a private person.

Lumi went back to Facebook. She looked for Magnus Sanders and found him. He hadn't posted anything for years except to make a few comments on baseball or football games, but he was friends with Cammie, who *did* have a very active timeline. A search through her many photos revealed a few shots of Nolan and the other members of the Sanders family. Cammie holding on tightly to a long-maned pony, her father beside her. Cammie and Magus dressed up with their dates for the prom. Nolan with a baseball bat and batter's helmet. A young Nolan tucked into bed under a Superman blanket holding a comic book. Nolan leaning against the giant, graffiti-covered rock in front of the high school, his body taller but still rail-thin. Another photo showed him—still looking underweight—with a petite, dark-haired young woman. He was holding her hand and smiling as they stood at the entrance to a dilapidated covered bridge. The caption read, "Nolan and Carol on their honeymoon in Brown County, Indiana." Lumi stared at the couple, a knot of jealousy forming in her stomach until she realized how disgraceful it was to be jealous of a woman who had passed away. She pushed the laptop across the bed for a moment to weep for those two young people. Carol, it seemed, had walked over that bridge, leaving Nolan behind to grieve for these past years.

Lumi was ashamed of that momentary barb of jealousy she had felt. Other emotions mixed together in her heart. She pulled the laptop closer and lifted the screen again. Taking a deep breath, she tried to make peace with the image and idea of Carol. When she hadn't known what the young woman looked like, Carol's history with Nolan hadn't solidified in her mind. Her thoughts had simply been that Nolan had once been married; they were very young; they were in love; she had died.

Seeing the two of them holding hands made a difference to Lumi. This woman, and this version of Nolan: thin, boyish, and carefree. The realization that Nolan had endured Carol's death and funeral within months of the photograph was startling. Lumi wanted to reach through time and hold him, but a moment later that seemed wrong. He had to find his own methods of moving on alone to mostly recover. And he had.

A few images of Nolan were more recent—after he had bulked up and had muscles all over—but there was something that wasn't quite right. He hadn't been photographed well. Or … he took a bad photo. Or … the angles weren't good. His face was not the extraordinarily handsome one she knew. The photos made him look … average. Good-looking, but not the hunk she saw him as when she was with him in the flesh.

The pictures of Nolan didn't represent the person she had talked and laughed with, had sat beside. Lumi remembered being absolutely bowled over by his good looks when he was teasing her at the auto repair shop. Even in the dim lighting of Sally's restaurant, she'd felt an electric spark radiating from him. Sitting next to Nolan, she kept stealing glances at him as if her eyes couldn't get enough of his handsome face and broad shoulders. He was already familiar to her heart, and he may have been familiar to her right from the moment she saw him standing on Maddy's doorstep.

Lumi downloaded the best of the recent photos of Nolan from Cammie's Facebook posts and made it larger. She examined his eyes, his nose, his lips. She covered the photo except for his eyes. They were the same. She covered everything except his mouth. It was the same. His nose was the same, and yet, seen all together, they didn't mirror the image of the man she carried in her mind.

Instead of reading another letter from Mama to Jackie, she went downstairs to rummage through the novels she'd bought earlier. Choosing one by Tammy Banks set during World War I, she made herself comfortable and switched her bedside lamp to a brighter setting. The writing and story were marvelous and moving, but the descriptions of injured and disfigured men made her uncomfortable. They reminded her too much of the stereoscope cards.

Could someone who knew Maddy from long ago have recently read the antiques newspaper article online? Were they retaliating? And if so, whatever for?

Lumi remembered snatches of what Maddy had said about the people she went to school with who were likely to be at the reunion. Could one of them be tormenting Maddy with those cards? The fact that it had happened close to when the classmates would be together may be the answer to why the cards showed up within the past several days, and why another recently arrived in her mailbox. Were they hoping to see her suffering at the reunion?

Since Maddy did have a shock of guilt while looking at the images, maybe someone who knew her long ago also knew of a crime or sinful act she had committed—a secret concealed or forgotten. The cards could be a veiled threat or a warning that at any moment, a stranger or a friend could wield their power to destroy Maddy.

Putting the novel aside, Lumi opened her computer again. She did a search for anything informative about repressed memories.

She read an article that said that if something terrifying happens physically or psychologically, your brain can push it away to where it can't easily be retrieved. It's a conscious drowning of the fact, letting it float for days, months, years, or forever, separate from conscious thinking and reacting. A trigger, however, can cause the protective waters to drain in a split second, letting the memory stand on its own again, fully formed or as a feeling of dread, fear, or pain.

So, this meant there was a chance Maddy had done something terrible long ago that was now being held as a weapon over her head. But what?

73

Did she murder someone? Kill them in an accident? No. The scenes in the cards showed blood and damage to too many bodies. Unless Maddy had thrown a grenade into a crowd, she couldn't possibly have been responsible for those terrible scenes.

Lumi read more about repressed memories. Certain specialists believed they were valid, but others thought they were false. She knew there were painful incidents in her past that she had purposely tried to forget. She had watched her grandfather die following a head-on car collision while he was driving and while Lumi was in the back seat. She saw a boy fall from a slide to the playground, his arm gruesomely broken. She'd been rejected by a boy she liked in front of other kids when she had asked him to a junior-high dance. In college, she had … no. No. No. She had tried to forget those things and more, but they came back to her throughout her life. Maybe repressing memories was beneficial, allowing peace to replace torment. Lumi knew she wasn't successful at moving beyond some of the most hurtful things in her life. She wondered if others had a skill she couldn't master.

She remembered that when she had first joined Facebook, a woman friended her that she hadn't seen since she was very young. They had been neighbors, and their brothers had been playmates. Sunny was older by ten years but was Lumi's first friend. Sunny posted on Lumi's timeline that she has a scar on her arm from the day Lumi had whacked her with a stick. "Remember that? Boy, was my mom mad! She stormed over to your house and screamed at your mom. My mom wouldn't let us kids play together for months!" It seemed like a significant event, but Lumi had zero memory of such a thing ever having happened. In fact, she protested to Sunny that it must have been done by another little girl.

"No. It was you. You had a temper!"

It had felt like Sunny remembered a whole, different child. If that was a real event that Lumi had purposely but absolutely forgotten, couldn't it also be true that Maddy honestly couldn't recall a major transgression from *her* past? Was there a level of the brain that hid terrible facts from itself while allowing reactions to them to continue forever?

Chapter Six

Lumi stretched her arms and back and sat up in bed. It was Tuesday, so she had another full day away from her shop to spend doing whatever she liked. But, she realized as she looked at her artfully-half-melted Salvador Dali-style wall clock and at the gray clouds outside her windows, she didn't feel like doing much of anything.

Maybe she would haul her purchases inside and price them at home. Or, she could spend the day reading, watching movies, cooking for the week ahead, or roller skating at one of the Indianapolis rinks. She hadn't gone skating since Brad had taken her in college. She sighed, rejecting the idea. It didn't seem like a thing to do by herself.

Her mountain bike, skates and helmet, boxes of books, her small kitchen table and chairs from her apartment, childhood diaries, favorite antiques she'd bought with allowance money as a girl, photos, dolls, toys, and winter clothes were mostly untouched since her move into her house from Indianapolis. They were in the two upstairs bedrooms that were otherwise unused. Lumi knew she should hang up her winter clothes, at least, but she didn't feel like working with bulky sweaters and corduroy pants in the summertime.

Every other Monday and Tuesday since opening her shop she had found plenty to do to occupy her time: auctions or thrift shops, mowing and planting flowers around the edge of the house, painting, cleaning, and cooking. She streamed movies or read. But none of those activities seemed appealing.

She padded downstairs and into the kitchen. She and Maddy had spent so much time in thrift shops and eating out that they hadn't found time to stop for groceries. Lumi held open her refrigerator door and scanned the nothing on each glass shelf. A single toffee ice cream bar was in the freezer. She ate it with two graham crackers left in the bottom of their box.

After changing into jean shorts and a Grumpy Cat t-shirt, she washed and dried a load of laundry that included the clothes she had bought the day before. The tops were cut lower and were more feminine and colorful than the ones she usually wore. The new shorts were more form-fitting, and the jeans hung lower on her hips than her other jeans and pants. She felt blood rush to her cheeks as she imagined Nolan's reaction to seeing her dressed more provocatively.

She fought with herself. It was cliché. It wasn't like her. She adamantly did not want to go down the slippery path of romance.

75

Lumi sat on top of the dryer, swinging her feet. The clothes flopping around inside the machine were her enemies, and putting them on would be admitting something to the world at large. It would be saying that she wanted to be admired from the outside as well as from the inside. Did she?

She had fought against caring about her looks—or at least appearing to care—for years except when she needed to dress up for a fine art or high-end antiques auction. Could Nolan only find her attractive if she wore makeup and sexy clothes?

Lumi was angry at herself for all the things she was feeling and worrying about for the first time. This flirtation wouldn't help her business. It wouldn't furnish her home. There were goals she wanted to meet before she thought too deeply about her personal life. Things were getting all out of order.

When the laundry was dry and folded, Lumi went out to shop for groceries. After a quick stop home to put the food in her refrigerator and cupboards, she went out again to the dollar store, hoping to find red, white, and blue decorations for her shop. She did, but she also found Cammie in front of her as she got into the checkout line.

Cammie pulled her credit card from the reader and punched a few buttons. Putting her card away, she noticed Lumi. "Well, hey, Lumi." She looked down. "Girl that is a *whole lot* of patriotism you've got stuffed into your cart."

Lumi glanced at her haul. "They're for my antique shop. I've never decorated it before, so I wasn't sure how much to buy. Too much, do you think?"

Cammie considered. "Maybe not. What's your square footage there?"

Lumi lifted her purchases onto the conveyer belt. "Um, about twenty-two hundred. That includes my storage area and a restroom. The upstairs is available if I ever want to expand. My landlord has his own stuff in storage up there for now."

Cammie nodded. "Well, I think you bought about the right amount. I used to work at Don's uptown—the hardware store. I was in charge of decorating, among other duties like firing slackers, ordering stock, and fetching lunch."

Lumi paid and put her bags into the cart, then walked with Cammie to the strip mall parking lot. The sky had grown even darker since she'd gone into the store. "I don't know how small businesses manage to hire workers. Thinking about paying my *own* bills every month makes me nervous."

76

"Well, Don needs quite a few floor workers and service people who make house calls. They do appliance repair, furnace work, electrical, plumbing—that sort of thing—anything simple where a real specialist isn't needed for the job. I met Mike at Don's. He's still there, but he's training at night to become an electrician."

"Great!" Lumi avoided a pothole before swerving her cart closer to Cammie again. "I've been antiquing my whole life. Mom and I even had a booth together when I was a girl. I almost can't believe I have my own antique shop now."

"So cool! I envy you. I've always wanted my own business."

"It's fun, but kind of frightening. No one is paying my salary except for me, and no one is on hand to help me."

Cammie raised an eyebrow. "Well, you must have friends you can call on. Right?"

Lumi looked across the parking lot. "No. I'm friendly with Mrs. Rasmusson, but that's about it. Girls I knew in high school don't seem to have any time for me or any interest in making time. Everyone has moved on."

Cammie looked concerned. "You sound lonely, Lumi."

"I am," Lumi said, pausing while a truck backed up. She regretted admitting such personal things to someone she barely knew. "But I'm used to being independent. I'm okay. Really." She smiled, hoping she looked like she meant that smile. "Maybe a few of my regular customers will become friends in time. I haven't been open that long."

"There's Nolan. You two are friends, right?"

"I don't think so. We've only just met. Mrs. Rasmusson introduced us when he went to her house on an errand for Magnus. He happened to be at Sally's. He happened to feel sorry when he saw I was sitting alone."

Cammie's expression changed as if she knew something Lumi didn't, but she didn't say anything more.

The wind shifted, flinging down fat plops of rain. The ladies parted ways to run to their cars with their purchases. They waved at each other as they both drove away, eventually into opposite directions.

Lumi pulled into a parking spot in front of her shop and sat for a while, looking at the weather report on her phone. It was only going to get stormier during the next few hours. She unloaded her thrift-shop purchases and dollar store decorations while the rain was barely falling.

"Need any assistance, ma'am?" asked a man's voice behind her as she was putting the last of the bags inside the door.

She turned in surprise, the wind whipping her long blonde hair uncontrollably. "Nolan! Hi! Uh, no ... thanks, though. Everything's inside already. Unless you want to help move stuff to the back of the shop. Oh, wait. You're working. Never mind. I can take it from here."

Nolan followed her inside out of the wind, letting the door close behind him with a jingle from the bell at its top. They stood near a full-length vintage easel mirror and an art nouveau swing-arm floor lamp.

Lumi was out of breath from lugging things into her shop, but she knew she'd have felt like panting around the man even if she had been lounging on a beach for the past hour. His black police uniform complimented his muscular build perfectly.

"I was passing. Saw you were fighting the wind and lugging a box into the store. Are you sure I can't help?"

Lumi shook her head. Trying to seem casual despite her thrumming pulse, she said, "I was talking to Cammie earlier at the dollar store. She was advising me on my decorations."

"Oh." He stepped a few inches away until his back was touching the door frame.

"So, you grew up in town here, too?" Lumi asked. Her legs felt weak. Her shirt was heavily splotched from the rain—that dumb white Grumpy Cat shirt, she realized. And she didn't have makeup on. And her hair was damp and scraggly.

He nodded, and a light seemed to flicker behind his brown eyes as he reached out to swing the lamp's shade closer to the wall.

The only thing Lumi could think about when he did that was that it was a good idea. That way if they lunged at each other for a wild embrace, nothing would get damaged. "I don't remember you. What street did you live on?"

Nolan shyly scanned her body and then met her eyes again. "Rupert."

"That's in the subdivision, right?"

He nodded.

They didn't say anything for a long moment. The rushing urgency of the wind felt to Lumi like the sound of blood whirling through her veins.

He pushed the lamp's shade farther against the wall, his eyes locked on her face and eyes. He wasn't smiling—there was something more emotional in his expression.

Lumi panicked, wondering how to run from her attraction. She didn't dare hope he was feeling something for her in return. If he *was* attracted to her, did she want that? Could she handle that?

Nolan took a hesitant step forward. "Windy out."

"It is," she agreed. Then she heard herself saying words that the rational part of her brain couldn't believe it was hearing: "You never

know *what* fun things will blow in through your door on a day like this."
Lumi saw that her words had struck him as funny, but also as meaningful.

He adjusted the slant on the easel mirror and stepped forward once more. "You're not open today?"

She didn't answer except to blink, holding her breath.

He moved closer again.

Lumi reached behind her and found the edge of a dresser. She took a half step to lean against it, feeling the need for support. "I'm not open on Mondays or Tuesdays. I … I'm here alone." She had whispered it. Why did I *whisper* that? she asked herself, her face heating.

Nolan met her eyes hopefully. He reached a hand forward a few inches, nearly touching her, but then let it drop.

Lumi panted lightly, fearful and excited at the same time.

"Oh," he said, almost whispering, himself. His own breathing quickened.

Lumi's eyes went to Nolan's lips. She glanced up and was startled to find him staring at her lips, too.

"Listen to that wind," Lumi said. "Feels urgent."

Nolan gulped. "I don't hear a thing other than your voice."

Lumi shook, scared of her feelings. Unsure of her feelings. What had he meant? Was it a compliment, or was she annoyingly loud?

He stepped closer. His eyes glanced down, then met hers again. "Nice shirt. Wet. Nice."

Lumi stopped breathing as a million thoughts raced through her mind. Was he flirting? Was he joking? Did he mean something sexual when he remarked about her shirt? Did he merely come in to see if she needed help, or was he interested in her personally? Had he been checking for her to show up at her shop all day, and that's why he was there at the same time she was?

A staticky voice crackled over Nolan's police radio. It seemed to rouse him from a slow-motion dream. "I should go."

She nodded, relieved but also disappointed.

Nolan whispered, "Lumi."

She searched his face. It hadn't been a question. He had merely said her name, but the *way* he had said it seemed significant. It was as if he were asking her if she was feeling everything he was in that moment.

"Nolan," she said back to him. She was saying yes—she was feeling everything, too. She knew she was breathing hard but couldn't help it. Her toes wanted to curl as a wave of desire washed over her.

His eyebrows flicked up, and his smile returned as he backed through the door and went out of sight, the jingle of the bell seeming like a sound-effect denoting something magical had taken place.

She caught her breath, then stepped out into the wind and rain to lock her door. For a moment she didn't know if she was happy or sad that a handsome cop wasn't standing mere inches away anymore. She hated to lose control.

"What was *that?*" Lumi asked herself when she was securely behind the wheel of her SUV again, trembling, her heart thumping. "What in the heck just *happened?*"

Lumi made layered meatloaf and put it and baked potatoes into the double oven she'd had installed two months ago. The meatloaf would be enough for dinner plus leftovers for three more nights.

While dinner baked, she went upstairs intending to put on warmer clothes since the rainy early evening had turned cooler. Opening her drawers and closet, she ultimately decided against dressing again and instead took everything off. It was gloomy outside and lonely inside her house, so she wrapped up in a bathrobe and read another letter from Mama.

Dear Jackie,

Well, as you know, Pearline is here. She gets on your dad's nerves, and she gets on long-suffering Waller Bee's nerves, but she's here. You asked on the phone how long she would be staying, but I couldn't say then. I can't say now, either. I guess it's open-ended, which also gets on your dad's nerves. He likes to know what a plan is, and right now there isn't one.

When we were first moving her in (she's in your old room, I hope you don't mind!), Pearline was exceedingly quiet. I think she had a fight with your grandma that last morning they were together. Which also worries your dad. What if Grandma won't take Pearline back!? Ever! Lordy! I get the worst glares now from Waller, and he grumbles like he's asking me when she's moving out again and off his bed that was your bed. I hope your dad and the dog settle down soon!

I think if P had money to spend, she's spent it, but good. If I don't give her something, she doesn't have it. This is going to lead to more trouble with your dad—I can smell it coming like a skunk who ate rotten eggs. Now it doesn't seem worthwhile to ask her where she got money from, or what she was doing to get it.

Nancy Jo asked me out to lunch today. I took P with me, but P looked bored the whole time. At least she's not sick anymore. NJ was in Boston for a week. She brought me an orange t-shirt with one of those dumb sayings on it. I guess I'll have to wear it if I do anything with NJ, but it's sure not my style! We went to the Hula Hoop for lunch. They make the best food! I had hoopla rings and a Hawaiian turkey club sandwich. Pearline complained about grease upsetting her gallbladder. She ordered a peanut butter sandwich off the kids menu. I don't know if I told you, but P used to be equal parts adorable/loving and annoying when we were girls. I keep hoping for the best, that she'll settle in with us and be happier eventually.

I didn't bring up the tragedy to P again. I'll wait until we're comfortable around each other again. Well, I'll write again soon, or call you. You and Marty should come up on the weekend if you can. I know, I know. I hardly made it sound enticing after moaning on and on about Pearline this whole letter!

Take care and hugs to you both,
Mama and Dad

The envelope contained two photos: one was of a cow-patterned cat relaxing on a porch step. ("The stray is getting mighty close to coming inside, whether we think it's a good idea or not.") The other was of Waller Bee, lying with his head on the floor and his eyes rolled pathetically skyward. ("What does WB think of the cat? You can tell from his face, I think.")

Lumi laughed at the inscriptions, and then again when she flipped the pictures over for another look at the animals. She put the photos and letter back into their envelope and took out the next one in the box.

Dear Teensa,

I wish I had good and happy things to write about. I should call you, but I never feel really alone in the house anymore between your aunt and your dad hanging around all the time.

Betsy is very sick. They took her cast off and her arm is okay, but while she was there in the doctor's getting her cast cut off, she confessed to her mom and the doctor that she had been feeling really sick but hadn't wanted to have her appointment canceled and take a chance on having the cast on a moment longer. Well, Jackie, they put her in the hospital right away. She has a form of meningitis! I think it's not the worst kind, but we're all horribly scared now! I have gotten close with that girl and her mom lately, and I feel every bit as bad for myself as I do for her mom! I don't want to lose her!

Your dad feels terrible. He is sweet on Betsy, too. What will happen if she doesn't pull through, or has lasting effects? Oh, God!

Just wanted to write it out.
Love from Mama

Poor Betsy! What if she dies? wondered Lumi, her stomach in a knot. She glanced at her clock. There was a lot of time left before the meatloaf would be done.

Dear baby J,

I am praising all that is Holy! I called you, so you know Betsy has passed through the storm. I don't know how long she'll stay in the hospital, but she should be mostly okay. There may be lingering effects for a while, or for her whole life, but for now she is doing good.

Having Betsy be a scare in our lives, your dad and I have become different people, you might say. We no longer are bothered in the least little bit about Pearline acting up. And, you know what? That seems to have changed her heart, too. We are in a much better place all together. P didn't know Betsy, really, but she was so upset right along with us that the little girl might die. Pearline says she wants to go home to Grandma's house soon. She kind of needed a break for a while to see things more clearly. Now, I know, the next thing coming will be to work on your grandma. She wasn't here having the spiritual breakthrough that the rest of us did! I think she's enjoying life without Pearline.

I put the throw pillows you made us on the couch, one at each end. They really brighten up that old slouchy couch! Your dad looked worried and I asked him why. He said it made the couch look shabby, and now maybe I'll be asking for a new one to go with your pillows.

I was sitting on the porch step peeling carrots before supper last night when I had unexpected company. That cat keeps coming around. I'm not sure Waller would approve if we took the kitty into the house. I think he is trying out a few different locations in the neighborhood. Seeing who has the best food and the most comfortable digs. I'm certainly not going to compete for his bestowments, but if he chooses us, what can we do?

I finally managed to talk to Pearline some more about the tragedy. I feel like we're closer than we have been in decades. I told her she is denying herself a happy life by carrying around so much guilt. I asked her to think about therapy, with or without Grandma. I think your grandma would rather sit in mud with pigs for fifty minutes at a stretch than see a therapist, but maybe Pearline will go. She said she's open to the idea. I offered to go with her. We'll see, she said.

I also told her that I feel the burden of her guilt, too. She didn't understand what I meant, I don't think, but maybe she'll think that over, too. We all need to keep growing and changing in this life, or why are we on the planet?

I'm writing this late at night. My lamp with the dark green shade looks pretty. Sinatra is on the stereo, singing barely loud enough for me to hear, and his album is on the last song. Every time I hear the last song on an album I get a little lonesome for the other songs and want to right away lift the needle back over to the start. However, my eyes are getting droopy and my hand is cramping up a little. If you were here tonight I would hold your hands in mine and dance you out to the kitchen (one two three, dip two three, twirl like this, one two three) and we could have bowls of cup of noodle soup together before bed. If I close my eyes, I can picture it and almost smell the soup and feel the warmth on my tongue. I see your darling, smiling face and your little hand holding a spoon, and you're giggling because you've just slurped. I miss having my girl here in the house! And I think (don't be shocked!) I'm also going to be lonesome for my sister when she goes.

Love to you and Marty,
Mama

Lumi lowered the letter to her lap, her eyes filling with tears, desperate loneliness crowding out every other feeling. She wiped her eyes and nose and glanced at her clock again. Dinner wouldn't be ready for another forty-five minutes.

She reached for her phone, cleared her throat, and called her neighbor. "Hi, Maddy. It's Lumi. Um, do you have Nolan's home or cell phone number? Oh. No. That's okay. I was maybe going to ask him to come over for a meatloaf supper. I was lonely enough to be brave and impulsive. I … please … forget this call. I was being all emotional. I'll snap out of it soon, I'm sure. Have a nice evening, and I'll see you soon. Goodnight."

She sighed and reclined onto her pillows. Staring at the ceiling, she chided herself for that last call. What was she thinking? "I guess those letters are having a strange effect on me. I should stop reading them," she said to herself.

After thirty minutes spent alternately chastising herself about the call and feeling disappointed that she hadn't been able to invite Nolan over, Lumi went downstairs to the kitchen. She put frozen beans and corn into pots of water on the stovetop without turning on the burners, and took butter and sour cream from the fridge. She switched on the 1960s blue and white plastic Philco radio that sat between two potted plants on a sill near the dining table and found a song on an AM station that matched her mood: "Hello" by Adele was just starting. The gloomy evening made it dark enough outside so that Lumi could see her reflection in the windows of the dining room. Her hair was tangled, and her fuzzy peach robe was open loosely but tied off at her waist. "I'm doing this to myself," she said aloud. "I'm making myself lonely now. I never used to feel it. Not like this, anyway. I need to get my mind back on my store and on fixing up the house, and then—"

Knock knock knock

Lumi jumped. The trio of knocks felt as familiar as a voice. Which was silly, she realized immediately. She adjusted the knot on her robe to hold it more tightly closed and crossed the living room to peer through the door window. No one was in sight. She twisted the switch for the porch light and jumped again. It was him!

Without opening the door, she called, *"Nolan?* What is it?" Her heart was suddenly drumming at double time.

"I was invited over for meatloaf."

She looked down at her robe and bare feet. "I … how?"

"It's misting out here. Can I come in?"

Lumi panicked for a moment but forced herself to calm down. "How did you know I was going to invite you?"

"Mrs. R called Magnus. Hey, are you going to send me home, or may I please come in? Seriously, it's miserable out here."

She took a deep, bracing breath before calling, "I'm going to let you in, but keep your eyes closed, okay? I'm in my robe. I'll let you in, but then I need to get dressed." She turned the lock and the knob, pulling the door open but staying hidden behind it. Once Nolan had stepped in from the porch, Lumi closed the door and turned toward her stairs.

A hand on her wrist stopped her.

He pulled her body against his. Gently. Not threateningly. His face hovered above hers, his large, expressive eyes melting into her eyes. The restrained strength of Nolan's arms wrapped around her was startling. Sensual.

Adele's singing felt too loud, too romantic.

In a gruff whisper, he said, "You look perfect. *Perfect.* Don't … go … anywhere."

She shivered, her eyes widening in alarm. He must have assumed she was a grown woman who had invited a man to dinner and then met him at the door in a bathrobe and nothing else. He must have assumed she'd *meant* for him to find her that way.

Nolan's lips were nearly touching hers. So close, so close. She could smell toothpaste and shampoo. He was barely a millimeter away.

The emotional part of her brain yearned for contact, but the sensible, scared part forced her hands to push against his chest, easily freeing herself. Lumi took a step away, one hand in her messy hair and the other clutching the front of her robe at its neck. "I told you not to *look*. I've got to run up to change. Please, um … have a seat. I'll be back in a few minutes."

Nolan reached for her again, but she was faster and had hit the stairs running.

After a few seconds, she crept back down to see if he had left or stayed. Adele was still singing her achingly beautiful song. The kitchen was warm and lit with soft yellow lamps. Nolan pulled out a chair at the close end of the dining table and sat, his back toward her. She couldn't believe she had gotten herself into such a situation.

After combing her hair and dressing in faded jeans and a white knit shirt, she walked in her bare feet around behind him to turn on the burners under the beans and corn. "Everything should be ready in a few minutes."

"Everything?" he asked, a note of teasing in his voice. He hadn't turned around.

"Um, yes. After dinner, I have cherry ice cream for dessert, if you'd like some. And …" She was horrified that she couldn't make her voice sound as casual as she wanted.

Nolan pushed away from the table and stood. His dark blue t-shirt and jeans fit him superbly. He faced her, but this time he didn't reach for her.

His lips and ears, and his brown hair and eyes, were sublime. How could she explain wanting him to come to her for dinner, but that she hadn't meant it to be a date, exactly? She had been lonely, and he'd come to mind for company. She didn't want a romantic entanglement. She wasn't ready!

Well, even if that were true, what should she say was the reason she'd wanted him with her? Lumi thought about Maddy and the stereoscope cards. She could use them as an excuse. But … Maddy hadn't wanted her to involve the police. She turned to stir the vegetables.

Nolan strode the few steps between them and stood behind her at the stove. "Mmm. Smells great."

He slid his arms around her waist as he moved her hair aside with his chin, exposing her throat for his lips. His warmth against her back was defeating her resolve. She instantly reacted at her core, her breath rushing out of her. The stubble on his cheek was rough and delightful, and his hands on her waist were possessive yet not demanding. Lumi continued to weaken. The delicious shock of having a man touch her in that way for the first time was acting like a drug, and the pleasures of his mouth, his warm breath, and his arms were overwhelming her senses. Gooseflesh swept up her body from her legs to her neck.

Nolan, encouraged, breathing harder, moved one of his thumbs higher, barely skimming the underside of her breast.

She twisted away, desire changing to fear as she stammered, "N-Nolan, this isn't what it seems. I … I just wanted to talk to you." Her face heated with embarrassment.

He raised his brows in a silent question and shrugged, not moving toward her again. He put his hands into his pockets. "About what?"

"About … what may be a crime. I want to talk to you about it off the record. But if that isn't possible, I think I'll have to keep silent."

He folded his arms and leaned against the refrigerator. "It *isn't* possible. If you want legal advice, I'd recommend a lawyer. No conversation about a crime is ever off the record with any officer." His body language had changed from warm and desirous to cold and professional.

She nodded, turning again to stir the vegetables that had started to simmer. "It's nothing I've done, but I *do* know about something that is happening to a friend. She's distraught. I'm trying to help her solve the mystery surrounding the crime, but I'm not getting anywhere, and I'm afraid she's putting herself into danger."

Nolan's voice behind her warmed again. "What can I do? If you won't tell me the particulars, I can't be of any help."

Lumi sighed, adjusting the heat under the burners. She turned again, feeling less embarrassed. "I was hoping to talk to you as a ... learned friend. I see now that I either need to shut up entirely or tell you the whole story."

He took one of her hands in his. "I'm not buying it, you know."

A line appeared between her brows. "Not buying what?"

Nolan rubbed her fingers. "You're scared for some reason. I think you made up the story about the friend to slow me down or to put me off entirely. Am I right?"

She kept her eyes on her hand and the way he was massaging it with his strong, masculine fingers. She thought fast, reviewing her options. "Do I take back my confession about a crime? No. That would be lying. Tell him I'm a virgin and immature about relationships in general? Too humiliating. Tell him I'd gotten lonely after reading the letters I shouldn't be reading? Betray Maddy and actually go ahead and tell him about the stereocards?" She felt trapped between lies and things she didn't want to admit or reveal.

"Lumi? What's really going on here?"

She mentally spun a wheel and picked a random response. Taking back her hand at last, she said, "I guess I should tell you about myself. But first, let's dish up and sit at the table." After taking the meatloaf and potatoes from the oven, she opened her glass-fronted cupboard and pulled down two dinner plates decorated with Picasso-style cows and chickens, then got out two tall cobalt-blue canning jars and filled them with ice and tea.

They loaded their plates and ate for a few minutes to the accompaniment of Lionel Richie singing his own song titled "Hello."

"Must be a theme tonight," said Nolan.

Lumi smiled, but then quickly frowned. "I don't know where to start," she admitted, turning down the radio. She'd decided to protect Maddy, at least for a little while longer.

"How about at the beginning?"

"Well, there *is* no beginning to this. Not really. It's just that ... I've never been serious with a boy or a man. I'm mortified that you think I invited you over here while purposely wearing nothing but my bathrobe." She took a sip of tea, her face heating as an image of opening the door to Nolan returned. She turned her head to look at the evening sky through her front room windows. "I've never done *anything* like that. I don't know how to say why I wanted you to be here with me for dinner, but please don't think I meant to ... be some sort of a ... because I'm *not.*" Her face grew even hotter, and she was sure it was bright red.

Nolan dug into his baked potato. A fluffy white mound sat on his fork, but he didn't raise it to his mouth. "I'll admit I was surprised at the invitation. We don't know each other very well, but I *have* felt that we've shared a mutual attraction every time we've been in the same room. This afternoon left me crazy. *Crazy.* When I heard you wanted me here tonight, I thought you were doing me the supreme favor of acting first." He finally ate his forkful.

Lumi glanced at him, flattered and grateful that he had said such a thing. She couldn't hold back her smile. "Oh, Nolan."

"I'll back off," he said after swallowing. "You don't mind if I wish we had dashed up to your bedroom tonight, do you?" He winked and stabbed a few green beans.

Lumi's face lost some of its heat as he made her feel more comfortable. "I think I need to explain myself a little more."

"You don't have to. This was all premature. I was jumping ahead, hoping you had, too. We'll slow down." He took a breath. "I'm having a great time simply being at the same table with you."

His flattery was not really flattery at all. He was sincere, which felt harder to take, Lumi thought. Her chest constricted, but she pushed away the rush of fear that wanted to make her run from the table. "I'm not someone who dates. I never ask anyone out. How did you end up here? How did I end up having dinner with you tonight?"

He shrugged. "It was time." He drank again, looking into her eyes when he'd lowered his glass. "I should tell you something, too, now that we're having a more personal discussion."

She relaxed. "I know you're a widower, Nolan. I'm sorry you've suffered that loss."

He took a breath and held it for a long moment. Looking at his plate, he said, "We didn't get much time together. Seven months. No time at all. Two seasons. Spring. Summer. We'd dated a short while. We were married for only two months." He shifted in his chair. Looking at Lumi, he went on, "I know she wouldn't want me to stay stuck in our past. You … make me feel ready to …." He swallowed, looking away again. "God, I'm not sure how to say these things."

Lumi wanted to hold him, to comfort him, but he was sitting so stiffly that it felt like he'd put up a wall even while he was revealing his heart's struggle. They ate without speaking for long minutes, letting ballads on the radio fill the space between them. She knew she should say something, but nothing that seemed right came to mind. "I'm bad at this," she admitted as she pushed her plate to the center of the table.

Nolan put his hand over one of hers. He directly met her eyes. "Even if there will never be a 'you and I,' I think we both needed this. I haven't touched a woman the way I've touched you since my wife was so ill. You said you've been lonely, too."

Lumi bowed her head, staring at her tea glass. "I've had a boyfriend, but he wasn't interested in me." She looked up. "That's odd, isn't it? I think he used me as an ear to talk to, so he wasn't talking into the air. I was a companion. He never swept me off my feet, literally or figuratively. Maybe he wasn't interested in women romantically. But," she said, and then took a breath, "I guess I used him, too. He kept other men at bay for four years. I'm not sure why I wanted that, but I did. It allowed me to stay shy and antisocial, which I liked. Now, though," she turned her hand over so that her palm was under his, "I'm tired of holding myself captive in my own tower. I have no idea how to deal with you. That's the most honest way I can put it. I have no idea how to react to your presence. I don't know if you mean what you're doing to me—the way you're looking at me or the way you held me. I wonder if you're playing. I don't feel deserving of your attention."

He squeezed her hand, frowning. "I don't want to scare you off. I … I *want* to get over mourning and avoiding. I want to find a woman to love someday. I want to trust what I see in your eyes, too."

Lumi inhaled in shock, her lips parting. The "L" word? Why was he using the "L" word so soon? But he wasn't saying it to her. She watched his face, understanding that he'd just admitted something very difficult and may be regretting saying too much.

She took back her hand and wiped her eyes with her fingers. "I think you've held on to those feelings for too long already. I'm *sure* your wife wouldn't want that for you. I'm hardly in a position to give out relationship advice, but I do see that both of us have clung to feelings we should have let go of a long time ago."

Nolan gratefully met her eyes before a corner of his mouth went up. "Don't worry. I saw your reaction to the word 'love.' I was just stating a fact. Maybe we'll never feel that way. I *do* think you're adorable and gorgeous, and I think you like me as much as I like you, but we'll go nice and slow. How does that sound?"

Lumi grimaced. "It sounds like you're a grown-up man who realizes he has to deal with a squirming, immature virgin."

He laughed, relief and grief all mixed together in that laugh. He got up from the table, pulling her from her chair into a friendly hug. "I don't mind a bit, my luminescent Lumi."

Lumi's arms went around him. Over the course of a few seconds, the friendliness and innocence of their hug seemed to change for her. She grew aware of Nolan's muscles, his heat and hardness, and the comforting, exciting way her body fitted against his in all the right places.

He took a single step back to meet her eyes again. He raised a brow nearly imperceptibly, and then a crease appeared there as if he wondered if he should say what was on his mind. His eyes went to her lips, then back to her blue eyes. After a moment, he breathed, "Oh, Lumi. I want to kiss you."

She was surprised. It felt like Nolan was placing the responsibility of meeting his lips onto her instead of waiting for him to do it. Moving away, she felt awkward and flattered. She raised the back of one hand against her cheek, trying to cool her face. Looking through the windows, she admitted, more boldly than she felt, "I've wanted to kiss you ever since you swung that lampshade out of the way. Or before that, when you bit your lip at dinner. Or before that, when I could see you watching me drive away from your brother's garage. Nolan, I think I've been wanting … you …"

Reaching for her again, he slid one hand under her hair at her neck and another around her back, tenderly but firmly. He waited until her eyes rose to meet his. He didn't move. He didn't breathe. It was as if he wasn't sure he could go through with the act of kissing her.

Lumi fought her shyness to say, her heart pounding, "Nolan … yes."

He hesitated. His look of uncertainty changed to pleasure as it seemed to sink in that they were absolutely, positively going to—

Unable to wait, Lumi leaned forward in what felt like slow motion, her arms rising to his back. She pulled his muscular chest tighter against her breasts. Nolan's rough beard stubble added satisfying friction to the kiss, and she moaned in pleasure, surprising herself. She wanted more and more but felt her inexperience in that moment. She had never kissed like this before.

Still holding her closely, Nolan took a break to kiss her temple before whispering, "Darling Lumi … your tongue … keep it soft for me. We're not fighting each other. Soft. Feel what mine does to yours. Do it back to me. You are *so* sexy. *God.* You feel *fantastic* in my arms."

His direction and compliments emboldened Lumi. Her fingers dove into Nolan's short hair, then trailed down his neck to his back, pulling him closer, exploring his muscles through his shirt. She did relax her tongue, and the new sensations he caused shot through her body, making her ache for some unknown something, and making her fear some unknown something, too. The combination was intoxicating.

Nolan groaned, nearly pulling away, but then renewed his attention to her lips, a quiver of emotion jolting him.

Lumi's mind floated between disbelief that he wanted her as badly as she wanted him and the pure exhilaration of touching and being held and kissed as never before. The sound of Nolan's breathing, the feel of his hands urging her to stay in his arms, the ministrations of his lips all blended into a blur of thrilling sensations that went on and on until her legs felt weak.

With a sound of regret, Nolan broke their embrace. Standing mere inches away and radiating desire, he said hoarsely, "That was *amazing.*" He hugged her again, saying, "But I have to get out of here—*now*—or I won't want to leave you at *all* tonight."

Tingling, breathing unsteadily, she didn't reply. She followed him into the living room and leaned against the back of the sofa to help herself stay upright.

Nolan opened the door and turned to her. He looked happy and nervous. "Yes. All those times you mentioned, Lumi. And more." He smiled. "Me, too." He stepped onto the porch and closed the door behind him.

Alone again, she flung herself onto the sofa. Joy, frustration, longing, and misery pounded through her body and soul. *"This* is what it's like," she said aloud. *"This* is what I should have been feeling. *This* is what I've been missing in my life for so, so long!"

Chapter Seven

Lumi cried in the bathtub, and then she cried in bed. She knew why she was upset. She'd never let anyone get that close to her heart and body before. It was a terrifying feeling, like discovering your car brakes don't work while speeding down a mountain. And she was upset because she'd never taken a chance on real romance before. She'd denied herself the wild exhilaration for no reason that she could understand, especially now that she was willingly soaring off the edge of a cliff. Sleep came after a long time, after the moon had been swallowed by clouds and stayed hidden.

In her dream, Lumi was a girl again, riding a few blocks from her childhood home on her tricycle all the way to Mrs. Rasmusson's house. The woman stood with her hands in her apron pockets behind a short white picket fence, her dark hair knotted into a tight bun. A middle-aged man sped out of the house behind Maddy, screaming, his hair caked with blood, but Mrs. Rasmusson never reacted. She never heard him, never turned to see who was behind her and coming toward her holding bandages that he was trying to wrap around his head. The woman smiled at Lumi as if nothing more interesting in the world was happening other than a little girl with blonde braids was passing on the sidewalk. When the man nearly reached Maddy, the dream ended.

Lumi sat up, breathing hard. What did that dream mean? Was it a memory from childhood, was it a mix of old and new memories, or was it a total fabrication?

She tried to make herself remember as much of the dream as possible. Was the man Mr. Rasmusson? Maybe. Lumi couldn't remember him very well. But why was Maddy ignoring his cries for help? Why wasn't she hearing him? Why was she smiling as if no one was running up behind her?

Lumi put her elbows on her knees, and her forehead on her crossed arms. The details were fading fast, but the feelings were still swirling through her. She almost felt a twinge of hatred toward the older woman. How could she be that cold—that unfeeling toward a man in need, bleeding badly and suffering?

She remembered how she had felt about Mrs. Rasmusson ten years ago … twenty years ago. Maddy had been stern and strict, and yet Lumi had always felt that if she needed help, Mrs. Rasmusson was someone she could turn to. She was never unkind, but she was forbidding. Now that they lived across the street from each other, she saw a very different woman. Everyone in the neighborhood and around town seemed to like her. She played bingo, volunteered, and was friendly with everyone she encountered. What had changed Maddy since Lumi had last lived in Barnwood? Was she different because her husband was gone? Had he controlled her, and in a way made her into that woman she used to be?

The bloodied man came to mind. Was he meant to be symbolic of the images in the stereoscope cards, or of Mr. Rasmusson? How had Mr. Rasmusson died? Lumi didn't know. "Dreams are just dreams," Lumi's mother had told her once when she'd had a nightmare. "Let them go or learn from them."

As she sat cross-legged on her sofa eating oatmeal, she tried to transport herself back in time, to remember the personality Maddy had long ago. Could that stern, almost cold woman have done something horrible in the long-ago past? Were the images on the cards an accusatory reminder meant to threaten Maddy? *Was* someone planning revenge? If so, for *what?*

Lumi had forgotten the names and most of what Maddy had said about the classmates who would be attending the reunion in a few days. Was it dangerous for her to go? Maybe having Chess at her side would be enough of a deterrent if one of them meant her harm.

Lumi sighed and finished getting ready for work. She'd left her purchases inside the front door of her shop, so she knew she should get there early to clear the path.

Her thoughts drifted to Nolan. He was wearing his uniform, standing in her store, swinging the lampshade out of the way. It seemed to her like the sexiest move he could have made at that moment. In her fantasy, she *had* rushed at him, wrapping her arms around his muscular body, tasting his lips, her fingers in his soft hair pulling him even closer against her yearning mouth. She was stroking his tongue with hers, lost in passion, moaning with desire, letting him go farther, pleading with him to—

But, no. No. No. She had to stop this wild ride. Nolan—even the fantasy of him—was ruining everything. She couldn't get involved with him. There were reasons to avoid men and relationships. She simply couldn't let the lusty part of her body and soul take over.

There were more people in town than usual—relatives home for the holiday and tourists passing through on road trips. She almost hated to lock up at six o'clock in case there would be another rush of customers, but the busy day had worn her out, and she wanted to get home to read another one or two of Mama's letters. But instead of walking into her own house ten minutes later, she crossed the street.

When Maddy came into view, Lumi shook her finger at her friend. "I wanted to check on you and to chastise you for tracking down Nolan."

Maddy grinned and held open the screen door. "I saw his truck when I left for Chess'. How'd it go?"

Lumi followed her friend inside. "Maddy, you really shouldn't have *done* that. Do you know what? When I didn't end up calling Nolan, I never put on clothes for the evening. I only had on a robe. And then there he came, knocking on my door, ready for a dinner date! Imagine my horror!"

Maddy put a hand to her mouth, her eyes widening. "Oh, *dear!* I never thought a thing like *that* might happen. Oh, dear. I should've called to warn you that I'd talked to Magnus. Lumi! Oh, *no.* I'm so sorry! Was he shocked?"

"I changed right away, and he was very understanding." She smiled to herself, remembering how he'd pulled her close while she was still only in her robe.

Maddy moved Tony from a chair and motioned for Lumi to sit. "Well, I hope you had a real nice dinner together. You sounded lonesome and sad on the phone. I knew I had to try to get Nolan over there to you. Did you have a good time?"

Lumi felt her face warming.

"Oh, I see!" said Maddy, sitting on her sofa. "That good, was it?"

"Maddy!"

"Well, youth should not be wasted on the young. You *should* be dating, Lu. Enjoy yourself, dear girl. I like Nolan. He's always been a nice boy, and now he's a nice man."

"He is." She sat up straighter. "Maddy? I had a dream about you last night. It was the version of you as you were when I was a girl. I was riding my trike on the sidewalk. You were in an apron standing behind your fence. A man ran out of your front door behind you, bleeding badly from a head wound. He was shouting at you for help, trying to wrap bandages around his head himself. Does any of that make sense?"

The older woman folded her hands on her lap. Tony jumped up beside her on the sofa, rubbing his furry forehead against her arm. "No. For starters, I never wore an apron. My mother did, and I never liked the look of them. My husband never had an injury like that. No one in this house ever did that I can remember."

Lumi glanced away. "Okay. It was only a dream that meant nothing."

94

"I'm not saying it meant *nothing,* Lumi—just that it might not be a real memory you had. The stereocards have been invading my dreams, too—every darn night, as a matter of fact. If I wasn't in the same house with Chess, I think I'd be frightened out of my mind, truth be told." She welcomed Tony onto her lap, hugging him to her chest. "I wonder now if I should stay home from the reunion. Talking to you about the boys I went to school with made me a little fearful. What if one of them is responsible for the cards? I mean, I feel as though we all know each other well, but maybe we don't. Should I stay home?"

"I had the same, exact thought."

"You did? But which one of them could be making those darn cards? Why?" Maddy scratched the cat under his chin. Tony raised his head to encourage her, his whiskers expanding in pleasure. "I never did a thing to any of those boys. Or girls. Not really. Like I said, I maybe didn't return feelings, but I never degraded anyone. I wasn't the snippy sort. I knew girls who enjoyed putting boys down, and I thought that was cruel. When I met my husband, I had a clear conscience."

Lumi took in a deeper breath than she'd meant to before asking, "Was he good to you? Mr. Rasmusson, I mean."

"Oh, sure! But Ras was so generous in spirit and heart, and with money, too, that I had to fight against him. I had to keep him in check, I guess you'd put it. He would have had homeless folks living in the attic if I'd let him. He'd hear about a family down on their luck, and he'd pay them a visit and push a few dollars into their hands. He forced me to be a harder-hearted woman than I would have liked. I had to be sure we, ourselves, didn't go starving. Ras was equally generous with me. He had given me his whole heart, and how could I have possibly lacked for anything when I had a spare?" She smoothed Tony's neck fur. "Isn't it funny you asked me about him? I was thinking about Ras earlier today, wondering what he would have to say about Chess taking over his job of protecting me."

"I'm sure he'd be glad. It sounds like he was a wonderful man."

"Yes, yes. But perfect men can be hard to live with. I always felt like less of a good person around him in contrast. It's nice to be with someone who has some faults. It lets you be comfortable with your own faults, too."

"I think you're right. Which gets me into trouble, doesn't it?"

Maddy stopped petting Tony to look up. "How?"

Lumi pinched her lips together for a second before answering, "I'm getting interested in one of those faultless sorts, myself."

The older woman laughed. "Oh, I'm sure you'll find Nolan's shortcomings eventually. You two hardly know each other."

Lumi nodded. "Well, I should go home. Is Chess coming here, or are you going over there tonight?"

"I'm leaving for his place soon. We had been changing houses every night, but now we're playing it by ear. Chess' part of town is much quieter at night. No close neighbors—no close fireworks going off at all hours like there have been near here lately. I hate to leave Tony, though."

"Take him with you," Lumi suggested, standing.

"I probably could, couldn't I?" She asked the cat, "Would you like to spend the night with your old pal, Chess, Mr. Tony?"

Tony squinted up at her.

Lumi stepped back to the sofa to pet the cat. "You're a very good boy, aren't you?"

"Yes. He is such a love doll and *such* good company for me. Oh, would you do me a favor? Stay here while I phone Chess. If he says yes to Tony for company tonight, I'll have you put a jug of cat litter in my car for me."

While Maddy was on the phone, Lumi toured the living room's fascinating antiques and primitives, noticing several things she hadn't before. A miniature painting of a Saint Bernard dog encased in a large pendant hung from a gold chain around the neck of a tall, peacock-patterned art glass vase. A three-volume set of books on the history of electricity in medicine were shelved near a mysterious wired device Lumi had never seen the like of before.

A few family photos in ornate or primitive frames sat on the tallest shelves. One was of a smiling Mr. Rasmusson. He was holding a little girl's hand as she stood on top of a beach picnic table, the girl's ponytails wet and her free hand holding a large seashell. There was one of Maddy and another woman of about the same age, back when they must have been about eighteen or twenty. Mostly hidden behind other items and very dusty were formal black-and-white portrait photos of Maddy and her husband. Mrs. Rasmusson was undeniably beautiful when she was young.

Maddy called from the kitchen, "Chess says to bring his buddy over, and that he's sorry he never thought of it before. So, I *do* need your help, please. I have a spare litter tray in the basement that I don't know why I haven't thrown out. It's got wear and tear, but it'll suffice for a night or two, and I can just leave it at Chess'. I'll show you where the litter is, and I'll put kibble in a baggie." She stepped into the living room and turned to the cat, her hands on her hips. "Tony? Where did your mother

96

put your carrier? Let's see, the last time I used it for the vet we came in through the back door, didn't we? It must be in the boots and coats closet."

"What pretty people you all were, Maddy," Lumi said. She carried the portraits with her, putting them on the table in the kitchen as she passed before following the woman to an unused main floor bedroom where the litter was stored.

"We were. Of course, we were both all dolled up that day, but yes—we *were* an attractive couple when we were young. Okay. Here's the jug of litter. I'll leave it here for you to haul out to my car. Now, if you will, run down to the basement for the spare pan. It's blue, I think. It should be right around where the wooden sleds are, up against the far wall. I'll get Tony's food."

Lumi started down the sagging stairs that had no backing supports. "Maddy, these stairs are *dangerous*. Don't go down here unless you absolutely need to, okay?" she called.

"I don't anymore. I usually ask Tim to get what I need from there. I should have those steps replaced."

Three bare bulbs gave off enough light for Lumi to see that the concrete basement floors were cracked and that the walls were constructed of large irregular stones with pitted mortar between them. Dust-laden cobwebs were everywhere, and the air smelled dank and loamy. She was glad that her own basement had been well taken care of and that it was a dry space if she would eventually need to use it for extra storage.

She found the litter tray and carried it upstairs where she found Mrs. Rasmusson quietly crying at the kitchen table.

"Maddy! What's wrong?" Lumi asked in alarm as she leaned the litter tray against the closed basement door. She quickly washed her hands at the sink and grabbed a towel. Pushing her hair behind her shoulders, she asked again, "What's wrong?"

"I ... had a flash of memory. Of blood. Head wounds. All kinds of wounds."

Lumi put an arm across the woman's shoulders. "I'm sorry. I guess that's my fault. I shouldn't have told you about my dumb dream."

"I don't think so, dear. Honestly, I think it has something to do with the photographer—the one who took those larger photos of Ras and me."

Lumi pulled out a chair at the table and sat facing her friend. "The photographer? But the ones he took are *beautiful*. Why would they make you think about those terrible things?"

Tony wandered past the women to sniff at his old litter box. A motorcycle roared past the house, spooking the cat and several sparrows who flew out of the bush near the kitchen window.

"I don't know why." Maddy sighed, staring at the floor. "I could see blood. People hurt severely. The cards have all that and more, but there are different visions in my head than the ones the cards show. I can't think why, but I *know* deep down that everything is connected. Lumi? What should I do? Go to the reunion or not? What about Chess? Should I tell him I kept the cards and that another one came in the mail today?"

Lumi was surprised. "Another one showed up today?"

Maddy nodded, concern and sadness showing in her eyes. "It's in the rolltop desk in its envelope, hidden under the leather writing mat."

Lumi went to the living room to retrieve it. Bringing the envelope into the kitchen, she sat and took out the card. It was the same sort of image as the first five, but this and the other mailed card were more gruesome. She took photos of the card with her phone, making sure to hold her hands steady. "So much ... horror in this one."

Maddy gulped. Shaking her head, she asked, "Should we report it to Nolan? Oh, but I'm honestly afraid to. I still think I'm guilty of .... I get such a feeling in the pit of my stomach when I see the cards or remember what's on them, and now the connection to the photographer is in my mind. But how? Do you suppose that same photographer is responsible for the stereocards? Does he know something about me? Oh, this is all so *confusing.*" She met Lumi's eyes pleadingly. "Please, Lumi girl. Tell me how to go forward."

"I wish I had the answers." Lumi put her phone on the table.

"I hate to sound like I care what gets said about me, but I do. I think I do want Nolan's help, but I don't want everyone reading about it in the paper. Does it have to be a formal police report? I'm scared, Lu. I'm scared, and I feel guilty. And why won't this *go* anywhere? If I'm meant to be threatened, why isn't there a note?"

"I don't know. As to telling Nolan—well, I'm sure a ton of these little incidences don't end up in the news. I'm not belittling what's happening to you, but it isn't exactly a murder or robbery or anything."

"Yet."

"Yet."

"Well, Lumi Leski, I think that you ought to talk with your Nolan." She inhaled. "I feel better now that I've made that decision. Let's get the litter and pan and food and cat out to my car for the night, please. I just want my Chess." Her face brightened. "Oh, dear! Don't let him hear that

I called him 'my Chess' or he'll be after me to marry him with even *more* enthusiasm!"

Lumi ate leftovers sitting on the sofa in front of the TV. Her Canadian bacon, mozzarella cheese, and beef meatloaf tasted better than it had the night before when she was self-conscious about chewing in front of Nolan and couldn't fully enjoy it.

Nolan. Her heart beat faster as his face flashed before her eyes. His lips very nearly kissing hers, his eyes half-closed with yearning. His hands holding her hands. Her back warming against his ... his ...

She forcefully yanked herself out of her fantasies. He hadn't phoned. He hadn't come into her shop. He wasn't knocking on her door now that she was home and free for the evening. Disappointment and confusion welled up inside her chest. Had she done something wrong? she wondered. Was she a bad kisser? Was she too immature?

Heading up to bed early since the next day was the Fourth of July and she would be going to Magnus and Alisa's party after she closed her shop, she decided to skip a shower until the morning. She closed her eyes, feeling the pillow change from cool to warm and uncomfortable. She turned on the air conditioner with the remote and closed her eyes again, listening to its humming sound. A firecracker snapped in the distance. Giving up at last, she turned on her bedside lamp, took another letter from the lunch box, and propped herself against her pillows to read.

Dear girl,

Betsy is home! Her doctor said she may have permanent hearing difficulties, but it seems that's all that remains of her meningitis! We are joyful, let me tell you, baby girl! Betsy was over here earlier, carrying that black and white cat in her arms. She wants to adopt him, and I think that's a wonderful idea. Her mom is supposedly only thinking about it, but Betsy said her mom was feeding him and petting him already.

So that's a terrible time over and done with. I feel wrung out! And Pearline is gone, like I told you on the phone. We talked a long time every night since Betsy went into the hospital. Every night we had a talk. It did me good, and I think it did her some good, too. I feel like I have my sis back in my life. I told her I wish she would move here to town, but she said she has some heavy reasons to stay with Grandma. Stuff I hadn't known about. So, I guess she had to move back, at least for now. I told her she should find a nice fella to date, but she shrugged. She says if she does, she'll wait until Grandma passes. I pointed out that that might be decades from now, but she shrugged again, saying she doesn't need a man. If anyone means it when they say that, I have a feeling Pearline is one who does.

P left here saying she'll get a therapist if Grandma will pay for it. Which worries me. She might be okay with P going to talk to someone, but if she's also got to pay for it? Hmm. I guess if P gets a job and pays for a therapist herself, well, then what can Gma say about it?

I have been going to a ladies exercise club. I'm hoping it will strengthen my legs more than walking. Plus, too much walking gets me into as much trouble as too much sitting! I'll let you know how that goes in my next letter.

The potatoes are all ready to dig up. Your dad is in the garage getting his shovel and gloves. He's wearing his rust-colored coveralls and that belt with the big ugly purple glass thing in the center of the buckle. I may go out to sun my legs in a while, after I put a cake in the oven. I'm making my mayonnaise chocolate cake with the white frosting on it for Betsy and her mom. If I can find a birthday or other small candle, I'm going to put it on top to blow out as a celebration.

Okay. My hand is tired of writing, so I'll close. Say hi to Marty, of course.

Love from us
Mama and Dad

Lumi was relieved to read that Betsy was home from the hospital and that Pearline and Mama were close like when they were girls. She was tempted to read another letter but didn't want to take a chance of learning anything alarming or worrisome, sure she'd endured enough of that in her real life for one day. She put the letter back inside the lunch box and turned out her light. Every evidence of the sun had disappeared for the night at last, so she stretched out on her back, closed her eyes, and tried to relax into sleep.

Knock knock knock

Lumi's eyes opened. Had she heard knocking?

Knock knock knock-knock-knock

She grabbed her robe and turned on her hall light to see to go downstairs. The persistent pounding sounds continued, but when she reached her door and opened it, no one was in sight on the porch.

Pop pop pop-pop-pop-pop-op!

Fireworks! Oh. *Fireworks,* not knocking.

She went back to bed and turned the air conditioner higher to try to cover up the popping sounds with constant soft noise. It worked reasonably well, but she couldn't calm down. Every firecracker blasting in the distance felt like Nolan knocking insistently on her door, waiting to be let inside to pull her into his arms.

Knock knock knock

Was that really a knock this time? It sounded much closer than the fireworks, and it had a different rhythm. Again, she turned on her hall light and went down to the front door to the sound of renewed knocking.

She twisted the switch for the porch light. Nolan stood outside, squinting beneath the bright bulb.

Without thinking, and with a tremendous smile on her face, she unlocked and opened the door. "What are you doing here this late?"

"Not that you mind?" he asked hopefully. He stepped inside and closed the door behind him. "You look nice."

She glanced down at herself. She was wearing only a thin, short nightie. She crossed her arms and gasped. "Oh, crap! Sit down. I'll run up for my robe."

He was in the kitchen leaning against the marble countertop when she returned. "Nolan, why are you here at night like this? Is something wrong?"

He took his phone from the pocket of his jeans. "Yes. I don't have your phone number. I couldn't text or call you to say goodnight."

She smiled. "Oh. I didn't think about that." She reached for his phone and entered her cell number and email address into his contacts list.

It was dark in the house except for a dim lamp over the stove and the hall light shining from the upstairs ceiling, but Lumi left the other lamps unlit. She debated starting a conversation about Maddy and her mysterious cards but found she had no energy for it.

He shifted his feet, his lower back against the edge of the countertop again. His eyes met hers, and he looked happy despite his exhaustion. "I had a long, busy day. There was a lot to do to get ready for the parade and for everything that's happening at the park tomorrow. I wanted to see you during my lunch break, but I never got around to taking one. I grabbed a couple of hot dogs from that cart in the park." He took in a breath, then exhaled slowly, frowning. "I missed you."

Lumi felt her heart pounding, but she couldn't think of anything to say that felt like enough but not too much.

Nolan stepped closer. She stepped closer. She wrapped her arms around his neck as he held her waist securely. They hugged for a long moment.

"This is heaven," he said. His breath was warm when he pulled her long hair away from her neck on one side to touch more of her skin.

She nodded against him, agreeing silently.

He whispered, "I should go. I'll see you at the party tomorrow. Do you have the address?"

Lumi nodded, not releasing him.

Another minute swept by. The firecracker pops and whizzes sounded farther away. She felt so relaxed in Nolan's arms that she wished he would carry her to bed and caress her and …

He stroked her back, his hands under her long hair. "I'll go now, Lumi. I'll text you."

She moved away from him at last. "I'll leave my phone on until you do. Goodnight."

He walked with her to the door, then turned. The light from the upstairs hallway shone brightly on them, and he inhaled in surprise when he saw tears wetting her lashes. "Well, if you feel *that* way about it, I can stay." He searched her eyes, his voice dropping an octave as he asked, "Do you want me to take you up these stairs to bed and hold you all night long, Lumi?"

Lumi shivered at the thrill of his suggestion. She stepped back, wiping her eyes with a sleeve. "I think my tears are from … relief." Lumi sat on the arm of her sofa, her hands pressing into her knees. "I thought I'd done something to make you stay away. But now you're here, and there was a simple explanation for why you didn't visit or call me." She looked up. "Nolan, can I say something?"

"Please, Lumi. Tell me."

"I'm … struggling. I've always thought being a strong woman meant I didn't need a man in my life—at least not romantically. I was proving to myself that I could do things on my own just fine. But … *you* happened. I'm fighting you off even as I'm … not."

"You *are* a strong person, Lumi. That's one of the main things I admire about you. I would never try to block your independence. But I *do* want to be needed."

Lumi nodded. "You are, but it scares me that right off the bat I'm feeling trapped."

"Trapped?"

She sighed. "In a good way. Captured. Taken. I think about you too much. Fantasize too much. I've always had this stubborn sense of control that you're messing up. I don't like it. I feel like I'm on a roller coaster. I hate it. And," she said, standing, her eyelashes wet again, "I love it."

"I could have said all the same things myself. We're in that same boat. But maybe I'm more ready for a change than you are. I'll wait for you to catch up. We'll be okay."

Lumi hugged him again, happy he understood what she'd confessed. "There's more to it, Nolan. Last night was … my first kiss. Like *that,* I mean. P-passionately. Not just a peck on a cheek or lips."

He stood back from her, grinning. "Fast learner."

She giggled, her cheek on his shoulder. She wanted to stay glued to him, not taking things farther. It felt wonderful to be held by Nolan's strong, reassuring arms. "Do you have to leave this minute?"

"No. I'm worn out, but if you don't need me to mow the lawn, I'd love to stay for a while."

She released him from their hug and walked to her closet under the staircase, grabbing a pillow and two plush winter blankets from the shelves. "Follow me. I want to talk in the fresh air instead of in the air conditioning."

They were soon lying on the blankets in Lumi's back yard.

"This is unexpected," Nolan said, reclining on his elbows.

"There are lights on the house that point out over the lawn, but they don't work. The power in the bedroom on the other side of my bathroom upstairs doesn't work, either. I'll have to get it fixed. Mind being in the dark out here?"

He lightly laughed, then rolled onto his side to face her. "Silly question."

She rolled onto her side, too, tucking against Nolan, her back to his chest and stomach, her head on his arm. She pulled her hair out of the way, and he kissed her neck, sending shivers of pleasure along her spine.

"Tell me about yourself," Nolan said. He lowered a hand to her waist, pulling her even closer.

"Oh, I'm pretty boring. I grew up down the street. Two older brothers, Curtis and Charlie, who live in California not too far from each other with their families. My folks are in Florida, living the retirement life. I went to college and auctioneering training. You know all that, though. Hmm. Well, for the past few years, I had an apartment on the southeast side of Indianapolis. All very dull. No dating. No friends other than nodding acquaintances, really, and they were all people at work. I love to read. Love to play around with antiques. Mostly I can talk about what I used to do and things I used to like as a kid. My adult life has been … lonely. I missed you." She inhaled sharply, surprised at herself for admitting such a thing.

"I missed you, too, Lumi, darling. I certainly missed the *hell* out of you." Nolan wrapped the sides of the top blanket around them, cocooning them together, then resettling, his head on the pillow, his arm more fully under Lumi's head.

"Tell me about yourself, Nolan. What did you do before I came along?"

"I've just said—I missed you."

She could feel him lightly shake, adding to the sensation of honest emotion that accompanied what he'd said.

"Tell me about how it is to be a cop, then. Or how it is to be Nolan Sanders, part of your family. Something. Start."

They talked for long minutes, embracing, their voices blending with the sounds of frogs and crickets, the occasional passing car on the street on the other side of the house, a distant train, and firecrackers near and far.

"Turn toward me," Nolan said during a break in their conversation.

She shook her head.

He stroked her arm with his fingertips, then found her hand and squeezed it. "All right. I'm happy holding you like this. I won't try to kiss you, Lumi. I won't do anything you aren't ready for."

She frowned. "I know we've already done that, Nolan, but … I feel like I'm in deeper with you now. If I start kissing you, maybe my heart and soul and body won't want to stop, and I'm not ready for more."

"I didn't come here tonight to seduce you. I swear. I *mean* that, Lumi."

She shivered. "Even hearing you say the word 'seduce' makes me feel like a kid inside. I'm too immature for you. I'm spooked—sliding in reverse to save myself from my need of you. I don't know how to explain these feelings. My arms want to open. My legs want to part. If I don't stay lying on my side, I know—"

"No. I wouldn't let anything like that happen, baby. No."

She breathed harder. "Thank you. I trust you. Let's just talk some more and stay right like we are. I'm on top of the world tonight. The very top, Nolan. Understand?"

He nodded against her head. "I'm on a high, too. Feel my heart racing? That's for you. The way you fit against me is perfection. Your every word is a luxury of togetherness, inching us closer together. Sex is sex. This is *real* lovemaking, Lumi: holding you, hearing about your life and what you enjoy and who you are inside. It's sensational to talk to you, too, feeling like you're interested. I haven't had a conversation like this in forever. I never get very personal with anyone."

Lumi smiled and kissed his bicep. "I'm going to want sex, too, you know, just not tonight. It might take me a long time to get there, mentally. Is that … off-putting?"

Nolan delicately kissed her neck. "One step at a time is fine with me. And, honestly, it isn't a make-or-break. It sounds like I can't mean that, but I do. I didn't make love with Carol that many times. She was fragile—seriously sick not long after we were married. I know from that experience that sex is fantastic, but not the be-all and end-all in a relationship. I'll never force anything on you, as I've said. You're in charge. I'm happy to be right here, holding you."

She smiled. "I'm not fragile, Nolan. When we do … get together that way I'm going to be a tiger."

He laughed once. "You mean a tigress."

"No. A tiger, just as a cat is a cat and a dog is a dog. I'm going to be all over you, using all my energy, matching you like a tiger. I know it. We're going to be muscles on muscles, mouth on mouth, and hearts slamming into each other."

She heard Nolan's breathing alter, coming harder, faster. She knew she'd said too much.

"Turn toward me, Lumi. God. Please."

"No." She groaned, angry at herself. "I shouldn't have said that stuff. I fantasize too much. I shouldn't have said those things, feeling comfortable enough to share my fantasy. Forget it. I was jumping ahead, Nolan. I can't act on what I admitted."

Nolan turned her body around, pulling her waist against his own. His lips slightly parted, but he didn't kiss her. One hand in her hair, he said, "You're my every fantasy, too, Lumi. I'm branded. Tied up." His breath became uneven, but he still didn't kiss her. "I'm stripping you naked in my mind, but I'm leaving you with my body. I'm going. I'm going." He stood and went around the side of the house.

After a long, yearning and frustrated moment alone in the back yard without Nolan, she stood, gathered the blankets and pillow into a wad, and went inside. She shakily turned off the porch light, locked up, and went to bed.

Her phone pinged ten minutes later. She reached for it, its charging cable attached. In the dark room, the message seemed very bright.

"I should have kissed you goodbye."

She smiled and replied, "I should have kissed you goodbye."

"Want me to come back and take care of that oversight?"

"I do. But don't, Nolan. I'll see you tomorrow. Goodnight."

Chapter Eight

When Lumi was a girl, the Fourth of July was the most significant event of every summer. She'd dress in red, white, and blue, eat a quick breakfast, then hop onto her decorated bike to get a good spot to watch the parade. Afterward, she'd join scores of other kids pedaling behind the last fire truck, avoiding the piles of horse droppings all the way to the park for a long day of games and food and listening to various country and rock bands with her friends. Her parents rarely went to the parade or the park, but after a cookout in the evening at home, the whole family walked together to watch the fireworks.

This year, however, she would miss the parade except for whatever she could see of it through her shop windows. It would be more of any parade than she had seen for several years, she realized as she walked through her antique store turning on lights and unlocking the front door an hour earlier than usual.

Lumi stepped outside where it was wonderfully warm. The Indiana skies were clear, and the air was fragrant. A lawyer's office next door had flower boxes out front, filled with sweet-smelling blooms. The parade wasn't due to start for an hour, but the sidewalks were full of people walking, talking, sitting, eating, laughing, and trying to control their excited little kids who were running after each other, weaving through the crowd.

Scatterings of people were sitting on lawn chairs and on the concrete curb along Main Street, and several empty chairs reserved spots for those who had wandered away to visit with friends and neighbors in groups. Every other business had a flag out front and patriotic decorations in their windows. Lumi cringed. She hadn't thought of putting out a flag, and all her decorations were distributed around and over and among the antiques and books inside the store, not in her windows. She went back inside and removed several streamers and tiny flags from various shelves and tables and taped them to the windows or artfully situated them among the items in her front display.

"There," she said aloud to herself, her hands on her hips as she looked over the shop. "Crisis averted."

Ready, she flipped the sign on the door to "open" and walked back to her checkout counter to work with items in boxes. After the parade had energetically and noisily marched through downtown Barnwood on its way to the park, Lumi had an hour of explosive, booming sales. Most of the customers said they hadn't known an antique shop had opened in town. Several left their contact information so she could let them know if she got in the items they wanted. Five had all wanted the same thing: a Hoosier kitchen cabinet. She had to admit to each customer that she wasn't buying larger items at this time, but she would keep their information on file.

Working solo definitely had its drawbacks.

After a young girl and her mother had left with an original Teddy Ruxpin doll two hours later, Nolan pushed open her front door and rang her bell. He walked behind the counter. "I feel like I'm not sure that you'll be at the party later. I'll be as disappointed as a squashed bug if you don't show. Coming?"

Lumi didn't answer. Her stomach flipped. She knew she was smiling but couldn't help it. His brown eyes, once he'd taken off his sunglasses, were doing things to her heart.

"Stop looking at me that way," Nolan complained.

"What way?"

He sighed. "All Lumi-ish. Now I can't think straight. I won't be able to do my duty the rest of my shift."

She smiled at him, admiring the way he looked in his crisp black short-sleeved uniform. "I wish you were off duty *now*," she wistfully confessed, almost as if she hadn't meant to say it out loud. "I would do things to you. Maybe."

His brown eyes sparkled with shock before they softened, then they hardened again with desire—all in the space of two seconds. He glanced around to be sure they were alone before leading Lumi by her hand out of sight into the unlit storage room in the back of her shop. Pinning her gently against the open door, Nolan stroked her cheek with his thumb and kissed her lips tenderly before enjoying them more forcefully. His fingers tangled in her long hair then roved her back. "You're so exciting. Oh, my *God*," Nolan breathed, meeting her eyes. "Beautiful. Lovely."

Lumi eagerly kissed him in return, surprised at her level of excitement.

He touched her lips with his thumb, feathered kisses on them, and finally found her tongue with his, immediately driving her crazy. He pulled away to say, his lips moving against her ear, "I thought we were going to go nice and slow with this romance."

"I *am* going slow. Aren't you?"

"It feels terribly slow to me," Nolan said. He delicately and leisurely nibbled a breath-warmed trail along her jawline before tasting her lips again, together and then one at a time, hungry and sated, then hungry again. "You smell fantastic. You feel fantastic. Lumi ..."

The hard edges of the equipment on his policeman's belt dug into her as she hugged him closer. Her hands explored his muscles through his uniform shirt, but again, he didn't match her movements. She wondered if he was giving her permission to do what she wanted without worrying things would go too far.

He held her around her waist, then inched his hands higher until they were barely at the edge of her breasts without touching them directly. The effect was startlingly intimate to Lumi, who wanted to moan and encourage him, but knew it would be wrong since they were both supposed to be working.

"Oh, Nolan," Lumi sighed, coming up for air after another long kiss. "Where have you *been?*"

"Far away, I think," he whispered. "It's great to be here, though. I wish I could stay." He took a step back, then seemed to be debating if he should kiss her again or leave.

"I won't be able to work the rest of the day if you touch me another second," Lumi said, closing her eyes. "You should go." Keeping her eyes closed, she was excited to feel Nolan's breath near her lips. No part of him was touching her, but she was enveloped by his body heat from head to toe as if he were a mere inch away, struggling to discipline himself. The sound of his breathing was close, yet he did as she had asked—he didn't touch her again.

After Nolan silently left the room, Lumi stood where she was, missing his warmth. She heard the jingling of the bell signaling that he'd gone through the front door. Her legs felt too weak to walk farther than the checkout counter, so she sat there until she'd regained her composure.

By two-thirty, no one had been in Lumi's Curiosities for nearly half an hour. She closed the shop, drove to the ATM, then headed for home.

She hadn't eaten much all day, but she didn't want to have a meal in case it ruined her appetite for food at the party. As she ate a banana standing in the kitchen, something occurred to her. How could she go to a party without bringing a passing dish, wine, or anything else that was usually brought to a gathering?

Lumi opened her refrigerator. She closed it again, dismayed. Sighing and embarrassed again by her lack of knowledge about social norms and niceties, she went up to take a shower, staying under the warm spray long after she felt as rinsed of suds as she was ever going to get. She usually let her hair air-dry, but this time she used a blow dryer to try to add volume.

In her bedroom, she flopped onto her bed wearing only a bra and panties, deciding to stay home the rest of the day and night. No one would miss her, she knew. The Sanders had only invited her to their barbecue because they felt sorry for her. Nolan wouldn't notice she wasn't there. He was attentive to her as part of his job—making sure a local businesswoman felt welcome in town—that sort of thing. He was faking when he kissed her and held her. It was all an act.

She wallowed in self-pity for a full fifteen minutes, talking herself out of the party as best she could.

Her phone pinged.

"Where are you?" It was Nolan.

She sighed, not knowing how to reply. She got up to look at the clothes she'd bought on her trip to the thrift shops. They were folded in a laundry basket on a chair in the corner near the closet. None of them looked like anything she'd usually wear. They looked … alluring.

"I'm getting dressed," she texted.

"I'm getting lonely."

"I don't have any food to bring. I feel terrible!"

"Get over here. There's so much to eat already. Don't even think about that. Come. Now."

"Okay. I'm nervous."

"Don't be. We're friendly."

"I know. I'm shy, tho."

"Just come here. Please."

She paused, debating. "Okay. I need to get dressed and stuff. Should I buy anything for the party?"

"No. Come over. Now."

She hesitated another few seconds before replying, "Okay."

Lumi tossed her phone onto the folded yellow blanket on the end of the bed. She dumped the laundry basket upside down near the phone and selected the most festive-looking shorts and sleeveless shirt from the bunch. Putting on the top and standing in front of a long mirror on the back of her closet door, she saw the tight-fitting, pale pink tie-dye shirt had a faded white heart at its center that sat right between her breasts. It was cut much lower than she'd expected when she picked it out, but she was happy to see that it did look good on her. She pulled on slim red jean shorts that had a button fly and laced up her strappy black sandals before applying more makeup than usual—including the mascara and lipstick she usually avoided—and brushing her puffed-out hair.

"I look like someone else," she told the mirror as she admired her own revealed curves.

She grabbed her phone and texted Nolan. "Done. On my way."

"You'd better be," he sent back. A kiss-face smiley arrived in a message a few seconds later.

"Tough cops don't send smileys, you realize."

He shot her another text of a winking smiley with its tongue hanging out.

Blushing, she was again convinced that she was in way over her head with Nolan. She'd never read the rules to the game she was playing. Almost everyone else her age had them memorized.

Lumi grabbed her phone, keys, purse, and long jeans and a sweater in case the mosquitos turned fierce after sunset. She went downstairs and turned on her porch light, knowing she wouldn't be home until late. Her phone rang as she was putting her things in her SUV.

"Lumi!" It was Mrs. Rasmusson. "Happy Fourth of July!"

"Same to you, Maddy!"

"I have something for you, dear. Can you come over for a minute?"

"I was about to leave, but I'll pop over your way first."

Maddy walked out onto her porch. "You look *stunning!*" She motioned for Lumi to follow her into the house. "I'm glad I caught you. I made dessert for you to take along."

"Take along?" Lumi looked confused. "You mean to the cookout?"

They stepped into the kitchen together. The delightful scents of baking hung in the air. "Yes. Here. It's a peach and lemon cake with rum frosting. It's my own recipe, and it's delicious if I do say so myself. I'll put it in a carrier for you."

"But Maddy ... how did you know I was going to—"

"You told me. Remember?"

Lumi scowled. "Honestly, no. In fact, I wasn't super sure I was heading over there until a little bit ago."

"Well, now you *have* to go. You have a cake, after all." She grinned, looking impish. "You must, and you must have a *good time.* That's an order!" she ordered, pushing the carrier into Lumi's hands.

Lumi placed the cake in its carrier onto the table. She hugged Maddy tightly. "Thanks, Mrs. R. It looks fantastic!"

"Pish tosh." She pulled out of their hug. "I hope this is only the first gathering you'll have with the Sanders of many, many more to come." She eyed Lumi from head to toe as if seeing her in a new light. "Unless you want to play the field. This town has a *lot* of nice single men. Whatever you decide, that's fine with me. I want you to do what makes you happy."

Lumi lifted the carrier again and walked toward the front door, unsure how to say she'd found her someone special. "Maddy, if I talk to Nolan about the cards today, will you be upset?"

The older woman blinked twice. "Oh, my dear. I don't know what to say. Play it by ear, okay? Mostly I want you to go and have a grand time. Eat. Enjoy the company. Watch the boomers in the sky tonight. If you feel like there's an opening to talk about my troubles, you have my blessing. I woke up this morning thanking the good Lord that this was a holiday and I couldn't possibly get anything terrible in the mail since there wouldn't *be* any mail. I've had enough. I can't pull a solid memory from my old brain to fit together the puzzle of those cards. I get snatches of feelings and visions, but I'm not solving anything by giving in to fears and staying secretive. You'd better handle it now by telling Nolan."

"All right. If it isn't tonight, I'll try talking to him tomorrow. I worry about you. Are you staying here tonight?"

"Chess and I are going over to a friend's house for a while, and then we'll come back here to be with Tony. That poor kitty didn't settle down all night when he was at Chess'. Because the house was unfamiliar, I guess. The firecrackers went on and on until after *midnight* in his part of town, even though we thought it would be quieter there."

"They'll likely go on and on until very late again tonight. I love the fireworks show the town puts on, but when I see little kids running around with explosives and sparklers, it makes me want to grab those firecrackers right out of their hands." She raised an eyebrow and smiled. "Not that I didn't love sparklers when I was a girl. Gave my mom a fit, which I can understand now."

Maddy winked. "You're going to make a great mother."

Lumi rolled her eyes, saying, "I think I need to worry about being an adult, first."

Lumi pulled up to the curb in the general vicinity of Magnus and Alisa's house. There were at least fifteen vehicles in the driveway and on the street. She hadn't known if the party was going to be the same small group that sat together in Sally's or if others were coming. She retrieved the cake from the passenger side, inhaling deeply, wondering if she should give in to her nerves and speed away for home. Then she pictured Nolan texting his impatience to see her and knew she simply had to take the walk around to the back yard—she just had to be sociable.

"Lumi! You made it!" called Cammie. She was floating inside a large blue pool in the back yard, her head and feet visible above its edge.

Lumi waved, took another deep breath, and kept walking, weaving around the many kids and adults, most of whom were in bathing suits or swimming trunks. The sun was bright and hot, and she wished she'd brought her sunglasses and sunscreen. Faint smoke from the grill conveniently wafted away from the crowd, but the aromas of cooking food on the patio were very noticeable. She found an empty spot on an umbrella-topped picnic table and placed the cake in its carrier next to a punch bowl full of pink liquid, strawberries, and an ice ring.

Alisa stepped from the house through a sliding screen door, her pregnant stomach leading the way. She had on a one-piece black bathing suit and a flowing white cotton skirt. "Lumi! Glad to see you, girl. Can I get you a beer or wine, or would you like tea? I have pink lemonade, and there are sodas in the cooler."

Lumi smiled, surprised to get a hug from the woman she barely knew. "I think I'll have lemonade, thanks. I fall asleep if I have alcohol." She scanned the crowd. "Is Nolan here?"

Alisa craned her neck but also didn't see him. "Nole!" she called. "Hey, has anyone seen Nole? His girlfriend is here." She shouted even louder, "Nolan! Your girlfriend has finally arrived!"

Girlfriend? Lumi wanted to fall to her knees and crawl under a table. How could Alisa just shout it right out loud to all these strangers like that? Lumi turned as casually as she could and walked across the back yard, along the side of the ranch house, and out to the street. That was enough of that! She was going home. Other people might be able to be happy little partygoers and girlfriends, but she couldn't. Hearing it shouted above even the level of the stereo's music was too, too much! She clicked her remote to unlock the door of her SUV.

"Lumi! Where are you going? Lumi! Wait!"

She opened the door, her face burning from embarrassment.

Nolan, wearing faded jeans and a red 10K race t-shirt, trotted up to her as she was sliding behind the wheel. "I know, I know. I can't believe Alisa did that, either," he said, slightly out of breath. He prevented her from closing the door between them, his eyes worried. "She meant well.

We're all so comfortable around each other that we don't think about how it would feel to come into our midst as a stranger." He bent to see her better, smiling warmly. "Please. Stay here. You'll really like everyone as soon as you get to know them. Alisa is only going by what I've said. I *have* told my family that you're my girlfriend now. She didn't know you'd get embarrassed."

Lumi sighed. Then she laughed. "Oh, my *God!* I could have died!"

Nolan was relieved her mood had changed. He laughed, too. "Please. Stay here. No one will be anything but happy for me that I have such a gorgeous woman in my life at long last. It'll mortify Alisa if she thinks she's scared you away. Please. Come back."

Her smile left her lips. She shook her head, her eyes fearful and protesting. "I *can't*, though. What will I *say?* They'll all know I ran off like a kitten in the cowshed."

He grinned at her simile. "Make up something."

She sighed, gripping the steering wheel. An idea occurred to her. She got out after Nolan stepped aside and opened her rear door. "Perfect!" she said, grabbing a paper bag. "Okay. Let's go back."

"There they are," said Cammie. She was wearing a jade one-piece bathing suit that was still wet from the pool, carrying two red plastic cups. She handed one to Mike, who was tending the grill in nothing but ripped and holey red, white, and blue shorts and a chef's apron. His tall, slim build reminded Lumi of the alligator-chef serving tray she had sold in her shop.

"Cammie," Lumi said, sounding as casual as possible. "I had to run back to my car for a minute. I forgot I'd brought you an addition to your collection." She gave Cammie the bag as she felt around behind her back for Nolan's hand, glad when he gave hers a squeeze.

"For me? Thanks. Is this what I think it is?" She stepped to a nearby picnic table and placed her cup there before opening the bag to pull out her gift. Her eyes widened happily. "Oh, Lumi! I love, love, *love* it! Look, Mike! Isn't this *perfect?"*

He peered through the haze of smoke at the colorful, fringed thing she was holding up. "Um, what *is* that?"

"It's a stuffed bowling pin, of course. Sheesh! Anyone can see *that."*

"Oh, yeah. Of course." He flipped a series of burgers before putting one on a waiting teen boy's hamburger bun. "It matches everything else you own, that's for sure."

"Look at these colors! Lumi, I don't know what to say. You'll *have* to come over to my house to see how great it'll fit in with my other stuff."

"Oh, definitely. I'm glad you like it."

"I do. Thank you!" Cammie slipped the bowling pin back into its bag and took it into the house.

Nolan squeezed Lumi's hand again. "That was fantastic," he whispered to her. Louder, he said, "Let's get you a plate. The cold salads are in the refrigerator so they won't get gross out here, and Mike has hot offerings on the grill. Buns and beans are on the table there, and various drinks are here, there, and everywhere."

Lumi went inside first for salads, then grabbed a bun and visited Mike.

"Dog or burger or turkey burger or brat?" he asked, pointing out each with a long-handled spatula.

"Dog, thanks, Mike. Everything looks great. I appreciate the invitation to your party." She looked around. "Trimmings?"

"Kitchen again. We had an unfortunate incident last year. We've learned our lesson. Anything even halfway perishable is staying in the house or fridge and out of this wicked hot sun. Oh, and Cammie put your cake in the house, too. We weren't sure how susceptible to heatstroke it was, so we decided not to take a chance."

She nodded, imagining a yard full of partiers bent over chairs and tables in misery, hot dogs clutched in their hands. She ladled out a cup of the pink lemonade, took a sip, and went back inside.

Nolan was in the kitchen, opening the cake carrier. "This looks like Mrs. Rasmusson's peach cake. Is it? I remember it from a charity bake sale held in the police station community hall. The gumdrop halves are her signature decoration."

"It is. Maddy called me right before I took off for here." Lumi put down her plate and cup. "Nooolan! I get to spend the *whole day* with you," she said, but then wished she hadn't sounded like a four-year-old heading to Disneyland.

He stepped behind her, lifted her long hair, and said as he kissed the back of her neck and bare shoulders, "Nuh-*uh*. It's *me* who gets to spend the day and night with *you.*"

She shivered, enjoying the sensation before she corrected, *"Evening."*

He lowered her hair and stepped around her to replace the cover on the cake, shrugging. "Your call. But that tiny pink shirt is doing criminal things to me, you realize."

She gasped in mock exasperation, secretly pleased he appreciated her seductive outfit. "Lots of people here. I didn't know how many were coming."

"More should be here later, but a lot of these folks will probably go home, too. My parents will come over when it's closer to dinner time, and a few of the guys from the station will show up later, too. Mike has a bunch of steaks and fresh fish waiting to grill for the next round of people, and we'll have a bonfire going when it starts to get dark. My friend Bruce usually brings his guitar."

Lumi's mouth hung open. "Your *parents?*" The two words came out as a squeak.

"I *do* have some, you realize."

She glanced at her outfit. "I'll have to change."

Nolan laughed. "God, no! You look fan—"

"Like a hussy!" she whispered, her eyes horrified. Through the door, she saw Magnus reach into a cooler for a root beer.

"Oh, hardly, Lu. Have you looked around the yard? Everyone is in bathing suits. If anything, you're overdressed." He checked the vicinity to make sure no one was very near the door to the patio. He stroked her arm and shoulder, then looked into her eyes and said sincerely, "This is the best day I've had in too long. You have no idea what it means to me to spend time with you like this and to have you meet my folks. They'll see for themselves how happy I am. You make me *fantastically* happy, Lumi."

"But we've barely met. It's too soon. We haven't had a real date, even. How can you introduce me to your parents?"

Nolan considered. "It's about feelings rather than a schedule, isn't it?"

She nodded. "I agree, but … meeting your parents? Isn't that a thing for like *months* from now?"

"We can go out to dinner instead of staying here if you'd like."

Lumi frowned. "I'll stay here. I'll meet them. Just don't oversell me, Nolan. You don't want them to think I'm a better catch than I really am."

"You're an *amazing* catch. I'm over the moon. Floating. It feels like Christmas landed on the Fourth of July this year."

They kissed standing next to the ketchup and mustard as sounds of happy squeals from kids filtered in through the screen door.

Nolan stepped back. "I'm going to put on shorts. Might as well get in the pool now." He paused, looking away, and then back to her. "Um, I hope you don't take this the wrong way, Lu."

"What?" she asked, wondering what could be coming.

"I love your lips, but I hate lipstick."

She was surprised. "Do you mean it?"

He nodded, sliding his hands into his pockets. "You're prettier without it, and you taste all wrong with it on."

"I hate it, too, but I thought you might like the added color."

She grabbed a napkin and removed as much as she could, glad to be rid of the taste and texture.

He tilted her head back with one hand and kissed her again, finishing with a light flick of his tongue and a tugging, gentle bite to her bottom lip. Holding her closer, he kissed her more passionately.

Lumi felt lost in desire, scared and happy at the same time as his tongue stroked hers, then sucked it. She felt him relax his embrace and slow his kisses incrementally, reluctantly, until there was electrified space between them again.

Nolan stepped back, meeting her eyes greedily, breathing raggedly. "There. Better. Now … now you taste like Lumi."

She couldn't move. Everything within her tingled. She wanted to run, and yet she wanted to grab him at the same time. As a young girl opened the sliding door, scooped up a serving of potato chips, and skipped out again, Lumi pretended to take Nolan's kiss in stride. She squirted mustard on her hot dog, saying, "I didn't bring a suit." She lowered the bottle. "Which is just as well. I'm not much of a swimmer. When I *do* get in the water, I need to wear those awful granny-style nose plugs." She picked up her plate, winking at him. "Still think I'm a good catch?"

He winked back, leaving the kitchen to walk along the shag-carpeted hallway.

Lumi went outside, feeling unprotected without Nolan beside her. She carried her plate, fork, napkin, and drink to a mostly empty picnic table and sat.

"Sorry about that low-class shout out earlier," said Alisa, sliding her legs under the table to sit facing Lumi. "I doubt anyone was even really listening, what with the music and talking and the kids running around like maniacs. Anyhoo, I hope you didn't get too freaked out."

Lumi swallowed a bite of potato salad, shaking her head. "No. It's fine. I was laughing about it a minute later. It did sort of …" she paused. "Okay. I *did* freak out," she admitted. "I can't even tell you when or if it's been said right out loud in public that I was someone's girlfriend."

Alisa shifted, trying to get comfortable on the hard bench. "So, you're *not* his girlfriend?"

"Oh, well … yes. I mean, I guess you could say that. It's all super new. I'm super new at … everything about this kind of thing." Lumi speared a cube of chili pepper chicken and cold noodles.

117

Alisa seemed confused. "New with Nole, or new as in having a relationship at all?"

Lumi held her fork aloft. "I guess the second. *And* the first. I've had a boyfriend before, in college, but it wasn't the same thing. He was more of a bodyguard. I could keep my walls up, and no one bothered to try to knock them down when Brad was around. I suppose I used him as much as he used me for companionship. But that was about it. No … fireworks, to put it in a way that suits the holiday."

Alisa's face softened. "And with Nole?"

"Way different," Lumi answered, then took a bite.

"Ah. Good." She patted Lumi on the hand that wasn't holding a fork. "Nole is stoked. He's a new man now, let me tell you."

Lumi, tired of blushing at everything, forced herself to concentrate on eating.

Without greeting Lumi again, Nolan walked past her table and went up the short ladder on the side of the pool. In a smooth, powerful dive, he was in the water and across to the other side.

Lumi coughed into her napkin to cover her reaction to seeing the man in nothing but cut-offs and his bare skin and muscles.

Alisa grinned, understanding. "I have to go to the bathroom. For like the tenth time today. I'll be *so* glad when the baby comes." She struggled to stand.

"Is this your first? When are you due?"

"Yes, and three-and-a-half weeks. It's a boy. You missed the gender-reveal portion of this party. If you wonder why everything around here is more blue than red, white, and blue—that's why—although pretty much everyone already knew a long time ago. Mag and I suck at keeping secrets, apparently." She was finally standing. "Ungh! I am simply going to have to move into the bathroom sooner or later. Put a little TV and fridge in there. A footstool. And my favorite books and parenting magazines."

Lumi hurriedly ate and tossed her plate into the receptacle. Carrying her cup, she went to stand poolside. Nolan watched her watching him for a while before swimming up to her. He rested his elbows on the edge of the pool. She liked that his chest had just the right amount of hair on it. His whole body was so—

"Coming in?" he asked, interrupting her thoughts. He reached for her, a half-wicked smile warning that he meant to pull her in.

She backed up in time to avoid his grasp. "No. I'm here to watch."

"We *are* going to end up in this pool together, you realize."

She took another step back. "Never."

He pushed off, floating on his back, the sizzling sun shimmering on his wet, muscular body. Stray strings of his cut-offs clung to his thighs, drawing her eyes to his midsection.

She walked back to the edge of the pool for a better look. Nolan turned his head and met her eyes. Lumi saw power and rawness in his stare. Sexuality. Heat. She was excited by the feelings rushing through her veins, but another sensation was gaining power right below the surface of her heart.

Two young boys pounded across the lawn behind her, rumbled up the ladder, and jumped into the pool, splashing her as they landed in sloppy cannonballs.

"Boys!" called a woman nearby. "Watch that splashing!"

The dousing brought Lumi to her senses.

Nolan was a real man with real desires and expectations, and yet she knew she was merely playing dress-up, pretending to be a grown woman. Her clothes, her makeup, her hair—everything suddenly seemed fake. She was a child inside who wanted to be a woman but had years to go before she would feel mature and capable of being Nolan's suitable partner.

Lumi was suddenly drowning in apprehension. She knew it was horribly wrong to run away from Nolan again, but she couldn't stop herself from panicking.

Ten years of avoiding men.

Ten years of *no no no no no.*

Ten years of fear and determination to be left alone rushed up at her in a punch.

Nolan's expression changed. He seemed to be able to tell Lumi was about to run off again, and he stopped swimming to stand in the center of the pool, unmoving except for the slight bobbing caused by the waves the boys were making as they played.

She shook her head, backing up a step. Her eyes widened.

"Lumi," Nolan said, finally striding forward. There was a pleading tone to his voice, but also defeat.

She plopped her drink onto a table, fought her way through a group of partiers, and ran to her SUV. In the distance, she could hear Alisa calling, "Nole! Nole! *Hurry,* dude!"

Lumi was off like a shot down the street, driving and crying at the same time. She didn't dare go home. She had to go where Nolan couldn't find her. She was panting, nearly blind from panic. Everything felt out of control, and she needed to be alone to think.

Chapter Nine

After slowly, tearfully driving several country roads around Barnwood, Lumi turned south, heading to the northern edge of Indianapolis. Emotionally exhausted, she pulled into a deserted area of a mall parking lot, lowered her windows, and angrily killed her engine.

"He thinks I'm a *woman*. A *real* woman. I'm *not!* I'm like eight years old emotionally. I can't *do* this. Not for real. He wants more. Hell, *I* want more, but I can't face dealing with it. I want Nolan! He wants *me!* Why can't I be a mature adult? What is *wrong* with me? Why did I run away like a chicken? He must *hate* me now! I embarrassed him twice in the same half hour! I can't ever see him again. He must hate me, anyway. I hate *myself!* Hate that I'm so immature in everything that counts!"

Lumi went on and on for several minutes, berating herself aloud, swearing and sweating and miserable in the heat of the SUV. She turned on the motor and air conditioning and cried heavy, heaving sobs. She soon realized that he hadn't called her. To be sure, she checked her phone. Nothing. No text. No message. The fact that he hadn't reached out to her was a harder blow than she was expecting. She was hyperventilating severely and worried she might faint. She'd lost the feeling in her extremities and face and felt dizzy.

"I've done it now, but good. Oh, Nolan. Oh, *baby*. What did I *do?*"

She thought about getting a motel room in Indianapolis, but it was only mid-afternoon, and if she could calm down, there was no reason not to drive the forty-five miles back to Barnwood. Since Nolan hadn't called, she knew he wouldn't be waiting for her at her house, either. He was, understandably, done with her.

In her mind, she could see Nolan, his eyes yearning. She imagined his hands on her, gently backing her against a door, pulling her against his body, pushing the hair away from her neck for his lips. Lumi remembered his smile as he reached for her from the edge of the pool, the water sparkling on his skin in the sun. She could hear his laughter, the words he whispered into her ears, the teasing, the comforting.

"All of it gone, now and forever."

She pounded the steering wheel. Misery gave way to anger at herself. Nolan had done everything right—everything to make her feel wanted and at ease and safe, yet desired. She had hurt him. This was a first for him, too. This was the first time he had dared to be interested in any woman since his wife had died.

"How could I have treated him that way? What is *wrong* with me? Oh, Nolan! Nolan!"

It was late afternoon when she pulled into her driveway. Her house looked silent and empty. She was sure that no one on the planet missed her or wanted her.

She rechecked her phone.

Not a single call or text.

Lumi went inside. Sliding into the tub, she let the warm, bubbly water console her. Her cell phone sat on the bathmat, waiting for a message from Nolan that never came.

Lumi felt every bit as miserable and regretful in the morning as she had the night before. There hadn't been a word from Nolan. He was truly done with her.

"As well he should be," she said groggily to her rye toast. She had left her phone on, and the volume turned all the way up throughout the night. Every time there was a notification of an email, she would startle awake, hoping Nolan was writing at last.

Sighing, she switched on her vintage radio. As if the airwaves had been influenced by her situation and misery, a station from Anderson was broadcasting Emmylou Harris singing, "I Still Miss Someone." The song made her heavily emotional. In her mind, she edited the blue eyes of the lyrics to brown.

She walked to the living room to look through her front window. Maddy's garage door was up, so she was probably gone to do her errands for the day. Lumi wouldn't need to leave for her shop for another hour, so she went upstairs to dress for the day and to read another letter. Maybe Jackie's mother could offer some comfort.

Dear Jackie,

Well, the cat Betsy and her mom have now officially adopted was christened Essanpee. I think that's how it's spelled, anyway. As in salt and pepper. Maybe it's actually S and P? I don't know. I'm thinking of it as Essanpee, and that's how I'll refer to him from now on. He's fully under their care. Even took a trip to the vet for a look-see. He's definitely a tom cat. And he's definitely got worms. Taking pills for that. And he has fleas. And scratches and old wounds, like any longtime street soldier would have. He's getting good and taken care of, Betsy reports. I'm glad. I told you she has hearing trouble in mostly one ear since her sickness. I keep hoping that will clear up in time. Such a little dear! I can't believe we lucked out and her ears are the only thing to worry about now after such a bad, bad scare when she was in the hospital all that time! A miracle!

The potatoes are all dug out of the garden and in the root cellar in the basement now. The onions are there, too. Your dad let them get pretty big. He pulled them out too soon last year, really, but I think he waited too long this time. Oh, well. They'll eat just fine. I really scrubbed out the root cellar before the vegs went in there. I haven't washed that room for maybe five years. I don't know that the vegs mind dirt on the floor and a dank smell, but it made me feel better to get that handled. My legs hurt again, but I will say I was surprised at how long I could work without needing to rest. I think the ladies exercise group is doing me some real good. Dad says not to overdo it there or at home, and I can see his point, but I feel much better today than I did even many years ago.

No word from Pearline herself lately. Grandma called yesterday. She said P has been down to the unemployment office. That's all she said, and I didn't press. It's up to her or P to let me know what's going on. I am done being nosy and pushy with those two. I've learned a lesson and I have had a big change of heart since P stayed here. She and Gma are okay. I don't need to butt in and ask a lot of questions. I think P is going through something with Gma that we don't know about. I need to stay out of it and just be an ear to hear if that's ever what they want. It will be real interesting to know if P got a job. I wonder what she'll do?

At the ladies exercise group, I met a woman who used to drive a semi truck. Can you imagine? I guess I knew there are women truckers, but I've never met one before. She's retired. Her back is all messed up, and she has a sort of skin problem on the side of her face and the arm that got the sun coming in through her window. That is a tough job for a man, let alone a woman. She says she's had to be real strong and strong-willed her whole life but now she wishes she had someone to take care of her. Isn't that sad? She never married, and now since she's been on the road for so many years she doesn't have close friends. I've been thinking I could help her a little. We'll see. Dad says do I need another project? I don't think I need one, but that doesn't mean I shouldn't take one on.

It's almost dinner time. The roast, potatoes, onions and carrots are about done in the oven. Can you smell them? Nice to have fresh vegetables from the garden!

Love to you and Marty
Mama and Dad

Lumi bent her knees to her chin and wrapped her arms tightly around her legs. Mama had pain and worry, and yet she was thinking about helping a woman she barely knew. There was a lesson there, Lumi realized. If you have heartache and pain, fill your life, your time, your heart by helping someone else.

She was putting away the letter when she saw a photo in the envelope. It was "Dad with Betsy and Essanpee." They were sitting on the wide stump of a cut-down tree with flowers all around. Waller Bee was not in the photo. Was he purposely avoiding the cat? Dad was holding Betsy's formerly-broken arm, pointing to it as if to say to the camera that he was happy her cast was off at last. Betsy was African American, cute and thrilled to be right there, a cat in one arm and her friend, Jackie's dad, beside her on the log.

Lumi wondered why she was surprised to see that Betsy wasn't white. She thought about a lot of what Mama had written. She couldn't remember her saying anyone was fat or short, skinny, or rich or poor. She described people in other ways. Mama was a seer of and minds and souls, far less concerned with exteriors.

Lumi questioned herself: did she treat people differently based on their outsides? Not too much, she hoped. Did she like Nolan because he was drop-dead gorgeous? She remembered seeing photos of him in Cammic's Facebook postings. He was the same man in the photos, but also *not* the same man. In person, she thought he was extremely good-looking, yet in the pictures, something was different or missing. There was no three-dimensional, full-fledged personality visible in those flat photos. She liked the flesh-and-blood, warmhearted Nolan who glowed from his soul, and that's the version of the man who intrigued her.

Lumi thought about Maddy, about how she seems prettier around Chess. Every prickly inch of her softens and pinks up. Did Maddy see Chess as heroically handsome? Does the whole world see the person they love through different eyes? Was this a secret everyone already knew except her?

It was a totally new phenomenon to Lumi, and it was astounding to realize.

Lumi opened her shop a few minutes before ten o'clock. She took a broom and dustpan outside and swept up the assortment of confetti, drink cups, political flyers, streamers, and ant-covered candies from in front of her own store and the businesses on either side of her. Kyla, her next-door neighbor and a lawyer, appeared at her front door and rapped on it to get Lumi's attention before waving her thanks.

Dumping the last panful into a wooden trash can attached to a light pole, she studied the way her front display looked from the sidewalk. Several of the flashier antiques and toys had sold the day before. It almost seemed like there were more holiday decorations left than items for sale. Turning to go back inside, she noticed a police cruiser parked in a spot three doors down. Her heart leaped with a mix of emotions before she saw a policewoman walk out of the alley and get into the driver's side of the car.

Lumi flipped the sign on the door, turned on the lights and stereo, and went to sit behind the checkout counter, her stomach tied in knots. "He's never going to walk in here again. He's never going to kiss me again. I'll never see him smile in my direction again," Lumi told herself miserably.

Soon a new feeling crept into her heart.

Relief.

She didn't have to try to be sociable except with customers. She could crawl back under her rock where it was comfortable and safe. She liked hiding in her emotional hole—all her old, familiar feelings were there, waiting to welcome her back. She had Maddy for a friend, and that was enough. She'd gone almost twenty-eight years without real romance, so why not forget about that uncomfortable side of life altogether?

"This is what you wanted all along, isn't it?" a voice inside her head accused. "You sabotaged things with Nolan! You ripped him out of your life on purpose. Lumi, you little baby! Grow *up,* already!"

She realized she had hit on the truth at last. She was afraid of the intensity of her feelings and had ruined her budding relationship herself. The fact that she would never see him again was a balm to the part of her spirit that had been outlandishly afraid. Her immaturity and avoidance were what she was used to. Nolan had pushed her into situations that made her excited but uneasy. She couldn't psychologically age fast enough to keep up with her attraction to him, and now she could retreat at last. The storm was over. She was safe again within the dark hole of her loneliness.

Lumi brushed tears from her eyes. "Well," she thought again, "I got what I wanted, and I certainly got what I deserve. Now, what?"

Now she was free to concentrate on her business again, on getting her home more furnished, and on solving the mystery of Maddy's stereoscope cards.

As she walked around her shop tidying the antiques on shelves and tables, picking up a lot of the decorations and selecting things to put in the front windows, she reviewed what she knew about the photo cards and the images on them.

Five cards had been in Maddy's oak box in the house—but for how long? Two had come in the mail since. They depicted horrible, bloody scenes. They felt threatening, but no note had been included with the original five cards or with the two that had been mailed. There was nothing written on the cards. Maddy had suspicions about no one.

Lumi wondered about the photographer who took the professionally posed photos of Maddy and her late husband and the many people Maddy had given a key. The last two stereocards had arrived in the mail after the locks on her house had been changed, and that felt significant.

And there was the article on her collection. Someone who held a grudge against Maddy could have searched for her name on the internet, read the interview—which would likely be nearly the only information about her online—studied the photos, and decided to retaliate for a long-ago crime they felt the older woman had done. But to do so by creating fake stereocards?

Lumi took out her phone and searched for the article on Maddy's antiques. It came up on the original antiques newspaper site that had posted it, but also on several other sites and blogs. She cringed. Maddy's collection had exposure the world over!

Lumi loaded shopping bags and a box full of the decorations she had removed from around the shop and put them on the top shelf in her storage room. She left the rest where they were, liking the effect of the metallic stars and foil strips among the antiques and books. They could stay until autumn when mini pumpkins and leaves would take their place.

She sat again, trying to think harder about the stereoscope cards. What possible motivation …?

Thoughts of Nolan invaded her concentration, but she pushed them aside, convinced again that her self-sabotage had spoiled everything.

She sighed. It all boiled down to self-sabotage. No sooner had the realization presented itself to the prickly forefront of her brain than another thought came rushing in behind it.

Self-sabotage!

What if *Maddy* had created the stereoscope cards?

What if Maddy had done this to *herself?* Maybe even without knowing she had done it? Was that possible? Was she pretending to be afraid? Was that why she hadn't wanted to tell the police? Did she worry they would figure out that *she* had made the cards instead of someone else who was trying to threaten her with them?

Lumi's heart pounded, this time with resentment and anger. How *could* she? How could that woman a make up this whole, terrible situation?

She was still fuming when a young couple walked into the shop. They browsed for a minute before approaching her.

"Hello," Lumi said. "Are you looking for anything in particular?"

"Do you have any jewelry?" the man asked. "Specifically, any wedding bands?"

The question irritated Lumi. "No, sorry. That is one thing I'm sure I'll never have." Realizing she was speaking gruffly, she modified her tone. "The jeweler on First Street has a large display case of vintage rings. His prices on antique jewelry are quite reasonable."

The woman smiled and took the man's hand in hers. "Thank you. I'm sure we'll be back when we get settled. I love your shop!"

Lumi smiled, hoping she didn't look as miserable as she felt.

Thinking about the mystery again, she told herself, "No. It isn't possible. Maddy is genuinely upset and afraid. She has plenty of love and attention. It can't be that she would do something merely to get more attention."

She mentally apologized to Mrs. Rasmusson for thinking she could have been the creator of the cards, but a part of her brain filed away that suspicion, as cruel as it was to do so. Because if Maddy hadn't done it, who had? she asked herself, biting a hangnail. She stared blankly ahead. *Maddy. It was Maddy herself. No. It couldn't be.*

If she hadn't made the cards, who had? It was that same question again. What had caused the woman to have frightening memories after looking at the studio photos? What was the connection? What *could* be the connection? The photographer's address had been in Indianapolis. Would the photographer still be alive and in business after what must be thirty or forty years?

Lumi used her restroom. When she returned to her worktable, she saw Nolan, in uniform, standing on the sidewalk looking in through the front door. He glanced up when he noticed she had returned to the main part of her shop. His expression was unreadable.

She froze. Her heart cried out for him, and her lips parted in silent panic, but she didn't move. She couldn't. The shock of seeing him again was heart-wrenching.

He seemed to be waiting for her to signal to him, and when she didn't, he walked out of sight as if all he had wanted to do was to make sure she was safe there in her shop and not hurt or missing.

Lumi precisely remembered what Nolan had said to her when he had been in her home for dinner: "I understand you a lot better now. I don't want to scare you off. I … I want to get over my guilt. I want to hold a woman and love her someday."

Tears filled her eyes as she stood in the same spot for long minutes, staring out at the street for a man who didn't reappear. She couldn't breathe. She wanted to run after him, but she felt she'd done the unforgivable and that there was no use trying to apologize.

She ached inside and out, worse than before she had seen Nolan. When she saw him again and could tell there was no feeling left in his heart for her, it was as if the floor had suddenly opened and she'd been dropped into a pit.

She drank most of a bottle of water, begging her brain to concentrate on Maddy's mystery instead of Nolan. She thought about the tangled issue of repressed memories. If Maddy hadn't made the cards herself, and if they *did* represent a real event in her past, why couldn't she recall what that event had been? Had it been insignificant at the time? Or, had it been so horrible to her that she'd forced herself to forget?

As she sat mostly ignoring a sandwich later that afternoon, she reviewed the pictures she'd taken of the cards. The first stereocard showed a black-and-white image of a woman's body that was almost entirely crushed under stone or concrete. A river of what appeared to be blood was draining from her, and she seemed to be laying in a puddle of water mixed with blood. It was eerie, and to Lumi, it felt like it was meant to be a threat to Maddy.

Maybe the woman in the photo *was* Maddy, back when she was a young woman. No. There was no way she would have been able to survive such a terrible crushing. She flipped to the next image on her phone. It showed a large room full of dead or probably dying people. Was it from World War II? There were men's fedoras on the floor, and most of the women were in dresses and the men were in suits. The bodies were surrounded by rubble. It was either from a formal event in more modern times or a typical scene from long ago. The photos reminded her of ones in the old *Life* magazines from the 1940s of bombed-out buildings in Europe and the wounded who were victims of the war.

Why was this a memory trigger for her neighbor? She wasn't old enough to have been a victim of World War II. She would have been a baby or toddler at that time, and she certainly wouldn't have memories of such a tragedy.

Lumi looked at the next photo. A man's bloody arm hung limply from the edge of a table. A blanket or coat covered the rest of his body and his face. The next photo was of a baby being pulled from the ruins, and the next showed a crying man with a crude head bandage supporting a limp, bloodied woman. They were splayed on the floor amongst broken seating, and a popcorn box sat near the man's feet.

So, thought Lumi, it was probably an event that had taken place in relatively modern times. The popcorn box looked like one that could have been made today, and yet the way the victims and survivors were dressed made the photos seem to have been taken decades ago. Were they all from the same place and day? she wondered. Was it a scene from another country? Was it even real? Could it be a staged event? Where did people typically eat popcorn out of a clown-faced box? At a circus or play, a theater or a fair.

Staged … was this a movie set? Unlikely. The emotions on the victims' faces seemed genuine.

Lumi kept thinking about the hats. She flipped to the last two cards—the ones that had been delivered to Maddy's mailbox. They were more gruesome, even depicting people's torn-open innards.

The more she thought about the cards, the more she was sure Maddy hadn't created them herself. Lumi wished she knew what to do, especially now that she couldn't ask Nolan to help or advise.

Lumi did a reverse image lookup on the clearest of the photos. An amazing number of near matches came up as a result, but none of them were very close to the shots on the cards. Most were scenes from wars, fires, protests gone wrong, mass shootings, the Jim Jones tragedy, massacres in foreign lands, and the Holocaust. Nothing seemed right. The way the people were dressed, and the box of popcorn were clues, she was sure. But to what?

She used search terms, but the results were so varied that there was no way to choose a direction of focus and research.

The day dragged into night. Her arms felt empty without Nolan. Her heart ached without Nolan. The shower offered no warmth. Her bed no comfort. The radio no pleasure. The rain on her roof was noiseless. The food on her plate tasteless. She had robbed herself of love and romance. She had sabotaged herself. She had hurt Nolan for no reason. Sleep was a long time coming, and even her dreams seemed cold and cruel.

Chapter Ten

Before leaving her house for work Saturday morning, Lumi's phone rang. No longer holding out hope that Nolan would call her, she wasn't surprised to see Maddy's name on the screen.

"Dear, will you pop over for a minute?"

Lumi glanced at the clock on the microwave. She had a little time to spare before she needed to drive to work. "I can. See you in a sec."

Maddy was standing on her porch, waiting. "I need to ask you to do me a huge favor. I would hate to bother you if you have a date with Nolan tonight, but would you please go with me to my reunion instead?"

They went into the kitchen to sit down. Lumi inhaled, bracing herself for what she had to say. "I don't have a date. And … I won't *be* having any dates, ever."

Maddy frowned. She adjusted her glasses, clearly saddened. "I hate to hear that. I really do. Oh, Lumi. I can see from your eyes how very upset you are."

"It was my fault, not his. I honestly don't know how to have a grown-up relationship, Maddy. He tried and tried with me, but in the end, I …" She broke off to avoid crying. She nearly cried again when she noticed the cake carrier on the countertop. Nolan must have returned it. He must have been in Maddy's kitchen recently.

The older woman cleared her throat and swallowed. She met Lumi's eyes. "I feel sorry for you both. Well, maybe this time apart will be a good thing. If you didn't say anything in anger or do anything terribly regretful, a little time apart can make for a more honest, fresh start if you want to try again."

"Didn't Nolan say anything to you?"

Maddy looked confused, then she noticed the cake carrier, too. "Cammie returned it. We visited about her and Mike and their unusual conglomeration of collectibles, but she never said a thing about how you ran away from the party. Twice."

"Oh, God."

Maddy patted her arm. "I know, baby. I guess it is a little messy right now, but I'm sure this will blow over in no time."

Lumi wiped the corner of one eye with the edge of a finger. Changing the subject, she asked, "Why do you want me to go to your reunion? Can't Chess take you? Do you need a ride?"

"Chess is certainly going with me. It isn't that. I want you there to act as detective. You know … sniff out potential criminals. Ask questions.

Dig around. See if you think any of my classmates could have sent me those cards. How about it? Will you go with us and play Sherlock Holmes?"

Lumi's face suddenly drooped. "I want Nolan back."

Maddy patted her arm again. "I know. I know."

"You *don't* know! I can barely *eat.* I can barely *sleep.* I see his smile everywhere. I want him to come back to me, but I ruined *everything.* You don't know, Maddy. You don't know what I *did* to him."

"I know *you,* though. Therefore, I am quite sure you didn't do anything as ruinous as all that to Nolan. I think you *did* do something terrible to yourself, however. Am I right?"

Lumi nodded, tears clouding her vision.

Maddy handed her a tissue. "If you really feel this deeply for him, I'm sure you'll find a way to repair the damage to yourself and to him. Like I said, a little time apart can be a good thing."

Lumi blew her nose. "He stood looking in through my door yesterday. Nolan. But he didn't come in."

"He was probably checking up on you. Being protective. Did you run out to him and ask him to talk things over?"

"No. I didn't move at all. Stood like a garden statue waiting for a bird to poop on my head."

"Oh. Well," Maddy said, standing. "I suppose you need more time to think about how terrible you are. Nothing wrong with that. It helps you grow and heal and figure out what *not* to do the next time. Can I get you a cup of coffee?"

Lumi shook her head even though the rich aroma was the first thing that had seemed appealing to her for a long time. Her insides felt empty. "I need to get to the shop. What time is the reunion?"

Maddy poured herself a cup. "Eight. It's at the Lions' Club. Do you know where that is?"

"I think so. At the corner by the fire station."

"Yes. Wear whatever you'd like. It's just us old-timers sitting around wondering who else will show up or who's died off since our last get-together. Eat dinner first. There will be homemade snacks and coffee, but that's about it."

Lumi stood. "I'll see you there. I'll drive myself over in case I don't want to stay as long as you and Chess do." She paused, wiping her eyes again. "Thanks for letting me vent about my miserable love life—or lack thereof."

Maddy playfully tugged at Lumi's hair to lighten the mood. "A bump in the road, baby girl. A little bump. If there's real affection on both sides, you'll work things out. Don't let yourself get too downhearted, okay? We'll have fun tonight, and you'll get to play sleuth. I think I'll write up a few notecards for you so you'll have some idea of what to ask."

Lumi nodded and hugged her friend. "I'm not sure *what* I would do if I didn't have you, Maddy. No one else on the planet is here for me. Everyone is angry at me now. I super screwed up."

Maddy smoothed her back comfortingly. "Lumi, that's not at all true that you don't have anyone, but I'll take a hug. It feels good to hug someone who isn't made of rocks."

Lumi tearfully giggled, then cried again against Maddy's shoulder.

Not long after settling in to price more items from her storage room at her worktable, Lumi noticed a woman looking into the shop through the display windows. It was Cammie. Lumi raised a hand and smiled, glad to see a familiar face.

Cammie reacted by balling her fist and hitting a window. Hard. *Bam!* Her eyes shot daggers of steel.

Lumi stood to walk toward her, but Cammie immediately turned away and crossed the street without even checking for traffic.

That blow was meant for my chest, Lumi thought. That woman would fight anyone to defend her friends and family. It was admirable, but Lumi dearly wished she was on the other end of things instead of being the enemy.

Cammie's fist-pounding caused Lumi to wonder what was going on with the Sanders family. Poor Nolan! Humiliated, he probably left the Fourth of July party and moped alone at home all night. His sadness probably damped the spirits of everyone else in the family, too. Lumi was supposed to meet Nolan's parents, and he was going to proudly show them that he had found a woman to have at his side again. He hadn't had a romantic relationship since his wife had died, and Cammie and Alisa were elated that he had opened his heart again.

Lumi pushed her fingers through her hair and rubbed her scalp in frustration. What had she *done?* How could she have been that *awful?*

Feeling weak and sick, Lumi considered going home to sleep the day away. But, she knew, being closed on a busy Saturday was death for any new business; she had to stay and tough it out.

The day dragged and dragged. Lumi swung from emotion to emotion when she wasn't helping her customers, trying to keep her mind on pricing antiques and books and linens or on the stereocard mystery. The vision of Cammie's furious eyes and her beating fist kept swirling in her brain.

At nearly closing time, she took her phone from her pocket, determined to face what she'd done. She wrote a text to Nolan: "I'm horrendously sorry! I'm sick with shame. Nolan, I'm—" but didn't send it. She couldn't think of a way to say exactly how she felt, and she didn't want to put him in the position of feeling obligated to forgive her.

She deleted the first and wrote another text. "You can't forgive me, I know. I won't ask you to. But I want you to know that I'm sick with remorse. No undoing it now. I honestly meant my emotions toward you. I still do. But I can't be what you need. I regret my immaturity. I regret hurting you. I am desperately sorry my fears have ruined everything!"

She hit "send" and let it go through time and space to Nolan's phone. She imagined him hearing his phone chime. She could see him checking the sender's name and then ignoring it or deleting it without reading what she'd written.

A minute later, her phone pinged.

"You think I'm not afraid, too?"

Her pulse tripled. She texted back: "Nolan." It was a cry to him from her heart.

He didn't reply. Lumi waited, standing in the middle of her shop as orchestral music on the stereo added a tune to her racing heartbeat. Five minutes later, she stopped hoping he would respond with even a single word. She texted one more message: "Oh, Nolan."

"Crowded! Where should I sit?" Lumi asked Chess, being a smart aleck. While putting on a summery short dress in shades of pink, and during the drive to the Lions' Club, she vowed to herself to think no more about Nolan until she got home. She was going to the reunion to do a job for Maddy. Taking a lesson from Jackie's mother, she would give of herself to try to forget her pain.

"Squeeze in by Mary Sue. She'll make room," Chess said, pointing to an older woman in a yellow chiffon dress at a large folding table. No one else in the Lions' clubhouse was sitting down, and only a dozen classmates and spouses were present.

Lumi walked to the countertop that opened to the large kitchen to pour herself a cup of iced tea from a pitcher. She put a wedge of lemon in it, grabbed a slice of apple pie, a napkin, and a plastic fork, and went to sit across from Mary Sue. Maddy was right when she'd said the woman's nose had taken over most of her face.

Lumi nodded, trying to think of a way to strike up a conversation. She was uncomfortable when striking up conversations with strangers, even though she forced herself to do it many times per day in her shop.

"Hot today," Mary Sue said. "Feels good in here, though. I don't have air over at our place. Do you?"

Lumi swallowed a chunk of pie, nodding. The pie was the first thing she had eaten all day other than a few stale cheese crackers she had brought to the antique shop months ago. Her stomach was full of missing Nolan, and it had no acreage for happy things like food. She was glad for the distraction of the reunion and tried to force herself to stop thinking about her own situation, at least for the rest of the evening.

She glanced around, not seeing Maddy. "So, you're a classmate?" She knew the answer but didn't want it to seem like she'd been informed.

Mary Sue nodded, sipping coffee. "No one thought to bring any coffee creamer. I hate it black."

"Oh. That's too bad. Want me to run to the store?"

Mary Sue looked surprised. "Do you work here?"

"No. I was just offering."

"Well, no, young lady. You sit and enjoy your pie. I've got to go off and find the ladies'."

Lumi felt unequal to the challenge she'd been given. Where was Maddy with her notecards?

"Chess," Lumi called softly.

He walked to her. Chess looked different all dressed up in a white short-sleeve shirt and black slacks—like a freshly painted tugboat. "You rang?"

"Where's your girlfriend?"

He grinned. "She ran home again. She'll be back in a jif."

"Home?"

Chess leaned close. "Forgot your cards with the hints and questions on them."

"Oh, crap. I wish she hadn't bothered—I'm not going to be able to do her any good."

"There she is now. Relax. You sit and listen to us talk. I'll do your job for you as a talker and questioner. You take mental notes. How does that sound?"

Lumi stuck her tongue out in a show of relief. "Perf. Thanks."

Maddy, in a lilac pants suit and white sandals, walked across the clubhouse toward Chess and Lumi. She surreptitiously pointed to her white purse, letting Lumi know the cards were inside.

Lumi walked partway around Maddy, admiring her. "Your hair looks great, Mrs. R. Did you get a perm?"

"Curlers." She glanced from classmate to classmate. "Big crowd this year."

Lumi wasn't sure if she was being sarcastic or not at first, but then decided she was serious. "I was conspiratorially whispering to Chess. He wants to do all the talking and questioning for me while I listen. Is that okay?"

Maddy nodded but seemed to feel let down. "But I made up these cards."

"I'll look them over, Mad," said Chess, his hand out.

She opened her purse and secretly handed him the cards. "Don't let on what we're doing."

He flipped through the cards, finally pausing to read one. "Well, I'm not asking anyone *that.*"

Maddy rolled her eyes and sighed. She tugged at the hem of her top and shifted her purse higher to her elbow. "Do what you want. They're only suggestions."

"Should we start?" asked a man in an Elvis t-shirt, dyed-black hair and sideburns, and plaid pants. He and a few other older men had placed folding chairs in a circle nearby.

"Come on. You'll sit with us," Chess said to Lumi.

After everyone had taken a chair, the Elvis-shirted man held up a sheet of paper and read off a list of names. When he finished, he said, "And may we have no more of *that.*"

"Amen!" said Mary Sue loudly, stomping a foot from where she sat.

Lumi, sitting between Chess and Maddy, silently looked questioningly at Chess.

He leaned his head her way to whisper, "That was a list of the dead."

"Now," said the same man, "who has news?"

Chess sat straighter and cleared his throat, but Maddy reached across Lumi to touch his arm, shaking her head as her blue eyes flashed a warning.

"Donna's now head surgeon at Acorn," a woman announced.

"'Bout time," said another woman's voice.

There was a pause as the classmates thought about speaking up with their own announcements.

"We came up yesterday from Georgia. Spent three weeks with our son and daughter-in-law. It's hot down there," said a man wearing a royal blue and yellow letterman sweater that very much did not fit.

"Anyone else?"

Chess cleared his throat, diving in without permission. "I'm going around with Maddy Rasmusson now."

Maddy audibly inhaled.

"Around? Like … what?" asked a white-haired man next to Mary Sue.

"We're practically engaged, you might say," Chess said proudly.

Lumi's face reddened. She didn't dare look in Maddy's direction.

"Well, terrific!"

"That's great!"

"When did all this start, you two?"

"I can't believe it!"

"Good for you."

A man Lumi hadn't noticed before walked up behind Chess and stuck his hand out. "I'm happy for you two. When's the wedding?"

Lumi finally glanced to her side to see Maddy's reaction. She was smiling, but rather uncomfortably.

"We're not *engaged,*" Maddy clarified to the room. "We're just shacking up for now."

A great roar of laughter went through the room.

A tall, gaunt man dressed in gray slacks and a black sweater, and with heavy eyebrows, came to loom over Lumi. "Who's this now, Chess? Your granddaughter?"

Chess elbowed Lumi. "Naw. She's a pal of Maddy's. Jim Scott, this is Lumi Leski. She wanted to join us to see how the cool kids throw a party."

Jim Scott's caterpillars drew together over his Dracula-like eyes. "Leski? I think I buried a Leski a few years ago. Any relation?"

Lumi had no idea if her next move would be to laugh or run in fright. "Um … I don't think so."

"No, no. Now that I think about it, that family's name was Leslie. Shame," he added, then turned, his hands joined loosely behind his back.

Chess chuckled silently, his upper body shaking under his crossed arms.

Lumi stood, intending to get herself a cup of coffee, and Chess took her chair to be closer to his girlfriend.

"Joplin!" Mary Sue called from the back of the room near the display of pies and cakes.

136

Lumi swiveled, as surprised as anyone else that the candidate had come to the reunion. She glanced at Maddy and then at Chess. Both crossed their arms and exchanged a look.

The whole atmosphere of the room altered, but in two distinct sections. The folks near the entrance were apparently happy to see Joplin, but the others distinctly were not, and they gathered into a knot around Maddy and Chess at the center of the room, silently commiserating.

The group surrounding Joplin suddenly laughed together. Lumi saw that the man was gesticulating and talking loudly. At a distance, his slicked-back silver hair looked like an artist had drawn it on with a few swoops of a pen. He wore a Hawaiian shirt, black slacks, and black dress shoes, as if he had never worn such a shirt but stopped by a store on the way to the reunion to try to fit in.

Joplin noticed he hadn't won over the rest of the room, so he waved once to excuse himself and strode up to his detractors. "Hey, kids. What's going on over here? How's the coffee?" He glanced at Lumi as if expecting her to get him a cup.

She didn't move.

"Hello, Pinky," said Chess, his arms still folded.

At hearing the nickname, Joplin's face reddened, but then he breathed deeply and smiled with his mouth. He turned only his head to look at Maddy. "I'm back in town, Missy."

"I see," Maddy answered.

He eyed her for a moment. "You've gotten older, but I can still see the girl you were back in school. I heard you're named Rasmusson now."

She nodded and put her arm through Chess'. "My husband passed some time ago. I'm with Chess now."

Joplin took a cup of coffee from Mary Sue and nodded his thanks. After a sip, he asked, "What are you protesting now, Missy?"

She shrugged. "Old age."

Joplin laughed, spilling a few drops of coffee on his hand. He shook it dry, then slid that hand into his pocket. He seemed to be considering his next words carefully. "Not like when we were kids. That was lots of fun. I have *lots* of memories of those radical days when you were on the march."

Lumi didn't like his tone, and she didn't like Maddy's reaction to what he'd said. Wanting everyone to be rid of him, Lumi said in a mock-friendly voice, "Mr. Rooney, it was nice of you to pop in on your old classmates like this. I suppose you're in a hurry to get back on the campaign trail. You must have dinner plans."

He seemed pleasantly surprised that she was giving him an out. "I do. Heading to … Carmel for drinks with … well, for drinks." He couldn't find a friendly face in the group around Chess and Maddy to say something along the lines of a happy goodbye to, so he put his full cup of coffee on a table and went back to the front of the room. There, he loudly laughed and patted shoulders, and then was gone.

"My hero," said Chess, standing. He nudged Lumi's arm with an elbow. "That deserves another slice of pie, at least."

Maddy strode to the ladies' room, looking upset. Chess held out his hand to prevent Lumi from following her. "She'll be fine. That guy is a turd. I can't believe he showed up here, and I can't believe any one of us was honestly glad to see him."

"Did he do something to Maddy? Back in the day, I mean."

"I don't think so. He … wasn't like the other kids who protested the war and everything else. He was a troublemaker. Pinky and his friends always managed to ruin any protest they showed up for, Maddy once said, taking the focus off the message and putting it onto whatever mischief they were making."

"Hmm," said Lumi, her eye on the restroom door, waiting for it to open again. "Should I be suspicious of him, then? After all, I'm here undercover to sniff out suspects."

Chess shook his head, sitting again with a sigh. "He's still only interested in himself. I'm surprised he didn't have an official photographer along to take shots of him mugging with his hometown classmates, and I'm surprised he didn't hang posters up once he was in the building. That's the kind of guy he is now, from what I've read and heard—which isn't that different from Pinky the kid. Naw … I can't picture him playing with a paste pot, doing home crafts."

Maddy rejoined them, looking like she'd put Joplin's appearance behind her.

"Coffee, Maddy?" Lumi asked. "There's no creamer, though."

"I'll take a cup, yes. A lady is always prepared for such an eventuality. I have some packets of powder creamer in my purse." She cleared her throat. "And a spoon and a little sugar, please."

Lumi was back with them in a minute. "It's hot," she warned, handing over the coffee.

"Feels good in here, though," said Mary Sue, coming up behind Chess' chair. "Nice to hear your news, Maddy. I always thought you two would get together when we were young people."

Maddy didn't answer as she sat next to Chess. She seemed to be sorting out her feelings on another matter and wasn't really listening.

138

A man with bowed legs stood leaning on a cane, holding what appeared to be a yearbook. He took a seat on the other side of Maddy, turning toward her with a little difficulty.

"Hey, Ralph," said Chess. "Any news?"

"I got married since I was last in town. Wendy, her name is." His voice was a combination of gravel and whine.

Maddy's mouth opened for a few seconds before she said, "Ralph! That's *wonderful*. Where are you living now?"

"That's her over there." He pointed across the room to a salt-and-pepper-haired heavy-set woman in a spring-colored skirt and white sweater who was tossing away a coffee cup. "We're in Ohio. I retired a while back, but she works as a special ed teacher in a school south of Columbus."

"How did you meet?" Lumi asked.

"On the internet. There's an old people dating site for duffers like us. I got lucky."

Wendy joined them. *"I* got lucky, you mean." She smiled and put a hand on Ralph's shoulder. Lumi liked looking at her. She wore a small bouquet of clovers on the front of her sweater. Her eyes twinkled with friendliness.

"Sandy!" Chess called, holding out his hand for a handshake.

An attractive silver-haired man in a polo shirt and dark blue shorts took Chess' hand, smiling. "I hear you're due for congratulations. I thought you two seemed mighty friendly at our last reunion."

Chess grinned, still sitting. "Buy up any more golf courses lately? That Spring Mile course is *tough*. Almost as bad as Purgatory. Since the Barnwood course closed, there's nowhere nearby for us awful, twenty-yard hitters to play."

Sandy pushed his hands into his pockets. "I'm done with all that now. Sold everything except the house and two cars and one of my small boats. Our kids need the money now. Why not help them out while they have families to raise? We don't need it, and I don't miss the hassles."

Over the next two hours, Lumi barely said a word, but she listened. When poker chips and cards were brought out from a storage room, Lumi said goodnight and left.

On the drive home, she felt disappointed. It wasn't like on TV or in a movie where the amateur sleuth went to a party or funeral and casually asked questions and figured out the identity of the murderer or thief. She hadn't learned anything helpful. Jim Scott was a creepy character, but that seemed to be a part he was playing to match his looming appearance.

Joplin was a typical sleazy politician, but maybe he was playing a role, too. *The Case of the Stereoscope Cards* was still far from being solved.

Lumi pulled into her driveway minutes later, and as she walked around the corner from her side yard, she had a shock that stopped her in her tracks. Nolan was sitting on her front steps. "Nolan!"

He didn't move. He didn't even look her way, and instead stared straight ahead at the road.

"How long have you been here? Why didn't you call me or text me? I would have come right back."

The distant street and porch lights were the only illumination since she'd forgotten to leave on her porch lamp. Nolan glanced at her, noticing the way she was dressed. "From your date, you mean? That wouldn't have been convenient."

"My date?" She walked closer, but there seemed to be a wall between them she couldn't break through, so she stopped ten feet away. "I was certainly not on a date, Nolan. Tonight was Maddy and Chess' school reunion. Maddy asked me to tag along."

"I've been here for two hours, talking to myself instead of to you, hating you a little more with each minute. Separating. Distancing. I have no idea why I'm even still here. Inertia, maybe." He looked away again. "I was falling for you, Lumi. You know that. You *know* that. I was slapped hard when you took off. And then when I stood in front of your shop, you did nothing at all." He exhaled loudly. "Slapped again."

"Nolan, please come inside and talk to me. Please. I'm begging you. If you ever cared for me, let me talk to you." Her eyes were wet with tears that hadn't fallen, and her lips quivered as she feared she wasn't going to convince him to go inside.

His eyes burned into hers, hurt and angry. "If I ever *cared* for you? What in the hell did you *think* I felt? I was bursting with joy. You were playing around, apparently—flirting and shit—but not me. *I* was falling in love." He stomped a foot. "And that 'tiger' speech. You gave me visions I'd kept at bay for *years*. *Why?* What kind of a *sick game* were you *playing* with my heart?"

She swallowed her humiliation and wiped her eyes with her fingers. "Nolan. Please, Nolan. Come inside. It isn't what you're thinking. Honestly. Honestly."

He finally stood but walked away down the sidewalk to his truck, parked three houses down. He got in, sat behind the wheel for a full minute, then retraced his steps. He pointed silently to Lumi's porch, his expression blank.

She went up the steps and unlocked her door and held it open for Nolan, then shut it behind her as he sat on the green sofa.

"I … want to explain," Lumi started.

"I'm not stopping you." He crossed his arms, staring at the blank TV screen.

"There are things about me I can't tell you. I can't face them. I can't say them out loud, Nolan."

"Same here."

She sat on the coffee table, not touching him, afraid he would react like a feral cat if she tried. "I got scared when you were in the pool at the party. Your eyes were hot with sex and lust. Your half-naked body was too much. I had sensory overload. I'm a full-on virgin, Nolan. I'm almost twenty-eight years old, but I'm way younger on the inside because I've had this determination to stay a virgin and to stay away from love and yearning. You represent everything I've ever avoided all rolled up into this perfect, awesome package: love, romance, sex, heat, attraction, weakness, fantasy, reality, relationships, friendship, and … it's all coming at me at once. A cannonball of everything I've avoided and let myself be afraid of for forever. And you're handsome, muscular, and manly. I can't *handle* it. I can't *take* it. I can't even tell you how scared I was in that moment, with the sun glinting off your abs and chest, and your eyes full of the pleasures of the bedroom."

Nolan leaned forward and put his hands over his face, his elbows on his knees. "Bullshit. *Bullshit,* Lumi. That *can't* be what happened."

"You're too perfect. I'm way, way down below you in the readiness to actually date and make love. I'm way less attractive. Way less fantastic. Way immature for you. It hit me *hard* how I can't ever be good enough or what you deserve, Nolan. I panicked. I screamed inside watching you swimming, wanting me. I had to run away, don't you see? I had to run away and hide in my damn hole again, where it's comfortable and normal, where no one wants to kiss me or undress me or even get to know me personally. I sabotaged us to make it all go away so I could be my usual, antisocial-but-comfortable self."

He looked at her, frowning. *"No.* That isn't what happened. You rejected me because I'm not good enough for you. *Admit* it. You used me to have a little fun, then when you got a clear look at me, you were laughing inside, and that's why you ran for the hills."

141

"Nolan! Why are you … why on … are you *serious?* Have you ever even looked in a mirror?"

"Have *you?"*

Lumi's lips parted. "Can this *be?* Can it be that we're *both* members of the low-self-esteem club?"

Nolan frowned again. "Why didn't you just *talk* to me about what you were feeling?"

She took a breath, trying not to cry. "I was all emotion. It was like I was taken over. And once I'd done that to you, I couldn't face you again. I was ashamed. Miserable. Tied up in self-hatred and very sure you would never want to have anything to do with me again."

He pulled her hand and she shifted from sitting on the coffee table to the sofa beside him. He lifted his arm so she could tuck under it. "Shit on a cracker, Lumi—all this heartache and *pain.* Why didn't you tell me more of what you were feeling? How could you be *scared* of me? I'm half in love with you already." He took a breath. *"I'm* not good enough for *you.* I'm not man enough for you. You deserve so much more than I can offer. How can you have it all backward?"

"I want to release you, knowing I'm probably bad for you, but there's this flashing neon sign in front of my eyes now."

"What does it say?"

"'We are *not* ending things, Nolan Sanders.'"

He hugged her tighter. "Lumi. *Lumi.* You are *so* very far from being bad for me."

With a stronger, clearer voice, she said, "Can we try again? We'll start over. We'll date and get to know each other better. There's a local auction I want to go to tomorrow night. Come with me if you're not working. You'll see that part of my world. We'll have a little fun together. No expectations."

He tucked a strand of her hair behind her ear and kissed it, and then said, "You should date other guys. Now that you know you can be up close and personal with a man, you should find out what you really want. I was just the first one to pound on your door."

She almost smiled as she said, "Oh, Nolan. 'Date other guys.' I'm sure that was the dumbest thing you've ever said in your whole life."

He laughed once, looking exhausted.

"Let's do this," she said. "Let's be friends." She put her head on his shoulder. "Friends who hug. Does that sound okay?"

They stayed sitting together in silence for a long time, hugging each other back to life.

Chapter Eleven

Lumi woke when bright morning light streamed through her living room windows. She was surprised to find herself on the sofa under the blanket, but then remembered details from the night before.

"Nolan?" she called into the house. "Are you here?"

No reply came.

She stood and stretched her arms and back. She wanted to text or call Nolan, but a second wave of uncertainty hit her. *Had* they reconciled? He had held her until she fell asleep, but did that mean he had forgiven her?

Feeling the need for a bath even before breakfast, she went upstairs. As she soaked, she imagined having Nolan's company in the tub. Would such a thing ever happen? Would they ever even kiss again?

Reluctantly, she forced herself to think about the high school reunion. None of Maddy's classmates seemed capable of hurting or threatening her with those awful cards. They were all dears, as far as Lumi could see. Except for Joplin. The friends all seemed to care for each other in their various ways. Even gloomy Jim Scott was shown to be too sweet to be guilty of anything as the evening went on, laughing and joking and wiggling his humungous eyebrows at the ladies.

Lumi scrubbed the makeup from her face and sunk lower into the nearly hot water and suds, trying to float. The sensation reminded her of the sight of Nolan on his back in the pool, sunlight gleaming off every bead of water on his chest, his muscular stomach, and his powerful legs. She was there with him in her mind, floating and warm.

A worm of worry pushed into her thoughts about his muscles. Did he use them to apprehend criminals? Lumi had only briefly seen him in his police uniform, and she certainly had never seen him working as a cop. Was he continually getting into dangerous situations? If she became seriously involved with Nolan, would she be pacing the floor day and night, fearful he was going to be shot or stabbed? Would she, too, be in danger from retaliating criminals?

She sat up, the water sloshing. "Wait," she told herself. "This is Barnwood, not Indianapolis."

Even so, she thought, there was *some* crime in town. Probably more by far than when she was growing up.

Lumi stood to shower off the suds, dried, and dressed.

While boiling eggs and making toast, her phone on rang. She went to the coffee table to answer it. Seeing Nolan's name on the screen made her fearful and overjoyed at the same time.

"I miss you," she answered.

Nolan laughed. "I hope you saw my name before you said that."

"Oh, yes. Seeing it was surprising, though. I wasn't sure you'd call. I feel … worried. I'm not sure you forgive me."

They didn't speak for a long moment. Lumi returned to the kitchen to turn off the heat under her pot of eggs.

"You're open on Sundays?" he asked.

"I am. Almost every antique shop is open all weekend, and we take our break on Monday and Tuesday. The bigger stores and malls are open every day, but they have employees. I've just got me."

"Well, you've got me, too."

She smiled, feeling reassured that they could go on being together. "Not at my shop."

"No. But you've got me."

"Oh, Nolan. I'm glad. I'm happy you said so."

There was another pause. "I heard what my sister did yesterday. Sorry about that."

Lumi smiled. "I love that she did it. It shows how wonderfully loyal she is to the ones she cares about. It helped bring me to my senses, honestly. I owe her a lot for the symbolic beat-down she gave me."

"Cammie can be a beast, but she is the kindest person, too. I hope you don't hold that against her."

"I don't. We'll be good friends eventually—I know it."

"Listen, I have to go. I don't usually work on a Sunday, but everything that was set up in the park needs to be taken down now that the holiday weekend is basically over. I've got to help supervise the city workers and handle several chores myself, and there's paperwork involved."

"I was thinking about you during my bath earlier. I worried about why you have so many glorious muscles."

He laughed at the compliment. "There *are* rough tools out there, but you shouldn't worry, Lu. I work out as a hobby. It helped me emotionally when I was alone for too long. There's a small gym in my apartment building." She heard him take a breath. "I love that you were thinking about me in the tub."

She paused, embarrassed. "Um, my eggs are ready."

"Let's not get ahead of ourselves."

For a few seconds, Lumi didn't know what he meant, but then it hit her. "Nolan! The eggs in the pot on my stove in my kitchen are ready to eat. *Those* eggs! Gah!"

"I'll call you later about the auction. Bye, Lumi."

"Goodbye, you goof."

After eating and getting ready for work, she walked across the street.

"Lumi, dear! How are you this morning? You missed the real fun last night. Having a bigger group made poker much better than in some recent years at our reunions. Too bad you weren't there for Chess' best one-liners."

Lumi followed Maddy into the kitchen.

"Here. It's a fresh pot." Maddy poured.

Lumi put both hands on the mug, feeling its warmth. She smiled with her eyes. "I've got big news."

Maddy sat facing her. "Nolan?"

Lumi nodded. "We made up."

"Oh, I *am* happy for you both! I mean, I knew it would happen, really, but I'm tickled to hear you say it." She grinned. "How did you do it? When?"

Lumi grinned back, but not enthusiastically. "Last night. He was waiting for me on my front steps. I guess he'd been there for a couple of hours while we were at the reunion. He was hurt that I'd apparently gone out on a date."

"A date? Oh, dear! How could he think such a thing?"

Lumi swallowed a sip of coffee. "Long story short: we talked everything out, and then we made up."

"And there you were, worried he was gone forever."

Lumi frowned. "He almost was."

Maddy cleared her throat before changing the subject. "Now, about your impressions of my schoolmates—get any ideas last night?"

"No. Sorry."

Maddy stood to retrieve her full mug from the countertop. "But ... where does that leave us? Does it mean that a total *stranger* is out to hurt me? Or is there someone from my long-ago past who's threatening me?"

Lumi thought. "I was reading on the internet about repressed memories. Do you think there's something you've done years ago but forgotten—something you did to cause this kind of retaliation? I'm not saying I think it was on purpose, of course."

The older woman sat again with a sigh. "There must be. I mean, I protested the war. I protested racial inequality. I marched for gender equality. There *were* fights, and even a few bloody fights, honestly. I wasn't one of the most active protestors in the 'sixties, but I did more of that than my girlfriends did, to be sure." She stared at the steam rising from her mug. "But the scenes in my memory don't match what's shown in the cards—not at all. I never saw blood and guts and babies and kids. There certainly were no men and women in dresses and suits. We wore shabby clothes to carry our signs and banners."

Lumi sighed. "How about the studio photographer? Could he have sent you the cards? Do you think he broke in here and put the first five in your collection?"

Maddy shook her head. "Why, though? Why?"

"I don't know, but I have this feeling he's very much connected to the mystery. Let me look at the name and address on his photos and take a picture of them. I'll see what I can find out about the studio while I'm at work."

During a lull between customers that afternoon, Lumi took out her phone to examine the posed photo of Maddy. The photographer's name, Phillips, and the street address were printed on the corner of the photo. She searched for the address and found that a convenience store had taken over the location.

Looking at other search results, she saw newspaper ads from the 1960s, '70s, and '80s for the studio. One of them had the photographer's first name: Desmond. Lumi searched for "photographer Desmond Phillips Indiana." His website was the top search result. Mr. Phillips appeared to be about seventy-five in the photo on the "About me" information page.

"Maddy? It's Lumi. Hi. Guess what? I'm sure I found that photographer. Uh-huh. He's still in Indy, but not at the same address. It looks like he works out of his home on Keystone Avenue. He advertises that he does weddings and commercial work. What should we do? Do you want to go there and talk to him?"

There was a moment of silence before Mrs. Rasmusson said, "I … what do you think we should do?"

"I think we should go. How about if I call him for an appointment? I could say I want an appraisal for a shoot of my antiques and the shop."

"You handle it, Lumi, dear. I'll go along with whatever you want. But if you say you want him to photograph your shop, won't he just go to you? Don't we want to go to him?"

"Hmm. I don't see any reason why one way is better than the other. All I want is for you to see him in person to try to jog your memory. We'll go from there, okay?"

"Fine. But, Lumi—what if he's the one responsible for the cards?"

"Well, I guess we'll confront him and get to the bottom of this whole ordeal."

"I'm scared."

Lumi waved at a woman who had come into the shop. "Don't be. I'll be with you. I think we've got to end this once and for all. I'll let you know the details."

"Well, all right, dear. I trust your judgment. Goodbye for now."

Lumi waited on a string of Sunday shoppers and talked with browsers. When the store was empty nearly an hour later, she called the photographer.

"Is this Mr. Phillips? I have an antique shop in Barnwood. I don't have an online presence, and I think it's overdue. I'd like an estimate from you. Should I go to you, or can you come here?"

"I do take clients, yes, but there's no need for an official appraisal. I work for a set fee per hour, plus my travel time and gas. Have you looked at samples of my work? My fees are posted on my site, too."

Lumi paused, not expecting actually to have to hire the man. "Um … couldn't we meet first, though?"

He sounded exasperated. "I don't have time for anything but work, I'm afraid. I have two weddings this week, and I'm shooting industrial photos at a factory under construction on the south side. Hire me based on my fees and samples, or don't."

Lumi had one new idea. She turned off her stereo and stepped into her storage room where it was very quiet. "I do have another question, please. Do you know Maddy Rasmusson in Barnwood?"

She listened for any hint of a gasp, any indication of recognition in his breathing or in his voice. "Who? No." He seemed to be waiting. "So, would you like to hire me or not? I can schedule you for early August."

Lumi told him she would look over his work again and get back to him. She was convinced he'd had no reaction to the name.

She called Maddy. "I don't think he's responsible. I would have had to hire him in order to meet him, and I don't have money to spare for things like that right now. I was hoping we could get a meeting with him to get an appraisal."

"Hmm. How about if *I* call the photographer? Give him a false name. Say I want to talk to him about my wedding in person. Is it worth a try?"

"Maddy! *What* wedding?"

Her friend laughed. "Pish-tosh! I was making up an excuse to see the photographer, Lumi girl!"

"I got excited."

"Don't. Not happening."

"Too bad. You two are perfect together," Lumi teased. "Okay. You call him. Here's the number. Ready to write it down?"

A few minutes later, Nolan, dressed in his uniform, pushed into her shop. He met her eyes. "How's your day going?"

Lumi walked to meet him, loving that he smelled of freshly cut grass. Her lips trembled. "I was nervous about seeing you again."

Nolan nodded. "Me, too."

"I feel like a different person today."

He nodded again. "I was up half the night. I left your place about one o'clock—about half an hour after you fell asleep after our long talk—and then I drove the back roads for a while to unwind."

She bit her lip. "Here we are, after all that emotion. How are we doing?"

He glanced around to make sure they were alone before reaching for one of her hands. "I'm sorry and ashamed of myself. I jumped to the wrong conclusions, feeling inadequate. Feeling rejected. There are important things about me that I haven't told you. I guess they prevented me from understanding what was actually going on with us."

"I was my fault as much as yours. More." She looked away and then back at him. She paused, remembering something Maddy had said. "This can be our fresh start."

Nolan looked into her eyes. "I have this tired-out feeling in my bones. I came here because I knew seeing you in the clear light of day would clarify things. Show me if I really *do* want to be with you again."

She nodded. "I'm scared now. I don't want you to—"

"I'm falling for you all over again."

Suddenly on the verge of relieved tears, Lumi asked, "I hope you know this one thing, Nolan—I want your heart more than anything."

Seeing her eyes moistening, he looked alarmed. "Don't *do* that, Lumi. I can't handle tears right now. I have a ton of paperwork waiting for me back at the station. I've been in the park all day, but there are things to do that I need a clear head for."

"You're not leaving me again so soon?" she asked, upset.

"I have to, but—" he looked around again, "I can do this." He led to the unlit storage room and leaned against the open door. Barely touching her arm, he whispered, "I want to kiss you, darling Lumi. Badly. I want to hold you again."

She faltered. It would feel like a first kiss all over again, she knew. Since Nolan was practically asking permission like he had the first time, she understood he was feeling the same way. She wiped her eyes, put her hands on his chest, and said softly, "I've been wanting to kiss you ever since you swung that lampshade out of the way. Or before that, when you bit your lip at dinner. Or maybe even before that."

They kissed for a long, slow, healing minute.

"This is very unprofessional of us," Lumi said, wrapping her arms around Nolan's waist, hating that the equipment on his duty belt dug into her. She wanted to feel his body against her and nothing else.

"This is perfection. Right here. This feeling you give me." He kissed her throat, then lowered his lips an inch, and then lowered them yet another inch more. "I love the way you smell and taste. I love this little freckle that I know is there, but I can't see in this light. I love the place where your breasts separate above your heart. I love the dimple in your cheek that only shows when you smile a certain way." He kissed each part of her as he described them.

"Stop!" she protested, still holding him close. "What if someone comes in?"

He lifted his head, smiling, his eyes mischievous in the near darkness. "We'll blame it on renewed ardor."

She took one of his hands and placed his palm over her heart. "I guess renewed ardor should take the blame for this pounding pulse you're feeling, too."

He let his hand remain where she'd put it, but said, "I didn't think we'd kiss again so soon after last night. I thought we'd agreed to be 'friends who hug.'"

"That was silly."

"I honestly didn't think we'd end up in your storage room when I walked in here."

Lumi nodded, her eyes staring into his in the dimness. She was almost dizzy from the boldness of Nolan's touch, and at her own boldness for wanting his hand to stay where it was. "I'm dying for you to touch more of me. I … can't believe I'm saying this, though." She kissed his ear, then whispered, "You'll have to stop us. You'll have to be the one to stop us."

149

"Shh. Don't talk. Let me enjoy this a while longer."

Lumi whimpered, excited. Aching. Hating that it was daytime and that they were supposed to be working.

Nolan swept an arm around her shoulders, pulling her into another kiss, waiting for her lips to part, and groaning when they did. He broke away to lightly glide the tip of his tongue down her throat, painting a trail of desire. He traded positions with Lumi, guiding her back to the door before kissing her lips again and again, his hands holding hers against the door above their heads, fingers entwined, his hips pressing intimately into hers.

Lumi caught her breath, then said, "You're taking me over, Nolan."

"I hope so."

Still holding her hands over her head, he sucked on her lower lip, then kissed her harder as one of his knees parted her legs a few inches, letting her feel his excitement.

She broke their kiss to whisper, "Don't. I can't know that, Nolan. I can't know you feel that … intensely. It scares me. It scares me."

He put an inch of space between their bodies, let go of her hands, and held her face, kissing her more delicately.

She smiled against his lips, feeling more in control, yet happy she did have a sexual effect on his body. It was a strange, confusing mixture of emotions.

His voice gruff with desire, he whispered, "I freakin' can't get enough of you, but I need to go." He lowered his hands to her waist and made sure she was looking into his eyes as he said, "I want your heart, too, Lumi—I do—not just every fantastic inch of your body. See you tonight."

That early evening, Lumi rushed home to change into tight jeans and a black, sexy sleeveless top, to put on makeup, and to make sandwiches she and Nolan could eat during the sale. They drove separately to an auction barn a few miles north of town already full of bidders and spectators by the time Lumi arrived.

"Hi," she said, finding Nolan examining a set of pewter horse bookends on a table right below the elevated auctioneer's station.

His face lit up, and he put an arm over her shoulders. "Look at me, the guy who gets to put an arm around the most beautiful woman in the … world."

"You were going to say, 'in the vicinity of the auctioneer,' weren't you?" she teased.

"No. Almost said 'universe,' but toned it down."

"Ha!" She smiled and kissed his cheek, stepping out from his embrace. "I need to register for a number. You should get one, too."

"I did already," he answered, pulling a white bidding card from the pocket of his black jeans. He looked up as one of the auctioneers stepped past him, a group of papers in his hand. "Hey, Steve. How's it going tonight?"

"Hey, Nolan. Good. Nice turnout, not like that dry spell we had for most of June," the man answered before disappearing into the crowd.

Lumi scowled. "Nolan?"

"Yeah?"

"How do you know his name is Steve?"

Nolan glanced around at the other offerings on the tables nearby. Holding a small box lid filled with vintage fountain pens and picking through them with interest, he answered, "Been coming here on and off for years." He held up an orange pen with a gold band. "Oh, look—an early nineteen-hundreds Waterman. In great shape, this would be worth a *lot.*"

She scowled again. "Nolan?"

"Yeah?" He looked at her when she didn't speak again. "What?"

"Anything you want to admit to me before I clobber you?"

"Clobber? Why, that would be assaulting an officer. You'd be looking at twenty years in the pokey, at least."

"I'll deal with you later," she warned, trying not to smile.

In the line leading to the office, she spotted a high school classmate. Lumi was dismayed to see Bobbi was still beautiful and dressing to flaunt her bountiful curves, and her softly flowing brown hair looked both unkempt and perfect at the same time. Lumi's stomach churned. Every boy she had eyed with the merest of interest was the one boy that Bobbi would flirt with and win over. She had deliberately stolen Cal Griggs, the one crush Lumi had hoped would ask her out for over a year—the one boy she was sure wouldn't fall for Bobbi's lure. Lumi had no idea why Bobbi had repeatedly mistreated her while pretending to be a friend.

Bobbi, turning to talk to the woman behind her, noticed Lumi, and her eyes registered recognition. "Lu! Lumi Leski! I haven't seen you in forever, girl!"

Lumi faked a smile. "Hi, Bee. Still living around here?"

"Downers Road now. God, girl. *Look* at you! You're *gorgeous!* Can you believe it's been about ten years since we were in school?" Bobbi eyed Lumi appreciatively from head to toe. "Look at you, kid! Hey, are you back in Barnwood again?"

Lumi's wariness subsided. "I am. I bought a house on the same street as my folks' old house, and I have an antique shop downtown." She had whispered that last part, not wanting to give away her expertise to the room.

"Cool! We should totally sit together. I'll find you later," she said before stepping up to the office window.

After registering for a bidding number, Lumi searched for Nolan. He was kneeling over a row of box lots of books on the floor near a wall. She put a hand on his back possessively. "I know I just went ahead and registered, but I think we should leave."

Nolan stood, surprised. "Leave? Didn't we just get here about five minutes ago?"

"I know, but … if you like me even a little bit, you'll agree to go somewhere else with me. Now."

"There you are, Lu!" Bobbi said, suddenly appearing in front of them across the boxes of books. She smiled first at Lumi, and then at Nolan. Her eyes widened as she took in the glory of his muscles. "And who's *this?*"

Nolan said, "Hello. Are you a friend of Lumi's?" He held out his hand.

Bobbi took his hand in hers but didn't shake it.

Lumi held her breath for a second before saying, "This is Nolan Sanders, Bobbi."

Nolan took back his hand, glancing between the two women. He kept his eyes on Lumi for a moment, as if trying to read her thoughts.

"Are we going to sit together, Lu? I think I see a group of three seats near the side door. Want me to go and claim them?" Bobbi asked, her eyes back on Nolan.

"Yes," said Nolan. "You go ahead and sit, thanks. We'll look things over for a few minutes before we join you."

Lumi's heart dropped to her feet. *It was happening again.*

Nolan looked over the rest of the books, did a three-hundred-and-sixty-degree turn to scan the contents of the sale, and then he pulled Lumi to the other side of the room.

"I've got our seats, Nolan," Bobbi cooed, patting a chair beside her own. "Sit here and tell me about yourself."

In a move so sure and swift that she never saw it coming, Nolan swung Lumi into a tight hug and kissed her. His thumbs dug into Lumi's back pockets, holding her firmly against him for an even more enthusiastic kiss. Letting her go, he grabbed her hand and strode out through the nearest door to the parking lot.

Lumi couldn't control a giggle. Her giggle turned into a laugh, and in her state of jocularity, she nearly fell to the gravel between two pickup trucks.

Nolan held her upright until she sobered.

"You have *no* idea what you just *did!*" she said, her heart soaring.

"I most certainly do," he argued, leading her to her SUV once he'd spotted it. "Can you drive, or are you still on the verge of giggles? I think 'driving while tittering' is illegal."

"Tittering!" she laughed. "Oh, stop! I'm going to fall over!" At her car, she pinned him gently against her rear door, feeling the joy in her heart change to desire. She took a breath and forced her head clear of such notions. "I want to kiss you so much right now, but I'll *never* be able to come to this auction again if we're seen making out in the parking lot. Especially after what you just did."

"I know a man-stealer when I see one," he said. "I could tell you were feeling defeated. I'm guessing you two have a history together."

"Yeah. Bobbi and me—frenemies." She stepped back. "But, Nolan— you grabbed me right there in front of everyone! How are we going to live that down? Especially now that I know you're secretly an auction-goer, yourself."

He let go of her hands. "No one was looking at us with all those box lots to dig through." He smiled and stepped back a foot. "I'm a man of mystery, right? I knew about your store even before you opened, but I never buy anything in antique malls or shops. I only buy from auctions, and very little at that. I like to go for the fun of it to get the occasional bargain, and stuff I really need."

"You wanted the pewter bookends and pens."

He hugged her and said, "No. Looking is not the same as wanting. I thought my kiss in there was proof of that."

She hugged him back, still elated.

Nolan broke their hug. "Hey—it's way early. Let's head over to Sally's for dinner."

She nodded. "Will it be only the two of us?"

"No. It'll be the same gang as last time. They invited me, but I said I had plans. I think they're probably sure I'm sitting at home alone. Let's go, okay? I want them to see that we're the new and improved Nolan and Lumi."

"Did you say anything to your family about us being ... well, that things are good between us?"

"I purposely didn't."

"Why? They'll probably attack me when we walk in. Cammie, especially."

"No, no. I'll talk to them first. Make them put away their brass knuckles before you get to the table."

Lumi opened her door and sat, adjusting the steering wheel and putting on her seatbelt. She gave Nolan a doubtful look, but said, "I'll see you there."

"Know how to get to Sally's from here?"

"I think so, but I'll follow you." She smiled again. "I think I'd follow you anywhere."

He squinted. "Cheesy."

"I know. I couldn't help it, though."

They walked into Sally's minutes later. Nolan waved to the group of Sanders at their usual table. He asked Lumi to stay at the bar until he signaled for her to join him.

Lumi couldn't hear what Nolan was saying over the loud country song that was playing, but she saw that Magnus and Mike seemed happy, but Alisa and Cammie did not look pleased.

Nolan signaled to her at last. She took a bracing breath and made her way to the table. Nolan hugged her from the side, giving her strength.

Magnus and Mike greeted her warmly, but the women were silent, eyeing each other in concern.

"This is a good thing, Cammie," Nolan said. "We're sticking this time. You don't need the details; you just need to know that Lumi has my heart."

Cammie shrugged, looking away. "She's going to break it."

"She has, of course—you know that. But we're stronger now that the break has healed. It was all a misunderstanding. She's the one I want. The *only* one," Nolan insisted.

Cammie raised an eyebrow, then looked at Mike to see how he was reacting to this news, surprised that he was smiling.

Nolan took a chair from an empty table and put it next to his.

Lumi swallowed and took a seat next to Cammie as Nolan sat at her right. Surprising even herself, she grabbed Cammie's hand under the table and held it firmly, not looking at her. After a tense moment,

154

Cammie gripped her hand in return. Lumi summoned the courage to face her. "I'm glad you showed up in front of my shop like that."

The jukebox was finally silent, and everyone at the table was listening to their conversation.

Cammie sighed. "You treated Nole like dog poop."

"I did." Lumi released her grip. "Your long-distance attack was a wake-up call. I was only seeing my side of things."

Alisa wiped tears from her eyes with a pointed tip of her napkin, trying to keep her makeup from smearing.

Lumi looked around at their faces. "I need to apologize and explain. I've never had a serious relationship. I've been going through an emotional growth spurt because of Nolan. It's been overwhelming. I'd been alone for so long that this thing with your brother has sometimes been *petrifying*. I don't want to embarrass you more by going on and on about it, but I do owe you all an apology."

Alisa's lips quivered. She slid a hand toward Lumi across the large, round wooden table, too far away for a touch. "I feel you, Lu, girl. I see it now. I was pushy, too."

Lumi cleared her throat and glanced at each of the faces watching her. "You couldn't have known I was fragile."

Cammie made a sound through her nose that may have signaled exasperation. She leaned closer to warn, her eyes flashing, "Don't … hurt … Nole."

Nolan said, "That's enough, Cam. I'm a big boy."

Lumi gulped. "She cares about you, Nolan." She turned to Cammie. "That means we're on the same side."

Cammie relaxed. After a moment, she glanced across the table and shared a faint smile with Alisa.

Mike, looking uncomfortable, opened his menu. "What are we ordering? I think catfish is one of the specials tonight."

"Ooh! Catfish!" Alisa said appreciatively. "The baby got excited when you said that." She looked at her stomach, patting it. "How about fries? No? Twice-baked potatoes?" She waited, then laughed and nudged Magnus. "Taking after you already with his spud preferences."

"As well he should," Magnus said before half-standing to try to read the chalkboard near the end of the bar. "They've got a deal on chicken wings tonight." He sat again and spoke to Alisa's midsection. "How do you feel about sharing a basket of hot wings with your mom and me?"

Alisa's beautiful, dark eyes widened. "Oh, no, you don't, mister! Don't you dare talk the baby into spicy foods. I don't want him to pop out *tonight.*"

Lumi held Nolan's hand under the table on his thigh. She smiled at Alisa and Magnus. "Do you two have a name picked out yet?"

Alisa snorted, tried to say something, then laughed again and gave up.

"What?" asked Lumi.

Magnus closed his menu, grinning. "We talked about names again last night. We like 'Colonel.'"

"No!"

"Not that again!"

"You wouldn't!"

"Why not?" giggled Alisa when she could finally speak.

"We would spell it like the corn thing, not the chicken guru," Magus said. "K-e-r-n-e-l."

"No."

"That's *awful.*"

"Dude, don't," said Mike as he shook his head. "With you as his dad, that kid is going to have it hard enough. Don't pin that name on him, too."

"But we live in the corn belt. It fits."

"Mag … *no.*"

"Well, then," Alisa said, finally not cracking up, glancing around at everyone at the table, "we should tell you that for real and for sure we've decided to name the baby 'Jeremy.'"

Lumi felt Nolan react. His hand in hers tightened as she said, "Oh, Alisa! I love that name! Jeremy has always been one of my favorites."

Everyone except Nolan and Lumi laughed or nudged someone next to them. Lumi was confused. "What?"

"That's Nole's middle name," Magnus said. "Didn't you know?"

She then understood Nolan's physical reaction to hearing their name choice. Looking at him, she saw how touched he was. The corners of his mouth were drawn down, and he seemed unable to raise his eyes beyond his glass of water. "I didn't," Lumi answered, feeling emotional herself. "What a beautiful tribute to your brother."

Mike, seemingly to give Nolan some time to collect himself, asked, "What's *your* middle name, Lumi?"

"Oh, geez. You don't want to know." She rolled her eyes.

"Well, if I didn't want to know it before, I sure do now," Mike said, smiling.

Lumi paused before saying, "Hella."

No one at the table said anything. They seemed stunned.

"It means 'tender' in Finnish," Lumi clarified.

"Maybe so," said Alisa, "but that's used constantly as a slang term now, you realize."

Lumi sighed again, her shoulders slumping. "I realize."

"That's a hella good girlfriend you got there, Nole," quipped Mike.

Nolan's expression lightened after the shock of hearing his future nephew's name. "I know."

Their usual waitress appeared between Lumi and Cammie. "Ready, Sanders family, or do you need another minute?"

They ordered and ate, talking between bites. Lumi felt herself bonding with the group; it was as if there had always been an empty chair waiting for her at their table.

Alisa went to use the ladies' room, and when she returned, she said, "Let's" to Magnus. He patted his full stomach but soon nodded. He took Alisa's hand and led her to the dimly lit dance floor on the other side of the short wall near their table. A bouncy country song from the jukebox had the other dancers energetically jumping around, but Alisa and Magnus moved together to their own slow rhythm, their baby between them. Lumi couldn't stop staring at them, mesmerized by how happy and in love they seemed.

After a moment, Mike finished his ice water and pulled Cammie to her feet to dance, too. They were excellent dancers and seemed to have a routine worked out for the song.

Nolan leaned closer to Lumi. "I haven't ever danced, really. Not with a girl. I just tap my feet when the music moves me." He watched his brother, sister, and in-laws. "They're *good,* aren't they? I always leave after eating so the other four can dance without worrying about me sitting here alone."

Lumi nodded, "I've never danced, either. Well, not with a boy. At high school dances, I would get in a circle with my girl friends, and we'd all kind of bop around. During slow songs, we'd go sit down or get a drink or use the bathroom and pretend we didn't want to dance with the boys, anyway."

They sat companionably at the table, enjoying the music from the jukebox and watching the others sway together or kick up their heels. Their waitress returned to refill the water glasses. She stepped to Nolan's side and said something to him that Lumi couldn't hear.

Nolan pushed away from the table to stand looking down at Lumi. Wordlessly, he pulled her from her chair and out onto the dance floor as a country ballad was beginning. The lights were turned very low except for a few dim reflections from the metallic ball overhead. He shifted his weight from foot to foot in time with the beat, holding her tenderly, his arms around her waist.

She put her arms around his back, relaxing as he led their movements.

To Lumi's great surprise, Nolan knew the words to the song. He lowered his head, pressed his cheek against hers, and sang near her ear as they rocked together. She could barely tell the recorded voice from the one coming from the man in her arms.

Lost
I have never felt so lost, my darlin'
When you left me standing all alone
My world was dark, and I was cold
Lost
I never thought I'd make it home

Found
Here you are again, wrapped in my arms
Dancing like we've never danced before
The music's never felt this sweet
Every note and every beat
Found
I've found you, and I'll hold you evermore

I can't believe it—here you are
Where I've wanted you to be
Dancing slow and easy
Like heaven in my arms
Our hearts are close together
Right where they belong
Whispering to each other
Things we haven't said so far

If I knew every love song
From every singer on the earth
None could say a single phrase
My heart could not outdo.
So, dance with me, my darlin'
Don't leave me standing here
All alone with no one in my arms …
This music is so empty without you."

Lumi was nearly swooning. The surprise of Nolan's beautiful voice, the rhythmic closeness of being on the dance floor in his arms, and the sentiment of the song's loving words combined, rushing enchantment straight into her soul. Her eyes dampened as Nolan held her tighter. She rested her head under his chin, feeling the rumble of his humming as he let the recorded voice finish singing.

The music ended, and no other song followed. Everyone went back to their seat.

Lumi paused before they reached their table. "Nolan, why … what did the waitress say?"

He linked his arm through hers. "She said, 'In lieu of my tip tonight, I want to see you two dance.'"

"She should still get a tip," Lumi said, playfully bumping her hip into Nolan's as she wiped her eyes.

"Double, I'd say," Nolan agreed.

Chapter Twelve

Nolan and Lumi arrived at her house an hour later, each in their own vehicle. Lumi parked her SUV in the driveway and then walked to sit in the truck.

"That was such a special dinner, Nolan. I was honestly super frazzled and worried about Cammie and the others on the drive to Sally's. I hadn't known what to expect, but it turned out to be a lot of fun—after the initial confessional was over, of course."

He nodded, gripping the steering wheel and looking ahead to the street, avoiding her eyes.

"What's wrong?" she asked, turning in her seat.

He exhaled in frustration. "I have no idea what to do with you now that we're not in public. Now that we're starting over like this."

"Tonight was perfect. All we have to do now is find our ending."

"How do we end it, though?"

She thought she knew what he meant. "Well, we can shake hands. Or, I suppose we can hug goodnight." She smiled. "Or, we can have a nice kiss."

Nolan glanced at her and then away again. "I've got to say that I don't know if I *can* have 'a nice kiss' with you anymore, Lumi."

"Oh."

"I have it bad."

"Oh." Her legs were vibrating from nervousness. "In that case, we'd better just shake. She held out a hand to him, trying to lighten his mood.

He took her hand and placed it lightly on his thigh. His yearning brown eyes met her fearful blue eyes. "I've gone and fallen hard for you again."

She inhaled, looking down. "Everything feels … I don't know—crazy. Romantic. The energy between us is powerful." She looked up again. "At the same time, I'm trying to keep my head above water. I could easily drown, and we aren't ready to drown together, Nolan."

Nolan whispered, "I am. Let me in tonight, Lumi. Let me show you how much is in my heart."

They were silent for a moment. She finally moved her hand from his leg. "This is all new again. I mean, we were flirting and having fun and getting close, and then I messed us up. And now … this time what we do and say is more meaningful. I'm not afraid; I'm coming toward you slowly to make sure things are even sweeter."

Nolan was silent for a while, then he raised the steering wheel and turned, leaning across the armrest so he could kiss her.

She kissed him back, but with restraint. She pushed against his chest. "I want more time. I honestly think you do, too. We need to find our footing again."

Nolan inhaled, a note of frustration coming from his throat. "So. Not tonight. All right." He looked away, then back at her again. "I'm certainly not angry, but I am more than ready to show you how I feel. I will never force you into doing anything you're not as … desirous of as I am."

"Oh, Nolan," Lumi said breathily, liking him even more for taking his foot off the gas pedal. "I *do* want you to come inside tonight—but to talk about a mystery I'm puzzling over. Can you do that? Just talk about something that isn't our potential lovemaking?"

Nolan ran his fingers through her long hair, letting them get tangled halfway down her back. He closed his eyes, admitting, "God, I got excited just hearing you say the word 'lovemaking.'"

She smiled but got out of the truck. "Follow me inside if you'll talk to me about Maddy." She stepped back and shut the door.

He hesitated, watching her go, but was with her by the time she had the house unlocked.

"Want a drink? I have soda, juice, and iced tea. Or hot tea," Lumi called from the kitchen.

"I'd like a glass of water, thanks."

She brought two tall glasses of water to the living room and put them on the coffee table in front of the sofa. She stood admiring him for a moment. Nolan looked comfortable, as if he belonged on her furniture, in her house, his eyes meeting hers. Finally sitting beside him, she said, "I hope what I tell you can stay between the two of us—well, the three of us. Maddy has reservations about making a formal complaint to the police. I am, however, talking to you with her blessing."

He took a sip, the ice clinking. "You understand that if I hear any mention of a crime from you tonight that I have to take it seriously. No joking, Lu. I won't sit here if you don't understand that."

"You have your Serious Cop face on. It's adorable," she teased, forgetting she was trying not to seduce him.

He put his glass back onto the table, sighing. "I mean it." He stood. "Sit here a minute while I use your bathroom. Think through exactly what you want to say to me. If you decide your story involves criminal activity, and if you think Maddy wouldn't want full police involvement, don't talk to me about her situation. That's as fair as I can be. However,

I will say that it makes me very upset that she felt she couldn't come to *me* right away. That she had to ask you to be her voice in whatever this is."

Lumi exhaled, agreeing silently. She said, "I have a half-bath on this floor, but the water to the toilet and sink were shut off before I moved in. I was told there's some issue, so I'll eventually have to hire a plumber. The full bathroom is upstairs."

While he was gone, Lumi stood at her front window. No lights were on in Maddy's house. Lumi wondered if her friend had made an appointment with the photographer or if she had changed her mind about calling.

"Okay," Nolan said as he stepped back into the room. He turned off the upstairs hall light and the light over the sofa and television. "Are we talking about Maddy, or have you decided to stay mum."

"Why did you turn off the lights?" she asked, a note of panic in her voice.

"So I won't see as much of your glorious curves. Or your long hair curling over your shoulders and breasts. Your legs in those jeans. How beautiful your face is, or how full your lips are, made to be doing something like this." He tried to pull her into his arms.

Not cooperating, Lumi held him at bay, her eyes letting him know she wasn't as resistant as she was acting. "Nolan, *please.* Stop. I actually need to get around to talking to you about a mystery I can't solve."

He sank onto the sofa. "Okay." He drank more water. Lifting one bent leg to a cushion to sit sideways, he asked, "What do I need to know?"

Lumi collected her thoughts, ignoring how great he looked in his black jeans. "Well, you know Mrs. R has all these antiques, right? And you've probably seen her French stereoscope viewer."

He nodded. "You're sure you want to have this talk? This is my last warning. You're positive?"

Lumi walked to the light switch, turning on the front room's modern hanging lamp again. "I am." She took her purse from the coffee table and got out her phone. "Look at these images." She sat beside him, her legs crossed. "Five stereoscope cards were planted in Maddy's box of antique cards. They're obviously not old, and not even very good attempts at making believe they are." She opened the gallery on her phone to show him the five out-of-focus photos and the two sharper images of the cards that were delivered in the mail.

Nolan held the phone and flipped back and forth between photos. "Hmm. Weird. So, you're saying there's a crime here, right? Someone entered her home and put these gross cards in with her views of birds and mountains?"

"Yes. You knocked on Maddy's door right after she first showed them to me." She paused, recalling seeing Nolan for the first time. She fought the urge to climb onto his lap. "Remember?"

"I thought something was going on with her. That explains why she said she was too upset to drive herself home from Mag's shop."

"I wanted her to tell you right then and there, but she said no."

"Why?"

"She said that when she looked at the images, she felt a memory just out of reach ... one that filled her with guilt. She wanted to try to figure out what the pictures represent on her own."

Nolan scowled, handing Lumi her phone. "Guilt? Maddy Rasmusson? What could *she* have to do with these kinds of gruesome scenes? This doesn't make sense." He added, "I remember her when she taught Sunday school. She was nobody to mess around with. We made felt animals for the manger and sang songs, but we sure didn't get out of line. She's a sweeter pepper now than she was years ago, but even so, she can't possibly be to blame for suffering of the kind that these cards show."

Lumi moved to sit on the coffee table where she couldn't feel the heat of Nolan's body. She took a long drink of water, crossed her legs, and said, "I've been going around and around with her about this ever since that day. Those last two cards—those last super terrible cards were mailed to her. It feels like someone is threatening Maddy. Or they are trying to blackmail her. Or make her feel ... terrorized. She's so strong-willed that she isn't freaking out, but I can see it's scaring her. Chess knows about the first five cards, but he's never seen them. I suspect there's a deeper reason she lied and said she destroyed them, but I can't get a real sense of what that is. I don't know much about Chess—or Maddy, when it comes right down to it. I barely knew her before moving back to town. I once suspected Maddy had made the cards herself as, like, self-sabotage, but I don't think so now. Why isn't she sharing the images with Chess? She feels he's overprotective enough as it is. He's staying with her every evening and—"

Nolan prompted, "And?"

"And they go back and forth between their houses. One night she stays at his place, the next he stays with her across the street. *All* night."

"Ha!"

"It's a platonic arrangement, Maddy says, but I know there's real love there. She thinks he'll smother her even more if she lets him see what's on the cards. And, of course, she hasn't mentioned the ones that came in the mail. Is she protecting *his* feelings or her *own* by keeping them a secret? I can't tell. Maybe both."

"I don't know Chess at all, other than by sight here and there around town. He seems nice."

"He is. I like him a lot. But something is holding Maddy back from taking their relationship to the next level. She'll sleep with him, so to speak, but won't commit to more. He's even asked her to marry him."

Nolan smiled, then got them back on track. "So. Those last two, the clearer images, were mailed? I doubt that's a criminal act—unless there was a threatening note included."

"They were mailed separately, but there were no notes. I don't understand this. They all seem to show an incident that happened a long time ago—maybe during World War Two, or later by ten or twenty years. It's hard to tell. I'm making a judgment by looking at the fashions alone. Well, by the hats strewn around, and because the women are in dresses. I'm … stumped. What is your impression of the scenes?"

Nolan thought for a moment. "Well, you said Mrs. R has a vague memory when she looks at the cards, and that she feels guilty. I don't think she was around during the Second World War—it must be from a more recent event. If she has any memories of what went on, then we're talking … nineteen-fifties? 'Sixties?"

"She said she marched and demonstrated, but no one dressed up in nice clothes for a Vietnam War protest, I'm sure."

"No."

Lumi sighed. "And there's the thing about a photographer."

"The one that took the photos on the cards, you mean?"

She shrugged. "We don't know. What I'm referring to, though, is her reaction when I was looking at a couple of studio photos of Maddy and her husband that were taken decades ago. I found them behind her antiques on a shelf. When I brought them out where she could see them, she got spooked. She had a flash of a memory of blood and head wounds when she looked at the portraits of her and Ras."

"Huh. Has she had any personal contact with the photographer over the years, do you know?"

"She said no. I called him and—"

Nolan slapped his forehead. "You *called* him?"

Lumi rolled her eyes. "I called him to ask if he would meet with me about taking photos of my shop for my upcoming website. I would go to him, or he could come to me, and I'd have Maddy at my side. I was hoping seeing him in person and hearing his voice would complete the mental circuit—that he would be the missing piece of the puzzle, and all her memories would fit together."

"Sounds like a bad idea. He could very well be the one sending her the stereocards."

"I doubt it. I asked him if he knew anyone named Maddy Ras—"

"Lumi! *What?*"

"But he had zero reaction to her name."

Nolan slapped his forehead again. "Oh, Lu."

"I asked him to meet with me about an estimate, but he wouldn't. He said his rates and photography samples are on his site. I can either hire him or not. That was that until I talked to Maddy. She said she would call him herself to try to get an in-person meeting with him to discuss wedding photos."

"Wedding? What wedding?"

"Hers and Chess'. Well, their fake wedding. It was meant to be a way to get to meet him."

Nolan leaned back and crossed his arms, frowning. "Maddy has guts, I'll say that. As scared as she is of it possibly being this guy who's been sending the cards, she's brave enough to do something to solve her own mystery. But I don't like this."

"I don't know if she was able to get an appointment with him. Honestly, Nolan, what could it hurt to see and talk to the photographer?"

Nolan looked beyond Lumi to the blank television screen. "Were there *ever* any notes with the stereocards?"

"No."

"So, no outright threats. No blackmail."

Lumi shook her head. "It's all so odd."

He yawned. "I don't see anything much to investigate as a crime unless she wants us to investigate how the cards ended up in her collection—find out if it was it a case of breaking-and-entering. The images aren't pleasant, but is this serious harassment? I don't know. People send each other photos in the mail constantly. Without a note, these creepy double images are merely anonymous … well, terrible gifts. I'll talk to the higher-ups tomorrow at the station. Maddy shouldn't be scared about talking to the police. Whatever she thinks she's guilty of, I'm sure the reality of it all isn't anywhere as frightening as what she's imagining." He yawned again. "I'm heading home. Last night was too short. Must have had only four hours' sleep." He stood and stretched. "I'm glad you told me, but I wish you ladies hadn't put yourselves through such misery."

Lumi silently agreed. "Goodnight. Thanks for listening. I am honestly very worried about Maddy. The two cards that were mailed were beyond awful. I hate to think what could arrive next. They make me feel there's an urgency to solving the puzzle. What if ominous or threatening letters start coming next?"

"That *will* be a crime, even if nothing else has been. Let me talk it over at work tomorrow. We'll go from there."

She hesitated before standing up next to Nolan. He had taken a lot of the burden from her shoulders, and without hesitation or complaint. "I feel more for you every day."

His body quaked in response to her words. He lifted one of her hands and held it against his chest. "The way you said that … like it was an off-hand comment on the weather. Feel what you did to my pulse?"

She closed her eyes, slightly embarrassed by her own admission. Her knees weakened, and she wondered why she was letting him leave, why he wasn't holding her, kissing her.

Was he afraid she would run away again?

Would she?

He released her hand, ran a finger along her collarbone while her eyes were still closed, and then left the house.

In a sudden rush of longing, Lumi followed Nolan outside. "Wait!" she whispered urgently, jogging down her front walk.

He turned to lean against his truck.

A few feet away, she stopped, not knowing what to do. Crickets chirped, and a streetlight softly hummed. "I … didn't say goodnight."

He opened his arms, taking her into them when she stepped forward.

"I'm no fun, am I?" she asked, her head under his chin. "I don't know what to do with myself around you, and I keep pushing you away when I *want* you to stay with me. I'm … fighting a lifetime of living behind my walls. You've torn them down, Nolan, but mentally I can't get used to my freedom. There's this other stuff from my past that doesn't want me to relax into a relationship. It's hard to explain, but know that I don't want you to feel rejected or hurt again. I want us to keep getting closer and closer."

Nolan held her tighter. "I'm not going anywhere, Lumi. As long as I know where we stand, going fast or going slow is fine. You take the lead, and I'll happily follow. I mean, I would love to pick you up in my arms and carry you to a bed of rose petals and ravage you all night long, but I can see it coming, and that's enough for now."

She pulled his head down to hers, leaning the whole length of her body against his, luxuriating in his kisses. Pressing her cheek against his

166

shoulder, listening to frogs sing in the distance, to leaves rustle in the trees nearby, she whispered, "Have there been other women since Carol? That you've ravaged, I mean."

He exhaled and put a hand under her chin, guiding it away from him to look into her eyes. "You know there's been no one. *No* one."

She stepped back. "How can that *be?* You're handsome and sexy and … a cop. Women must throw themselves at you night and day. Like Bobbi did."

"They don't. And what she did was far more about you than it was about me. People sense when someone isn't available romantically, and I haven't been. I haven't sent out signals that I'm looking for love or sex. Well, until recently, that is. How can you be surprised? We've talked about this. We've both been walking around under a cloud of low self-esteem. I'm equally astounded that you feel undesirable. You're drop-dead sexy, and your eyes are spectacularly beautiful. Your body and your sense of humor are irresistible. I can't understand how you haven't dated. Haven't you had a lot of guys hitting on you your whole adult life?"

"No." She hugged him again. "I mean, a few of the older men who were usual bidders at the auction house I worked for would tease around with me during the sales, but I knew they didn't mean anything by it. My coworkers knew I was all business. I've been good at hiding behind my walls." She ran a hand from his shoulder to his waist. "You're the only man who has ever told me such things."

"Not possible," he insisted. "How? How have you never had an intimate relationship before, not even with your college boyfriend?"

Lumi shook her head clear of a memory, then said, "My time with Brad was almost brother-sisterly. I was annoyed with him more than I liked him. He was a guy to have around, to do date things with. We had a bond that started a week after my first year in college. We'd gone through … well, I needed him. He was important to me. He kept me in school, really, and I think I kept him going, too." She pulled herself emotionally free of the past. "And, Nolan, maybe I'm not attractive to anyone except you."

"That's crazy. You must know you're …." Instead of telling her again, he showed her using more kisses. "Go inside. Call me tomorrow about Maddy and the photographer. If she did arrange to meet with him, please don't let her go alone if you can get away from work. Otherwise, I'll try to go with her. All right?"

Lumi nodded against his shoulder. "All right." She didn't let him go. Her hands around his back crept lower than they ever had before.

Nolan growled. "You're actually killing me, you realize."

She nodded again, smiling to herself. "You have the most excellent ... backside. You can't see it, so maybe you don't know. But ... *wow.*"

He patted her waist. "Right back atcha, darlin'. Damn. You have no idea how badly I want to see you naked—to explore you with my eyes and hands and lips."

Lumi gasped at his shocking words, her spine tingling. "Don't *say* such things. *Jesus,* Nolan."

"Why not? I'll say more if you let me. Talking is a big part of foreplay and lovemaking. I want to turn you on in every way possible—touching, kissing, talking."

"I can't handle that. It's ... *embarrassing. Too much.*"

He grinned, pulling on the hem of her sleeveless shirt. He whispered, "I want to pull this top over your head and whip off your bra. I want to see the glory of your milky white breasts and your hard nipples as you anticipate my tongue licking them, biting and sucking them. I want to hear you moan with every tug of my fingers, Lumi. I want to hear you *beg* for my teeth to softly, sensuously bite your—"

"Nolan!" Lumi hissed as she stepped back, her mouth open, her eyes wide. "S*eriously,* dude. *Stop* that!"

He was breathing harder, turned on by his own words to her, his eyes radiant. "I'll stop talking, but I won't stop imagining doing those things and way more to your fantastic body, Lumi."

She crossed her arms as if defending herself against his fantasies, then walked toward her porch. Turning, happy to see that he hadn't yet left the spot where they had stood together, she said, "Goodnight, Nolan. I lo—I'll call you tomorrow."

Twenty minutes later, her phone pinged. *"I can't stop thinking about you. I swear I can still feel you against me. I can feel your tongue on mine. Your lips."*

"I can't stop thinking about you," she texted back, smiling, her face heating. Suddenly worried Nolan would think she was starting to have a bad habit of simply repeating what he wrote, she added, "Almost there. But please don't push me. I can't get the words you whispered out of my head. I feel pushed."

"Well, don't. I'm having so much fun falling into you that I don't mind waiting. Much."

She sent back a heart, reminding her that she'd almost said "I love you" to him earlier. Undressed at last after having a snack and washing up, she slipped on a nightgown and got between her cool, white sheets in bed. Lumi allowed herself a long, luxurious memory of dancing with

Nolan, hearing his voice singing to her, his arms holding her as they swayed, and the rumble of his voice against her heart. It occurred to her that she hadn't looked around for Cammie and Mike or Alisa and Magnus when they were on the dance floor. The whole rest of the world had disappeared.

Then she replayed his sexy words as they hugged against his truck. She couldn't handle it. Couldn't take it. She wanted to run away from his desire even though he was miles away.

Lumi knew she'd have to think of something other than Nolan if she wanted to go to sleep, so she reached for the lunch box of letters despite having little interest in them. Her own life was so exciting that things a mother had written to a daughter long ago didn't seem appealing.

Dear Sweetie girl,

My legs hurt me real bad tonight. I'm trying not to take one of the pain pills the doctor prescribed. I don't like feeling dependent on them, which is probably dumb. Taking one every so often won't get me hooked like a drug fiend. I realize that in one way, but I have a fear. Ever since the tragedy. I don't know if I've told you this, but I was hooked on pain pills back then. It took a long time to feel like I could live without them. The doctor kept giving me prescriptions, sometimes without even seeing me in his office. I don't think a doctor would do that now. He'd find out why I kept asking for more. So, that's why I'm scared to use them. I remember how hard it was to climb back to normal life after being on them for too long.

I think a lot about the tragedy lately. I don't know if we've ever talked together as grown-up ladies about what happened when my legs got crushed. It's a horrible memory, and Pearline was devastated, too. She bought a ticket to that ice show, but at the last minute she didn't want to go. She was like that all the time. She was anti-social one minute, then wanting to go to a party the next. Anyway, she and a few friends bought tickets to the ice show. Then she felt suddenly shy about the fact that there would be men along with the ladies in her group, so she sent me. I was elated! Pearline let me wear her yellow dress and carry her matching purse. Off I went on the bus with the gang of my sister's friends. We were singing and happy the whole way there. We got inside and the show was terrific.

But then the explosion happened. Bodies were thrown into the air and were mutilated or burned. There was screaming and crying all around. Thankfully, I was unconscious after a minute or two. I woke up in the hospital, after I'd had surgery. That was just the first surgery, Teensa. I had several. The pain was writhingly unbearable when I wasn't on a fresh dose of pain medicine. I hate to write this, baby. I hate for you to know, but I asked the nurse to kill me one night. I did! She was taking my pulse and I grabbed her arm and I begged!

They put me by myself in a nicer room after that and never left me totally alone until I got to go home a long time later. I had so much damage I didn't think I'd ever walk again! I saw a specialist, and he set me on the right path. But Pearline never recovered. She cried and cried for weeks after I got home. We never had the same relationship again! Guilt is a terrible thing. It eats at flesh and soul as bad as any mange or disease or vicious animal. A year later, I got married. Got pregnant. I delivered you, suffering the pain of having my legs spread wide apart as you came from me. Your dad wouldn't let me go through it again; he had his operation to prevent another pregnancy. But I'm so happy to have you that I would gladly suffer it daily to give you life!

Even now, I see those bodies and the blood at night before I fall asleep, although I blacked out fast. I remember a little boy lying beside me on the ice, reaching a hand out. He was pinned under chunks of rubble, too. I'm haunted. Just haunted! It was many years ago, but when something that horrible happens you either carry the images in your mind constantly, or you try to push them out of your brain as fast as you can and never see them again. I often think about men and women who go to war and experience those horrors. They and I know the same hell, but I was blessed with closing my eyes to it after a minute or two. Imagine seeing such things for months or years? Oh, Teensa! Terrible!

To end this on a lighter note, Essanpee the cat is doing good. He's gaining weight and his ails are fixed up or nearly so. Betsy's one arm is skinnier than the other, but she is not in any pain. She'll be back to her old self by autumn's end, I'm certain. Your dad really gets tickled by her! What a sweet, sunny dear she is for the whole neighborhood to have around! I haven't been back to my exercise group for a while. My legs need a rest. I'll go back soon, and then maybe I'll try talking more to the trucker lady who's retired. Pearline went in for two job interviews this week! I didn't ask what jobs she tried out for. That's part of my new policy of not butting in. I'll take what information she wants to tell me and be happy.

Thinking of you often. Love to Marty. Hope he likes his present! Tell him I'm proud of him, will you? I don't say that sort of thing to him, but he's got to know Dad and I feel that way. We're proud of you, too. You're

*a good girl. Always have been the light of our lives. I wish you were here.
I'd love a Teensa hug right about now.*

Love, Mama

Lumi folded the letter, shouting, "Ohmygod! Ohmygod!" over and
over. She unplugged her laptop from its charger and did an internet
search for "ice show tragedy Indiana." She nearly fell off the bed when
the news stories and photos appeared on the screen.

"Hundreds of all ages injured. Seventy-four Hoosiers killed."
"The deadly Coliseum explosion of 1963, were you there?"
*"Holiday on Ice gas explosion kills dozens, young and old, and leaves
hundreds with devastating injuries. Popcorn machine to blame."*
*"The finale had begun. A remarkable pinwheel formation. Smiles in
the audience and cheers. But a leak in a valve supplying propane to the
popcorn warmer sparked a blast of orange flame that shot forty feet up
through the south side seats, catapulting people and chairs through the
air. It has become known as the Halloween Holocaust. Concrete chunks
and body parts rained down, many charred from the blistering inferno.
Numerous spectators fell on the ice on the south side of the arena, while
others fell into a crater caused by the explosion and were buried
underneath huge slabs of concrete. Suffering of survivors is immense.
Indiana is still in mourning weeks later."*

The photos were eerily like the ones in the stereoscope cards forced
upon Maddy. In fact, Lumi recognized two of them as being the exact
same photographs. How could such a terrible event have happened in
Indianapolis without her ever having heard about it? Tears filled her
eyes. She had chills.

She jumped from bed, shaking with the effects of her discovery,
walking around and around the room anxiously, her mind reeling from
what she had read about and from the horrific photos online.

Lumi looked at the time on her phone. It was late. She texted Nolan.
"OMG Nolan! Are you awake? I need to talk to you about Maddy asap!"

She paced her floor again. Should she run over to Maddy's? Was she
there tonight or at Chess'? She looked at the time. Too late. She thought
about calling her mother in Florida but knew her parents went to bed
about ten each night. Her brothers? No. No one had been told any of the
details, so she would have to start over from the beginning, and she didn't
have the patience for it.

Still not hearing from Nolan after a few minutes, she decided to call him. "Nolan!"

"Lumi! What's wrong? Are you okay?"

She was immensely happy he'd picked up. "No, I'm not. I mean, I *am,* but emotionally, I'm a wreck. I've discovered the answer to Maddy's stereocards."

He yawned. "Should I come over?"

"Would you? I know how tired you are, and I hate to make you lose even more sleep like this, but I'm *overwhelmed.* " She caught her breath and forced herself to calm down. She was being silly. "Wait. No. It'll keep until tomorrow. I don't know why I got so excited. I mean, nothing can be done about it tonight. I'll talk to you tomorrow. I have the day off. Come over when you can take a break. Or come for breakfast. Okay?"

"I'll come now."

"Nolan, you don't have to."

"Honey, you don't know what your voice sounded like when you first called. I think you *do* need me over there. I'm coming."

"But it's super late. I'm sorry I called and woke you up."

"Stop. Let me go so I can get dressed. I'll be there in a few."

Chapter Thirteen

Lumi left the sofa and unlocked her door when she saw Nolan's truck headlights through her front window. She stood on the porch with her fuzzy peach robe wrapped tightly around her. The night breezes were cool on her bare legs and feet as she watched Nolan walk toward her and step up to the porch. Seeing him rushing back to her when she needed him meant more to her than she could ever have expected.

She raised her arms to his neck, smiling. "You didn't have to come. I'm glad you're here, but this is crazy. You'll be *supremely* tired tomorrow."

He hugged her hello before they went into the house. "I wouldn't have been able to go to sleep again after our call, and I'm always happy to be with you—for any reason."

Lumi switched on the overhead light in the living room and sat on the sofa, motioning for Nolan to join her. She opened her laptop but didn't show him the articles.

"Nolan, remember that lunch box of letters I got at an auction? I had tried to give them back to their owner, but she didn't want them. I was supposed to toss them away, but I've been reading them. I know, I know. That was terrible and snoopy of me, but ... I guess I'm terrible and snoopy."

"What has that got to do with Mrs. R?"

She thought about how she could explain the connection. "The letters are from a mother to her daughter. The first ones were written in the mid-nineteen-eighties. The daughter is newly married. Her name is Jackie. The mother, who I know only as 'Mama,' wrote several times about trouble with her legs and how she's had a hard time walking and pain ever since some long-ago tragedy. Well, I read another letter after you left tonight to take my mind off missing you."

He smiled.

Lumi held his hand, noticing how strong it looked even against the background of her fuzzy bathrobe. She looked at Nolan again. "This latest letter was startling. Mama wrote details about what happened to her legs. Her sister gave her a ticket to an ice show to go in her place, which then made the sister feel guilty ever since. And Mama wrote about dead bodies and blood, rubble and hurt children."

Nolan's expression changed. "Oh, yeah?"

"I did a search on a few of those keywords, combined with 'Indianapolis.' Nolan—look at what came up." She showed him the search results on her computer, putting it on his lap.

He was speechless, astounded by what he was seeing and reading. Finally, he said, "Let me see your phone—the photos you took of the cards."

She ran back upstairs to get it, then handed it to him.

Nolan swiped open the gallery, flipped past the photos Lumi had taken of the reunion, and then carefully looked at the cards, comparing them to the online photos. "This one and ... this one are obviously the same shots."

Lumi nodded. She stayed silent, letting him read the articles. After a while, she went to the kitchen to put mugs of water into the microwave. She added tea bags and placed chocolate chip cookies on a plate and brought them out to the coffee table.

Nolan didn't look up from the screen when he said, "I have a vague memory of hearing about this when I was little. An older neighbor may have been there. It seems sort of familiar, but I had never read anything about it. I never saw photos. This is tough to learn."

Lumi sighed, sitting again. "Think about *all* the tragedies from that period. What a terrible time to live through."

He closed the computer and put it on the table. After taking a sip of tea, he said, "But we haven't solved the mystery of the cards, or how this event involves Mrs. R. Why harass her about an event that took place so long ago, and one that she couldn't have done anything to change? She must have been about twenty, right? It wasn't a bomb. No one did anything intentionally. This doesn't make a *bit* of sense."

Lumi raised her feet onto the sofa cushion, holding her mug as she turned to face Nolan. "Or ... what if ... what if someone *thinks* she had something to do with what happened? I mean, people get weird ideas."

"This is years and years after the fact. Why now? Why do it with stereoscope cards?"

"Yeah."

They ate together in silence, thinking.

"Extraordinary. How freakin' weird that you read those letters, and that right there in one of them was a passage about the ice show explosion."

She nodded, sighing. "Well, think about it—the letters were written in Indiana, and the event was in Indiana. Even though I wasn't aware of it, and you weren't, not really, it has to be a *super* huge deal for older people in this area."

"I guess. But still—the *odds! How serendipitous!"*

Lumi remembered the first time she'd taken a letter from its envelope in her antique shop. So much from that moment on had been altered by what she'd read. The loneliness they made her feel led her to invite Nolan to come over for dinner. The lessons she had learned from Mama about family and friendship and how to see souls instead of merely bodies. Now the letters had led her to a discovery about the ice show tragedy. She took another sip of green tea, letting the fading steam rise against her face as if she saw everything from the past through an enchanted fog.

Nolan finished the last of his tea, then slid the laptop and his James Dean mug to the center of the coffee table.

She placed her Garfield mug onto the table more forcefully than she meant to. "I have to talk to Maddy tomorrow." She twisted to lean comfortably against Nolan's arm. "I wonder what the connection is to that photographer. Maddy said seeing his posed photos of her and Ras gave her flashbacks to scenes like the ones in her stereocards."

He put his arm around her, closing his eyes. "You feel mighty good. Mind if I stay on your couch tonight? I'm just about asleep right here, right now."

"Want to go up to my bed? To sleep, I mean."

"Couldn't possibly climb the stairs."

Lumi got up, turned off the lights, locked the door, drew the curtains on the window behind the television, unfolded a throw from the back of the sofa, put a pillow from the closet under Nolan's head as he shifted, and then stood over him. "Put your feet up. I'll take off your shoes. There." She unbuttoned the top button of his jeans, stretched out alongside him under the thin blanket, and loosened the knot of her robe so the tightness at her waist wouldn't keep her awake. They breathed together in silence for a long moment. She smiled. "I had a sudden thought. Probably my neighbors think you rushed back over for … you know—something else."

"I did," he mumbled into her hair. He shifted, lessening his hold on Lumi while continuing to cradle her.

A minute later, she could hear the change in his breathing as he gave in to sleep.

Lumi had been awake for a few minutes, luxuriating in the warmth of Nolan's body behind her, when she finally sat up and checked the time on her phone. It was almost seven-thirty. "Oh, geez, Nolan! Look at the *time*. When do you need to be at the station?"

He stirred and stretched. Realizing where he was, he grinned and reached for her, hugging her under the blanket again and sighing with pleasure. "Nine. Why? What time is it?"

"Seven-thirtyish."

"Hmm." He held on tighter, sliding a hand into her robe to cup her breast. "Heaven."

Lumi didn't breathe. She was starting to panic. No man had ... his hand was on her ... he had done it as if it were the most natural ... it felt ... really fantastic, she realized, calming down. It felt glorious and comforting. His fingers weren't moving, and he clearly wasn't trying to excite her. His hand was seeking closeness and intimacy, nothing more.

After another few minutes of relaxing together, she sat up again. Turning to face him, she asked, "Are you always this adorable in the morning?"

He didn't answer.

She tried to memorize his features, glad he was resting and unaware that she was luxuriating in staring at his features. Nolan's eyebrows were as perfect as his eyes and lashes. His forehead was tanner than the rest of his face. His morning stubble was manly. He reminded her of a young Joel McCrea, but with fuller lips and a more handsome nose. Gazing at his lips made her ache to hold him and kiss him for hours. Remembering he had to get to work, she sighed and asked, "Taking a shower here or at home?"

"Are you joining me?" he asked hopefully, looking up at her.

"No."

"Humph. Might as well go home." He frowned playfully.

"I can get you breakfast first. I don't want to send you out into the world all starving and pitiful."

"Breakfast would be great, thanks." He reached for her and they kissed. "Good morning, hon bun."

Her eyes twinkled. "Oh, wow—I'm somebody's 'hon bun' now. Feels awesome." She giggled, then her expression sobered. *"Wait.* I forgot I'm a strong, independent woman, not some hunk's 'hon bun.' I'm conflicted."

"Be both."

"Yeah. I'll be both. Okay, Nolan. Up and at 'em."

Fifteen minutes later, Lumi put a plate of pancakes and sausage links in front of Nolan at the dining table. "I'll make myself some later."

"So, did we resolve anything last night?" he asked, pouring syrup.

Lumi blushed for a moment, then realized he was talking about Maddy and her cards. "We're a hundred times closer to solving the mystery than we were before, but I'm not sure how close that really is, to be honest."

"No 'who' for the 'what,' and no 'why' or 'how.' And yum, Lu—this is *outstanding.* Your meatloaf dinner was great, too. I think I was too preoccupied that night to say so."

She patted his hand.

"I usually eat bland and protein and healthy after a workout in the morning."

She pushed a yellow Depression glass butter dish across the table. "Poor Nolan! Here; have more butter."

He laughed. After eating for a while, he grinned and said, "We spent the night together, you realize."

"Really? I had no idea. Did we have fun?"

"We slept soundly, I'm afraid."

Lumi winked. "I have the day off. Too bad you don't."

He swallowed. "Well, *someone* has to get out there and defend Barnwood."

"Actually—I almost forgot. I have a dental appointment. I haven't had a checkup since moving back to town. I'm seeing a new dentist today." Lumi glanced around at what she could see of her house. "I feel nervous about having you here all night and now for breakfast—like my mother is going to walk in on us at any second."

"Nice, though. I'm loving this."

She watched the pleasure he took in sitting with her as he ate. Her nervousness faded away, and a new feeling blossomed. She saw future nights and mornings with him, his face stubbly before he shaved. Teasing and laughing, sitting together for meals and movies. Talking about dentist and doctor appointments. Waking up together. Going to bed together and holding each other. Making love. Reading together. Walking in the woods. Setting an alarm or sleeping in late. Kissing whenever the urge struck.

"What's that dreamy look about?" he asked, finishing his milk and then wiping his mouth.

Lumi didn't answer. She reached for his hand under the table and looked away.

He stood, tilted her chin, gave her a brief kiss that left her burning for more, and left.

After she'd washed their dishes and started a small load of laundry, Lumi took a shower and got dressed at last. Putting on sandals, preparing to cross the street to talk to Maddy about the ice show discovery, she was surprised to hear a knock at her door.

"Cammie! So cool you came over. Come on in."

"I asked Nole for your address a little while ago, telling him I wanted to smooth things over a bit more. He told me to leave my brass knuckles at home." She followed Lumi into the kitchen. Leaning against the refrigerator, she said, "And I *do* need to smooth things over. I shouldn't have hit your window like that—given you the death stare, either."

Lumi shook her head and tugged at her earlobe. "I told you that was exactly what I needed. I was so stuck in my own world that I hadn't stopped to realize how my actions looked to you all and how they would have made Nolan feel. It was the start of a better road."

Cammie crossed her arms. "I'm overprotective of him."

"I love that you did that. I mean, it's sweet that you care about your big brother that much. I was the enemy at that point, so …"

"Big?" Cammie asked, one eyebrow cocked.

"What?"

"Ha! Nole is our *baby* brother." She uncrossed her arms, smiling. "Didn't you know that?"

Lumi froze in place, stunned. *"Baby* brother?"

"Sure. Magnus is the oldest. He remembers you from school because he was a grade ahead of you. I was a grade below you. Nolan was last. Didn't he ever tell you his age?"

Lumi was the one who cocked an eyebrow this time. "No. I … guess I assumed he was the oldest. So, that makes Nolan about twenty-five?"

"He'll be twenty-four in September."

"Oh. Well. Huh. Four years younger."

Cammie suppressed a smile and swung her feathery brown hair behind her back. "Well, I guess you two *are* just now getting to know each other."

The two women sat at the dining table.

"Should we start over?" Cammie asked, holding out a hand. "Hello. I'm Camilla. Nole's sister. Mike's wife. Magnus' sister. Alisa's sis-in-law. How are you?"

Lumi took her hand and shook it. "I'm okay now. Done running off, probably."

"Good." She took a breath. "Lumi, I'm starting to doubt that you know much of what Nole's been through. You know he's a widower, right?"

Lumi nodded, thinking she should hear Nolan's private life from him directly.

Cammie put her palms flat on the table in front of her, shifting in her seat. "It was sad. We couldn't believe how fast Carol was gone. Nolan was left half the person he had been. I won't get into details, but he didn't have a great childhood. He was sick a lot, and our parents went absolutely broke from medical bills, even after insurance covered a big part of the expense. He felt angry and guilty in turns. When his wife passed away, we were worried he'd get sick again. Emotional trauma can do such crappy things to your body. So, Magnus and I made a pact to be there for him as much as possible. Mag told him to look into joining the military or the police force. Having discipline and physical work to do would get Nole's mind in a better place, he thought, and it did. Nolan got bulkier and bulkier working out every day, and the police department folks are like his second family. He knows so many more people in town now, and he's strong and stable. But," Cammie said, taking a breath, "we still worry about him. If you wondered why I was irrationally angry when you abandoned him, well … now maybe you can understand my motivation a little."

"I do, but I always understood it was because you love him."

Cammie looked into Lumi's eyes more directly. "If you feel like he's smothering you, don't let him. He is just about as inexperienced at relationships as you are. Carol was his first girlfriend and his last. There's been no one else before you, as far as I know." She stood. "I should go, but I wanted to clear the air."

Lumi paused, thinking about how to say another thing that she wanted to get out in the open. "I … don't have any friends in town other than Nolan and the older lady across the street."

"Well, you do now."

Lumi stood, too. "I wasn't fishing. I was leading up to this: you and Alisa and the guys have made me sad, in a way. I've been lonesome for a long time. Shy for a long time. Having Nolan in my life made me angry at myself, and sad, too. I had been missing out on just about everything by being determinedly alone. He is showing me what being … desired feels like, and how fantastic desiring in return is. And, well, being around all of you at dinners and the party has also made me sad. I've missed a lot. I almost don't know how to be a friend at this stage of my life."

Cammie met her eyes sincerely. *"This* is how. You're already doing it." After a pause, her tone of voice changed. "But, Lumi … be a little more honest with yourself, okay? I don't believe you're all that shy. Not like you feel you are. If you were, you wouldn't be able to run your shop and talk to strangers the way you do. Think hard. Are you actually shy, or have you avoided getting close and having real relationships for a different reason?"

Lumi pulled her damp hair off her neck and leaned against the edge of the table, reaching behind her for added support.

Cammie tried to explain. *"No* one is naturally good at being friendly with strangers. You have to work at it. If you do it long enough, it becomes a habit. If you're lazy, you're never going to feel comfortable. Flex your muscles. Put some real effort into caring about other people more than your own fragile ego. It's hard—especially if you've let yourself be self-absorbed for years and years."

Lumi blinked. She looked through her window, her face hot. What Cammie was saying hurt, but maybe that was because it was true.

Cammie went on, "It's the same thing with a romance. Maybe you've never had real romantic love in your life because you weren't willing to put any effort into a relationship. Here's a news flash: no one ever rushes up to anyone begging them to be their girlfriend. It's a two-way street, like every other friendship. I don't care how gorgeous or ugly you are— or think you are—if you don't meet someone at least halfway, nothing will ever come of it."

Lumi took a few breaths, thinking.

Cammie added, "It sounds like you'll have to do some soul-searching, Lumi. But, if you want friends, you'll have them. I don't just mean the Sanders clan. You're smart. You're funny and interesting. You *are* likable. Open up your heart to people around you, at least a little, and I think you'll be surprised at what comes in return." She paused, reading Lumi's expression. "Lumi, I know you don't like some of what I've said today. Please, though, think about it. I already care about you. I say these things because I *do* care, not because I hold any bad feelings toward you. All right?"

Lumi nodded, her face feeling hot. "I get it. But I … feel like I've been in emotional boot camp lately."

"I'm glad Nolan has you." Cammie smiled. "That's the most important thing to take away from my visit. The others of us are, too. I'll let you in on a secret: we felt like you were taking Nole for a ride. You're very pretty. We didn't know if you were using him as a plaything or *what* you were doing. None of us could have imagined that you were some sweet, inexperienced girl afraid of Nolan's … manliness."

Lumi's brows drew together. She saw things from their point of view. "Did I come off as that shallow?"

Cammie shrugged. "I was worried my brother had fallen for someone wholly different than you turned out to be. You are very much the opposite of who I thought you were when you ran from the back yard on the Fourth." She smiled. "Seeing you in his arms on the dance floor—that was what *really* melted my heart. He was singing to you. I haven't heard him sing since he was in school."

Lumi frowned with emotion. "I want to earn your family's trust as much as Nolan's."

Cammie bit her lip, looking a little like Nolan when he did the same thing. "Don't feel like I'm pressuring you to change, but if you want to be more sociable, think about what I said. Put yourself out there. As to the Sanders ... we'll soon understand you better, and you'll understand us better. And there's no goal line to rush toward. Take whatever time you need to realize that you're very welcome at our table."

"Maddy?" Lumi called through the screen door.

"Come in. I'm in the back."

Lumi found her in the laundry room. "Hi." She leaned against the washer.

"Hi, yourself." Maddy blushed as she studiously concentrated on folding an uncooperative navy blue fitted sheet.

Lumi wondered why her friend seemed embarrassed. "Uh, Maddy?"

"Yes, dear."

"Can we talk?"

"Shouldn't you be talking about these things with your mother?"

Puzzled, Lumi asked, "What?"

Maddy gave up on the sheet and pushed the wad of it into a wicker laundry basket. Tony eyed the basket as if considering making it his bed for the day. "About ... the facts of life."

"Maddy, I have zero idea what you're talking about."

"I know Nolan Sanders spent the night with you. I got here very early this morning and saw that his truck was out front. Not that I should have been shocked—you *are* an adult."

Lumi went to the kitchen and sat, putting her laptop on the table. She felt embarrassed and indignant. "We're not doing what you're imagining, Maddy."

"Not that it's any of my nevermind."

"Maddy, you say that you and Chess are spending every night together, but that it's strictly platonic. Right?"

Maddy inhaled and joined her at the table, folding her hands on her lap. She looked through her window at the birds and bees. "That's different. We're old. We're only good friends."

"I do believe you. Honestly. But, if you *were* having relations in those sheets you just pushed into your basket, would you want me to judge you?"

The older woman's eyes dampened. "I'm just worried about you."

"And I appreciate it. A little. I think."

Maddy suddenly laughed. She slapped Lumi's hand. "Maybe I'm all huffy because I'm jealous."

Lumi smiled, then laughed, too. "Ah. *There* it is. Confession is good for the soul."

"Well, how would *you* feel if you spent evenings and nights with a man who claims to love you but who never even once tried to jump your bones? Even though I *have* invited him into my bed on a few occasions."

"Maddy!" Lumi practically screamed. "Too much information! Too much information!" She covered her ears playfully.

"Well, Lumi dear, if you didn't come to me for tips on avoiding pregnancy, and if Nolan spent the night but wasn't able to successfully seduce you, and since you have your computer thing with you on this visit, I have to wonder: what's up?"

Lumi stood to pour herself a cup of coffee. "Firstly, I've been on birth control for years. I haven't needed it for its intended purpose, but still—contraception is not an issue. Secondly, Nolan is very seductive. I am not ready for the main event just yet, and I really don't think he is, either. Thirdly, I have to talk to you about the cards."

"Oh, yes. I did phone up that photographer. He's rather rude, isn't he? Turns out he isn't the man who took the shots of Ras and me."

Lumi sat and reached for a napkin to wipe up a drop of coffee she'd spilled. Surprised, she asked, "He's not?"

"The man said it was likely his father, who's passed on now. They shared the same name."

"Huh. Do you still you want to meet with him?"

"I really don't see a reason. The father is dead and gone."

Lumi sipped her coffee. Lowering her cup, she finally said, "I have a difficult thing to tell you." She paused, wondering how to start her story. She told Maddy about the box of letters, and some of the details in them, including Mama's painful legs.

"I don't think I know anyone named Jackie. I don't see much help there."

"Don't dismiss my story yet."

Maddy seemed surprised. "No? Why? How could a group of random old letters help us find out who's trying to scare me?"

Lumi lowered her cup to the table. "Because I now know how Mama's legs got hurt. She finally wrote it all out in the letter I read late last night. That's why I called Nolan to come over. Earlier in the evening, I'd told him about your troubles. When we were done talking about all of that and he'd gone home, I went up to bed to read another letter. In it, Mama talks about going to an ice show in Indianapolis, and about a tragedy that happened there. Her legs were crushed. She wrote about blood and death being all around her in the rubble."

Maddy's face drained of color.

Lumi was frightened as she watched it happen. She had heard the term applied to people who experience a shock, but she couldn't ever remember seeing the phenomenon. Pressing on, Lumi said, "I did an internet search. When I saw what came up on my screen, I called Nolan to come over again. He ended up sleeping on my sofa overnight since it was very late when we'd finished talking. Maddy, the images in your cards match photos of the nineteen sixty-three Coliseum explosion following an ice show on Halloween night. The stereocards were made from photos taken at the scene."

Maddy inhaled sharply, dropping her face into her hands.

Lumi opened her laptop and searched again for the news stories and photos. "Look. Here they are. Most are in black and white, like your cards, but some are in color. And there are archived television stories. They show the same sort of rubble, the same sort of injuries. The popcorn boxes match the one in your card—the chunks of the building match. The clothing styles are the same. The seating is in pieces everywhere. The wetness on the floor must be melting ice. I couldn't figure out why the floor seemed water-wet as well as blood-wet. This explains it."

Mrs. Rasmusson didn't look at the computer. She laid her head on her hands on the table, silent, unmoving. After a long moment, she raised her head enough to speak. "I know why I had such a bad feeling when I saw the studio portraits. I remember now."

Lumi, sensing her friend was struggling, moved closer in her chair, her eyes concerned. "Oh, Maddy. Oh, honey. Why?"

Maddy trembled, her eyes wet and sorrowful. "This is a long story. Let's go sit out in the sun where I won't have such a chill."

Lumi helped the woman to stand and led her through the squeaky screen door where they sat on the porch in white wooden rocking chairs. The sun's rays didn't reach them at that time of the day, but it was warmer than inside the cool house. Pulling her chair closer to Maddy's, Lumi asked, "What about the photographer?"

"I remember now, but I'll have to start with what came before the photographer." Maddy rocked forward, her elbows on the armrests. She tugged at the sleeves of her yellow blouse, stalling. "You see, when I was young, I worked in the Coliseum's concessions booth."

Lumi gasped, her eyes widening in shock. She nearly cried, dreading what was to come, feeling panic rising in her chest but fighting it away, knowing she needed to be strong for what her friend was about to reveal.

Maddy went on, "They paid more than other food places. I didn't have a college education, and when I heard about the rates they paid, it seemed like a good job compared to what I could earn here in town. I carpooled most of the time with friends who also worked in Indianapolis and lived in Barnwood. Coliseum employees usually got tickets to see the shows when we weren't working." She half-smiled. "It was a fun place—so many people, so much activity. The entertainments were grand, big, *spectacular*. I felt lucky to be a part of the events, even in a small way. The boys who worked there were friendly and good-looking, and we were a jolly bunch. I had such a wonderful year." Maddy's smile wavered, and a tear fell from her eye to her lap.

Lumi dashed into the house for a box of tissues. Back with Maddy, she leaned against the back of her rocker, her heart pounding, hating where the story was leading.

Maddy pulled out a tissue to hold, looking down at her shoes. "I even sort of loved one of the boys. He worked concessions, too. He was the main draw for me." She paused, seeming to remember more details. "Scoots. I don't remember his real name anymore. I know we called him Scoots. Blonde. Big, blue, impish eyes. He had Halloween off, and he wanted to take me to a costume party. I was scheduled to work that night, making popcorn and vending drinks—that sort of thing, but Scoots wanted to take me out. Our first time going on a date. I was supposed to work, but I told him yes, anyway." She wiped her eyes, a heartbroken expression on her face. "I drove halfway to Indy, and he met me halfway. There, I got into his big dented-in car from the nineteen-forties, and we went on to the party at his uncle's house." Her face brightened. "It was crazy and fun, oh my! I went as a cat. I wore a black leotard outfit and a white bib with shiny black buttons down the front, and a black bowtie. I'd made a long, skinny tail from black pantyhose. I made felt cat ears and glued them to barrettes for my hair. At the party, there was a little drinking and carrying on, but nothing too wild. When Scoots said we should go, he drove me back to my car in Noblesville at a diner parking lot where I'd left it. He kissed me when we were going to separate. I had drawn whiskers on my face with a ball-point pen, and I think I looked pretty juvenile, but he kissed me, anyway."

Lumi burst into tears, her fingers up to her lips. *"No,* Maddy. Oh, *no!"*

Both women sat on the porch and cried together, each on their own chairs, holding hands.

After a long, long time, Maddy whispered, "Scoots killed himself."

"What? Oh, *God,* no! Why?"

"He'd given his little brother …"

"Maddy! No!"

"… his little brother his ticket for the show. That boy died. Scoots lost friends. He felt responsible because …"

"He'd taken you out."

"He called me the next day. I can still hear the croakiness of his voice as he blamed himself for the explosion." Maddy covered her eyes with the hand holding the tissue, her lips quivering. "All those *people.* All that destruction and *suffering. Death* and *blood* and the *building* destroyed. So many injuries that people are living with to this *day!"*

Both ladies shook with sobs. Lumi sat on the white wooden floor, her hands gripping Maddy's tightly, her head on the woman's knee.

After a few moments of quieter crying, Lumi finally asked, "How did you not recognize the images on the cards?"

Maddy wiped her eyes again. "I never saw them. My mother wouldn't allow it, and I was still living at home. No newspapers. No TV. No one spoke of it around me. I never saw a single photo. After the first reports on the radio, off it went. Dad would have liked to have *thrown* the TV and radio right out the window—let me tell you—to protect my feelings."

"I can understand that. What a *terrible* time for you all." Lumi wept lightly. When she could bear to speak, she said, "Dear Maddy. I am very, *very* sorry. I don't know *how* I'll ever forgive myself for reminding you of these things."

The older woman smoothed Lumi's hair gently. "How could you have known? How could you have known that it would trigger such profound sadness and guilt even these many years later?"

Lumi looked up at her. "But you *do* realize now that you were in *no way* responsible for the explosion. You know that in your heart, don't you? You were no more guilty of anything than Scoots was. If you don't blame him, how can you blame yourself?"

Maddy dabbed her eyes. "My mom ordered me to forget it. No one talked about the tragedy around me except Chess."

"Chess?"

She nodded. "A great good pal. Built like a stone wall, and as solid as one. He let me talk about it. But I … I held back, even with him. I didn't tell him certain things. He never knew I went out to a party that night. He thought I wasn't scheduled to work, that I was only mourning the loss of my friends and coworkers. I never told him that I should have been working. I think … I think I made myself believe, over time, that *that* was the true story. I told myself I had escaped death by a twist of fate. I wasn't meant to be there. I wasn't assigned to be there. God wanted to spare me, so I wasn't scheduled for that night. And on and on and on."

Something didn't add up. "But Maddy—why have you carried such a burden of guilt? Skipping work on that fateful night didn't cause a chain of events that led to the explosion. How could it have mattered if you had worked or if Scoots had kept his ticket to the show?"

Maddy shook her head, a tissue to her nose and mouth. She squeezed her eyes tightly shut, forcing out tears. "I *know* it. I *know* it's the truth. If I had been there, I might have known there was a leak. I was such a careful worker. Maybe if I had been behind the concessions counter, I would have … *something*. I feel like I upset the balance of the universe by shirking my duties that night, simply to have a date with a boy I liked."

Lumi looked away, through the slats of the porch railing, beyond the driveway and the yards along the street. She could almost see one of the wounded men from the photos on the stereocards, a hand outstretched to the camera. "You *did* repress your memories. Self-preservation made you do that. It sounds like you had help from your parents, too. Even though they went overboard to shelter you at the time, don't you think it was the best thing? You may have ended up letting the guilt do to you what it did to Scoots."

Maddy gulped at air and nodded. "Survivor's guilt. I let people believe that's all that was depressing me. What I was suffering felt like a darker cousin to depression. It nearly ate me whole."

Lumi got up from the floor and returned to her rocking chair. She stared at the annoyingly sunny day and the flowers and green grass.

"Now, about the photographer," Maddy said hoarsely. "I married Ras a couple of years after the explosion. Mom encouraged us. She could see I was never going to leave home unless she pushed me out. I had no hope

186

in my heart. No plans for the future." She looked over at Lumi. "Oh, yes, dear—I may, indeed, have been about to follow in Scoots' path. Ras was such a sweet, funny, happy man. Generous. An antidote to the poison in my heart. I never talked to him about the explosion and my part in it. That was my mother's advice, and I followed it. We married. Had a daughter. I lost two more pregnancies, but we had Jem. One day for our anniversary, Ras set up a studio session so we could get nice pictures taken." She took a bracing breath. "We had our photos shot and were done in a few minutes. Afterward, instead of going out through the front door where we came in, and where the road was being repaired, the man said we could take a shortcut to the parking lot through his side door." Maddy stopped talking, frozen for a moment before she burst into renewed tears. Finally able to continue, she said, "We went through what looked like an art gallery room, but with photos instead of paintings. There were these large black-and-white pictures on easels and the walls. Poster-sized—probably three feet tall. They were images taken at the Coliseum that night."

Lumi felt gooseflesh rise on her body. "Oh, *no!* And you'd avoided seeing them for all those years, too."

"Ras wanted to look them over. Being his usual friendly self, he called for the photographer to come back to us to talk to him about the shots. I was horrified! Lumi, it was like I'd been sent deep into hell."

"Oh, Maddy!"

"I didn't know what to do. If I'd reacted, I would have had to tell Ras about my part in that night. I didn't know what to do. I pretended interest in the blown-up photos. I endured it, but once we got home, I said I had a headache and had to lie down." She breathed raggedly. "It nearly did me in. I was sick in bed for several days."

Lumi closed her eyes and lowered her head. "I'm *achingly* sorry. That must have been *torture.*"

Maddy's lips quivered again. "I willed myself to bury those thoughts once more and forever. I had a husband. A daughter. I had people around me who were counting on me day and night. I had to stuff the memories away in a mental drawer. I had to! But do you know what? The enlarged photos in the studio were not the ones on the stereocards. I think if they'd been the same ones, I would have known right away what they were. I suppose that man, and a lot of news photographers, were at the site of the tragedy. And maybe some folks who had cameras with them at the ice show also took photos after the explosion."

Lumi's phone pinged. She looked at the message that appeared.

"Have you spoken to Maddy yet?"

187

"It's Nolan. He's asking about you. What should I say?"

Maddy blew her nose and sniffled, frowning. "I guess maybe … can you do the talking to him now? I'm so tired. This is a terrible thing to relive."

"I don't want to leave you today. When is Chess coming over?"

"He won't be here until after supper, like usual. Don't fret, Lumi. You go on and do. I'll sit here a while and think about my baby and my Ras and my grandsons, and how I have Chess and church and friends."

Lumi knew a piece of the puzzle was still missing. Maddy wasn't telling her everything—she could feel it in her bones. She could almost hear Maddy start to say one thing, then change to another. She was positive that her friend was keeping yet more secrets. Feeling it wasn't doing any kindness to press for more details, she asked, "Where is your daughter? Can she come over to be with you today? I have a dentist appointment, I'm sorry to say. It's certainly not as important as being with you, but I want you to recover from your shock. If I stay, I'll keep reminding you of that terrible time."

"I don't know her schedule at the hospital since it changes week to week. I'll call her. See if she can visit."

"Do that. I'll wait here with you."

Maddy swallowed, her lips quivering. "I'm okay. I'm a little fearful, but okay. But Lu, we *still* don't know who sent those stereocards. Or why. *That's* what I'm scared about. I guess I'll always have guilt, but it's got to be like you said. If I don't blame Scoots, how can I blame myself?"

Lumi sighed loudly, wiping tears from her eyes and cheeks. She wondered if Maddy was saying what she thought Lumi wanted to hear instead of what she really believed.

The woman rocked, nodding as if the motion of the rocker was moving her head involuntarily. "I'm fine, baby girl. I'll call Chess if Jem can't come."

"I'm waiting with you until one or the other gets here."

"Oh, my dear—stay if you want, but please do the talking to your Nolan. I don't want to go through this story again."

"So, you're not going to tell Jem or Chess?" Lumi asked, surprised.

"No." She looked at Lumi. "Can you understand? Today has taken me on a walk through hell. Please … don't ask me to go again."

Lumi gripped her friend's hand. "You call Jem; I'll call Nolan. Here—take my phone."

"She won't answer a call from a stranger. I'll have to go inside to use my phone."

Lumi followed her, nervous. She waited until Maddy was almost ready to say goodbye to Jem before she grabbed the receiver. "Is this Jem? This is your mom's neighbor, Lumi Leski. Hello. Did you tell your mom you're coming over here? No? Okay. I'll have to see if Chess can come. It's *vitally* important that she has company today, and I do wish ... you will? That would be really, really great, Jem. Honestly, just perfect. I'll wait with her until you get here. Thanks."

Maddy protested. "She's busy. You should have let me call Chess."

Lumi replaced the phone onto its charging stand. "I think you need your daughter here today. She sounds very nice—very concerned."

The older woman blinked in agreement, then went to sit at the kitchen table. "A joy."

Lumi dialed Nolan on her own phone. "Hi. I'm with Maddy. We've had a long, terrible talk this morning. I'll explain everything when we can get together. I'm waiting with her until her daughter arrives. Can you get a break this afternoon? No? Okay. You let me know. Oh, and if you haven't spoken to anyone there about the stereocards, please don't. Everything will be clear when we can talk. Please believe and trust me when I say that keeping the story of the stereocards between us is a far, far better thing to do than making it public. Thank you, Nolan. Great. Me, too. Bye."

Maddy looked up, her mouth open. "Did ... did he just say, 'I love you'?"

"No."

"Well, *what* did you say 'Me, too' about?"

"I think he said, 'Looking forward to seeing you.'"

Maddy's face fell. "Oh. Disappointing."

Lumi laughed, happy to have the mood lightened. "You *rascal.* You and your Chess are one and the same in a lot of ways. When are you going to give in and make it official?"

Maddy shook her head. "I don't think I will. I like how we have things now. There's always more to a story. I have reservations."

"Yeah, but think of the savings if you have only one house and one set of utility bills and property taxes to pay."

"Listen, Lumi girl, how about *this* idea? How about if I stay out of your love life, and you stay out of mine?"

"Is that a possibility?" Lumi teased.

Maddy leaned back in her chair. "Oh, probably not, now that you put it like that."

They both chuckled.

"So many of us love you. Don't let this hurt you again," Lumi said sincerely.

Maddy's eyes darkened, but then they seemed to clear. "I'm glad you got Jem to come. I don't see enough of her. Or her husband. Or their two boys, now that they're grown." She reached for another tissue from a box on the table. Shifting position, she said, "Let me say one last thing about your romance, all right? *Embrace* it. You're given one life, baby girl. Don't let fears and your past dictate today and tomorrow. Don't be afraid to love. Don't be afraid to push it away if it isn't right. Find your own two feet. Take it or leave it, but if this man is good and kind and he turns your socks inside out just looking at him, let him know. Open your heart. Have sex or don't. Wait until you're married or don't. Have babies or don't. Do what feels exactly right without looking at a clock or calendar."

Lumi grinned. "Take your own advice, Mrs. R. Take your own advice."

"Mom?" a woman's voice called through the screen door.

"In here, Jem," Maddy answered. "That was fast, babycakes. You must have shot through red lights."

The squeaky door slammed shut. Seconds later, a middle-aged woman with short blonde hair wearing Kermit the Frog scrubs came into the kitchen. "I was in my car not far from here when you called. Is everything all right?"

Lumi answered for Maddy. "It is, and it isn't. Hi, I'm Lumi. I live across the street now, but I grew up a few blocks away. I think I remember you, but you were already grown and moved out when I was little."

Jem pointed at Lumi, smiling in recognition. "Pigtails and a tricycle, and later you had a bike with training wheels, right? Two older brothers at the willow tree house?"

"Yep."

Jem's forehead wrinkled in concentration. "I have a particular memory of you. One day you were out front on the sidewalk. A plumber had been working under our bathroom sink, and he managed to cut his head badly. He ran down the hallway and out the door trying to wrap a towel around his bleeding wound. I was right behind him, and I'll never forget the look on your face. You were *scared!* Bolted off on your trike as fast as your skinny little legs could go!"

Maddy and Lumi looked at each other, shocked.

"Of all the things to bring up, Jem!" Maddy exclaimed.

Lumi laughed. "How weird! I recently told your mom about a dream I had that must have been because of that incident." She took in a deliberate breath, her expression and voice more somber. "Listen, Jem—I had a long talk with your mom that deeply, terribly upset her. She doesn't want to talk about it, and I agree. It would be too much stress for her to get into what we discussed yet again. I don't want you to leave her alone today. Please wait until Chess comes over for the night before you take off."

Jem raised her eyebrows as she finally lifted her large denim purse onto the table. "Why would Chess Amberton be coming over *here* for the night?"

Lumi slapped a hand over her mouth.

"Just go, Lumi girl. I'll fill her in on those details," Maddy said, exasperated.

Lumi bent to whisper into her friend's ear before leaving. "But don't give out *too* much information, Mrs. R."

Chapter Fourteen

After her dentist appointment, Lumi didn't know what to do for the rest of the day. Emotionally drained, she thought about going back to Maddy's but felt she would open a wound if she visited too soon. Nolan couldn't take a break to see her, and she didn't want to work in her store and didn't want to shop or do housework.

Driving through downtown, she saw from its red-letter marquee that Barnwood's historic art deco tile-fronted theater was showing classic films during the day and new releases at night. She pulled into a parking lot and grabbed the brown sweatshirt she kept on her back seat.

"When does the next movie start?" Lumi asked a young man who was wearing a vintage crushed red velvet usher's cap.

"In about ten minutes," he said through the brass speech box in the ticket window.

"Good. I'll take a ticket."

"No need. The daytime shows are free. We encourage concession purchases, though. Enjoy the show."

She stepped inside the palatial entrance hall. Dark red, gold, cubed glass, and brass accents were everywhere in sweeping curves. Lumi checked for emails and messages and then turned off the volume on her phone. She bought popcorn and cola at the glass-and-brass neon-lit concession counter and went into the auditorium to find a seat. The popcorn nearly made her cry, remembering Maddy's story. The concession stand nearly made her cry, too.

Sitting in the center seat in the center row, she was almost the only person in the room. She put her sweatshirt over the back of the seat next to hers, the soda in a cup holder on her armrest, and munched her buttery popcorn, reviewing the conversations she'd had that day. She knew she needed to pull herself out of the depressing visions of the Coliseum explosion and her friend's part of that horrible event, and hoped that the movie would help.

"Is this seat taken?" a voice asked from behind her.

Lumi was startled as she looked up. "Alisa! Hi! Come and sit with me."

"I had a popcorn craving. I can't do a damn thing anymore, it feels like, so I visited Mag for a while at the shop and then decided to head over here for the afternoon." Alisa walked with difficulty along the row, her protruding belly bumping the back of the seats they faced. She sat at

Lumi's right, settling in with her drink and tub of popcorn. "This kid can't come soon enough!"

Lumi put her popcorn on the empty seat at her left and wiped her fingers with a napkin. "It just occurred to me that I don't know what movie we're going to see."

"Quiet Man."

"Oh, sorry," Lumi whispered, looking apologetic. "What movie are they showing?"

Alisa sputtered, trying to hold back, but then she burst into cackling laughter. "Girl, you're *hilarious!*"

Lumi smiled weakly, not understanding. Soon the long, burgundy velour curtains parted, and the movie screen flickered into bright life. When the title appeared, Lumi cracked up laughing, too.

Alisa elbowed her, and Lumi elbowed Alisa.

"I honestly had no idea there was a movie called *The Quiet Man,*" Lumi said softly.

"Hilarious!" Alisa said again, chewing. "I'll have to remember to tell everyone this the next time we're all together."

They settled more comfortably into their seats, and Lumi picked up her popcorn again. The movie was a revelation. It was from the early nineteen-fifties, but the plot's message spoke right to her as if it had been made solely to help her think more clearly about her relationship with Nolan. Too many silly things can block forward movement in a romance: stubbornness, false propriety, pride, and concern about the opinions of others. When the end credits rolled, Lumi was too emotional to stand to leave.

Alisa shook open one of her folded napkins and used it to blow her nose. *"So* good. Gets me every time I see it."

Lumi frowned in sympathy.

Alisa stared into her almost-empty popcorn box, checking for a last popped kernel among the old maids at the bottom. "I think Mary Kate is preggers at the end. That's what she's telling Sean Thornton before they high-tail it back to the cottage."

"I think so, too," Lumi agreed, coming back to non-cinematic reality. She watched Alisa struggle for a few seconds before standing to help the woman get out of her seat. They glanced at each other and then hugged for a long moment, the baby inside Alisa between them.

Back home, Lumi took a bath and brushed bits of popcorn kernels out of her teeth. She dried and curled her long hair, put on makeup and a blue-flowered short-sleeved top and dark blue capri pants. She carried her sandals downstairs where she watched a comedy series while waiting for Nolan to call or come.

He came, still in his police uniform. He knocked, stepped inside after she opened the door, and slumped onto the sofa, not greeting Lumi except with a light crease of concern between his eyes.

Lumi closed the door, turned off the television, and walked around the sofa to hug his neck from behind, her cheek against his.

He sighed, patting her arm. "Bad day."

Lumi went into the kitchen and poured two glasses of iced tea and brought them to the coffee table. Sensing he needed to relax in silence, she sat beside him, her head against his shoulder.

After a couple of minutes, Nolan sighed and drank down almost half of his tea. He ran his hand over his head and finally spoke. "Just the worst day. Feels good to be with you. I can't even express how wonderful it is to come here where you are at the end of the day."

Lumi frowned sympathetically. "I love having you. Of course. Of course. Want to tell me about it?"

"I don't know. Don't you have something to talk to *me* about? You called when you were with Mrs. R this morning."

She considered for a moment. "It can wait. No rush. We'll just sit here for a while." Lumi took his glass from him and put it onto the table. She unbuttoned his uniform shirt and helped him take it off so he was only wearing a white t-shirt on top. She undid his duty belt, and he put his police equipment on the table. She untied his black shoes so he could slide them off. She then stood and lifted his legs onto the cushions and put a pillow under his head. "I'm going to order a pizza."

"You look nice. We should go out. Let me go home to shower and change."

"I'd rather not, honestly. What toppings do you like?"

He closed his eyes, breathing what sounded like a sigh of relief. "Anything normal. No hot peppers. No pineapple. No anchovies. Anything else is fine."

She went into the kitchen to order the pizza from the restaurant's website, purposely staying out of the living room to make it easier for Nolan to take a nap before the pizza was delivered. She glanced at the back of the sofa. He remained out of sight, and the thin blanket wasn't in its place; he must have pulled it over himself.

Lumi switched off the air conditioner and then made a salad, folded laundry on the dining table, and checked auction sites on her phone for sales the next day, alert for sounds from Nolan or the delivery driver.

After nearly an hour, she heard a car door slam outside. Lumi tipped the driver and put the pizza on the kitchen counter as Nolan finally sat up.

He flung the blanket onto the back of the sofa and walked to the kitchen as she was putting out bowls for the salad.

"Ready to eat?"

"I'll run upstairs first. Back in a minute."

Lumi placed the salad, dinner plates, dressings, pizza, and forks on the table and carried the glasses into the kitchen from the coffee table and refreshed Nolan's tea.

When Nolan returned, he hugged her tightly. "I needed that nap. You were sweet to do that." He sat down and opened the pizza box, lifting out a hot, gooey slice for her plate and one for his own.

Lumi went to a drawer next to the refrigerator and pulled out a handful of napkins. "My house is your house. My sofa is your sofa." She sat but didn't start to eat. "Would it be better if we didn't have any serious conversation tonight? I don't know what you went through today, but I can see it must have been bad."

He put his fork on his salad dish and took one of her hands in his on the table, looking at nothing through the window. "I saw a child nearly die this afternoon. A little girl. She was playing with firecrackers near the park." Nolan cleared his throat. "I was nearby, over in the next block. I was there in a minute. She was injured badly. The ambulance came faster than I've ever seen one arrive, and when the ambulance was gone, and I was left there to ...." He rubbed the back of his neck. "I should be used to these experiences, but how can anyone that sees a child hurt that severely *not* be affected?"

She stood and hugged him from the side, her head on his. "Oh, Nolan." Part of her was panicking, a part wanted to erase his haunting visions, and another part was afraid she was doing everything wrong. She wasn't used to being needed, especially not intensely. She pushed the heavy table back and sat on Nolan's lap, facing him, straddling him, hugging him around his neck.

He didn't move, but he did make a sound from his chest that could have been a sob.

Lumi had a flash of thousands of nights ahead of them. Of the uncountable, terrible things Nolan would have to endure and witness. How had he gotten through these things when he was alone? How could he be the generous, loving man she knew him to be if trauma and tragedies were a large part of his life? Could she *do* this? Could she go through this with him now, and do it over and over again for a lifetime?

How can I not? she answered herself silently.

Nolan's forehead and throat were overheated and sweating.

Lumi switched on the air conditioner after leaving Nolan's lap. She went upstairs to the bathroom and returned with a warm, wet washcloth and a towel. Beside him again, she gently washed his face and neck, then dried him with a delicate touch as he sat very still.

When she had finished, Nolan took a few breaths. He scanned her body, seemingly lost in thought. "That felt … intimate."

She carried the towel and washcloth into the laundry room beyond the kitchen. From there, she turned and said, "I guess it was."

He began eating when she rejoined him at the table.

"Nole," Lumi said, using his family's nickname for him, "what I have to tell you—it's mighty upsetting. You decide: should we have all of our sad conversations out and over with tonight, or should I tell you the details about Maddy later?"

"I don't know." He took a drink and ran a finger across the condensation on the glass. "Let's get a little food into our stomachs for now. Turn on some music, please. What did you do today?"

She twisted the knob on the radio, found classical music, then lowered the volume. "Well, after you left, I did a few chores and got ready to go over to Maddy's. But—surprise of all surprises—your sister knocked on my door before I could leave."

"I figured. She asked me for your address this morning."

"We had a … clearing of the air, I guess you'd say, and I found out a couple of things about you. I was glad she didn't tell me too much. I'd rather hear about your life directly from you as we get to know each other better."

His brows twitched. "Aw, geez. What did she say?"

Lumi chewed a pepperoni and swallowed. "Well, number one—that you're the *youngest* brother, not the oldest like I thought."

Nolan shrugged. "We're pretty close in age, all of us. If you'll remember, I did try to get you to tell me the year you graduated. I could have revealed my junior status long ago."

Lumi winked, then her expression sobered. "Cammie said you were a sick kid. God, you'd never know this muscular hunk sitting across from me was ever sick a day in his life."

He wiped his mouth. He looked at Lumi and then away again. "Did she tell you it was cancer?"

"Oh, *Nolan.* Really?"

"Twice. About five years apart."

She shook her head. "How old were you?"

"Ten and almost fifteen."

Chills ran up her spine and arms. "What ... where were the cancers? What type?"

"Brain. Radiation treatment the first time. Surgery the second. I haven't had any issues since."

Lumi's lips parted, and her eyes widened as a flicker of anxiety crossed her face before she forced herself to control her expression. *Brain cancer! Twice!* A gasp escaped her that she tried to suppress.

Nolan took her hand. "You're not the only one in this relationship to have a fear-laced past." He concentrated on the sight of her hand in his as he said, "Carol ... I met her when we were both in the hospital fighting the same fight. I didn't see her again until we found each other after we were out of school. We dated. Got married right away. It wasn't very long before her cancer returned with a vengeance."

Lumi's lips parted in sorrowful surprise and her eyes closed against visions of Nolan holding the hand of the woman he loved as she died. How much pain had he endured before they had met? She heard an echo of Cammie's voice: "Don't hurt Nole." His sister was probably used to feeling like his protector. Lumi opened her eyes, seeing Nolan staring at the wall. "But you're okay now?"

He opened the pizza box and reached for a second slice. "I've had viruses and the usual little illnesses over the past several years, but never another sign of cancer. That's one of the reasons I work out. I feel like ... if I look strong and healthy, maybe I'll scare away cancer forever, and it won't dare to come back again."

Lumi nodded. "It'll work, I'm sure. But Nolan, why didn't you tell me about your cancer before tonight?"

He ignored the pizza on his plate, frowning. "That wasn't fair, was it?"

She looked toward the sofa. "I wouldn't put it that way. There are still significant things about me that I haven't even hinted at. I shouldn't have even asked why you haven't mentioned it before, because your medical history doesn't play a part in our relationship. It means I have another thing to fear in a vague sense, but it doesn't feel like it will be a significant part of our lives."

"But it *does* play a part in our relationship. It *does.*"

Lumi gasped again. "Has it ... are you ...?"

He shook his head. "No. I didn't mean to scare you, Lu. Sorry. No, it hasn't come back, as far as I know. But cancer *is* the reason we're together."

"How so?"

He glanced up to her face and then away again. "I was always known in school and in town as the sick kid. I was too thin, too weak. Girls had no interest in me. I saw myself as the sick kid, too. It sank into my spirit. My friend Bruce, his family, and my family were almost the only people who saw me as a worthwhile human being, it felt like. Well, the people at church were okay, and I was always hearing, 'We're praying for you,' from those folks, but you can imagine how it felt to hear *that* week after week. Some of the teachers gave me extra attention and made sure I didn't fall behind. But the kids my own age? They were not okay."

"I'm *very* sorry, Nolan."

He looked at Lumi more directly. "When I graduated, I got a job at the canning factory my dad worked at, starting at the ground level. It was pretty good pay, but boring. I wondered whatever happened to a girl from Alexandria named Carol I knew from a cancer club through the hospital. She understood me. We'd fought the same dragon. I looked her up online, and we started writing emails, then meeting. She needed someone as much as I did."

"I'm glad you had her, and I'm glad she had you."

Nolan frowned and made a sound. "I lost her. I *lost* her. It was like having a leg cut off."

Lumi sniffed, unable to say anything.

"I was beaten. Thankfully, Magnus wouldn't leave me alone. I moved in with him because it felt like a better way to go than to move back in with my parents. He talked me into police training, but I had to wait until I was old enough. While I was living with Mag, I started working out on his home gym, which helped lift my spirits. After training, I got a job on the force here in town. I passed the psychological test fine. I knew I was fine to work, too, but I had been alone for too long—without a girlfriend, I mean. Every girl in town even remotely close to my age still thought of me as the sick kid. I tried online dating, but that was depressing as hell. A couple of guys at the station set me up on blind dates. I wasn't ready, in a way. There was no chemistry with anyone. After a while, I gave up trying."

Lumi shook her head.

"When I was at Mrs. R's that afternoon when you were there, and after she told me that you had been out of town for ten years, I felt a spark of hope." He took in a deep breath. "Please, please don't take this the wrong way now, Lumi, but what I liked about you above all else when we first met was the fact that you didn't know me. You didn't know me as a sick and scrawny boy."

Lumi shrugged. "How could I care about such a thing now?"

"I felt like I had a shot with you, but I was nervous. I honestly had almost no idea what to do to ask a girl out or even how to flirt with any success. Then the weirdest thing happened: you *did* seem to like me. I felt more and more attracted to you—your personality, your sense of humor, your genuine sweetness." Nolan sighed. "Is this too much to admit?"

She looked at him, her face heating, her stomach aching. "It sounds perfect. Until I hurt you."

He shrugged. "I had sick-kid syndrome all over again. I was sure someone had told you about my cancer at the party, and that you were rejecting me."

"It wasn't that at *all*. You know that now."

"I can't tell you … God, I was hurt and *angry*. Really, really hurt. When you stood in your shop and didn't wave me in or move, I knew you didn't care about me anymore—if you ever had. But then you sent that text. It was convincing. After work, I cleaned up and went to your house. You weren't there, but I waited. When the minutes dragged on and on, I felt foolish for hoping you still cared. You *couldn't* want me back. But a part of me held out hope, so I sat on your steps even longer, and longer still. Another part of my brain told me how dumb I was to fall for a gorgeous woman who was callously playing around and then ran as soon as she heard I'd been sick. By the time you did get home …."

Lumi wept. She stood to run up to her bedroom, wanting to allow herself time to cry in private. Returning in a few minutes, she sat on the floor at his side.

Nolan held her hand on his lap. "Bless you for finding the strength and the words to tell me your truth and your real feelings for me, Lumi. Everything turned out to be the opposite of what I'd been thinking. You weren't rejecting me, you were actually …"

"Fearfully, fitfully attracted to you. Scared of our closeness. *That's* the truth." Lumi fought an urge to cry again, realizing they both needed to pull out of their downward spiral. She stood and then sat on her chair, her legs to the side to face him. She reached for his hand, and he gave it to her across the table. "I'm glad you told me everything. I feel like I've been putting a crapload of burdens on you this whole time, asking you to be understanding about my fears. I hadn't thought, really, about how my actions affected you or anyone else. I've been self-centered for ages—I can see that now. I've had my eyes opened, again and again, these last several days." She squeezed his hand, looking at him, making sure he was hearing her. "I'm sorry, Nolan. I'm not sorry you've told me all that you have; I'm sorry I was so absorbed in feeding my own fears that I hurt you. I never, ever meant to hurt you." She held back from crying, almost failing. "I'll tell you one more thing—you are the strongest man I know—and I don't just mean because you pump iron." She sniffed and smiled. "Not that your muscles aren't drop-dead super sexy."

He slowly exhaled, then glanced at her. "Are they?"

She walked behind his chair. Bending over him, she ran her fingers over every dip and rise of his abs and chest and shoulders through his shirt. Hugging him around his neck, her hands moved in a purposely slower, more enticing way.

"I should get to do that, too, shouldn't I?" Nolan asked.

She paused, standing away from him behind his back. After a moment of consideration, she stepped to his side, took his hands and placed them on her waist, giving silent permission.

He didn't move. He blinked and looked away.

She kissed his temple and whispered in his ear, "Yes. Tonight." Lumi couldn't believe what she was offering. It felt too soon, but a part of her was emboldened by the fact that he had backed away. It felt safe to move toward him even though she wasn't sure she was ready.

Nolan lowered his hands to his lap.

She sat on her chair, watching him, waiting for an explanation. The news announcer seemed like an intruder, so she switched off the radio.

Nolan picked up his pizza slice. "I don't want these heavy and dark feelings on my heart or in my mind when I'm finally touching you the way I want to and ... *need* to. I don't want there to be any distractions."

"I feel the same way." Something occurred to her. Her eyes widened. "Nolan!"

"What?"

"I was ... oh, *no*. I was supposed to meet your parents at the party." Her face reddened. "I can't imagine what they must think of me now."

"I left there a few minutes after you did. I don't know what Mag or Cammie told Mom and Dad, but they must know about the incident; otherwise, Mom would have called to ask me why I wasn't at the bonfire. But *absolutely* don't worry about it. Once they know things are good between us and that there was just some simple misunderstanding, they'll feel nothing but happy we're a couple."

Her spirits sank. "I hate that I did that to you." She shook her head. "And I mean I *hate* it."

"I jumped to the wrong conclusion. You jumped because I was rushing at you, wanting you badly." He tried to smile. "It'll probably make a funny story someday."

Lumi looked down at her plate. "I guess we needed to have that bump in our road, but I wish I'd stayed at the party and pulled you aside to talk things over instead of running away like a scared kid."

Forget it now. We're far beyond all of that. You were telling me about your day." He bit into his lukewarm slice.

She speared lettuce with her fork more forcefully than was necessary, angry at herself again.

"Lumi. Don't. I'm not hurting from what happened. We're all the better for it. Really." He playfully tapped her foot with his. "Tell me about your day."

She put down her fork and took a drink. Nodding, she said, "Well, after Cammie left, I went to Maddy's to talk to her about Mama's letters and what I found online." She looked up. "But Nolan—her story takes a horrible, outrageous turn. I hope you didn't talk to anyone at the station."

"No. I didn't get a chance, and then you called to warn me off."

"Good. We won't discuss it now, but it was very upsetting. I asked her to call her daughter to stay with her since I had that dentist appointment, and now I suppose she's with Chess tonight."

"Did her daughter know about Chess, I wonder? I mean, his spending nights with her mom?"

"Apparently not, but she does now. It was a gut-wrenching morning. I hated to leave her, but I also didn't want her to keep being reminded of what we'd discussed. I went to my dentist appointment, which was nearly a bust. I had to keep wiping tears from my eyes, and my mouth kept frowning when it should have been opening wide. After that, I was lonesome for you and didn't feel like coming home, so I went to see one of the free matinee movies downtown. Guess who I sat with?"

He shrugged. "Katharine Hepburn?"

"Who? No. Alisa. She and her unborn but enormous child sat beside me."

Nolan raised his eyebrows, incredulous. "How could you not know who Katharine Hepburn is?"

"Is she the mayor or something?"

Nolan slapped his forehead. "I can see that I've got to educate you on the old movie stars at some point."

"Oh, you mean like Marilyn Monroe? Is this Katharine like Marilyn?"

"She is not actually much like Marilyn Monroe, no. Never mind for now." He glanced sideways and then scowled. "Hey—wait a minute! You're an *antique* dealer. You know all about old stuff and vintage everything. How is it possible you've never heard of Hepburn?"

Lumi shrugged. "I'm twenty-seven, not *eighty*. How do *you* know about her?"

"I've seen zillions of classic movies. I love film noir, the old screwball comedies, the Marx brothers, monster movies from the fifties and sixties … silent films."

"I guess I've seen a few old movies, but I've never been into watching them. I'm a reader and an auction-goer. That kind of thing."

Nolan smiled. "In a way, I'm glad. I have something cool to share with you. If you want to, I mean."

Lumi picked up her phone and typed in "Hepburn." She showed a photo to Nolan. Glancing at it again, she said, "Looks like she was a tough broad. She *could* have been the mayor of a city."

"Yeah. Mayor of Tinseltown."

Lumi glanced away from her phone to look at him. "Where's that?"

He slapped his forehead again. "Lumi!"

"What?"

He smiled, losing his exasperation. "You're too cute."

"Is there such a thing as 'too cute'?"

"Come here." Nolan opened his arms.

She stood beside his chair, enjoying the hug.

"I feel much better now. Thank you, sweet stuff."

She ran her hands over his chest and shoulders. "No problem, pardner." She giggled. "Isn't 'pardner' an expression from those old westerns? And 'git along little doogies'?"

"'Dogies.' Not 'doogies.'"

She pulled back just enough to look at him, her eyes wide. "Really? Are you *sure?* I thought it was 'doogies.'"

"You're thinking of a teenage doctor on TV."

"Am I?"

He let her go to stand, laughing. "I think you're pretending to be culturally uneducated, trying to get me to laugh."

"Am I?" she teased as she carried their plates to the kitchen.

He helped to clear the table, taking a last bite of his pizza slice before bringing her their plates.

Lumi sealed the salad in a storage container. With a sparkle in her large, blue eyes, she said, "But seriously—how adorbs are Margaret O'Brien and her drop-of-a-hat crying talent? We definitely need to have a *Thin Man* marathon. Oh, and a Preston Sturges marathon, too!"

His face brightened with surprised happiness. "I *knew* it! You little faker!"

"Who? Me?" She batted her eyelashes, then elbowed him. "This was payback for that shock I got at the auction barn. You never said you were interested in antiques!"

He reached out to tweak her hair. "I like playing house with you."

She nodded. "It's a nice house." She put their plates and bowls into the sink and turned on the hot water. "But it's *perfect* when you're here with me."

He closed the refrigerator and leaned against its stainless-steel door. "Promise you won't ever buy a different sofa. Yours is *outstanding*. Seriously. I slept great on it all night. No kinks in my back or anything. Nice, wide cushions big enough for two."

"Well, if I ever kick you out of bed after a big fight, at least you'll be comfy down here on the sofa." She gasped, her hands frozen in horror under the running water. She hadn't meant to say such a thing out loud. "I mean ..."

"But we won't fight like that. Not us." He reached past her to turn off the faucet. From behind, he put one hand around her waist and pulled her hair aside with the other to taste her neck with the tip of his tongue, gliding it lower and then up again. His mouth went to her earlobe, sucking it, biting it gently. With his lips against her ear, he said, "We'll be too much in love to fight."

She struggled to stay upright as his tongue danced lower on her neck again, his body fitting against hers perfectly. "I-I think so, too."

After kissing her cheek, he said, "We'll be strong for each other, and weak for each other, too." The vibrations from his voice drummed against her back.

"Yes."

"There will be bad days, but they'll end with us kissing in the kitchen, wrapped around each other against whatever happened."

"I know."

Nolan's breath on her skin was pure ecstasy. His hands were tremulously exploring new territories on her body, tenderly branding them with warmth. He raised her top enough to sensuously stroke her stomach.

She moaned, shocked and thrilled at the same time. Her head fell back against his shoulder as she relaxed and welcomed his touches, not fighting what he was doing—loving what he was doing. Breathing out the only words she could think of, she said, "Nolan ... yes. Oh ... yes."

"And you'll ..." He turned her around, guiding her against the edge of the marble countertop with his hips. He lifted her to sit there, his eyes half-closed with yearning. In his delicate and searching kisses, a swirl of emotion seemed to pour from him: sadness and happiness, worry and thankfulness.

Lumi held onto Nolan's shoulders and wrapped her legs around his waist. Her tongue flicked at his throat, loving the wild intimacy and taste of his skin, renewing her energy.

He groaned and captured her lips again. His hands tangled in her hair; her fingers raked his back, pulling him as close as possible.

She lowered her legs to push him across the kitchen against the refrigerator, molding her body to his, letting her fingers inch lower and lower along his lean, firm muscles. She slid her hands under his t-shirt, and he trembled at her touch. She found his nipples and caressed them. Taking his hand, she invited him to do the same. Watching his hand disappear under her shirt, she quivered with desire.

Nolan hugged her again, kissing her softly, stroking her tongue with his in long, slow, deliberate movements, then let Lumi repeat what he had done. *"Ecstasy,* darling. I want you … I want you …"

Lumi lowered her hands to pull his pelvis against hers and looked down at where they were touching. Looking up again, she said, "It's like you're driving me crazy down unpaved roads. I want you, too, but I don't know where the twists and turns are, or how to navigate as they come into view."

He met her eyes. *"You're* in charge, and you're driving just fine. Tell me what comes next, Lumi."

"Come here to my mouth. There's so much excitement and emotion running all through me. Kiss me numb. *God,* Nolan. *Now."*

Nolan kissed her, sucking her lips one at a time, then teasing the tip of her tongue with his. He raised her shirt over her head, pausing, his eyes on her white, lacy bra.

Lumi lifted his shirt off, too, and felt a reaction throughout her body as she gazed at his torso. His lean, hard muscles were startling.

Nolan reached for her bra and lifted it over her head, his eyes revealing his desire. He cupped her breasts that fit his hands as if their bodies were made for each other. "God. Gorgeous. Magnificent."

Lumi whimpered, wanting to go farther but scared to go farther. She shook, waiting for whatever would come next. Her eyes looked shyly away, then back to him. His abs and chest were frighteningly masculine, overwhelming her as she fought for control.

"Kiss me, Lumi. That's all I'm asking for tonight." Nolan released her breasts to hug her gently.

Lumi nodded. She reached for him, kissing him softly, her breasts against his chest, her hands exploring his muscular back.

Nolan whispered, "You're so sweet, Lumi. *Jesus.* I can't believe what you're doing to me." He took a breath, then said, "Open your lips for me."

She moaned, doing as he asked, still shocked every time he said something erotic. Needing to catch her breath, she turned around, and his hands covered her breasts. Her head on his shoulder, she admitted, "I've never felt this way before, Nolan. Not *ever.* I'm *crazy* for you. Weaker. Stronger. *Crazy.*" Lumi turned again and met his eyes, pleading uncertainly, "T-take—take me to bed." She kissed a line from his throat to his lips.

Nolan broke their kiss, shaking. He held Lumi for a long moment, letting his breathing slow, softly stroking her back under her hair. "Darling … no. No. Not tonight." Suddenly stepping away, he picked up his t-shirt and put it on. He walked around the sofa, put on his duty belt, stuffed his feet into his black shoes, and grabbed his uniform shirt.

"Nolan, are you *going?"* Lumi asked, practically mewing in disbelief and desire as she grabbed her top and dressed, following him into the living room.

He looked at her, determination in his eyes. "I am. I'll see you tomorrow, though. Should we go out for dinner to try to get more food into us than we did tonight?"

She frowned, aching for him. "It feels like you're always going."

"I'm heading to the hospital. I want to check in on the parents of that little girl. I couldn't face it before, but you gave me strength." He kissed the air between them and went out through the door, his shoes still untied.

Chapter Fifteen

Left with only the vintage AM radio for company, Lumi sat at her dining table with the mug of green tea she had made after waking up from a nap she hadn't meant to take right there, her head on her arms. She stared at her reflection in the darkened window she faced. She looked messy and kissed. She rubbed her neck and throat, trying to stop it from aching for Nolan's lips and tongue.

Cancer. A little girl nearly dying in the park. Maddy's guilt and pain. Nolan needing her, wanting her. Friendships blooming. Stars crossing. Fate. Serendipity. The past and present and future blending into each other in print and reality. Photos and letters. Repressed memories rediscovered and fitted together. And cancer again. Nolan's expressive eyes a few inches from hers. Emotions pouring into their kisses, giving each other healing and bravery to do what must be done. Wanting each other. Wanting more and more of each other, from each other. Fears roaring up and dying away. Passion and desire and everything new and overwhelming.

At the sink, Lumi dumped away her cooling tea and went through her back door to stand in the shadowy yard, her bare feet in the colorless grass. Above the maple trees, the moon was shining in the sky, just as she'd hoped. Stars, though barely visible, were hanging from their unseen strings from the unseen somewhere beyond. So much was changing around her and within herself. The constancy of the solar system had always comforted her. Now, however, she was welcoming transformations and shifts. She wouldn't even have minded a snowfall, and she wouldn't have questioned why it had come in the middle of this particular summer.

She checked her phone and saw that it wasn't yet ten o'clock. She went back inside and looked through her living room window. Maddy's downstairs lights were shining through her sheer curtains. Lumi decided to go across the street.

"Mind if I come in? I'm restless."

Chess met her at the door wearing a green and blue paisley bathrobe, looking more accessible than he did in his daytime clothes. His bulldog jowls seemed to sag from tiredness. "Sure, Lu. Maddy went upstairs to get her old slippers on. Turns out she doesn't like the new ones she bought today. Come on in. Care to join us for cards?"

"Thanks, Chess." She patted his shoulder. "I'm glad you two are here tonight." She kissed his cheek and hugged him.

He flustered after the unexpected gesture.

Maddy came into the room. "Lumi? I thought I heard your voice."

"Hi, Maddy. Chess said I could sit in on your game for a while."

She glowered. "I hate those slippers. I don't know why I got a pair without backing at the heel. How does anyone tolerate those slide-ons? *Terrible.* They flip-flop around when I walk until they about trip and topple me over." Her glower changed to a frown as she remembered it was the first time she was seeing Lumi since their talk. She tried to smile. "Grab one of those chairs. Want a snack?"

Lumi kissed Maddy's cheek, too, smiling. "I do, thanks. I'll get it."

Maddy, frowning again, grabbed her friend tightly, kissing her hand. With damp eyes, she said, "Glad to see you, my girl." She sighed, saying everything with that one sigh.

When Lumi returned to the living room with a plate of cheese cubes, cocktail meatballs, chips, and a cup of water, Chess was whispering to Maddy at the card table in front of the television. Lumi hated to pass the threshold, wanting to leave them uninterrupted. She watched them a while, then joined them. "Same game as last time?"

"If that was rummy, then yes. Did I see Nolan's truck earlier? Did you two have dinner together?" Maddy asked as she dealt out three hands.

Lumi nodded. "He took a nap, and then we tried to eat a little pizza. Poor Nolan. There was a real ... well, he had a bad day."

"I heard about it at the barbershop," Chess said, knowing what Lumi hadn't said. He hid a frown, his eyes downcast. "I know her grandparents—the Millers. They sure do love that little doll. I've been praying it turns out that she'll be fine."

Lumi suddenly lowered her cards to the table, rippling the card edges with her thumb nervously, her eyes fearful. "Oh, Maddy and Chess—how can I *do* this with him?"

"Do what, honey?" Maddy sympathetically reached across the table to pat Lumi's arm.

"Go through these things that he must go through too often."

"Everyone has *things*, dear," Maddy said, picking up her cards again. "A doctor has things. A nurse. A construction worker. An electrician. A retired bandleader. *Every*one. That's life. You've put yourself apart from other people and their feelings for too long, that's all."

"It's good you're needed," said Chess, leaning back in his chair. "I wish I was needed more. I'm an old fart. Who has any need for an old fart?"

Lumi was astonished. *"Maddy* does, for *one* example."

Chess shook his head. "She doesn't need *me*. I need *her*."

Maddy looked wounded.

He went on, "No matter what I try, it doesn't work. We'll never be more than good friends, I guess. I'm giving up." He tried to smile at the ladies, but his lips wouldn't allow it. He rubbed a hand over his forehead. "I've done everything I can think of to get her to rely on me enough to want to get married and live together night and day, but I can see she'll never think of me that way." He wiped his nose with a cloth handkerchief taken from the pocket of his robe. "I love her, Lumi. But she has never, ever considered me to be any kind of a man to have a real romance with. Not when we were young and not now."

Maddy, her face awash in shock, demanded, "What do you *mean* you're giving up?"

"You don't want me hanging around all the time, and certainly not at night."

"You idiot! Why would I suggest you come across the hallway to sleep in *my* bed those times?"

He shrugged. "I know you didn't mean it … like I was hoping you meant it. You want some company. *Any* company. You don't have the same feelings I do." His eyes were tearful as he folded his arms against his chest, comforting himself. "I tried everything to convince you to marry me. I did … I did everything I could possibly *think* of."

"Oh, nonsense!" Maddy chuffed at him. "You just settle down now and—"

But Chess wouldn't settle. He went into the kitchen, made noise in the cupboards or refrigerator, and then went up to the bedroom that was not Maddy's own bedroom.

At home, Lumi sat at her dining table, a feeling of dread rolling around in her stomach. She turned up her air conditioning. She sweated. She turned on the radio to jazz music, the volume purposely too loud. She tried eating ice cream. Nothing worked to stop the heat of realization from hitting her over and over again.

She knew the heartbreaking truth at last, and in the morning, she would have to do something about it.

Too many revelations and too many emotions for one day were taking their toll. Lumi wanted to run away—to get behind her wheel and hide on a highway. She wanted to sit in a corner of one of the unused bedrooms upstairs. She wanted noise. She wanted silence. She wanted Nolan, but she was afraid of her feelings again. She hated everyone. She loved everyone. Nothing was the same as it had been a month ago. It had all happened in a rush. This new realization about Chess overwhelmed her. She wanted her mother, but what would she say? There was too much to explain. She wanted her mother to know what was in her heart without needing the details of all that had been happening. She wanted her mother urgently, like a lost child would.

Or, in her desperation, maybe a fantasy mother would be someone she could run to for comfort.

Yes. A fantasy would have to do.

Lumi ran up to her bedroom and dumped the letters from Mama onto her bed, urgently, frenetically feeling each envelope for the added stiffness that meant it contained a picture. "Mama! Mama! Where *are* you? Which one are you *in?*"

Even in her frenzy of handling and opening and checking for the photo she wanted, she made sure to keep the letters in their same envelopes, and then returned the pictures to those envelopes after looking at them. After taking out several photos that weren't of Mama, Lumi finally extracted what she was looking for.

There she was, in her suntanning station on a strappy lounge chair, a drink on the little bench beside her. Mama, in the photograph's fading colors, was shielding her eyes from the sun as she looked up at the camera, smiling, the other hand waving in a blur. She wore a red swimsuit and had a blue-striped towel over her legs. Her short hair was strawberry blonde with a hint of curl at its ends. Her face was as familiar as a memory but as unclear as a dream. Mama was happy. Mama had found her place in the sun. Waller Bee must be nearby. Dad was probably taking the photo. After sunning, she would go inside and write a letter to Jackie about Pearline's next problem or Grandma's complaints. Betsy would be over before supper, showing Mama how her arm was getting muscular again. After dinner was eaten and the dishes were done, Mama and Dad and Waller would walk to the Dairy Barn and sit outside on a picnic table eating strawberry sundaes. They'd hear the pinging thwack of a softball bat, and Waller would want to run across the street to the park to fetch foul balls. The kids would be cheering, calling "ayyy, batter-batter-batter," and a few birds in the grass near the picnic table would hop closer and chirp, asking Dad to toss something their way. Mama would hold Dad's arm on the walk home, and her legs would be too sore to climb the stairs for the night, so they would sit together in the living room, watching a summer rerun and holding hands on the sofa. After an hour, Dad would help her upstairs, help her undress, and help her into bed, telling her she was still a knockout, kissing her lips tenderly, reaching for the lamp switch. The room would be dark except for a sliver of light slipping under the closed door from the hall after Dad had left her.

Lumi put herself in Mama's bedroom. "Mama! I'm here. Should I put on a record? I bought 'I'm Not Lisa' for you today. We can sing it together. The record liner has the lyrics. Mama? I'm glad to see you. How are your legs feeling tonight? Can I get you anything?"

Lumi imagined Mama smiling, saying no to her. Suddenly, Jackie was there with them, on the other side of the bed, taking Lumi's hand and then Mama's. Mama said she wanted to look at Lumi and Jackie until she could fall to sleep. That was all she wanted. Her daughters were with her. She was glad they were friends as well as sisters. She let go of Jackie's hand and put her arms under the covers comfortably. She closed her eyes and said she only wanted to sleep, covered over in sod, her feet in the socks her girls had picked out for her.

It was a crazy fantasy, its parts all mixed together into a jumble of hopes and fears as tears rolled down her cheeks. She held the photo a moment longer, and then put it back in its envelope with a letter Lumi hadn't read—a letter she would never read.

The sound of her phone startled her. Nolan texted: *"The girl will be okay. Her legs are hurt badly, and an arm is, too. Probably no lasting damage. Maybe some scarring from the burns."*

Lumi stretched across her bed, the green envelopes around her in disarray like the leaves of a willow tree.

"Thank God," she typed in return. He didn't reply, and she could understand why. She turned off her phone and threw it to the end of the bed.

Lumi cried weakly, the envelope that held a photo of Mama under her hand for comfort until she, too, slipped into sleep with her lamp still on, and to the faint jazz tunes hushing through the floorboards.

Lumi checked the internet for Chess' address the next morning. She watched for him to leave Maddy's, and at about nine-fifteen he did. Lumi easily followed him in her SUV, never needing the address she'd looked up because the man was a slow, careful driver.

She pulled into Chess' driveway after he had gotten out of his car, startling him. For a moment, he seemed pleased to see Lumi, but then, sensing she was upset, he leaned against his taillight and waited. Lumi hesitated, almost changing her mind about confronting him. She rolled down her window but wasn't entirely sure she was getting out until he started talking. Anger boiled in her blood. Outrage.

"What's up, buttercup? Is there a problem with Maddy?"

Lumi got out of her SUV, not even shutting her door before accusing, "It was *you.*"

Chess wiped his nose with a handkerchief. He seemed confused. "Did I run a stop sign?"

"It *was* you!" Lumi yelled again. She put one hand on a garden gnome's red plaster hat for support, her eyes hard. "How could you *do* that to her? *How?*" She walked the lush front lawn of Chess' ranch home, her hands in her pockets. "Of all the unexpected … you. It was *you* the whole time."

The man didn't respond, watching her pace.

"You made and sent Maddy those stereoscope cards. *You* did that! Oh, my *God,"* cried Lumi. Realization of more details dawned on her. "That's where Maddy's playing cards are—in the rolltop, right next to her stereocards. That's how you slipped your handmade cards into her box of antique views. You made them from scenes of the Coliseum tragedy to scare her into feeling the same way she did when she used to be close to you and dependent on you when you were young. You were the one she turned to for comfort after the explosion." She stopped to glare at him. "Isn't that right, Chess?"

Chess scowled. "Lu, girl—what in the gol-darned heck are you *talking* about?"

Lumi scowled, too. Things were off-kilter. His reaction didn't fit her expectations. "Chess, you … you go and sit somewhere."

He followed Lumi's orders and went to sink onto his porch glider, out of the bright morning sun. A pair of finches argued in the walnut tree above them.

She followed, standing in the yard a few feet away from him. "Did Maddy talk to you about the Coliseum explosion yesterday or today?"

He seemed confused. "No. We most definitely have not talked about that since back when it happened. In fact, I was sure she'd forgotten about it. What's this accusation about those cards?"

Lumi forcefully exhaled, her eyebrows raised. "Okay. What we have here is a disconnect." She tried to piece things together in her mind. She wanted to pace, but didn't, feeling drained. "Chess, you love Maddy. You liked her when you were young, maybe even in high school, but she didn't return romantic feelings toward you. However, you felt close to her while you were comforting her after the Coliseum exploded. You knew she wasn't allowed to talk about it at home, but *you* were there for her, listening, maybe even holding her when she cried. You were the one she talked to. She could tell you how depressed she was, and how she was miserable about losing her friends." Lumi paused for a few breaths, thinking fast. "Cut to the near-present time. You and Maddy are both without spouses again. You get that old, loving feeling when you two are together. You enjoy being with her and you fall head over heels. But, again, you aren't on the same page. She likes you, obviously, but as a friend—just like in the 'sixties."

Chess stared at his garden in the distance.

Lumi moved closer to stand in front of the porch's potted palms and rolled-up bamboo blinds. "Desperate to find a way to make Maddy need you on a deeper level, you devise a plan: why not go back to a proven formula? Why not make Maddy afraid again, and even of the same thing? The Coliseum explosion. Remind her—subconsciously—that you were there for her when no one else was. She would run to you, need you, be comforted by you, and you would win her heart. Suggest spending all night together every night for her protection." She shook her head. "I'm seeing how it went now. You found photos online or at the library, printed them out, and made fake stereoscope cards." Lumi bit at a hangnail, preparing her speech's ending. "But there's a hitch. She isn't scared enough to get married. What's a man to do? Up the game. Find even more disturbing photos and make them into cards, too, mailing them after she changed her locks. But Chess," Lumi said, standing in front of him, her face hard with accusation, "you didn't merely *frighten* her. You did a bad, bad thing."

Chess held up a hand, his eyes steadily locked onto hers. "Lu, you are so far off the map with your theory that I don't even know what to say. I *did not* make those cards. I never even *saw* those cards. They were of the *Coliseum?*" He stood, his face as serious as she had ever seen it. He leaned on the porch railing in front of her, his face red. "Listen to me— I love her. You've seen the way we are together. We love each other, whether Mad wants to admit that to the world and to me or not. I would never do anything to frighten her." He shook his head, then sat again. "And you had better start telling me what 'bad, bad thing' someone *else* did to her. I will most certainly join you in the battle."

Lumi continued, not wanting to believe him, still certain she'd solved the case. "You don't know the whole truth from that Halloween night in nineteen sixty-three. You have no idea what pain, what guilt, what *horror* she endured back then. You *couldn't* have understood because Maddy never told you the whole story. She suffered more than any person should have to. You sliced open an old wound, Chess, and the result on her spirit is worse than the blood and guts and terror that were shown in the cards you made her look at. Far, *far* worse."

Chess ran a hand over his bristly jaws. Meeting Lumi's eyes again, he said, "Lumi. Please. Stop this. I *did not do it!* And how could there be anything I don't know about that night? How? I was her only confidant at that time. I'm *sure* she told me everything."

Lumi stood straighter, and her eyes widened. Her voice sounding like a judge about to give a death sentence, she said, "No, she didn't." She revealed everything she knew about that night at the Coliseum, about how Maddy was supposed to work but skipped for a party, about repressed memories, survivor's guilt, and how what he had done to her was unintentionally deplorable. Worn out, she sat next to Chess on the glider.

His face was splotched from sobbing as he'd listened to the depth of the horror Maddy had endured long ago.

"You have to hear me, Lumi," Chess said, wiping his eyes and face with a handkerchief. "I understand how you came to this conclusion, but you're so very wrong. I'm *horrified* by what you've told me. Sad to the core that Mad held this secret for decades. It may have changed the course of our histories if she had confided these things to me long ago, but she didn't. She had reasons, and maybe I wasn't the person who should have been told. She had a good, good husband. I had a lovely wife. We both have grandchildren. Things are as they were meant to be. I told her this morning that I was sorry for getting upset last night. I didn't mean it that I was giving up on us. I was upset about the Miller girl but took out my frustration on Maddy. She and I had a good talk this morning, and we'll be okay. But here you are, telling me these heartbreaking stories, accusing me." He sniffed, shaking his head. "It wasn't me. I didn't make those cards, Lumi. I *did not make* them."

Lumi was stunned she'd gotten it all wrong. After a moment, she accepted the truth. "I'm relieved. Oh, Chess! I'm relieved!" She put her head on his shoulder, crying. "I'm relieved." She held one of his large, weathered hands. "I was so sure. It all fit together. I thought it had to be you." She gulped, worry churning in her stomach. "But … oh, Chess. This leaves me without a solution."

Lumi drove slowly toward home, weary, happy, and miserable in turns. It wasn't Chess. Her brilliant powers of deduction had been a figment of her imagination.

At a red light, she glanced around at the downtown buildings. The architectural salvage company that had been at that location for decades was still thriving, which was a good sign that her own, similar business would do well for many years. A vacant lot had been turned into a community garden. A small coffee and doughnuts vendor sold from a cart near the new benches that had been placed in the garden last month. A gallery that went out of business in the spring was now the campaign headquarters for Joplin Rooney. His likeness was on a banner hanging inside the large window, and bumper stickers were on every other inch of the glass. A pharmacy worker carried a white paper bag out to a parked car where an elderly lady sat behind the wheel. Upstairs in an apartment, red-patterned curtains flapped in the breeze of an open window. Kids rolled along the sidewalk on bicycles, enjoying the warm morning before the day turned hot.

Lumi pulled into a parking spot in front of her shop, planning to work alone for a while even though she wouldn't officially be open to customers. Kyla, the lawyer who had an office next to her antique store, stepped outside to water her plants in the window boxes. She saw Lumi and waved, and Lumi waved back, smiling, wondering why she had never visited such a friendly-looking woman who worked right next door. The woman reminded her of the portrait of Maddy that had been taken long ago at the photographer's studio. The memory made her miss her friend, so she decided to drive home instead of going into her shop to work.

"Maddy? Are you home?" Lumi called through the screen door a few minutes later.

Maddy stepped to where she could look through the screen, a dishtowel over one arm, her hair loose and her glasses off. "Come in. I'm putting away the breakfast dishes."

Lumi opened the door and followed her to the kitchen. She took a breath and held it a moment, watching her friend put away two mugs. "We need to talk. Do you have some time?"

"I sure do. I feel nice and energetic this morning. The sun is so pretty." She smiled. "Chess and I made up over breakfast. We didn't really fight, I know, but we talked things out." She slipped the towel through the handle of the oven door. Her smile faded as she turned toward Lumi. "You look mighty serious. Is it Nolan? The Miller girl?"

Lumi shook her head, pulling out a chair at the kitchen table. She nervously smoothed the wrinkles on the blue tablecloth with her fingers. "No. Nolan is okay. He said the little girl should be okay, too."

"Oh, that *is* good news."

Lumi rubbed her forehead, frowning. "There's something else." She looked at her friend, hating what she had to say. "I ... oh, I did a *terrible* thing to Chess."

Maddy sat, her face incredulous. "To Chess? You? What are you talking about?"

Lumi frowned, trying not to cry again. "I accused him of making those stereocards."

Maddy looked at her pig-shaped salt and pepper shakers. "What did he say?"

Lumi was surprised. "Did *you* suspect him, too?"

"He was the only one who made sense, even though that theory totally *didn't* make sense at the same time. I think ... I guess that's why I didn't want to let him know I'd kept the cards. Why I didn't show them to him. I didn't want to see his face. I didn't want to learn the truth. As long as it was only a suspicion, we could go on being good friends. I could go on enjoying his company and protection. Do you see? I suppose that's why I didn't want to think very hard about it."

"He didn't do it."

Maddy searched Lumi's eyes for the truth.

"Maddy," Lumi shook her head, "it *wasn't* Chess."

The woman bowed her head and dug her fingers into her gray hair, her elbows on the table. "I can see that you're sure. I'm glad. But I don't know if that makes the situation with the cards better or worse."

"First of all, I need to tell you that when I went to see Chess just now, I talked with him about what you told me yesterday. I'm sorry I was the one to do it, but I was ... on a roll. Had my detective hat on, accusing him and berating him for terrorizing you. I revealed too much of your private story."

Maddy stood and walked to her sink, staring through the window at what she could see of the periwinkle sky. "Don't let it bother you, Lumi. That's a conversation I was going to have with Chess soon, anyway. I couldn't marry him without having that talk. It's time. It's time we set a date, too."

Lumi got up. She put an arm over Maddy's shoulders and watched the sparrows on the bush outside the window. "You and Chess, married at last. Everyone will have to start calling you Mrs. *A* instead of Mrs. *R.*"

Maddy patted Lumi's hand, then turned to wrap her arms around her friend. "This will be quite a change. I haven't had sex in forever."

"Me, neither," laughed Lumi. "Literally."

They chuckled together, hugging, then sat at the table. After a moment of silence, Lumi stood again and poured mugs of coffee from the electric pot near the sink.

"Here. I'll get your half-and-half. We still need to solve your mystery." Lumi grabbed a small carton from the refrigerator and sat again. "Now. Maddy. Think. What haven't you told me about the Coliseum explosion?"

Maddy sighed, stirring in a spoonful of sugar and then adding cream to her coffee. "Probably a terrible thing. I'm sure of it."

"I'll bring you back in time. You listen and remember. You *have* to try."

The older woman sipped her coffee. "Bring over that plate of oatmeal cookies, first, will you? You look like you haven't been eating much lately."

Lumi did, and then she pulled her chair closer to her friend. She closed her eyes, saying in a monotone, "It's nineteen sixty-three. You've graduated. You have a job at the Coliseum in the concession booth. You have friends there. You live at home with your folks. You protest."

Maddy inhaled sharply.

"What?" asked Lumi. "Protesting? What did you remember?" Maddy quaked, so Lumi put her a hand on her arm. "Tell me. What popped into your head?"

"I'm not sure. I could see a gang of boys—young men—gathered around me."

"Is it at a protest march?"

Maddy covered her eyes with her fingers. "Keep talking."

"Nineteen sixty-three. You still live at home. You work in the concession booth at the Coliseum in Indianapolis. An ice show is the featured attraction. You want to go to a party with Scoots. He's cute, and you maybe love him. But there's another memory coming to you. It has to do with protesting. A gang of young men. They're standing near you. They're … what? Talking to you, harassing you? Hurting you?"

"Talking."

"Talking to you. They're not your friends. Or they are."

"Not."

"They're friendly. Or they're nasty."

"Pretending to be friendly. I have a bad feeling about them. I think."

"They're pretending to be friendly. They're at the protest, talking to you. What are they saying?"

"They're … oh, they're asking me questions." She sobbed, saying, "Don't. *Stop* now. Please."

"They're asking you questions, Maddy. You're upset because they were terrible questions, weren't they?"

Maddy cried louder.

Lumi went on, keeping her voice even yet firm, "Those questions. *They* are the problem. They're the solution. Maddy, what did they ask you?"

"About work."

"They were standing with you, pretending to be nice, but they were asking uncomfortable questions about the Coliseum. That's right, isn't it?"

Maddy covered her face with both hands, nodding.

"Those questions, Maddy. *What* questions? Who were the young men?"

Maddy shook her head.

"The young men. You hate their questions. They're frightening you. Terribly. You're surrounded, scared. Who are they? What are they asking?"

With a cry of anguish, Maddy said, "I remember. I remember it all. You ... you can stop hypnotizing me."

Lumi moved her chair back to its usual place at the end of the table, then sipped her coffee, waiting.

Maddy looked up at last. "I remember about Pinky."

"What?"

"Pinky ... Joplin. It's an *awful* memory, Lu."

"That guy. I got such a bad feeling from him at the reunion. The way you reacted told me *something* had gone on between you two."

"One of the boys asked me where I worked. I think he already knew." Maddy paused, taking a drink, swallowing loudly. "He said he didn't like Coliseum show spectator types of people. I told him that was dumb—all kinds of people went to see those shows. Another boy disagreed, saying they were all rich people and the tickets cost too much—something like that. Pinky asked what I did there, and I told him I worked concessions. They eyed each other. Pinky asked what kinds of food I sold. I mentioned drinks and sandwiches. Popcorn. He latched onto that."

"Oh, no," said Lumi, shifting to the edge of her seat.

"He asked how it was made—the popcorn. I described the huge poppers. When I mentioned propane, he looked at his friends again. 'Really? There must be a ton of huge tanks of that stuff there. Those are ugly suckers. They must store them somewhere out of sight.'"

Lumi stood and walked the length of the kitchen floor. "Oh, holy *crap.*" She stopped and leaned against the edge of the sink.

"Pinky smiled when I told him where they were stored, and that some were kept in the concession area. He then stepped up to me and kissed me right on the mouth while his friends laughed and cheered. I was so humiliated and disgusted that I ran home and didn't attend the march."

"Oh, Maddy. Oh, *Maddy*. That creepy *asshole.*"

"The explosion happened the very next night. I heard through the grapevine that it was caused by a leak in a propane tank that kept the popcorn warm in the poppers. It was ruled an accident. None of the tanks had safety caps on them. The valves were rusty on some of them. There was a bad leak in at least one of the tanks, and when the gas met the flame of the popcorn heaters …. It was a freak accident that happened when forty-three hundred people were in the building. A freak accident."

"Oh, God!" Lumi cried, sitting again, stuffing her hands under her thighs. "Maddy. Did those guys *do* that? Did they kill all those *people?*"

Maddy closed her eyes. "It was all I could think about—the coincidence of those boys quizzing me about where I worked and the propane tanks. They were troublemakers. I was dumb to say one word to them."

"But Maddy—did they *do* it?"

Maddy looked to the ceiling, then back at Lumi. "Pinky was waiting outside my folks' house the day after the cause of the blast was announced in the news. He was white as a ghost. He told me he and his friends were at a Halloween party that night in Anderson. Lots of people saw them. He handed me a piece of paper with the phone number and address for the family who hosted the party. Made me promise to call it and talk to them. He needed me to believe him. He was crying. Apologizing for the kiss. He hugged me, scared to death that I could ruin his life and the lives of his friends if I reported his questions to the police."

"Did you call that number?"

"I went to a payphone outside a gas station. The father of the family answered. He knew Pinky well, so he knew right away who I was talking about and verified that he and his friends were there all night, at least until midnight. I called information and asked who the number belonged to. I didn't recognize the last name. At least I know Pinky didn't give me the number of one of his friends who was pretending to be an older man on the phone. I found the house the next time I went to Anderson. I didn't knock at the door, but it gave me another layer of proof for Pinky's alibi—at least in my mind."

Lumi felt goosebumps on her arms. "This is … incredible."

"The next time I saw Pinky, we were in the drug store. He pulled me outside to the sidewalk, then into the alley. He hugged me again, asking me to be his girlfriend. I knew why—he wanted to make sure I kept my mouth shut. I swear, that guy would have *married* me to keep my mouth shut. But I could see what was really going on. When I laughed at the thought of dating him, he turned on me. He threatened to bring me down with him if I ever said anything about the questions he'd asked and that we talked about propane tanks at the Coliseum on the night before the explosion. He would make sure the police put me right in there with his gang, and he would say that I had thought of the whole thing myself."

"Holy crap! Maddy! What a ... piece of work."

"I knew I was trapped with that young man forever. Joplin Rooney would forever have power over me, and I would forever have power over him. It was a standoff. If I'd had a knife in my hand, Lumi, I probably would have used it—on him or on myself. I can still see his eyes, dark and threatening. Chilling. He'd locked me in a cage and threw away the key."

Lumi was almost gasping, her heart pounding. She stood and went out to the front porch, seething. She pictured Mama from the letters and how she was there that night. Lumi's imagination widened, seeing again the images of numerous dead and injured people at the ice show; seeing the crater of the explosion.

The screen door complained as it opened behind her, then slapped shut.

Maddy crossed her arms over her brown blouse. "And now he's not only back in town, but he's running for state senator."

"How the hell does he *dare?*" Lumi asked, taking a seat on a rocking chair.

"That guy. He has balls."

"Or he's so sure you won't say anything that ... well, there's your answer."

"What is?" Maddy asked, sitting.

"There's the answer to the stereoscope cards mystery. Now you know who did it. Now you know why he did it: to keep your mouth shut. To remind you that you were in it together, or not in it together, as the case may be. He sent you cards to terrorize you into keeping quiet about the questions he'd asked you in nineteen sixty-three. You feel guilty about the images because he *wants* you to feel guilty—too afraid to bring the whole thing up to block his run for office. He sent you those cards on the off chance that, even though you hadn't said anything for decades, you may be considering blabbing to thwart his chances of getting elected."

Maddy rocked for a moment, thinking. "But he hasn't been here in my house. The first cards were in with my other stereocards. The last two were mailed, sure, but the first five were in the house."

Lumi scowled. "He must have walked in when you were gone to the store. You told me you never locked up through the day if you stayed in town."

Maddy shook her head. "But he wouldn't know that. No, there's something else we're not thinking of. Some other way he got them into my home."

Thinking, Lumi ran through her original list of suspects. Only one of them really seemed to be a possibility. "The paper delivery man."

"The paper man. Sure!" Maddy agreed, excited. "He's new in town, struggling with three jobs and with a baby on the way. He had never been here before. I honestly thought he was like most other people when they first see my collection—they want to look around. He asked to see my stereoscope viewer, and then I got out the cards. He must have slipped them into the box when I was putting one of the cards in the viewer, not paying attention. Pinky must have paid him to do it."

"I'm calling Nolan," Lumi said, reaching into her rear pocket.

"What will you tell him?" Maddy's face registered fear and apprehension.

Lumi put her phone down. "Here's what I want you to do for me. Right now. Get that worried look off your face for now and forever, as far as Joplin and the explosion are concerned. That pink turd has done enough damage to your soul. It ends *now.*" She dialed. "Nolan? Can you come to Maddy's? It is police business. I guarantee it. No, you won't need a partner, but please come soon. It's about the stereocards, and it *is* a police matter. Okay. See you soon."

Maddy stood and went back inside the house, saying, "I'm making you and Nolan sandwiches."

Lumi shook her head, but she didn't protest. She suddenly did feel very hungry. "Chicken?"

"Close. Egg salad."

"Even better," Lumi called.

Nolan was there when the sandwiches were ready, pulling up to the curb.

Lumi jogged from the porch to meet him. She glanced inside his cruiser, a thrill running through her at the sight of her handsome boyfriend in his crisp, black uniform. She was dating a cop! It was far more real to her at that moment.

Her face must have revealed her feelings. Nolan laughed once as he opened his door and stepped out, pulling off his sunglasses and tossing them back onto the dash. Winking, he said, "That's how I feel when I step into your shop. 'Holy shit! I get to kiss an *antique dealer.'*"

"Ooh! Well said. Bonus points." She grinned, forcing herself to resist touching him, remembering she had asked him to come on an official police matter.

He followed her past Maddy's fragrant flowers along the walk to her porch steps. Lumi heard radio chatter coming from the cruiser as she led Nolan into the house.

"Nolan, dear. Here. I made you and Lumi something to eat while we talk." Maddy placed a plate with four thick white-bread sandwiches cut into halves onto the kitchen table. "Milk? Water? Coffee? Soda? What can I pour?"

"I guess we're eating lunch early today," said Nolan, glancing at the electric 7-Up clock over Maddy's stove.

Lumi and Maddy sat with Nolan, telling him how Lumi had thought Chess was responsible for the stereocards, but that he wasn't, and then the essential facts of events in 1963 with Joplin and the propane tanks.

Nolan wiped his mouth and fingers with a napkin when he'd finished eating and listening to the details they revealed. "First things first. Mrs. R, thank you for lunch. Secondly, Lumi, even though you were wrong about Chess, you did have reasons to suspect him—don't beat yourself up about that. You didn't give up; you kept at your case. Who knew you were a hypnotist? Great work!"

Lumi smiled, her face flushing from his praise, but also from a renewed feeling of embarrassment that she had so wrongly accused Chess of making the cards.

"Where do we go from here?" Maddy asked.

"To the newspaper office for the name and address of your delivery man so I can interview him. Once we have his confession—and I agree, very likely it was him who put those cards in your collection—move on to Rooney's campaign headquarters." Nolan stood to bring his plate and glass to the sink. "But I need to ask you something, Mrs. R."

She turned to look at him. "I can guess."

"What's your answer?"

Without a beat of hesitation, Maddy said, "Make him quit his campaign."

Nolan put a hand on her shoulder from behind. "As you wish."

Chapter Sixteen

Back at home after sitting another hour with Maddy, Lumi texted Nolan that she was going out of town for the day and would be back in time for their dinner date. He had called Maddy ten minutes before, telling her that her wish had been his command: Joplin Rooney was quitting his campaign, and he was quitting Barnwood altogether. His run for office had been the only reason to move back to his hometown, so he was leaving again as hastily as he had arrived.

Nolan messaged, *"Detective Leski, have I told you lately how fantastic you are?"*

She replied, "Thank you again for handling the messy details! Maddy was extremely relieved. XOX"

She checked her emails and called her mother for a quick check-in, saying nothing about all that had been going on. She felt that the events deserved a long, handwritten letter after she ran a very important errand.

Driving south, Lumi clicked off the air conditioner in the SUV and opened the windows, breathing more deeply than usual, loving the sun and summer colors everywhere. She glanced at the lunch box on the seat next to her and frowned wistfully, already missing the letters she hadn't read. At a roundabout, she turned right and found Jackie's home, the last trailer in a park along the river. A sun-faded red compact car was out front.

Lumi looked for a number on the house to be sure she had the right address before knocking on the dented aluminum door.

"Yeah?" a woman's voice called from inside.

"Jackie?"

"Yeah?"

"I have a box for you."

"Leave it on the steps."

Lumi hesitated. "I'm not UPS or anything. I'm ... we spoke on the phone a while back. I have—"

The door swung open, and a middle-aged woman with short, uncombed blonde-gray hair and a stern expression on her face stepped to the threshold. Lumi backed away to the lawn again.

Jackie glanced at the lunch box in Lumi's hand and growled, "I *know* what you have! I told you to get rid of those."

"But, they're ... precious."

"I know what they are."

The woman looked conquered by life, but her defeat had come long before Lumi had knocked on her door.

Jackie shook her head and disappeared into her house.

Lumi went up the steps, twisted the metal doorknob, and pulled. "Please. Let me talk to you."

"Walk right on damn in, why don't you?"

The inside of the trailer was neat and clean but packed with an excessive amount of homemade crafts. The interior of the home was unexpectedly charming and colorful.

"Want a drink, then, girly?" In the kitchen, Jackie held a beer in one hand and a ginger ale in the other.

"Sure. The soda." Lumi felt the handle of the lunch box in her hand, her thumb pressing into the ribbed ridges. Part of her wanted to leave and take the letters with her, saving them, but she stood firm, nervously wondering what she would say now that she had arrived and was in the house of the woman she had only had an imaginary image of while reading the letters.

After another minute, Jackie joined her, holding two ginger ales and a wheat-bread sandwich. "Here. Eat. You're too skinny."

Lumi looked for a place to sit that wasn't taken up by beautiful, well-made patchwork dolls and artistically original hooked-yarn pillows and soft toys. She finally moved a giraffe-faced pillow and sat on the sofa, putting her drink and the lunch box on the floor instead of making a clear area on the coffee table that was full of cloth scraps, yarn, and craft magazines.

Jackie seemed to really see the lunch box. "Flintstones. Ha! I didn't pick that out, you know. Marty did. Meg hated it. I only made her use it a month before I got her Hello Kitty."

Lumi bit into the sandwich, which turned out to be cranberry chicken salad—and good. She cracked open her can of soda and sipped. After swallowing, she said, "I want to give the letters back to you."

"I *know*. I *said* I know, all right? I know. Just sit there and eat your sandwich." Relaxing after a moment, she said, "Marty and the Flintstones lunch box. Sounds like the title of a teen adventure novel."

Lumi wanted to smile but didn't dare.

Jackie remained at the opening to her kitchen. One hand was up and bent at the elbow as if her muscles were accustomed to holding a cigarette aloft for many years and their old habits hadn't yet died out. "I know how you're feeling. You think I secretly want the letters back so I can have and hold Mama and her words again. Blah, blah, blah. *No.*"

Lumi shrugged. "I'll take them home, then."

"You'll do *no* sucha thing with those. They'll go *right* out into the burning barrel. I'll light the match myself."

Swallowing more of her soda, Lumi thought fast, trying to come up with a way to soften Jackie's mood. "So, you like teen novels? I do, too. I read them all the time as a girl. I loved the ones written in the 'eighties. They had those posed photos of high school girls and boys on the cover. All moody and preppy. After that, I moved on to adult romances."

"Did I say I liked those books? When?"

"And romantic mysteries. I never fell in love or had a romance myself, but I loved the stories."

"What the—? Why are you even *talking* to me?"

"Listen, Jackie—I read your mother's letters. Some of them."

"You did *what?*" Jackie turned to steel again. "Who gave you the right to snoop?" Her eyes closed for a few seconds as if restraining herself from committing murder. "And then you come here and you *tell* me about it? Are you nuts?"

"They changed my life."

Jackie lowered her empty hand to snap open her own can. She threw several stuffed toys from a chair to the floor, sat, and hit the remote, turning off *The Young and the Restless.*

"So, you bought them at my auction sale, and that gave you the right to read those letters? Then you come here, in my *house,* and talk to me about them? Is that what you're saying? Lady, you are all kinds of …. Who goes around *doing* that?"

Lumi chewed, thinking about what she could say next. "How's Betsy?"

Jackie shifted and gazed through her open door. She sat with her knees apart comfortably, as if she'd always seen her mother sit that way and had learned to imitate her. "She works with hearing-troubled little kids."

Lumi smiled. She took another bite of her sandwich and chewed for a moment. "How about your dad?"

"He lives next door in the double-wide. Moved in after Mama passed. Him and his yellow furball cat."

"Oh, I'm super glad, Jackie. How's Marty?"

Jackie rolled her eyes. "Stupid."

"Is he? Your mom said she was proud of him, you'll remember."

"Now *how* would I remember *that?* Was it *me* who read those letters just now, or *you?*"

"How's Marty?" Lumi asked again, trying to meet Jackie's eyes.

Jackie tugged her pants' fabric looser at her knees, then pushed her fingers through her short hair as if remembering it hadn't been combed that day. "Fine. He's fine," she said begrudgingly. "Went to the store before you pulled up. He retired last summer, and now he's here all the time, smothering."

"Good."

Jackie glanced through her screen door and then back at Lumi, letting out a long breath. *"Proud* of him? What *for?"*

"I don't know."

"Well, I guess we're okay together. *Dad's* a pain, though. He misses mom. He was so used to taking care of her full time that he doesn't know what to do with himself now. Meg's got two kids with her girlfriend. She comes to visit often and never makes me babysit, even though I'm willing. I have to practically *beg* to take them kids off her hands. Dad's in pig-swill heaven when those boys come over."

"Nice. That really sounds nice."

"You're a *chirpy* little piece, ain't you?"

Lumi grinned. "I guess. I feel like I know your mom and dad. Pearline and Grandma. Betsy and a cat named Essanpee. Waller Bee, too." She remembered another detail from the letters. "Still love boiled turnips?"

"Radishes. *Radishes,* not turnips. And not boiled. I like them pickled best."

There was another moment of silence except for the bird calls that seemed louder and more plentiful there by the White River.

"I hate the fact of those letters," Jackie said. Her voice had mellowed; her eyes were surprisingly damp.

"Why?"

Jackie put her drink on the floor and wiped her face with both hands in a motion that seemed to pull away a veil she'd been wearing. She shifted her feet. "They remind me of how dumb I was. Happy little dip-wad, thinking I knew how my life would be. How it would turn out to be a fairytale full of backyard barbecues and playing wife and mama right alongside my school girlfriends who also got married too damn young. If I could only get *going.* Get *married.* Get a man—*any* man to take me. I was bound and determined to prove to my mama that I could do what I set out to do. She wanted me to wait." Jackie yanked at the hem of her blouse, seeming to release tension from her body. When her face hardened again, it was clearly from anger at herself. "I knew *better,* didn't I? I had it *all* planned. Find a man. Marry him. He'd work all day while I played house. I wasn't going to get stuck living with Mama and Dad forever like Pearline got stuck with Grandma. I knew better." She

225

frowned. "Well, I *didn't.*" Jackie inhaled, holding her breath a moment. "I found Marty down at the rail station. He looked good. I snagged him. But I didn't know how to do anything on my own, or for a husband. Mama's letters came week after week. She wrote to me like I was doing fine, living the life I wanted to. We barely had a dime, Marty and me. I couldn't tell my folks how it really was. Marty tried. He's stuck by me, and he's always tried. I was dumb not to go to college like my folks wanted. They wanted me to live a little. Grow up some. Look around at what's what. But I knew better. Those letters are like ... paper nails pounding into me."

Lumi bit her lip. "I'm glad you told me, but listen—please reread them now with fresh eyes. Your mom wasn't ever judging you. I never got that impression from her letters. She was worried, naturally, but any mother of a newly married daughter would feel that same way. She sounded positive, really, when she wasn't writing of her own woes and pain. I think she was willing you into a good life by writing about how loving and happy her marriage with your dad was, even many years into that marriage. She was encouraging you to feel like ... it only gets better with time."

"I'm a disappointment to her. I mean, I was—before she died."

"Jackie, I really, really don't think so."

"Well, then ... I'm a disappointment to myself."

Lumi glanced at the lunch box. "Money isn't everything. Backyard parties and lunching with the ladies don't stand as a measure of a life's worth. You've stuck with Marty. You have a daughter and grandsons. Your dad is right next door. You kept your promise to your mom in that way, too. I bet ... I bet you even remembered about the socks."

Jackie's hand went to her lips as if she subconsciously meant to inhale from a cigarette. It stayed there to cover a frown. "How do you know about the socks?"

Lumi pointed to the lunch box.

Jackie sighed, and her body tensed. "Those are *my* letters, after all. No one should touch them. They're home again. Mama wanted *me* to read them again someday, not a chirpy little stranger."

Lumi suppressed a smile, understanding that no match would touch a single one of Mama's letters. She wanted to ask about the mysterious source of Pearline's supply of cash all those years ago, but it seemed inappropriate. Instead, she asked, "Did Pearline ever get a job?"

"Yeah."

"Where?"

"Oh, she worked in a department store for a long time, back in the bookkeeping department. She was good on computers after she got the hang of them. Pearline worked and went on little trips with Grandma and my mom and other friends. They liked art galleries and museums and concerts. They were okay. Pearline seemed happy. Had a few boyfriends starting along about the time I had Meg, but she didn't marry. Stayed with Grandma till she passed. Now she's got an old geezer boyfriend who used to manage a casino. They go around on cruise ships or go on artsy vacations all over, and she even visited here once with that boyfriend. She and him were like teenagers around each other. Mama was here, with Dad. We were so jolly together." Jackie licked her lips, trying to hide the fact that they were trembling. She looked through the door window. "I miss Mom. I don't know how to get over losing her. I'm lonesome. Dad's lonesome. She was the center of the family."

Lumi smiled, leaning forward. "I hear your mom's writing voice when you talk. I feel close to you already."

Jackie looked slapped with surprise at such words. "What are you *saying?* You don't *know* me. How can you say such a thing?"

Lumi leaned forward a little more, her elbows on her knees, her expression and voice serious. "Like I said, those letters changed my life. I would never have thought of coming to visit anyone like this if it hadn't been for the gentle lessons your mom taught me. There are tons more letters I never opened. I'm leaving them all for you to read. I think Mama has a plan for you, now, too."

Lumi was holding her soda and what was left of her sandwich when she stood to go. At her left were framed photos under the windowsill. Dad as an old man, standing in bib overalls near a garden. A man that could be Marty sitting in a pickup truck in a campground, Jackie sticking her tongue out at him playfully. Mama younger and then older than the photo Lumi had held the night before. An older woman and a middle-aged woman waving out of a train window. There were pictures of curly-haired boys, and of women who were probably Meg and her girlfriend. One of Waller Bee in Dad's fishing hat, his eyes rolled up to try to see what was on his head.

Lumi wished she could have picked up each picture to talk to Jackie about the people in her family, but maybe that would be something to do on another day. She stepped around the craft-laden table, leaving the Flintstones lunch box on the sofa.

Jackie hesitantly rose from her chair as if she had no idea what to do.

"I'm not far away. I'm in Barnwood." Lumi reached into the back pocket of her shorts for the card she'd put there earlier, hoping she would have the nerve to give it to Jackie. "Here's my card. I have a little shop downtown. Come and visit me, or I can come back. I'd love to sell some of your beautiful crafts in my store. We can talk about consignment terms." Lumi gave her the card before stepping down onto the concrete steps outside. Halfway to her SUV, she turned on the cracked sidewalk to look at Jackie, who was standing in the open doorway.

Lumi remembered her fantasy of holding Jackie's hand over Mama in bed. The birdsong died away, and the wind picked up, blowing the white fluff of dandelion heads between the women before they settled gently on the lawn like snowflakes. Lumi looked at Jackie and was surprised to see her wiping tears from her cheeks before she turned to disappear into the shadows of her home.

Lumi drove on to Indianapolis, emotions surging through her veins: love and worry, jubilation and fear, excitement and joy. She shopped at a few thrift stores but couldn't concentrate on what was sitting on shelves or hanging from racks. She wondered how Chess and Maddy were doing, so she went home to find out.

She found Maddy dragging a plastic bag of topsoil from her garage.

Lumi jogged to her and lifted the bag into her arms. "Where do you want it?"

"Right over there at the chokeberry bush. A dog must have come along and dug under there as if he'd planted a bone long ago. I don't know how he made off with the dirt that was in the hole, too. This topsoil was from a gardening project that Ras did or didn't do."

"Leave it to me."

Maddy caught her breath, wiping her forehead with the back of her hand. "Thank you for doing this. Everything seems to get heavier for me by the year."

Lumi opened the bag with the jagged edge of her housekey and dumped the soil into the hole. She stomped it down, making it level. "Just the right amount."

Maddy looked to the sky as if seeing something in the few puffs of cloud.

Lumi wiped her sandals on the lawn, trying to scrape dirt from their sides, then stepped closer to her friend. "I know, Mrs. R. This has been a lot for you to relive."

"You figured it out—my mystery."

"Not by myself. I'm glad I could help stop those cards from coming. Since we've been through this war together and are now on the other side in a time of peace, I can tell you that I feel closer to you by far than I did before you called me over that fateful afternoon. Have you talked to Chess again?"

"He left a little while ago. I know you told him the details from nineteen sixty-three, dear, but I felt keenly that I needed to tell him everything, too. I didn't think I'd ever want to discuss it again after I confessed all and opened up to you, but I did. It felt less powerful to me the second time around, but what I told Chess drew something deep and mournful from him. When I also told him about Pinky, I almost had to sit on his lap to keep him from running off and killing that guy. Told Chess I want him in my bed, not off in a jail cell. I'm sure Rooney's in his own version of hell now that he had to slink off and quit his campaign."

"I can imagine Chess has a great deal of pain from this, too—for you, mostly; he loves you that much."

Maddy closed her eyes, remembering. "We had a long, long cry about it, Lumi. Oh, that man and I cried." She opened her eyes and picked up the empty plastic bag from near the bush. "He has a way of talking to my heart. You tried to make me see I was not at all responsible, despite my protestations, but hearing it from Chess—who had been there at my side the first time—made me see it was honestly true."

Lumi nodded. "Good."

"I'd been holding back with Chess. When those cards showed up, I suspected him of making them. We've been casual friends over the past decades—not at all close. He had his wife and family; I had Ras and Jem. We've been getting to know each other better, getting to love each other, really, over the past good while, but I wasn't fully certain he was totally trustworthy. I'd only ever really been with my husband and I had no experience judging the average man's soul, I'll admit now. I can see how wrong I've been. Chess is not only a dear friend, but he's dear in every way." She glanced away for a moment. "In my mind, I'd already said yes to marrying him. That's why I let him talk about us at the reunion. If I hadn't been serious about him, I wouldn't have even gone. I was sure he'd crow to the gang, and I let him say that we were practically engaged because that was the truth—I just hadn't gotten around to officially saying yes. And … well … maybe all this needed to happen, Lumi girl. Now my guilt and turmoil have been dug up like a dog getting a bone from beneath a chokeberry bush. It's dug out and gone, and all the old dirt with it." She tossed the empty bag into the metal garbage can in her tidy garage, then returned to the side yard. "Chess and I set a date. The last Saturday in August."

"That soon? Wow, Maddy—that's really great!" Lumi looked at her hands and feet. "If I weren't so dirty, I'd give you a hug."

"I don't mind dirt. It's good, clean dirt. My Ras wouldn't have bought dirty dirt for the yard he loved." She grinned. "Sounds funny, but you know what I mean." The whistle of a bird drew her attention. "See that cardinal on the birdhouse there? That's old Ras, I'm certain. Cardinals were his favorite. The males are bright red, shouting joy and gladness." Maddy walked closer to the birdhouse, stopping a few feet away. The bird remained perched where he was, not flying off. Maddy clicked her tongue to it, and the cardinal lowered its head toward hers, his black eyes shining. "Hello, Rassie. Good to see you. What do you think about Chess and me? Is that okay?" She waited a moment for the bird to sing two notes in reply. Maddy turned, winking at Lumi. "Blessings from Ras."

Lumi took a long bath, reflecting on how much had changed in her heart and mind since Maddy had called her over to look at the stereocards. She had come to understand a good deal about relationships of all sorts. Her soul felt as warmed and washed and afloat as her body was there in the tub. She stood to rinse in the shower, letting the prickly ends of sadness and worry circle the drain and disappear with the last of the suds.

Downstairs, she sat at the dining table in her bathrobe with a pen and pale green vintage notepaper she'd bought in an auction box lot.

Dear Mom,

If you have an old lunch box, put this letter inside. There will be more to come.

Where should I start? How about with this: I have a boyfriend. His name is Nolan. I love him. There. I've told you first before I've even told him. I think he knows already. We have a connection like you and Dad. You two don't always need to say everything out loud, and that's how I feel with Nolan.

I'm a new woman, Mom. I'm sitting here in my own house on a day off from my business. That's new, but that's not what I mean. My outlook and attitude are new. I thought being independent and being strong were the same thing. Even worse, I thought being independent meant being alone. I pushed and pushed everyone away until no one had any interest in standing at my side. No one knocked at my door. I thought I wanted that. I was roaring and roaring about my strength, but they were empty words shouted to the emptiness around me. Work was everything. Getting somewhere was everything. But where was I trying to get? When was I going to really stop and look around at the nothing I was fighting to hold onto?

I have all these Facebook friends who "like" and comment on my posts online, but I don't see those people in person. What is the point of a pretend social life? Maybe other people can thrive in both real and unreal worlds, but I can't. So, in having no face-to-face connections, I was hiding in a hole. I got to loving life in my hole. Then Nolan and Maddy and Cammie and Jackie and her mother and Chess and Alisa and Mike and Magnus came along, saw me down there in the dark, and they pulled me out by force. Or, maybe that's not quite right. Maybe they pointed out that I had a ladder all along.

I didn't like it. But then I loved it. But I freaked out. I'd gotten used to the dank and dark and invisibility. I ran away from Nolan, and we broke each other's hearts. That could have been the end, but it wasn't. We forgave each other but realized there wasn't actually much of anything to forgive. We just needed to learn to communicate better.

I didn't like people robbing me of my independence. I'm not sure where the conviction came to me that I was weaker when leaning on an arm. I have friends now—the start of good friendships, I'm sure. And do you know what? I'm stronger. Those arms around me are not holding me down. They're lifting me up.

Love to you and Dad,
Lu

Lumi sealed the letter in its matching envelope before going upstairs to dress and finish getting ready for her date. She decided to put on her most formal summer dress—dark blue with black satin straps. She'd bought it to wear while working the floor at an exclusive fine art auction, and then never wore it again. Checking for makeup issues one last time in her bedroom mirror, she smiled at herself. The woman looking back at her seemed far more mature than the girl she had been a few months before when she'd first hung the mirror on her closet door.

"I'm glad we went somewhere new," Nolan said after dinner in his truck. "I keep eating at the same two or three places. Plus, that dress deserved to go out to a fancier restaurant than Sally's."

"Sally's will always be my favorite restaurant. Don't knock Sally's." Nolan smiled.

Lumi gazed at Nolan as he drove, at his profile, at his hands on the steering wheel. He had dressed up, too, even though they hadn't prearranged to go anywhere special for the evening. "I forgot to tell you—Chess and Maddy are getting married."

"A happy ending for them, after all of that terrible trouble. This was a satisfying day, let me tell you. Seeing that sleazebag sweat was satisfying. I don't like bullies, and that guy was like something out of a comic book. He saw me coming through the door, and his eyes immediately registered why I was there. You should have seen him when I signaled through the window for the paper man to come in. Yep—satisfying."

"So, you've had enough satisfaction for one day, then?"

He took a hand from the steering wheel to tug her hair playfully. "Funny."

She stared ahead at the blend of night darkness and golden and colored lights from homes and streets and stores, lowering her window, wanting wind on her face. "I'm glad Chess and Maddy are getting married. Theirs may end up being one of the greatest love stories of all time."

Lumi saw Nolan in the dim light of his dash as he tried not to react. She put a hand on his shoulder until he glanced at her. "But there's room in the storybooks for yet another."

He smiled and stepped on the gas pedal, pushing them onward a little faster.

They sat in the truck at her curb, the motor off, the windows down. The night sounds seemed distant to Lumi, who was feeling a burst of joy simply sitting with Nolan.

He rapped his knuckles on the outside of the truck window frame. "Beautiful weather. Think I'll drive around a while before I head home."

"Oh, no, mister. You're coming in." Lumi unbuckled herself and Nolan.

He closed his eyes, putting his hands on the lower arc of the steering wheel.

She turned to him, perplexed as to why he wasn't touching her or looking at her. "What's going on, Nole?"

"You're … inexperienced. I feel like I don't have the right to change that. I can still hear you telling me to be the one to stop us."

Lumi lifted the padded armrest between them and got as close to him as she could in the truck. She put her head on his shoulder and took one of his hands from the wheel to hold it. "Nolan, every person on the planet has a right—or *should* have the right—to decide who may or may not touch their body. I've never met anyone before you who I was sure was the one person I wanted—and needed, frankly—to hold me in intimate ways. It's true that we *are* just getting to know each other, but in the ways that count, I know you very well. I know your tenderness and vulnerability. I know how strong you are. How much you value the people you love. How noble you are. I know you can go through fires and come out on the other side so much stronger than before. I can't say I've ever met a better man in my entire life, except for my father, maybe, and daughters are supposed to think their dads are superior. He doesn't count." She sighed. "I can't say that I've always known my own mind in some things, but I'm sure I can say I *do* know it now. That's because of you. I know my own heart better, too. That's also because of you. Tonight, though, I want to know *you* better."

Nolan made a sound as if he'd been holding his breath and hadn't wanted to let it out. "We can wait. We should wait, Lu. You've put this new, exciting penny in my hand. I don't know if I want to spend it this soon. I'm so sure of us that I don't want to rush in and mess things up. We can wait."

"Or we could go upstairs tonight because that's what we both want. Equally." She paused to smile at him. "Well, unless you'd rather not have me to do things like this to you all night long." She ran her fingers from his chest to his waist. "Or this." She put a hand under his white buttoned-down cotton shirt, her nails raking his skin, dipping into his navel, rising to his chest again.

He let her do what she wanted for a while. "Lumi," he finally said, half out of breath, meeting her eyes. "Darling—think, though. This is a big step. Pulling back a bowstring and shooting an arrow with it are very different things. When it comes right down it … and now that we're both really serious about heading to the bedroom together … is this too soon?"

She sighed and slid her hand out from under his shirt. Meeting his eyes playfully, she grinned and said, "You know what? You're right. I was going to make passionate love to you all night long, but I guess it can wait until next year. Or the year after that. Heck—we can just forget

233

the whole thing altogether." She leaned away from him and reached for the door handle.

At the last second, Nolan pulled her arm, holding her in place. "Oh, you're so *wicked.*"

"Come and get me," she teased, taking back her arm and opening the door. She jumped from the truck and stood on the sidewalk, waiting.

He was beside her in seconds, hugging her, laughing lightly.

Lumi broke their embrace to put her purse on the porch. "Let's walk to the back yard. There's a glorious moon tonight."

"It's cloudy. We won't see the moon or stars."

"They're all there, though," she assured him.

He followed her around the side of the house, sitting with her on top of a sturdy plastic picnic table.

"There's nothing but darkness out here, Lu. Other than a few porch lights."

She put an arm around his waist and adjusted a strap on her dress. "This table was here when I bought the house. We'll have to get a better one."

The cloud cover was thinning.

"Wood or aluminum?" he asked.

"Wood. Unless you'd rather have aluminum. Or, instead of buying a table, can you make one for our yard?"

"I can." He looked up to the sky, leaning back on his elbows. "The moon is trying to shine now." With one arm he motioned to the brightening moonlight. "You're doing this, aren't you?"

She smiled. "I am. Like it?"

"Reminds me of Jimmy Stewart and Donna Reed in *It's a Wonderful Life.* I feel like I should lasso the moon and pull it down for you." The last tendrils of a cloud mass drifted vaguely north. Nolan turned to look at Lumi, who was staring at the cloudless moon. Admiringly, he told her, "You're absolutely luminescent. It's like you're made of moonlight yourself."

"I was named after snow, not the moon, remember?" She kept her eyes on the clearing sky, watching for stars to appear. "I just wanted to sit here for a while with you. The moon has always seen me on my own. Every night when it opened its eyes to look to Earth, I've been on my own. Out here in my yard, in college, in high school, or gazing at it when I was little from my bedroom window. Or while sitting in my willow tree, looking for glimpses of its light through the flowing leaves." She swallowed, feeling the importance of the words she was about to say even before she voiced them. "I want the moon to know that from this night forward I'll be watching for it to grow from thinnest sliver to full and round while I'm with the man I love. There will be two of us now." She finally looked at Nolan instead of at the heavens. She smiled at him and nodded to let him know she was sincere.

Nolan watched as she searched for stars. "Lumi?"

"Yes?" she asked, already hearing his words in her mind yet aching for them.

"Does your old moon know I love you, too?"

She didn't react except to smile while still looking up to the sky. "I suppose so. I think so. Yes."

"If not, I can probably lasso that thing and pull it down a little closer so it can better hear me say it again."

"Say what again, Nole?" she asked in mock innocence, sitting straighter and turning. She ran her fingers through his hair, then lowered her hand to his arm.

Nolan looked mesmerized, as if the night, the moonlight, Lumi's eyes, and the fragrant, warm air were luring him into a spiderweb to be held captive forever.

She waited, not moving, not expecting him to say how he felt again. Her eyes half closed, and as if by magic, the moon slipped behind a wisp of cloud, giving them more privacy.

"Oh, Lumi. This isn't anything I thought I would say to a woman again. I was hurt and lost, determined to go through life alone." His fingers delicately tangled in her hair. "Being without you is the last thing I want now. I wake up to thoughts of Lumi. I go to sleep thinking of you and my heart pounds your name. It's more than physical, this attraction. You're a comfort and a puzzle to figure out. Every moment of the day without you feels like a wasted moment. The truth is … I do. I love you." He met her eyes. "It means everything to me to hear you say you love me, too." He stood and pulled her enthusiastically into his arms, holding her tightly, being held as tightly in return. "My arms are so full now." His lips sought hers, and he kissed her passionately, without any restraint of body or soul. Nolan took a step back to meet her eyes. He laced his fingers through hers and motioned with a nod to the front of the house. "Let's go inside now, darling Lumi. I'm going to stay."

The snow-white moon shed its cloud cover again, lighting a path to show the way that they should go.

Jenny Kalahar lives in central Indiana with her husband, Patrick, and their pets in an old schoolhouse full of used books. She is the author of ten books and has been published in several anthologies, in literary journals, and in her humor column in Tails Magazine. She and Patrick previously owned and operated bookshops in Michigan and Ohio, and now sell books via the internet. They are active in the poetry community of Indiana. Jenny is the publisher of the Poetry Society of Indiana, the founder and leader of Last Stanza Poetry Association, and the president of the Youth Poetry Society of Indiana. She was nominated for the Indiana state Poet Laureate position and twice nominated for a Pushcart Prize in poetry. When not writing, reading, or working with old books, she loves expeditions through flea markets and playing piano and percussion.

Made in the
USA
Lexington, KY